IRISH VOW

M. JAMES

PHOTOGRAPHY BY
WANDAR AGUILAR

ONE
ANA

My world is spinning around me. I feel dizzy, like I could faint. Dimly, I realize I'm grabbing onto the countertop for support, staring into the blazing green eyes of the gorgeous woman standing in front of me with her arms crossed over her chest, glaring at me as if I'm her worst enemy.

Which, I suppose if what she's said is true, I am.

"I'm Saoirse O'Sullivan. I'm Liam's fiancée. And just who the fuck are you?"

"What do you mean, you're his fiancée?" I manage, focusing on the first part in an effort to avoid answering the second. "I—he hadn't mentioned—"

"Well, he wouldn't, now would he, if he were keeping another girl in his house?" Saoirse looks disgusted, shaking her head. "I want to say I don't believe this, but in some ways, it makes some things make better sense—"

"No." I shake my head firmly, because even if she's quickly coming around, *I* refuse to believe it. "He doesn't have a fiancée. He would have told me, he wouldn't—"

"Wouldn't what?" Saoirse looks at me keenly, and I catch a glimpse of something sparkling on her finger in the light of the apartment, something that I don't want to look at too closely, so that I don't have to admit what it is.

But Saoirse clearly isn't going to give me that luxury. She raises her left hand squarely in front of my face, her own creased with anger, her lips thin and set.

"Aye," she snaps, that slight hint of a Gaelic accent slipping through again. I love hearing Liam's. It makes his voice sound smooth as cream mixed with whiskey, like an Irish coffee, and just as full of heat when it slips into his voice because he's aroused. I hate hearing it on this woman's voice, sharp and cutting, slicing into me and making me think of Liam right now, at this moment, like that—when there's a very real chance that he's lied to me. Or, if not actively lied, lied by omission.

How could he not tell me if he had a fiancée?

I'd been with Alexandre, I've fully admitted that, along with my feelings for him. But I hadn't been *engaged* to him. I hadn't—

I'd promised to stay with him, true. I'd said I loved him. Despite the fact that my bond to him had been one of someone who was owned, I'd meant those words when I'd said them. Deep down, I can't argue that Liam having been engaged prior to us is so different, but still—

How could he not have told me?

Saoirse waves her hand in front of my eyes, as if trying to pull me back to the present. "Take a good look at it," she snaps. "My grandmother's ring, put on my finger by Liam McGregor, in front of my father and uncle and Father Donahue, promises made by us both in front of all three of them and God. So whoever you are, I'd thank you to tell me what you're doing in my fiancé's apartment."

I open my mouth and close it again, stunned by the sight of the ring on her finger, the oval diamond glittering in the sun, flanked by emeralds the same bright green as her eyes. Natural emeralds, not the overly dark green that lab-created ones take on. They're set in yellow gold, the band filigreed on the sides. It looks like an heirloom piece, an antique.

I feel sick, thinking of Liam sliding it onto her finger with a promise. Her grandmother's ring. In front of a priest.

Those things hold weight. Not just to him and Saoirse and me, but also her family. And, in a more far-reaching sense, I suspect to the organization he runs, too. I don't know the ins and outs of Irish crime. I barely know the Bratva, and my father was involved in that.

The last time I got mixed up in the dealings of a crime organization, I was tortured nearly to death. Since then, I've tried to avoid it—clearly with limited success. First Alexei, and now falling for Liam, who is probably playing a dangerous game if this woman is to be believed.

But I can barely think about that. All I can think about is that he's promised to marry someone else. He's been in my bed, *inside* me, pleasuring me and calling out my name as I repeatedly did the same for him. He's sworn to me he loves me, held back his kisses and his desire waiting on me to feel the same, forcing us to wait to sleep together again until I'd forgotten Alexandre. And all the while, he's been doing that—while engaged to someone else?

I can't believe it. I *won't*.

Saoirse drops her hand, looking at me with frustration written across every one of her pretty features. "Are you an idiot?" she asks, narrowing her eyes. "I've asked you twice now—"

My thoughts circle back to something she'd said before. A name. "Father Donahue," I blurt out, and Saoirse narrows her eyes.

"What about him?"

"You said he performed your—your engagement? What do you mean?" The idea of that seems strange to me. I've never pictured getting engaged other than having the man ask me in some romantic setting. Sofia didn't so much get engaged as getting muscled to the cathedral between Luca and Don Rossi, and Caterina's engagement was decided without her present, and her wedding was equally rushed.

Saoirse sighs. "It's a tradition of the Kings, when their highest-ranking is engaged to be married. He signs a document with a priest, the bride-to-be, and two of her male family members present." She shrugs. "It's all very archaic, as many of their traditions are, but not without its charms. And," she adds, her eyes narrowing. "Liam performed that ceremony with *me*. So that brings me back to the question—"

"Father Donahue," I blurt out again, and Saoirse rolls her eyes, but I don't stop to let her talk. "He's in Manhattan. Is that where you live?"

"No." Saoirse looks at me as if I'm a bit slow. "I live here in Boston. With my father—"

"So how could he have performed your…your engagement?"

Saoirse lets out a long, slow breath through her pursed lips as if it's taking every bit of patience she has to keep talking to me. "We were in Manhattan when it was performed," she says, speaking slowly as if to an idiot or a child. "At Viktor Andreyev and Caterina's second wedding. My father wanted it confirmed before Liam left on some business trip—" Her eyes narrow again, and I see her putting the pieces together.

"I'll ask you again," she says finally. "What the fuck are you doing in my fiancé's apartment? And who are you to him?"

Much to Saoirse's plain disgust—and mine with myself, if I'm being honest—I burst into tears. Because I can't deny it any longer.

If she were lying, she wouldn't know Father Donahue. She definitely wouldn't have been to Viktor and Caterina's wedding—which she probably attended with Liam. The thought of them at a wedding together, holding hands, dancing, laughing, makes me feel sick.

I look at the ring on her finger, and I know she's telling the truth. It's in her bearing, how confidently she speaks, how all the pieces fit together. He's kept this secret from me, and this is how I'm finding out.

My knees feel weak. Tears are streaming down my face as I clap my other hand over my mouth, stifling the deep, shuddering sobs that are threatening to break loose. Saoirse shakes her head in frustrated disgust, turning away from me.

It takes me a second to realize where she's going—towards Liam's bedroom.

I follow her long enough for her to stalk inside, looking around as if she's searching for something specific. The bed is made up, and she turns away from it to yank open dresser drawers, his closet, stalking into the attached bathroom and then back out again.

"There's nothing of yours in here." Saoirse glares at me as if it's somehow my fault that she hasn't found the evidence she was looking for.

"I—I don't sleep in here," I manage through my tears, my throat choked. "I—"

"You don't sleep with him?"

I shake my head, and that much, at least, is true. She narrows her eyes as if sizing me up, and then pushes past me to stride through the living room again, towards the opposite side of the house.

Towards my room.

I try to catch up with her, but the guest room I occupy is the first one she enters. She looks around, standing in the middle of the room as she takes in the pink and white color scheme, the unmade bed, and the bathroom door open to show where some of my things are strewn across the counter.

"So this is where you sleep." Saoirse presses her lips together. "Did he have this room made up especially for you? I can't imagine him telling a designer to do—*this*—for any other reason." She waves her hand around at the admittedly overly-feminine décor, and I feel the air go out of me as she turns back to me.

"Yes," I admit quietly. "He had the room redecorated so I'd be more —comfortable."

Saoirse raises an eyebrow. "This is your idea of a well-decorated room?"

"Well—no, not exactly." I bite my lower lip. The conversation is ridiculous, but the longer we can keep from getting around to what Liam and I are to each other, the better. I'm still not sure how much of it I want to admit to her, how much I *should* say—not even for Liam's protection, but for my own.

"I used to be a ballerina," I finish lamely. "He just told the decorator that, and she—well, he said she kind of went off on her own, and this was the result. I was just happy to have somewhere to sleep."

Even I'd admit the last comes out a bit melodramatic, but it stops Saoirse in her tracks. She pauses, considering me again for a moment.

"What do you mean?" she asks finally. "That you were glad to have somewhere to sleep? What are you, some kind of charity case? A family member I don't know about?"

It's on the tip of my tongue to tell her that, yes, I'm some long-lost family member. But I'm not sure she'd believe it in the first place, and at any rate, it would come out eventually that I'd lied. I don't necessarily want to tell her the whole truth if I can avoid it, but something tells me that the fewer lies I weave around Liam and me to this woman, the better.

"Liam rescued me," I say truthfully, wrapping my arms around my waist.

"Rescued you?" Saoirse looks doubtful. "From what? Who?"

How the fuck do I condense this into a short enough story that she'll listen to—and even believe—me?

"I got mixed up in some dealings with the Bratva in Manhattan a while back. Trying to help a friend," I explain. "One of his brigadiers turned traitor. He kidnapped the Bratva leader's wife—"

"Yes, Viktor and Caterina. I heard the whole story, or some of it, anyway, from Liam." Saoirse purses her lips. "So you got caught up in that? That man that kidnapped Caterina and her friend and some other girl?"

Clearly, Liam left me out when telling Saoirse the story. I can understand it, I suppose—he probably wouldn't have been able to get away to come and find me so easily if he'd said plainly he was going after a girl he'd left behind. But at the same time, it hurts to think that he didn't tell her about me. I wonder what else he told her, if he told her that he'd participated in torturing Alexei to death, how clean she thinks the hands of the man that she's meant to marry are.

I wonder what she would think if she knew what kind of woman *she* is. A daughter of someone high up in the Kings, clearly. But is she like Sofia, who never wanted to know any of it until she was forced to, or more like Caterina, who was raised in that world and never flinched at the things that had to be done?

I think, deep down, that the woman standing in front of me has a strong spine. She hasn't cried or shouted, hasn't flown into a rage. She's angry, but she's talking calmly to me, though I can hear the thread of fury through every single one of her words. She's stayed composed, something that makes me think of Caterina, and it's that, too, that makes me believe she's telling the truth.

This is the sort of woman that Liam *would* marry, if he'd never grown to have feelings for me.

The question is, does he want to?

I don't think that's a question she could properly answer. And I'm not sure if Liam will tell me the truth any longer.

The thought nearly sends me into a fresh round of tears, but Saoirse snaps her fingers, her frustration showing clearly again. "Explain," she says curtly. "You were kidnapped?"

"Yes, I—I met Liam at the safe house in Russia, when he and Luca came there with Luca's wife and some of the others that were in danger because of what Alexei was doing. Because I'd had dealings with the Bratva before—tried to get information from them—Viktor had decided I was in danger too, so he wanted me brought there. That's when Liam and I met—"

"So you've said," Saorise snaps. "So the two of you—what? Became friends? And he 'rescued' you because of that?"

"I—yes." I lick my dry lips, feeling my heart racing in my chest. I have to tread carefully, now, if I don't want Saoirse to know what Liam and I are to each other—if I want to keep that to myself, until I have answers from him. "Alexei came to the safe house—"

"Yes, I know. And you were with them? When he tried to sell the women at that party?"

How much does she really know? "Yes. And someone bought me before Viktor, Liam, and the others could get there. I wasn't there when they rescued Caterina and the other women and Viktor's children. A Frenchman named—"

"And Liam went to rescue you from this—Frenchman?" Saoirse interrupts me, and I can see that her patience is getting thinner by the moment. "He what—rode in on a white horse, stole you, and brought you back here?"

"More or less," I whisper. Her version, in fact, is a *lot* less, but I'm not inclined to tell her any more. I don't want to share the mingled traumas and joys of my time with Alexandre or the inescapable pain of what he'd forced Liam to do. I don't want to be the one to tell this woman, who is engaged to Liam, that he was held at gunpoint and forced to fuck me to climax in front of Alexandre and his friends.

Liam should tell her that if she's going to know. Just as he should have told me about Saoirse in the first place.

"And you're telling me that you're just a friend." Saoirse looks at me carefully as if trying to surmise how trustworthy I am. "That Liam went all the way to bloody fucking France, burst in and took you away from this man who bought you—putting his own self and a great deal more in danger—and brought you here to his penthouse and a room he'd had specially decorated for you, and told me *not a single bloody thing about this*—because you're his *friend*? A woman he's known for—how long?"

"Not long," I whisper. I can't quantify it exactly. I couldn't even tell her how long I was at Alexandre's with absolute certainty. The days had tended to bleed into each other there, especially without a television or a phone or access to a computer. I'd been in a strange sort of bubble; it had almost felt as if time hadn't started back up again until Liam had whisked me out and I'd woken up in that London hotel.

Saoirse shakes her head, disgust starting to show on her features again, and she turns away from me towards the dresser. I don't realize what she's doing in time to stop her, and I'm not sure I could have even if I'd tried.

It only takes the first drawer for her to find something suspicious. She turns back towards me, the silk and lace teddy, the pretty sleepwear that Liam had bought me, and the pink and lace lingerie set clutched in her fists.

"What in the bloody hell is this?" She drops it in a pile on the floor, flinging it towards me. "He *rescued* you and brought you straight here, right? So he must have bought these things for you, right?" She dangles the pink and white collar from her finger, and I can feel my face flushing to the roots of my hair, just looking at it. Thinking about how many times I've imagined wearing it, and the rest of the lingerie set that came with it, for Liam. The way he'd bought it for me, even though I'd said I didn't need it, as if I might have a reason to in the future.

The memory of that day makes all the hurt come rushing back, flooding me with a pain that I hadn't thought he could make me feel. I remember the night he'd gone out, when he'd come home to me having a nightmare and what had come after, and I realize with a blinding certainty that he must have been with *her*. The way he'd been before he left, almost guilty, refusing to sit next to me on the couch or touch me—he'd been going to see his fiancée. At the same time, I waited for him to come back, unknowing. And that night—

I want to know if he's slept with her, and don't, all at once. It'll be a question I'll have to ask him if I can manage it. There's no way to ask her without giving away that I, too, have slept with Liam, for different reasons, on different occasions.

Once because I was forced to. Once out of desire, and I'd managed to ruin that too when I'd screamed Alexandre's name at the end. I still have nightmares sometimes about Liam scrambling away from me mid-orgasm, horror on his face, still hard, still twitching with the pleasure of his climax even as he'd looked at me with such pain that it had ripped me apart to see it, in the same way that I'd ripped him apart too, by doing it.

Now, we might never get a chance again after this.

"No," I whisper, abandoning any ideas about not lying to her. I can't face this woman and tell her flat out that Liam bought me any of these things or tell her about what we've done together. I just can't, not until I know the truth from him, because some small part of me is still holding out hope that *she's* lying.

Even though I know, deep down, that she's not.

"You're not fucking him?" Saoirse narrows her eyes, tossing the collar onto the floor to join the rest of the lingerie. "You're telling me you just—have all of this? That the two of you are nothing but friends? You're some charity case he took in and just—fucking forgot to tell me about?"

"Your engagement was arranged, right? Maybe you're just not that close?" The words come out before I can stop myself, even I know they're absolutely the wrong choice. I can see it even more clearly in the way Saoirse's eyes go round, as if she can't believe I've spoken to her that way.

"Tell. Me. You're. Not. Fucking. Him." Her words come out individually, enunciated, and I swallow hard before looking her in the eye.

"No," I whisper. "We're just friends."

"You're bloody fucking lying." Saoirse shakes her head with disgust. "But I suppose there's no point in trying to drag it out of you."

She pushes past me, back out towards the living room, and I follow her numbly at a distance, trying to hold back the tears. She gets as far as the front door before she turns sharply around, her eyes narrowed as she points one manicured fingernail at me.

"This isn't over," she says flatly. It's not a threat, not even said in that angry tone of voice. It's a simple fact, spoken like a woman who has a right to the man who lives here. "I'll deal with Liam when I get back. As for you—" she grits her teeth, and I can see her jaw working. "I'd be thinking of somewhere else to live if I were you. You won't be here on Liam's charity much longer."

When the door slams behind her, it shakes the entire penthouse. My knees won't hold me up any longer. I only just make it to the living room sofa before I collapse onto it, dissolving in tears.

How could he not have told me?

TWO
ANA

He took me away from Alexandre for this. He never even told me —

If I could stop to think, I would know that the thoughts and emotions swirling around my head don't make sense. But I can't think anything through. All I can see is Saoirse's beautiful, angry face in front of me, her engagement ring glinting in the apartment sunlight, her voice in my head over and over again.

I'm Liam's fiancée.
Who the fuck are you?
Father Donahue —
Viktor and Caterina's wedding —
Charity case —
Are you fucking him?

I can hear her, plain as day, and all I can think is that Liam should have told me. How could he think I'd never find out? Had he planned on marrying her in secret, keeping me somewhere else like some secret mistress, never telling Saoirse and me about each other? It seems so different from the Liam I know, the man who says he loves me and who I've been falling in love with more and more every day, the man who risked so much to come and get me away from Alexandre.

Alexandre.

This morning, it had been easier than I'd expected to refuse him, to hang up on him. To fight off the feelings I still have for him. But now, with this betrayal fresh in my mind and my heart aching with more pain than I've felt since the night that Alexandre was the one to betray me, all I can think is that maybe I'd been wrong to brush him off so quickly.

He'd said that Liam had secrets. *Was this what he was talking about?* I can't imagine how he knows, how he could possibly know something so intimate about Liam's life, but I want to know. I want to know if this was what he was trying to tell me about, warn me about, and if so—

I feel like I'm in a dream as I pick up my phone, like an out-of-body experience. I hit the button to call back the number that had called me this morning, wondering if it will even go through, if he called me from someone else's phone or a burner he'd thrown away. But it rings once, twice, and then a third time, and I hear that deep French accent that sends shivers of fear and desire down my spine all at once come over the line.

"Anastasia?"

"How did you know it was me?" It always feels odd to hear him say my real name, not my nickname. He only ever said it when he was angry with me or in the throes of desire, or sometimes when saying he loved me. It sends such conflicting feelings through me—it reminds me of being afraid of him and how much pleasure we shared together. It ties my stomach in knots just thinking about it.

"I saved this number, *petit*, of course. What is it? Have you changed your mind about seeing me? Have you called to say that you miss me?" There's a pause, and I know he's waiting for me to speak, but I can't. My throat feels closed over with panic, my chest tight and aching. My hands are shaking so badly that I can hardly hold the phone, and I know I'm on the verge of losing it.

"*Petit*, you sound upset. Tell me where you are, and I will come to get you. You shouldn't be alone in such a state. You know I can care for you—didn't I, in Paris? I can keep you safe, *petit*—"

"You said Liam had secrets," I blurt out, the words coming out strangled. "His fiancée. Was that one of the secrets you were talking about?"

"Ah, so you met the lovely Irish princess. Saoirse O'Sullivan, I believe her name is?" The name sounds odd in his French accent, nothing like how Saoirse had pronounced her own name.

"Yes." I feel a fresh wave of tears welling up, and I press my shaking hand against my mouth, sinking off of the couch and onto the floor as I try to keep myself from bursting into sobs all over again. "Was that one of the secrets? Alexandre, tell me, please—"

"I love when you say my name like that, *petit*. So sweet, begging me—"

"Alexandre—"

"Yes." His voice is slightly more clipped. "Yes, it was."

"Are there more?" I clutch the phone tighter against my face, feeling myself starting to shake all over. *What else could there be? What else is Liam keeping from me?* I hadn't wanted to believe Alexandre this morning. I'd thought he was lying, to convince me to come back to him by shaking my trust in Liam. But if he'd been telling the truth about this, he could be telling the truth about others.

Has Liam been lying to me about more than just Saoirse all this time? Keeping more things from me?

"You should ask Liam," Alexandre says tightly, and I can tell that he's displeased that I'm so concerned with Liam. "Since the two of you are so *close*."

The displeasure in his voice tips me over the edge again into fresh panic, fresh tears. I feel suddenly as if I'm losing them both— Alexandre because I've gotten so far away from him now, so much so that I don't know if I could go back to being his pet, his little doll, even if sometimes I still crave it, and Liam because I no longer know if I can trust him. I start to cry in sharp, gasping, gulping sobs that threaten to actually suffocate me, choking on the tears and unable to breathe, crying loudly into the phone.

"*Petit. Petit!* Anastasia!" There's a clear alarm in Alexandre's voice, the irritation gone. "*Petit,* please. Don't cry like this. You don't need to weep for him. Tell me where you are, *petit*, please. I'll come and find you." There's a moment's silence on the line, and then his voice again, rich and thick like smoke, like silk, wrapping around me the way it used to do in the apartment in Paris, lulling me into his grasp. "You shouldn't have left me, *petit,* my little Anastasia," he murmurs. "You belong to me. You know that you do. You should never have left. You thought that he could take you away, that you could escape—but you belong to me. Deep down, you know it's more than what I paid for you, *petit.* In your very soul, you belong to me. I awakened things in you that you never knew you could need or crave, did I not?"

I stifle another sob, closing my eyes as I tip my head back, wishing more than anything that I could disappear and that this could all end. Liam, Alexandre, who I love, who I want, who I should be with, who I can trust. I feel sick of it all, sick of trying to decide, trying to understand, and I choke out the only question I can think of to ask him, the only thing that could possibly matter right now.

"Did you love me?" I ask tearfully, the words coming out half-muffled. "Did you, really?"

"*Oui, petit,*" Alexandre says simply. "Yes. I loved you dearly, passionately, in a way that I've loved no other woman since—"

He breaks off, but he doesn't have to say who. I know who he's talking about—his stepsister, Margot, the girl he loved and lost horrifically so many years ago, which warped him into the strange and eccentric man he is today. "I love you, *petit,*" he says again, his voice softer now. "It is up to you if you believe it is true."

"If you love me—" I squeeze the phone so hard that I feel like my knuckles are turning white, holding it to my cheek like it's his hand as I try to understand. "How could you do that to me, then? How could you force Liam to have sex with me like that—in—in front of everyone, in front of you? How could you do it? If you really loved me, how could you watch?" I'm crying again now, stumbling over the words. "I was so scared, Alexandre, so scared, and I trusted you. You said you would keep me safe, and I *trusted* you!"

The words come out in a rush, more than I really meant to say, but the silence on the other end tells me that he's heard me.

"I'm sorry, *petit,*" he murmurs finally, his own voice thickening with emotion. "I meant to test you, to test your love for me. Yvette—" Alexandre breaks off again, and I hear him draw in a deep, shuddering breath. "I believed that you would take no pleasure in him, that you would realize you loved me only, and it would only solidify our bond, that you would know no other man could make you feel the way I did—"

"That's crazy," I whisper before I can stop myself. "Surely, Alexandre, you see how crazy it is—"

"Was it?" His voice sounds brittle as a twig, snapping after each word. "You were a bad girl, *petit*, if you loved me as you say you do. You failed this crazy test. And you left with another man, as you promised me you would not do." There's that deep breath again, and I swallow hard, feeling unsteady even sitting down from the yo-yo of his emotions in addition to my own.

"You can be my good girl again, *petit*," Alexandre croons, his voice rich and smooth again. "Just ask me to forgive you, and I will. We can put it all behind us, this ridiculousness, and be like we were before the Irishman ruined our peace. Tell me where you are, and I'll come for you. I'll take you home and protect you, as I promised I would. *Petit*—"

"I can't go to Paris," I whisper. "I have friends here. I have—"

"You will make new friends. I'll give you more freedom than you had before once we're together again and safe, once I know that I can trust you to stay, to keep your promise to me."

"I—"

"I would never cheat on you, Anastasia." There it is—my name. My real name on his lips as he begs me to come back. "I will never love another woman but you, my *petit*, my Anastasia, never want anyone except you, my beautiful broken doll."

It's almost hypnotizing. His voice, saying words that feel familiar, that feel, in a way, safe. Words that promise things I need, that I once wanted from him. Love, safety, pleasure, protection. I once wanted to be on my own, to face the world alone, but I don't anymore. It's too cruel, too capricious, too awful. I want someone by my side as I walk through it, someone to help me shoulder the burden. I don't want to face all my demons by myself.

With Alexandre, I didn't even have to face them. I only had to exist, to follow a few simple rules, and he was pleased.

But would it always be that way? And do I want to be with a man who doesn't let me choose my future?

Do I want to be with the one who's lied to me?

"Tell me where you are, *petit*." Alexandre's voice is more frustrated now, insistent. "Tell me—"

A rush of panic washes over me, scrambling my thoughts again. I can't decide, I can't choose. I don't know what to do, so I do the only thing I can with a single snap decision—I hang up. His voice cuts off, leaving only silence and the sound of my rapid breathing as my heart hammers in my chest.

The phone drops into my lap, and I sit there, shaking.

I'd only just started to feel safe again, secure, and now this. I don't know what to do. I don't know what I *want* to do, and out of my options, I don't know which of those I can trust.

I find myself reaching for the phone again, but this time I call the one person that I know I can depend on. The one person who has always been there for me, as long as I've known her.

Sofia answers after two rings. "Ana? Is everything okay?"

"No!" I say, my voice rising, and then I burst into tears again.

"Ana—Ana, whatever it is, just breathe. Tell me what's going on, just as soon as you can."

Sofia's voice is calm and soothing, and it breaks through the wall of my panic. "Ana, are you hurt? Are you safe?"

"I'm safe," I manage, sniffling through my tears. "And I'm not hurt—not physically, at least."

"What happened?"

I take a deep breath, holding back the tears long enough to talk through them. "Did you know that Liam had a fiancée?" I manage, biting my lip hard to stem the fresh wave of sobs that threaten to break loose just from saying the word aloud.

"What?" Sofia gasps, and it's clear just from that one word that she didn't have the slightest idea, either. "No, of course not, Ana! I wouldn't have left you there with him when we came to stay if I'd known. He was with a woman at Caterina's wedding, but I had no idea they were engaged. It was before he went to find you, too—I assumed that if there had been anything there, he'd broken it off—"

"The engagement was that night, according to her. Before he left."

The words come out numbly, like parroting something I've heard someone else say. "Luca didn't tell you anything about this?"

"No, not at all." Sofia pauses. "And if he knew, I'm going to have something to say about him not telling me once he knew you were staying there—"

She breaks off, and I can tell from the tone of her voice that there's going to be tension in the Romano household tonight.

"I'm sorry, Sofia, I don't want you and Luca to fight over this." I wipe savagely at my face, dashing away the tears. "I just—I never thought, he never even *hinted*—"

"I don't know what the fuck he's thinking, to be frank," Sofia snaps. "Ana, if you want me to come to get you, I will—"

"No, I want to see him when he comes home." The words feel choked, strangled in my throat, but I mean it. "I can't just run away."

"I'll come there, then. So if you need me, after—"

"It's okay." I take a deep, shuddering breath, feeling slightly calmer just from the sound of her voice. Somehow, calling my best friend made it feel more normal. All of this is horrible, but it's just guy problems. I've never sat on my floor sobbing to my best friend over the phone about them before. Still, I've definitely sat on *our* living room floor, or my bed or hers when we shared an apartment, complaining about guys, crying when one disappointed me. Back then, it felt much more low-stakes, but it's not that different.

I've gotten through worse. I can get through this.

"No," Sofia insists. "I want to make sure you're okay, Ana. I'll be there tonight, just as soon as the plane can be ready."

"Sofia—"

"I'm not taking no for an answer," she says gently. "Take a shower, or a bath, Ana, and a nap if you can. I'll be there soon."

When she hangs up the phone, I'm left on the living room floor, still trembling even if I'm not in a full panic like before.

It's evening when Sofia gets to the apartment. I've managed to take a bath between the phone call and then, but I'm still in my robe, my hair damp as I sit, curled into a ball on the couch. Only her knock on the door gets me up. Even then, my heart is hammering, afraid that it's Saoirse coming back to tear into me again even though Sofia just texted me.

Sofia takes one look at me as she comes into the penthouse and lets out a sigh. "Have you eaten at all today, Ana?"

I shake my head, tears already welling up in my eyes again.

"Okay. Come on, let's get you in some comfy clothes, and I'll make dinner. Or order it." She gently guides me down the hall, one hand on the small of my back, and I let her.

The pile of lingerie is still on the floor when we walk in, and I flush red, but Sofia doesn't even blink. She just scoops it up, tossing it all back into the top drawer as she fishes out a pair of loose, soft pajama pants and a tank top for me. "Did Saoirse do that?" she asks as she turns around, and I nod speechlessly.

"Bitch," Sofia says, spitting the word out with real venom, and I shake my head.

"That's the thing—she wasn't really." I take the clothes from Sofia, undoing my robe and tossing it across the bed. "I mean, I could tell she was pissed. And it's hard to blame her—if she really is Liam's fiancée, then we both have a right to be upset with him. But she wasn't really a bitch. I mean, she didn't yell or call me names or anything." I fiddle with the string on the pajama pants as I pull them on, reaching for the tank top. "She did say I should start looking for somewhere else to stay, that she was going to put a stop to Liam's 'charity,' as she called it."

"You're always welcome with us, you know that." Sofia perches on the edge of the bed as I pull the tank top on, sympathy written across every inch of her face. "And I'm glad she wasn't mean to you—but I have to say, I'm less worried about her than about you right now. You're my best friend, Ana. I don't care who Liam is; I'm not going to let him treat you badly."

"That's the thing." I sink onto the bed next to her. "That's why I don't understand any of this. He *hasn't* treated me badly. He's been nothing but kind and patient with me, even though things are difficult between us and there's so much baggage. I didn't even believe her at first because there's been nothing to make me think he'd ever do something like this. I just—I don't understand."

"How long before he comes back?" Sofia urges me up off the bed, herding me back down the hall and into the living room so that she can go about finding us some dinner. "Do you know for sure?"

"He said he'd be gone for about a week." I curl up onto the couch again, watching as she flicks through a food delivery app. "I don't know what I'm going to do until then. I feel like I'm going to go crazy wondering, thinking about it—"

"Well, I can stay for a few days." Sofia taps her phone, finishes the order, and sets it down next to her, tucking her feet underneath her on the sofa in a mirror of how I'm sitting on the other side. "I have an OB/GYN appointment later this week, so I have to be back in New York for that. But I can stay and keep you company until then."

"Luca's okay with that?"

"I didn't give him much choice," Sofia smirks. "I was pretty upset with him for not telling me about this fiancée. According to him, he and Viktor are flying in next week after Liam gets back to talk with him."

"About that?" I frown, looking at her nervously. "Why would they—"

"He wouldn't tell me all the details. He said with you being my best friend, it wasn't a good idea for us to talk about it too much. I don't—I don't really know what that means." Sofia looks at me apologetically. "I'm sorry, Ana. He was really adamant about not talking about it more after that. I wish I could give you better answers. But I have to be careful of my marriage too. Liam is in an alliance with Luca and Viktor, through the Kings, the Bratva, and the mafia, respectively. Liam's relationships can affect that. And with you and I being as close as we are—well, I can understand Luca's perspective, even if I don't like being kept in the dark. I wish I could tell you more."

"It's okay." I chew on my lower lip, picking at my cuticles as I look away. "I don't want to cause problems in your marriage. I just—I don't even know how to believe Liam at this point. I don't know if he's going to tell me the truth, if he hid this from me all this time, with everything we've done—"

"Hear him out." Sofia looks at me, her brow furrowed. "I'm upset with him too, Ana. But it's possible that there *is* an explanation for all of this. Men like Luca and Viktor and Liam—their lives are complicated. *Everything* about them is complicated. Maybe he hasn't been telling you because—"

"Because he doesn't think I can handle it?"

"Because he wanted to give you time to work through everything else before he threw that at you. Maybe he wasn't planning to go through with it—"

But even as she says it, Sofia's expression looks doubtful, and I feel my heart sinking. I know she's trying to make me feel better, and having her here does, at least a little.

I know that nothing can really fix it, though, besides hearing Liam tell me the truth.

And even then, I can't help but think that maybe this time, we've run into something that can't be fixed.

THREE
LIAM

When I come home, I can feel the foreboding before I even get off the plane. My texts and calls with Ana have been short and to the point all week—and while I'd chalked it up to her missing me and struggling with being alone, I can't help but feel that there's something else going on.

It doesn't make me feel any better that I haven't heard from Saoirse, either. Normally I would have been glad that I hadn't needed to call her, but the pointed absence of even a text left me more than a little concerned. It makes me feel like something has been going on while I was gone that I'm not aware of, which makes me even more unsettled.

When I step into the penthouse, my suspicions that something's wrong are instantly confirmed. The kitchen is a mess—a few dishes in the sink, things scattered across the counters, and the living room is the same. There are throw pillows haphazardly across the couch and on the floor, a couple of blankets half-on, half-off the sofa. It's not filthy, exactly, and I know there's still another day before the maid comes for her biweekly visit. Still, I've always kept the house up in between, and I saw Ana try to do the same. I'd assumed she had the same tendencies towards neatness that I do.

But compared to how it usually is, the apartment is a bit of a wreck.

Which instantly puts me on alert, thinking that Ana has spiraled while I was gone.

"Ana?" I call out her name, my stomach clenching with worry. I hadn't wanted to leave her, especially after getting the calls from Alexandre. I'd been afraid that something like this would happen, that she'd fall back into her depression with no one here. "Ana?"

A new fear grips me as I stride down the hall towards her room—that Alexandre has found her and taken her away. That he's scooped her up while she was out of the house going to one of her appointments, or evaded my security and broken in somehow, and taken her. But if the latter had happened, I would have been notified by now—

"Ana!" I push open the door to her bedroom and see her there, sitting on her bed wrapped in a blanket, scrolling listlessly through her phone.

My first instinctual feeling is relief. It washes over me, cool and clear, the moment that I see she's safe and still here. And then, the next is frustration.

I can tell that, despite our agreement, she hasn't been taking care of herself. Her hair is lank and listless around her face, and she looks as if she's lost a little weight over the last week, not gained it. That, combined with the state of the penthouse, all but confirms my fears that she's back in another depressive spiral.

"Ana," I say her name again, and this time she looks up, her blue eyes listless.

"Liam." The way she says my name is nothing like how I'd imagined she'd greet me when I'd thought eagerly about getting back home to her all this last week. She sounds tired—sad, even. Nothing about her tone of voice is what I would have expected.

"What's going on?" I step into the room, shutting the door behind me. "I've barely heard from you all week. The apartment is a mess, and you look like you haven't washed your hair in a few days or eaten—have you been going to your appointments?"

"Sure." Ana turns back to her phone, and I feel something tighten inside me, something almost angry.

"Anastasia." I never use her full name, but it slips from my lips as easily as the shortened version I'm used to, in my current mood. "Look at me."

Her jaw tightens, and she keeps scrolling.

"Put the fucking phone down and look at me."

Her head snaps up, and she finally does, dropping the phone onto the bed as she pushes herself upright a little more. "You can't talk to me like that," she says, pressing her lips tightly together. "You don't ever talk to me like that."

"If this is what happens when I leave for a week, maybe I should." I shove my hands into my pants' pockets, trying to battle the rapidly rising frustration. "What the hell is going on? You've never acted like this since I've known you, and I know you're lying to me about the appointments. We had an agreement, Ana—I would provide for you and give you a place to stay as long as you needed it, and you would take care of yourself, go to the appointments that I made for you—that I'm *paying* for—Christ." I run my hand through my hair, letting out a frustrated breath. "I sound like your fucking father. This isn't our relationship, Ana, so what the hell—"

"Maybe I don't need your charity anymore." She flings off the blanket, turning so that her legs are hanging over the side of the bed. Even though it's the afternoon, she's still wearing pajama pants and a tank top, the latter of which does very little to disguise the way her nipples are pressing against the thin fabric. After a week away from her, it's hard to ignore. But this also clearly isn't the time for that.

"My—*charity*?" I blink at her. "This isn't charity, you know that, Ana. I care for you—I *love* you, so what the hell put that into your head?"

"Not what," she mumbles, refusing to look at me. "Who."

Something goes through me at that, a pinging sense of alarm that warns me that whatever happened in my absence, whatever's about to happen now, isn't going to be good. But there's nothing to do but keep pushing forward, and find out.

"What do you mean, *who*? Ana, what are you talking about?" I take a couple of steps further into the room. She finally looks up at me, her blue eyes accusing and glittering with barely unshed tears.

"Your fiancée came by. *Saoirse O'Sullivan*."

She spits out the name, and the instant it comes out, hanging in the air between us, I feel my heart sink to my very toes.

Shit.

Fuck.

I'd thought I could handle the situation with Saoirse before Ana found out. I'd thought that maybe, she didn't need to know—or I'd tell her after it was handled when there was nothing left for her to fear. When it was certain that we'd be together, and it would just be a story to tell—a *this almost happened, but I loved you too much to let it.*

Clearly, I'd miscalculated.

"Ana—"

"Just tell me if it's true." Her voice is watery, the tears starting to brim on the edges of her lashes, threatening to fall. It rips my heart out to see her like this, and I kick myself mentally for ever thinking that this was the way to handle it, for not telling her and trusting her to be able to handle it, to be patient while I found my way out of this mess that I've gotten myself into.

I keep misjudging, at every step, how to best handle this, it feels like.

"Did she come here?" That thought makes me angry—I've never brought Saoirse back to my penthouse, never invited her here. The idea that she'd barged in on her own makes me want to throttle her, metaphorically, at least. I'd never actually hurt her. But I want to tell her never to fucking come to my apartment without an invitation again, that's for sure.

"Yes." Ana swallows hard. "She—I thought it was you, that you'd forgotten something. She came in, and—she said—the ring—" Ana starts to cry, her words breaking off as she claps a hand over her mouth to stifle it, and all I want is to go to her, to hold her and comfort her. But something tells me that wouldn't exactly be welcomed right now.

"Just tell me," Ana whispers. "Was she telling the truth? Are you engaged to her?"

I let out a breath, feeling all the air go out of me as my shoulders sag. "Yes," I say finally, and the pain that warps Ana's expression makes me wish that I could go back and do everything all over again, so that I could do it so much differently.

"It's not what you think," I start to say, and Ana's face twists, her eyes narrowing.

"That's what they all fucking say," she spits. "You're not really going to use that line on me, are you, after all of this? *It's not what you think.* Are you kidding me?"

"It's not." I grit my teeth, running one hand through my hair as I try to think of a way to explain before she completely melts down. "I don't love Saoirse, Ana."

"So what? You were going to marry her and have one of those loveless, rich people marriages and keep me as your mistress on the side? When were you going to tell me about that arrangement? Or was I never supposed to find out? What was going to be your excuse for moving me out of here into my own place, for not always being able to see me, for not being able to sleep over, for not—"

"Ana!" I cut in, my frustration rising as her voice does, glaring at her. "Ana, will you just give me one fucking second to explain, lass? There's an explanation here if you'll listen to it."

"I don't believe you—"

"I'm not going to marry her!" I almost shout it, staring at her as I try to rein in my own temper. "I've been fucking trying to get out of it since the minute I brought you back here, but it's a delicate situation—"

"She said you got engaged before you came to find me! So what was she, the backup in case you couldn't get me away from Alexandre? If I wouldn't leave, or you couldn't find me, you'd have her in your pocket to come back and marry?"

"No! Jesus, Mary, and Joseph, Ana, that's not it at all. Just let me fucking explain—"

"Alexandre called me." Ana tips her chin up defiantly, glaring at me. "He called me the morning before you left on your *business trip*, if that's really what you were doing. Or were you off finding another side piece, some other damsel in distress to rescue—"

"I absolutely was fucking not—Alexandre?" I break off, realizing what she said. My heart lurches in my chest, thinking of him calling her, of her hearing his voice, of what feelings that might have brought up in her. And then for Saoirse to show up not long after—

"He called me. He wanted me to tell him where I was, but I—I hung up on him." Ana looks at me, her eyes tearing up all over again. "I was so sure I wanted you. I had all these feelings, I felt so confused, but I couldn't imagine leaving you. I thought he'd give up if I ignored him. And then Saoirse showed up, and I—"

"Did you call him back?" I stare at her, feeling angry all over again. "Ana, you told me you were trying to get over him, to put it in the past—"

"He said I could go back with him if I wanted to. That he'd come to get me." Ana stares at me defiantly, and I feel my stomach knot with fury and fear all at once at the thought of her telling him where she is. At the thought of him taking her from me.

I should have fucking killed him when I had the chance.

"He only wants me." Tears are streaming down her cheeks again. "He swore it, over and over, that there's no other woman for him. Can you say the same now, honestly? Or have you just been fucking lying to me this whole time? How could you ask me—" Ana breaks off, crying harder. "You said you wouldn't let me tell you I love you, wouldn't sleep with me again until it was only you. How *dare* you, how fucking dare you demand that when you had someone else. How is that fucking fair, Liam? How could you—"

"I don't love Saoirse!" I nearly shout it, my hands in fists as I clench my teeth, trying to figure out how the hell to make her understand. "I've never touched her, Ana. I've never so much as fucking kissed her, except at the altar when we were engaged, and briefly at that. I've never made love to her. I've done everything I fucking can to keep my hands off of her because I want *you*, Ana. I don't want any other woman but you. I swear it, by anything you want me to swear on. And that's all I want in return—for you to forget Alexandre and want me, and me alone, because that's how I feel about you. It's only you, Ana; it only ever has been." I'm breathing hard now, staring at her fiercely, trying to break through the walls I know she's thrown back up. "Did you tell him where you were?"

"No, I—" Ana wipes at her face, but it's useless, she's still crying. Fresh tears immediately replace the ones that she wiped away. "I wouldn't tell him where I was. But it's not fair, Liam—"

"If you still fucking love him so much, why do you care about Saoirse?" I glare at her, struggling mightily to keep my temper in check, to think and speak rationally, but I'm quickly being overcome by my own emotions. "I know I should have told you sooner, but I had no plans to go through with it—"

"Why did you save me?" Ana looks up at me tearfully. "If you had this other engagement, this other promise, why did you come all the way to France to find me—"

"Because I fucking love you!" My voice rises, and I run both hands through my hair, feeling like I'm in danger of pulling it out. "Christ, Ana, how is it so hard for you to understand? My engagement to Saoirse was temporary, to keep things in order here while I went to find you, and when I came back—"

"You loved me? You didn't even know me then. You still don't know me, if you think—"

I let out a frustrated breath. "I want to know you, Ana. It's all I want. I've tried, day after day, to get you to let me in, but you can't. Not all the way, because you're still clinging to him. You're too—"

"Broken?" She cuts me off, her voice suddenly sharp, almost vicious in the way she spits the word out. "Is that what you were going to say? You haven't let me in either, Liam, or you would have told me what was going on in your life. You would have told me about Saoirse. Don't you think that's something I fucking needed to know?" She shakes her head, tears flying. "At least Alexandre loved me because I was broken—"

"He didn't fucking love you!" I stare at her, feeling as if it's impossible to get through to her right now, not knowing what else I can say. "He fucking collected you, Ana, like a piece of art or a first edition book, or some bloody thing like that. You weren't a person to him. Just like you said, you were his doll. A toy. Something to *own*. That's not love—"

"What you've been doing isn't love, either! Keeping your fiancée a secret from me while you *supposedly* try to figure out how to break things off isn't love! Lying to me isn't love—"

"I haven't lied to you, Ana, not once. Not ever—"

"A lie of omission is still a lie."

We both stare at each other, chests heaving, the angry words we've both spit out hanging in the air between us. Ana clutches the side of the bed, her eyes wild and furious and tearful, and I'm just as upset.

"I don't know what to do," I say quietly, looking at her. "I don't know what you want—if you want him, or me, or if even you know. I had made my decision, Ana, even if you don't believe me. I kept some things from you, yes. I thought it was the right choice. But I don't know what it is that you want from me, from us—"

"What do *you* want?" Ana stares at me, her lips trembling, and I want, more than anything, to tell her that it will be okay. But I'm not sure if that's true anymore.

"I want you," I say simply, holding her gaze with my own. "Just you, but I don't know how that's possible anymore. I'll lose everything for a woman that's still dreaming about another man."

And then, before she can say a word, before I can say anything else that I'll regret later, I turn on my heel and leave the room, the sound of her crying following me all the way down the hall.

FOUR
ANA

Without thinking, I leap up off of the bed and follow him. My heart is racing in my chest, tears streaming down my face, but I can't just drop it. Not like that, not when that's the last thing he said before leaving.

He wasn't going to marry her. Can that possibly be true?

Up until the moment Saoirse barged into the penthouse, I'd never felt that I had a reason to believe that Liam wasn't telling me the truth about how he felt. Everything he said, everything he did, pointed to him being a man who was truly in love with me, who was willing to cross oceans and make sacrifices for us to be together. I'd felt so guilty because all he'd asked of me was to stop loving a man who I perhaps shouldn't have loved in the first place, and I'd been struggling with it.

But Liam had been keeping secrets from me, too.

He's striding towards his own bedroom, and I have to rush to keep up with him. I can see that he's angry in the set of his shoulders, the way he leans forward as he walks, but I can't just let him go. Something inside me is screaming that if he walks into that room and shuts the door, it's done. That I won't be able to get him back—and I'm not at all sure yet that I'm ready to let him go for good.

He goes to slam the door as he steps into his room, but I push against it, following him inside. He turns on me as I do, his green eyes blazing, and I hold my ground as we face off with each other, the frustration on Liam's face as plain as the pain I can see shimmering in his eyes.

And there's something else, too, that I can see as his eyes flick over me. He wants me, even now. I can feel it, and I want him too. The rocky cliff that our relationship is hanging from makes it feel worse that we've never fully gotten to be together. Every time we get that close, something happens to ruin it. Liam stops us—or I accidentally call out another man's name.

What would have happened if I'd screamed his name instead that night? Would he have confessed everything about Saoirse, told me he was breaking it off with her, and we'd be fine now? Happy, even?

There's no way to know. But I'm not ready to call it completely, not yet.

"I've tried to forget Alexandre," I tell him breathlessly, closing the door behind me and leaning against it so he can't easily force me out. "I told you I hung up on him the first time he called. I was ready to tell you that I wanted to be with you, to put him in the past—I wanted to get there by the time you came home from your trip. And then Saoirse stormed in—"

"I was afraid Alexandre might call you." Liam rubs a hand over his mouth. "I should have fucking known—"

My eyes go wide. "What do you mean? How—what would have made you think—"

"He called me, too. First," Liam admits. "Out of nowhere. I thought maybe he was just trying to spook me into giving you up, but clearly—"

I stare at him, horrified. "And you didn't think to warn me? You knew he'd found us, and you didn't think that was something I should know? Why didn't you tell me? Hearing his voice out of nowhere was an awful shock. I—I wish I'd had some warning—"

"I didn't tell you because I was afraid of this happening!" Liam shouts, his voice rising again as he clenches his jaw with obvious frustration. "I was afraid of Alexandre coming between us again, of him ruining what little progress we'd made. I was afraid that if you knew there was a chance he'd come for you, it would confuse you all over again, and you'd remember how you felt for him. It's the same reason I didn't tell you about Saoirse."

He's breathing hard now, stepping towards me, and I move sideways, away from the door, but Liam is closing in on me. My heart is pounding wildly, and I don't know if it's fear or something else altogether making my breath catch in my throat as Liam backs me against the dresser, his face taut with half a dozen emotions that I can't pick apart.

"Everything we have is so fragile, Ana," he whispers, his voice rough, the words catching as he speaks. "I'm fucking terrified of losing it. I kept secrets from you because I was afraid of losing you, and now —" he lets out a breath, his green eyes shimmering with pain. "Now I might lose you anyway, and I—"

"What, Liam?" I'm whispering too; our voices suddenly hushed where they were raised a moment ago, close together in the space between his dresser and his bed. "Tell me—"

"You've made me feel things I've never felt before." His hand comes up, touching the edge of my jaw, brushing over the line of it. "You've made me want things I didn't know it was possible to want. I'd settled on the things that I'd been raised to believe a man in my position should have—and among those is an arranged marriage to a proper woman, a woman who fulfills the needs of a King. But I don't want a *proper* woman anymore, Ana."

He's very close to me now, his entire body rigid and taut, and I can feel the heat coming off of him. His voice is rough, tense, and it makes my heart race until I think surely he can see it beating wildly against my throat.

I can't breathe. Every hair on my body is raised, my skin prickling, and I don't know if I want to run from him or throw myself into his arms—if I even were to have a choice, right now, and I'm not sure that I do.

"I love you, Ana. I have loved you since the moment I set eyes on you, I think, and I—I can't fucking lose you. Not now. Not over this."

His fingers close around my chin, pulling me forward. "Liam—" I breathe, but it's too late. My eyes lock onto his, and I can see the wild desire there, the need for me that's taken him over.

I can't imagine him looking at Saoirse like that. Only me.

His mouth comes crashing down on mine, his other hand hard on my waist as he pushes me back against the dresser, holding my lips to his. His tongue snakes over my lower lip, pushing into my mouth, forcing it open for him, and I can't help but give in. I'm instantly swept away by the tide of desire that Liam always rouses in me. The moment he feels me start to kiss him back, my hands grabbing at his shirt instead of trying to push him away, that hand that was on my chin tangles in my hair.

His hand fists in my long blonde locks, wrapping them around his hand as he grinds himself against me. I can feel how hard he is, not just his cock but every muscle in his body, straining with the need to be closer to me. It almost hurts, how hard he's gripping my hair as his mouth slants over mine, devouring me, but I don't care. It feels good, too, and my hands tighten in his shirt, pulling him closer to me as if he could *be* any closer than he is now. I can feel the edge of the dresser digging into my lower back as Liam's hips press into mine. I start to go up on my tiptoes, urging him further to pick me up and set me on it so that he can be between my legs, so that I can wrap them around him.

Instead, I feel his hand on my waist drop lower, squeezing my hip before his fingers hook into the waist of my pajama pants and the thin cotton panties that I'm wearing beneath them, dragging them down. I gasp as I feel him yank them off, the fabric pooling around my feet as he goes for my tank top next, his hand fisting in the thin material as he drags it upwards, baring my flat stomach, my ribs, my breasts.

He breaks the kiss just long enough to strip it off of me. He stands there, still fully clothed and panting, looking down at my slim, pale, naked body as I grab at the edge of the dresser for support, my knees trembling with the emotions crashing through me.

"Come here, Ana," he growls, and then his hands are on my naked waist, burning into my flesh as he pulls me towards him while he steps back towards the bed.

Oh god. Desire, hot and furious, sears through my veins at the thought of him throwing me onto the bed. But instead, he drags me past it, almost picking me up as he moves towards the wing chair by the window.

"What are you doing?" I half gasp, half whimper, but he ignores me. I catch one glimpse of his face, his jaw set and his emerald eyes dark with mingled anger and lust, before he sits down, pulling me into his lap with my back to him.

"Liam, I don't know what to do. I—"

"Shh." One arm slides around my waist, his other hand beneath my jaw, pulling my head back to expose the length of my neck for him as he drags his lips down it, nipping lightly at the sensitive skin of my throat, his tongue tracing every inch that his teeth scrape across.

"Oh god, Liam—" I moan aloud, my thighs squeezing together. I'm suddenly painfully, achingly aware of how vulnerable I am, entirely naked and bare in his lap while he's still fully clothed. Wearing the dark, fitted suit trousers and crisp white shirt that he'd had on when he arrived, his sleeves rolled up above his muscled forearms—one of which is holding me against him, tightly in his lap.

I can feel the hard ridge of his cock nestled against my ass, and I can't help but arch backward against it, the sensation sending another flush of desire through me. His hand tightens on my jaw, his mouth sucking softly at my neck, and I hear him chuckle darkly.

"Liam—" I whimper again, feeling myself getting wetter, arousal pooling between my thighs until I know, with a flush of embarrassed heat, that any moment now, he'll feel it soaking through the fabric of his pants. But he doesn't seem to care.

"It's okay if you don't know," he murmurs, his fingers sliding from my jaw down my throat, tracing the line of it until they're curled around my slender neck, holding me in place as surely as the arm around my waist is. "I'll decide for you now, lass."

His lips rise to my ear as the hand on my waist slides lower, over my stomach, down to my clenched thighs. "I still haven't punished you for not obeying me while I was gone. You haven't taken care of yourself, haven't eaten since Sofia left, haven't gone to your appointments. You've been a bad girl, Ana, and it's time for your punishment now."

I can feel myself starting to tremble, the arousal growing until I can feel it, sticky against my inner thighs. I shiver with the sudden, delicious mixture of fear and desire that spreads through me at his warning.

"I'm not going to hurt you, Ana," he murmurs, his fingers sliding between my thighs. "I would never hurt you. I never want to cause you pain. But I'm still going to punish you."

"Pleasing me isn't a punishment," I whisper breathlessly, twisting in his lap so that I can see his face. "I don't understand—"

There's a dark look in Liam's eyes as he starts to push my thighs apart, a wicked smile spreading over his face. "Oh, believe me, Ana, it can be."

"I don't understand—"

He turns my face away from him, his hand gently pressing against my throat again as he pulls my head back against his shoulder so that I'm leaning fully against him, bare and vulnerable in his lap. "Spread your legs for me, Ana. Don't make me ask you twice."

I couldn't have if I'd wanted to. His voice is dark, mesmerizing, wrapping around me like smoke and lulling me into the soothing embrace of *obeying*, giving me what I needed, what I craved. Some small part of me, I know, was hoping for this when I'd disobeyed him. It hadn't been a conscious decision to spiral back into that dark place that would keep me from doing what he'd asked me to do, but I know a part of me wanted this. I wanted to find out what Liam would do if pushed, what he would do to *me*.

It's not what I expected at all.

Slowly, I spread my thighs open, squeezing my eyes tightly shut as my face flames to my hairline, pink with shame. The moment my thighs part, I feel the arousal trickling from my pussy, leaving a wet spot on his leg.

"That's a good girl," Liam murmurs, his hand stroking up my inner thigh. "Spread yourself wide for me, Ana, so I can touch all of that sweet pussy. I'd bet good money you're wet for me already, ah!" His fingers reach the upper part of my inner thigh, where my skin is already wet, and he groans against my ear, his hand on my throat flexing lightly.

"So wet already. You want this, don't you? You want to know how

I'll punish you, how I can turn pleasure into a reminder to obey me." His fingers slide higher, brushing against my slightly opened, swollen folds, and I gasp at the pleasure that jolts over my skin even at the light touch.

"I'm going to tease you until you come, Ana," he murmurs, his breath warm against the shell of my ear. "But you'll have to be a good girl and beg for it. Don't you dare come until I tell you that you can, you understand me?" His fingers brush over my folds again, teasing the swollen flesh. "Bad girls don't get to come without permission."

"Oh god—" I gasp, moaning as his fingers delve between, stroking around my entrance, sliding through the wetness gathered there. "Liam, please—"

"Already begging." He chuckles darkly, his fingers slowly tracing higher towards my aching clit. "Did you touch yourself while I was gone? How many times did you come while I was away?"

"None," I whisper. "I was upset, I—"

"No wonder your pussy is so hungry for me then, little lass." His tongue traces the edge of my earlobe, sucking it between his lips as his fingers crawl torturously upwards towards my clit. "You must need to come so badly."

"Liam—"

"Ah, I love when you moan my name like that, lass." He presses a kiss to my throat, just above where his fingers are wrapped gently around it, holding me in place. "I dreamed of you moaning it just like that, every time I stroked my cock thinking about you. And I'm still so fucking hard for you. Do you feel it?" He shifts against me in the same instant that his fingers finally find my clit, circling the hard, throbbing nub. I cry out with the jolt of intense pleasure that tightens every muscle in my body as he presses me downwards against his throbbing shaft.

"God, yes, Liam—" I gasp, grinding backward against him, sliding my ass against the thick ridge. I'm already so turned on that I barely care that I'm soaking the fabric beneath me even more as I grind on him. "I want it, please—please fuck me, Liam. I want to come with your cock in me, please—"

He chuckles again, his fingers still slowly teasing my clit. "You have to earn that, lass. We've talked about that already. Do you think you earned my cock, while I was gone?"

"No, but—" I whimper, still pushing back against him. "You want to fuck me, I can feel it—"

"This isn't about what I want." His hand tightens slightly on my throat, not hard enough to choke, but hard enough to remind me that it's there, and that, combined with the feeling of his fingers still circling my clit is enough to push me to the edge, my thighs trembling as a fresh wave of arousal gushes from me. "Be still, lass. Stop trying to make me lose control. I won't, not this time. This is about you. Your punishment for being a bad girl while I was gone."

The words slide over my skin, silky smooth, and I gasp, arching up into his hand. "I'm sorry, Liam, please—oh god, I'm so close, please let me come—"

"Not yet." His fingers pull away from my clit, sliding lower instead, towards my entrance again. "Christ, you're wet. One day I'm going to fuck this sweet hole, Ana, and I'm going to enjoy every second of feeling this hot, wet pussy clenched around my cock." Two of his fingers circle my entrance as he murmurs against my ear, and as the last words slip out, he pushes them inside, just barely.

My reaction is instantaneous. I push myself down, unable to stop myself from trying to get more of his fingers inside of me, wanting it, needing it. "Liam, please, please—"

"Such a horny little lass." His hand tightens on my throat warningly. "You get what I decide to give you, lass, until I choose otherwise. This is a punishment, remember?" He jerks his hand away, leaving me untouched and throbbing between my legs, and I swallow hard, nodding.

"I'm sorry—"

"Beg for me to touch you, lass." His voice darkens, his accent thickening. "Beg for my fingers on your pussy. Beg, and maybe I'll let you come."

"Liam—"

"I'd imagined this," he growls against my ear, his hand hard on my thigh. "You, naked and spread open for me, bare and begging on my lap. I thought of other things, too, like your pretty ass turned pink from my palm. I could do that instead, lass, if you'd like? If you don't want to beg?"

"No, Liam, please—please touch me, I need it, please—"

"Be specific, lass." His fingers stroke the side of my throat. "Where do you need it?"

"On my—" I can't say it. My face is burning red, and I feel him throb against me, his cock hard as iron against the soft flesh of my ass. Part of me wants him to do it, to lay me over his lap and spank me, to make me feel as punished as I know he means to.

"I don't want to hurt you, lass. I won't unless you choose it. So tell me what you want and where you want it, or I'll lay you over my lap here and now."

"Please touch me! Please, please, on my—" I gasp, squirming in his lap with the deep, aching need that feels as if it's spreading through every part of me. "My clit, Liam, please, I need your fingers on my clit. Please make me come, please—"

"Ah yes. There's a good lass." His hand slides instantly between my thighs, his fingers circling the tender, throbbing nub as I gasp with relief, pushing my hips forward into his hand. "I think for that, you deserve a reward."

His hand tightens ever so slightly on my throat as he pinches my clit, lightly, and then as I gasp, he starts to rub firmly, his fingers intent on driving me forward. "Come for me, lass. Whenever you please."

"Oh god! Oh god, Liam—"

I nearly scream his name as the pleasure tears through me, the orgasm almost instantaneous. My thighs splay open even wider, my muscles rigid and trembling as I arch my back, my ass grinding against the hard ridge of his cock. I don't know how he can stand it, how he can feel me writhing wildly against him as he fingers my clit and not throw me over the bed and shove himself inside of me. I feel as if I'm losing my mind with pleasure, my pussy clenching with the need to be filled as I cry out again and again, but he doesn't stop. He keeps rubbing, keeps the pressure on my clit as I come harder than I think I ever have. When I finally go limp against him, panting as I try to catch my breath, Liam chuckles darkly against my ear.

"You needed that, I think," he murmurs as his fingers lightly brush my outer folds, moving away from my oversensitive clit for a moment.

"That wasn't much of a punishment," I gasp. "You've made me beg for it before. You—"

"Oh, I'm not done, lass," he interrupts, and I feel him smile as he presses his lips to my throat. "Not even close."

And then, as I gasp aloud, his fingers dive between my thighs once again.

FIVE
ANA

"Liam!" I try to squirm away as his fingers brush my oversensitive clit. The hand that was on my throat drops instantly, his arm going around my waist to hold me in place as his fingers start to stroke again.

"You wanted to come, lass. So come, as many times as you can, until I decide I'm satisfied."

Oh god. I realize what he's doing, and a shudder of mingled anticipation and fear runs through me. I don't know how much I can take, how many times he can wring orgasms out of me, but my body is already responding again, my clit pulsing against his fingers as he rubs it gently. The position I'm in is utterly humiliating, splayed across his lap, wet and naked and orgasming while he sits there, composed and fully clothed, and it's so intensely arousing that I can feel myself already on the brink of another climax.

"Don't hold back," he murmurs, rubbing faster as he feels me starting to tremble. "Come for me again, there's a good lass, ahh—"

"Liam!" I try to squirm away again, but he's holding me tight. All I can do is writhe in his lap as a second orgasm overtakes me, making me cry out as the pleasure races over me. My swollen clit pulses against his fingers as I grind helplessly into his hand. It feels so fucking good and like too much all at once. The worst and best part of it is that I know he's not going to stop, that he's going to keep going, keep pushing me to another climax and another, until my body is so wrung dry with pleasure that I can't take another.

The moment he feels me relax into him again as the orgasm recedes, his hand slides lower, two fingers pushing into my drenched, fluttering pussy. I clench around him instantly, and he groans, his lips brushing against my jaw.

"That's right, lass. You want me to fuck that hungry pussy, don't you? So hungry for more, for my fingers, my tongue, my cock. This is all you get, for now, my little lass, until you show me how good you can be. But it's enough, isn't it? You're going to come for me again."

There's a commanding note to his voice as he pushes his fingers deeper that sends me even closer to the edge, his fingers thrusting into me as the pad of his thumb finds my clit, but he doesn't stroke them in and out of me. He just holds them there, buried inside as he starts to rub again, his lips on my neck as the arm around my waist tightens. "You look so beautiful, splayed out for me like this, Ana," he whispers. "Come for me, lass."

And I do, for a third time, moaning as I arch against him, pushing myself down onto his fingers as his thumb circles my clit, sending me crashing over the edge.

Then, just as I start to catch my breath, he begins to thrust his fingers inside me, curling them as he fucks my tight, aching pussy with his two fingers. His thumb starts to move again, slow and inexorable against my oversensitive, throbbing bundle of nerves.

After that, I start to lose track. A fourth orgasm, a fifth, until it's not individual orgasms any longer but a solid, cresting wave that rises and falls. Just when I think that I'm done, he changes his touch, does something different, and the wave crests again, so that I'm moaning and writhing, drenched and sticky and bare, spread wide in his lap as his fingers stroke and rub and pinch and thrust until all I know is a pleasure that feels like too much, like I can't bear anymore. At the same time, I don't want him to stop.

He pushes a third finger into me, filling me to the point that it's nearly as much as his cock, and I fall screaming into another burst of pleasure. "I can't take anymore," I beg him, panting as I slump against him, my hips still twitching against his hand. "I can't, please, Liam, I can't come again, I can't take it, I can't—"

"You'll take it until I've had enough," he growls against my ear, and just those words are enough to send another frisson of pleasure down my spine. "You'll take every orgasm I want to give you, little lass, until I'm tired of pleasuring you."

And then, the hand around my waist slides downwards, those fingers slipping between my thighs as the fingers inside of my pussy slip out, so drenched with my arousal that when he pushes them between the cheeks of my ass, I almost don't realize what he's doing at first.

"Liam!" I cry out as I feel the sudden pressure, accompanied by the fingertips of his other hand starting up the slow, circular tracing around my clit again. I squeal with mingled surprise, and no small amount of pleasure as the finger between my ass cheeks pushes deeper, inside by a knuckle, and then deeper still.

"You're going to come for me like this, Ana, with my finger in your ass, and you're going to love it." His voice, dark and full of lust, wraps around me, holding me there, bound in place as I squirm on his finger, the pleasure building again. "Come for me, little lass—"

"I can't, I can't—" I beg, tears filling my eyes, my exhausted body begging for him to stop. Still, the pleasure is coming anyway, unfurling through me, the shame of it turning me on more than ever. I'm exposed, drenched, and now the feeling of his finger thrusting inside of my ass as he rubs my clit fiercely is tipping me over the edge again, into yet another climax—

It doesn't stop. *He* doesn't stop. He keeps going until one finger in my ass becomes two, thrusting, his voice murmuring in my ear that I'm such a dirty girl, so horny, so needy, to come like this from him fingering my ass. And then, the hand on my pussy shifts, so that there are two fingers inside of me there again, and always one on my clit, rubbing, pressing down, pushing me higher and higher, until I'm stuffed full of him, and I'm still coming with tears pouring down my cheeks.

"Please, Liam, please, I can't, I can't—" I'm sobbing, tears dripping off my chin. However, I'm still shuddering, squirming, and still arching against him as he fucks me with his fingers in both of my holes. The intense pleasure pushes me into another of those endless, cresting climaxes. I lose all sense of where I am and what's happening. There's only pleasure, with his hands on me, his voice in my ear, and me begging him to stop and keep going all at once as I sob my way through the endless pleasure.

"That's a good lass," he croons, and suddenly his hands are on my waist, lifting me. He picks me up, setting me on the bed as I look dazedly at him, and I roll towards him, reaching for him.

"No." He steps back, out of reach, and I'm too exhausted to try to go towards him as he steps a little further away from the bed. "You'll have to be a good girl for longer than that if you want to earn this again."

As he speaks, his hand goes down to his belt, undoing it as I watch. Even as exhausted as I am, I crave touching him, the feeling of his hot, straining flesh against my palm, in my mouth, inside of me.

"Liam—"

"No, lass." He slowly tugs his zipper down, his heated green eyes raking over my naked, limp body as his hand slips inside the fitted black pants, and I know in another second he's going to expose all of that rigid, throbbing length to my gaze.

I want to see him. I want to touch him, to—

Fuck. He looks so good, hard and ready for me, his cockhead glistening with his arousal, the pre-cum already beading down the shaft as Liam wraps his fist around it. "I could tie you up," he says hoarsely, squeezing the base of his cock so that it stands up firm and pulsing, the head swollen and reddened with the ferocity of his desire. "I could tie your hands above your head and your ankles apart, so that you could feel just how open you are for me, how easily I could thrust every inch of this cock into you, even though I won't. And you *know* I won't, not yet, no matter how much you beg for it."

He starts to stroke as he speaks, his hand sliding up and down the shaft in long, slow movements that draw my eyes downwards. I watch him hungrily, and I can't stop myself from starting to squirm towards him, my eyes pleading, until he pins me with that stern, emerald gaze.

"Be still, lass," Liam says, his voice sharp and commanding. "Do you know why you're not tied up?"

"No," I whisper, feeling a throb between my thighs at the thought of it, even though I don't know how I could possibly come again. I don't know how many he's wrung out of me, but I feel completely exhausted, beyond the ability to reach another climax.

Not that I'd say that out loud because I'm not at all sure that he wouldn't try.

"Because I want to see you obey me. I want you to lie there, unrestrained, watching me touch myself, knowing how badly you want my cock. I want to see you craving it, needing it, but obeying me because you're trying to be my good girl." His hand speeds up a little, stroking, squeezing, his thumb brushing over the glistening tip and sending a shudder through him. "You want to be my good lass, don't you, Ana?"

"Yes," I breathe, licking my lips as I watch him, watch the pre-cum dripping from his head, the way he collects it in his fingers, smearing it down his shaft. I know just how good he tastes, the sharp saltiness of him on my tongue, and I know how good he feels inside of me. At that moment, I feel as if I'd do anything to have him like that again, to have him in my mouth, in my pussy, making me his in every possible way.

"Tell me you miss my cock." His voice is rasping now, thick with building lust as he strokes faster. His other hand pushes his fitted pants and briefs lower, cupping his balls, tugging them out so that he can hold them in his palm, stroking the tight flesh as he jerks his cock in front of my eyes. "Tell me what you want, Ana."

"I want to taste you," I whisper breathlessly, and despite myself, I feel my hand drifting to my inner thigh. "I want your cum on my tongue. I want to feel you in between my legs. I want you inside of me. I want you to fill me up—" The words roll off my tongue, dirtier than anything I'd imagined I could say. Still, I feel completely lost in a sea of arousal, the world narrowed down to the two of us and the almost suffocating heat surrounding us both.

Liam waits until my fingers are nearly at my clit before shaking his head.

"No, Ana," he growls. "You said you'd had enough, right? Do you want me to come down there and see how many orgasms I can wring out of you with my tongue? Do you want me to stuff you full of my fingers again while I suck on that hard, throbbing little clit of yours—"

He groans, and I shake my head, even as it's on the tip of my tongue to tell him yes. I can't take anymore. I know I can't, but the thought of his mouth on my pussy is almost enough to make me beg for it anyway.

"Fuck, Ana!" Liam's hand slides up over the head of his cock, squeezing, and he moves towards the end of the bed. My heart leaps in my chest, thinking that I've made him lose control, that he's going to fuck me now. That he can't wait any longer, either.

"Spread your thighs open, yes, that's a good girl," he murmurs as he climbs onto the bed, his hand still sliding up and down his swollen shaft as I obediently spread my legs wider, and he kneels between them. "You want me inside of you, don't you? You want me to fuck you with this cock, fill you up with my cum—"

"Yes," I breathe, feeling my skin flush pink, every inch of my body heating under his gaze. He's so close, and I can feel my pussy clenching rhythmically, wanting him so badly that I can hardly think. "Liam, please—"

"No," he whispers, and I let out a small, breathless sob.

"Liam!"

"This pussy is mine," he growls, moving closer, so close that I can feel the heat radiating off of him against my sensitive flesh. "You're mine, Ana. I want you more than anything else in the fucking world, and when I fuck you again, when I fill you up with this cock, it'll be because you know that. Because you want me, and only me."

He growls those last words as his fist flies over his cock, his hips pushing forward, and I gasp as I feel his cockhead brush up against my swollen, sensitive pussy. He parts my folds with it, and for a second, I think he's going to push himself inside of me, despite everything he's saying. But he doesn't. Instead, he slides upwards, grunting as I start to shudder too, the intense eroticism of the moment overtaking me, pushing me towards the edge.

"Liam, please fuck me, please, please—"

"No." He's panting now, his hand stroking himself hard and fast, his face tight with pleasure as he reaches the edge. "Watch me, Ana.

Watch me as I—" He groans, and I see him stiffen, his cock going rock-hard in his fist, visibly throbbing. "Watch as I fucking come—all over—your little clit—"

A groan of pure pleasure tears past his lips as he goes absolutely still, his cock shoved up against my throbbing clit as he squeezes his shaft, now glistening with my arousal as well as his. I feel the same pleasure suddenly unfurling through me unexpectedly as I watch, frozen with need, as the first hot spurt of his cum coats my throbbing clit.

The sight of it, the heat of it on my skin, sends me over the edge. I claw at the blankets, screaming out his name as my back arches. I hear Liam groaning mine as he starts to stroke his cock again, fast and hard, the head rubbing frantically against my clit as spurt after spurt of his cum drenches my clit, my swollen folds, my entire fucking pussy. It feels so fucking good, and I can feel Liam rubbing himself against me, his groans filling the room as we come hard together, and I can't help myself. My pussy is clenching, aching, and I wrap my legs around his thighs, arching upwards so that his cock slips downwards, sliding in our mingled arousal. For just a second, as his orgasm starts to ebb, I feel the blissful, perfect sensation of his swollen cockhead piercing me, stretching me, shoved inside of my aching body.

Liam freezes in place, and he grabs my hip with one hand, shoving me down and holding me still. I can feel him pulsing inside me, the last drops of his cum trickling out, and he stares down at me with his hazy, lidded green gaze.

"You want my cum inside of you that badly, little lass?" He growls the words, and I nod breathlessly, hardly able to speak.

"Please, Liam—"

He's still hard. I can feel him throbbing, and he closes his eyes briefly, his entire body shuddering as he holds himself there, barely inside me.

"I want to fuck you so badly," he murmurs. "I want you so fucking bad it hurts."

I don't know what possesses me to say it. If I'd kept quiet, he might have kept going. He might have slid into me then and there, let me feel all of him filling me, if only for a moment.

"But you want someone else, too," I whisper, looking up at him, even as my body tightens with the effort to hold him inside of me.

Liam tenses, his eyes opening as he looks down. "No," he says flatly. "That's you, lass. There's only one woman for me, Ana." His hands slide down my thighs, pulling my legs away from him, opening them wide. "I've never wanted anyone the way I want you."

He rocks forward once, letting me feel the friction of him just barely inside of me. And then he pulls free, standing up as he turns away from me to walk into the bathroom.

I lay there, watching him go, covered in his cum and trembling, my entire body taut with desire as if he didn't just make me come more times than I thought was humanly possible.

What the fuck are we going to do?

SIX
LIAM

I've never been to Saoirse's family home before. I'd called her, telling her that we needed to talk, and she'd agreed. "We most certainly do," had been her exact words, spoken in a clipped tone that told me this was going to be very far from a pleasant discussion.

The O'Sullivan manor is a huge, old stone house a decent distance from the city, on a sprawling piece of land that stretches farther than I can see, with rolling green hills and stables within view, as well as an equestrian course and a huge landscaped garden and greenhouse behind the main house. It's in that garden that Saoirse told me to meet her, so I do exactly that, glad to avoid the possibility of running into her father by not actually going inside.

Or so I hope, anyway. For all I know, he's waiting out back for me as well.

I open the wrought-iron gate that leads into the garden, walking down the well-kept cobblestone path, following it deeper into the manicured expanse of trees, flowers, and shrubs until I see Saoirse's dark strawberry hair, pulled away from her face and falling in heavy curls down her back.

She's standing by the fountain in the center of the gardens, and she turns towards me at the sound of my footsteps, though I don't know how she heard me over the sound of the splashing water. She looks as lovely as ever, dressed in dark jeans and an emerald silk blouse. I don't doubt that the color choice is intentional, meant to remind me who she is and why I'm meant to marry her.

"If you throw a penny into the fountain," Saoirse says, her hands resting against the cool, damp stone as she leans against the edge of it, "you can make a wish. What do you think I ought to wish for, Liam McGregor?"

She slides one hand into the pocket of her jeans, her left hand. The engagement ring sparkles in the bright sunlight, almost blinding. I know that, too, was calculated.

When she pulls her hand out, there's a copper penny clasped between her thumb and forefinger, and Saoirse turns her back to me, leaning towards the fountain.

"Should I wish for a faithful fiancé, do you think? Maybe one who is truthful and doesn't lie to me. Or should I wish for his older brother to appear so that I could marry the McGregor brother who would appreciate the princess being handed to him, gift-wrapped for the sake of his status and pleasure?" She straightens, turning back towards me. "That's what I'm meant to be, you know. A trophy. Something to prop up your position, to legitimize you even further, so that you can wipe away the stain on your family name with my virgin blood."

I shift uncomfortably, and Saoirse smiles, clearly enjoying my discomfiture.

"Oh, don't pretend you don't like the thought of it. All you men do. An untouched bride, one who will shiver with pleasure for your cock and your cock alone. You all *love* that. Everything I have to give you, everything I have to offer, could be nullified in one instant, if I spread my legs for some other man. It makes it tempting, honestly. Especially after what I found in your apartment."

Her gaze hardens. "Because it doesn't matter where *you* stick your cock, does it, Liam? So long as I'm pure on our wedding day."

"My lack of virginity can hardly be a surprise to you, Saoirse," I say dryly. "And after all, don't you want a man who knows what he's doing in bed?"

"I want a man who doesn't bloody lie to me." Saoirse's mouth thins. "I know what I'll wish for." She flicks the penny sideways, letting it splash into the fountain. "A fucking explanation, Liam McGregor. And quickly. Starting with your *business* trip after the wedding."

I cross my arms over my chest, letting out a sigh. "As I'm sure you've figured out by now, I wasn't away on business. When Viktor and I broke into the chalet where Alexei was keeping the women, Ana had been sold during his party before we could get there. She was the only one we weren't able to rescue. So I went after her."

"Did Viktor ask you to do that?"

"Well, no—"

"So you chose to go after her of your own accord. Why?" Saoirse narrows her eyes.

"Because I felt guilty. I couldn't leave her in the hands of a man who would purchase her like that. And it was easiest for me to go." It's partially the truth, enough of it that I think Saoirse will listen, perhaps.

"Easier for you, the head of the Irish Kings, to go after a trafficked girl instead of some of Viktor's brigadiers. I think not." Saoirse purses her lips. "Don't treat me as if I'm stupid, Liam. What is she to you?"

"We—I'd met her before, briefly. We formed a certain attachment. A friendly one. I didn't want to leave her rescue in the hands of others—"

"Friendly?" Saoirse smirks. "You're telling me that there's no romantic attachment between you, Liam. That you aren't fucking her, that you're not—"

"It wasn't about that—"

"Stop bloody lying!" She shakes her head with disgust, her voice rising, though she's careful to keep it pitched so that our conversation can't be heard over the splashing of the fountain. "I found the lingerie in her drawers. Lacy, pretty things, a nightie, a garter belt, a fucking *collar*." She raises an eyebrow. "I didn't know you were so kinky, Liam. Gives me certain ideas about our wedding night—or perhaps I'll have you wear it instead."

"Come off it, Saoirse." I glare at her. "I didn't buy those things for her to wear for me."

"But you did buy them."

"They caught her eye. She's been through a lot. I wanted to spoil her—"

"But not fuck her." Saoirse shakes her head. "I'm not a fool, Liam. I know men well enough, even if I've never been with one. I'm a virgin, not an idiot. I know you don't want to marry me, that you've been dragging your feet since well before the official betrothal. It stings, certainly, that you can't see what's in front of your fucking face, that you don't value me as you ought to. But there are plenty of women in my position, in arranged marriages that are cold and loveless. It's not what I wanted, but it's also not unexpected. But this—"

Her jaw tightens, and she steps away from the fountain, closer to me. "This is blatant disrespect, Liam. It's disrespectful to *me*, and I won't have it. I won't be treated this way. I'm Graham O'Sullivan's daughter, his eldest daughter. You'd do well to think of the ramifications if I were to tell him what—or rather *who*—I found in your apartment the other day."

I look at her carefully. "So you haven't told him?"

"No." Saoirse's hands are on her hips, her chin tilted defiantly up at me.

"Why not?"

"I'm not sure yet if I want you dead." She narrows her eyes at me. "As I said, I'm not an idiot. I know men in your position keep mistresses. Again, it's not what I'd hoped for. I wanted fidelity, at least in my marriage, if not love. But if you're going to keep one, she shouldn't be in your bloody home, Liam. If we're going to have the sort of marriage my parents had, an old-fashioned arrangement, then it needs to be done with respect. And rules," she adds, still glaring up at me with those shamrock-green eyes. "You can't simply do as you please, Liam. Not a man in your position. Not a man with as much as you have to lose."

"You can stop there." I look down at her, my own jaw tightening. "That's not the sort of marriage we're going to have, Saoirse."

She blinks at me, momentarily caught off guard. "No?" I can see the flicker of hope that crosses her face, whether she realizes it or not. It makes me feel guilty because even now, as angry and hurt as she is, she still wants what she'd believed this could be. She still feels there's a chance.

But I've come to disabuse her of that notion, once and for all.

"That's not the marriage we're going to have, Saoirse, because we aren't going to *be* married."

"I—what?" She stares up at me, her expression angry all over again. "What in the bloody hell are you talking about, Liam—"

"I'm going to find a way to break the contract between us," I tell her firmly. "There will be no marriage. I shouldn't have let this go on as long as I did."

"We were betrothed in front of a priest, in front of my father! We made vows—"

"I know. And I'm sorry for leading you on, Saoirse—truly I am," I tell her gently. "I didn't want to sign the betrothal that night. But if I hadn't, I would have come back from finding Ana to a civil war among the Kings. I knew it, and I made a snap decision to keep things from spiraling out of control here while I went to find her. I couldn't waste any more time—I didn't know what sort of man had her, what he might be doing to her. She'd been through enough, Saoirse, more than you know—"

"Stop." She waves a hand at me, her gaze bright and brittle, though I'd wager money I'll never see Saoirse O'Sullivan shed a single tear for me. She's not that sort.

"I don't need to hear the saga of poor Ana," Saoirse says. "I'm truly sorry for what happened to her and the other women. It's a terrible thing, and I've long thought there should have never been any dealings between the Kings and Viktor Andreyev, so long as he trafficked in women. But of course, I, myself, am a woman, so I never had any voice in that." She gives me a pointed look. "I was pleased to hear he's changed businesses. I don't think for a second that poor girl deserved anything done to her. But that doesn't mean I want her in your home. It doesn't mean I approve of whatever you're doing with her. And it doesn't mean I intend to sit by and let it happen or listen to this nonsense—"

"It's not nonsense, Saoirse." My voice isn't cruel as I say it, but it is firm. "We're not going to be married. As soon as I can find a time to broach the topic with your father, I will be breaking our engagement—"

Saoirse's eyes flick over my face, and whatever she sees there, she suddenly goes very still, her own expression hardening. "I would think about what you're doing, Liam," she says, her voice cold and quiet. "You're the younger son of a traitor, whose elder brother abandoned the table in light of his father's sins. I'm no King, but I'm the daughter of one, and I know them well enough. They won't take this insult lightly. You risk everything by setting me aside, and you know it." She narrows her eyes. "I don't care how sweet this girl's cunt must be to scramble your brains like this; you need to think this through. If you set me aside, as you're saying you will, you're risking everything. Not just your place at the table, Liam, but possibly your life as well. Is she worth that?"

Yes, I think, the moment she says it. But I don't say it aloud. I can't pretend that I don't feel for her. Saoirse is everything I should want—beautiful, intelligent, strong-willed, with a spine of steel and an understanding of duty and what needs to be done in our world. She would make a fine wife for any King. She knows who she is and what her place in this world should be. She doesn't fight against it or complain—but I can see that she's not one to always bend to it, either.

Saoirse is the kind of woman who takes what she's been given and molds it to her own liking.

As Niall would say, I should be falling on my knees with gratitude to be given such a woman. But I can't.

Since the moment I laid eyes on Ana, there's never been any woman for me other than her.

"I'm sorry, Saoirse," I say gently. "It's nothing to do with you—"

"If you keep talking and say what I think you're about to say, I'll kill you myself." She glares up at me, crossing her arms as she takes a step back. "I'll say it again, Liam. You should think about this. I won't say anything to my father for now. I'll let you have time to reconsider, to think if that girl back in your penthouse is worth losing everything that the McGregor name has left. If she's worth your legacy."

Then, she steps past me, sweeping by me with the barest brush of emerald silk against my arm. Saoirse makes it a few paces down the cobblestone path before she turns, letting out a sigh as her arms fall to her sides.

"I wanted you, you know." She bites her lower lip, her eyes flicking over my face. "I would have been a good wife to you, faithful and true. I could even have loved you, Liam. I *wanted* to love you and for you to love me. But now I know better."

Her eyes meet mine, cool and empty of any emotion, even anger. "It should have been your brother, Liam. It should have been Connor. Never you."

And then, without another word, she spins on her heel and stalks down the cobblestone path, leaving me there as she disappears into the huge, grand house beyond.

SEVEN
LIAM

After that, I can't go and talk to Niall. I know that for certain—I know exactly what he'd say. So instead, I call Max, who tells me to come to his hotel room and talk.

At least with Max, I feel less judged.

"I ordered up a bottle of whiskey," Max says with a knowing look as he opens the door for me to come in. "I thought you might need it. You sounded a bit the worse for wear on the phone."

I'm not about to tell him about my reunion with Ana—at least not most of it—so I opt to tell him about my meeting with Saoirse instead, sinking down into a chair in the living room portion of his hotel suite and reaching for the whiskey and a cut-glass tumbler. "I told Saoirse that I wouldn't be marrying her."

"Ah." Max raises an eyebrow, reaching for a glass for himself and sitting down opposite me, taking the bottle when I hand it over. "I gather that went about as well as any of us would have expected?"

"She didn't exactly let me." I frown, taking a deep gulp of the whiskey. "She told me to think it over, that she wouldn't say anything to Graham for now, until I had a chance to 'think about the consequences.'"

"And have you? Thought about them, I mean." Max leans back on the couch, observing me. "What it'll mean for you and the Kings if you stick with this plan."

"Of course, I've thought about it," I tell him snappishly. "I've done nothing other than think about it, every day, every fucking *hour* since I signed that goddamned betrothal contract and left for Russia with you and Levin. I know exactly what I'm risking. And yet—"

"And yet you keep pushing forward."

"I don't know what the hell else to do." I run a hand through my hair with frustration, taking another gulp of the whiskey.

Then, there's a knock at the door, startling me, and I sit up, glaring at Max. "Who in the bloody hell is that?"

"I thought it might not be only me you'd need to talk to." Max gets up, circling around the couch, and reenters with Niall in tow a moment later.

"Bloody hell." I glare at Max. "Who asked you, anyway?"

"You did," Max says cheerfully, handing Niall his own glass.

"Lady troubles again?" Niall clinks his glass against mine, taking a seat next to me on the opposite end of the couch. "Which one this time?"

"Both," Max supplies helpfully, and I glare at him.

"I came here for counsel, and you—"

"No, you didn't." Max refills my glass. "You came here to vent, and two pairs of ears are better than one for that. Liam here told Saoirse he's breaking things off," he adds, glancing in Niall's direction. "Just to get you up to speed."

"Jesus, Mary, and Joseph." Niall shakes his head, taking a healthy gulp of his own drink. "I take it she was none too pleased?"

"None," I confirm. "She said she'd give me a chance to think over the consequences."

"As well you should." Niall shakes his head. "You've gone on with this for a while, Liam, but surely you must be starting to see—"

"I don't think he is," Max says, leaning back once more. "How are you feeling about all of this, Liam?"

"Like I'm going bloody fucking insane." I rub one hand over my face, tossing back the rest of my whiskey and refilling the glass myself. "Saoirse is the proper choice. I know that. She was raised to be the wife of a King. She's beautiful, stubborn as hell, and tough as Irish hardtack. She'd withstand anything and come out of it without a hair out of place. But she's not the woman I love. I love—"

"Ana," Max says.

"The ballerina," Niall says it flatly, in tandem with Max.

"Yes." I glare at them both, but as I take another sip of my whiskey, I feel some of the frustration leaking out of me, replaced by utter exhaustion. "I've never wanted anything the way I want her. But God almighty, it's so fucking *hard.* I don't know that it's supposed to be this hard, this much of a fight." I take another long drink, tilting my glass back, and Max refills it without my asking. "It would be easy with Saoirse. *Too* easy, I think."

"So you want Ana because she's a challenge?" Niall frowns.

"I want Ana because I love her. I love her—and I have no explanation for why. We barely know each other. She's wrong for me in every way—she's Russian, the daughter of an executed Bratva brigadier, physically broken, mentally unwell in a number of ways, and yet—" I let out a long sigh, sinking deeper into the couch. "I fucking love her, and I don't know how to stop. And if I send her back to New York and marry Saoirse—"

I break off, looking at the two men who are now watching me with just a glimmer of sympathy—Max more so than Niall.

"I'll bloody regret it for the rest of my life, and I know I will."

"If that's the case, then—" Max starts to say, but I'm not finished talking.

"Is this the right thing, though?" I look at him, shaking my head. "I said I came here for counsel, and this is it. Is this good for either of us? Should I marry Saoirse, regardless of what I want, of what I'll regret or feel, and do what's expected of me?"

"You love her, right?" Max looks at me appraisingly. "Ana?"

"Aye." I tilt my glass back again. "But I'm not sure if it's enough."

Max leans forward. "So love her. Don't just try to fuck her. Take her out. Try to woo her. Show her who you are—who you *really* are, and discover that in her as well. And then you'll know if it's real, lasting love—if it's worth risking all of this for."

"Well said." Niall tilts his glass towards Max. "Say, you're a former priest, right?"

"Once upon a time." Max glances at him, taking another sip of his own whiskey? "So?"

"Have you ever actually been with a woman?"

I glance at Max, curious. I don't actually know the answer—for all that I've spent plenty of time with the man over the last weeks, there are certain things he's kept to himself, and I can hardly fault him for it.

Max grins. "No," he says, draining the last of his glass. "But that doesn't mean I don't know anything about them."

When I'd left Max's hotel, I'd been well and truly drunk. I'd come home to find Ana in bed, her lights off and her asleep, and I'd retreated to my own room and the questionable pleasure of my hand, as much as I'd wanted to wake her up and sink myself into her. Drunk as I was, it had been hard to resist the urge, but I couldn't stand the thought that she might wake up from her half-sleep and see Alexandre there instead of me. I couldn't stand the thought of her calling out for him again, so I'd left her alone, choosing to take care of the problem myself. On the one night that I would have preferred to actually have the problem of whiskey dick, my cock seemed insistent on remaining as hard as ever just at the thought of her.

I'm up and gone before she's awake in the morning, thanks to a call that I'd gotten on my way back from Max's. Much to my displeasure, Luca called me to let me know that he and Viktor were on their way to Boston and expected to meet with me bright and early in the morning. From the tone of his voice, I didn't expect it to be a pleasant meeting, and I could guess what it was likely to be about.

Sofia had come to stay with Ana after the debacle with Saoirse for a few days, and while I'm grateful that Ana wasn't left all alone while she struggled, at least not for the entire week, that also means that Luca has likely gotten wind of the situation—and passed it on to Viktor.

Like it or not, my decisions affect them as well, thanks to the alliance. It's clear that I've been avoiding those consequences that Saoirse mentioned as long as I could, and now the crows have come home to nest.

I'm presentable when I arrive, though my head is aching from too much whiskey the night before. Luca and Viktor are already waiting for me, seated on either side of the head of the table, the meeting room otherwise empty.

"Morning." I sit down, setting the coffee that I'd picked up on the way down in front of me. "Can I offer either of you anything?"

"No, thank you," Luca says in the same breath that Viktor says, tersely, "An explanation."

Jesus, Mary, and Joseph. That's three times in barely over two days that I've had an explanation demanded from me, and I'm quite frankly becoming exhausted with it.

"What do you mean?" I take a sip of my coffee, just as the door opens and Levin walks in, followed by Niall and another man I don't recognize.

Niall stands behind me, as he's accustomed to, while Levin takes a seat to the right of Viktor. The man I don't know—tall, dark-haired, hazel-eyed, and clearly Italian, takes a seat to the right of Luca.

"This is my underboss, Alessio Moretti," Luca says, nodding to him. "He's come from Chicago to take the position. Alessio, this is Liam McGregor, head of the Irish Kings here in Boston."

"A pleasure," I say tightly, nodding to him. "Now—Luca, Viktor, what's this about? It's not that I'm not pleased to see you, but this meeting was called…abruptly."

"We warned you, when you went to rescue Anastasia," Viktor says, his voice equally terse, "that she was not well."

"We both did," Luca adds. "We told you that she was physically and mentally damaged. You went after her anyway—at some urging from my wife as well, I later heard—and we were happy enough to let you do it. Ana deserved to be rescued."

Viktor frowns, and Luca gives him a pointed look. "You know as well as I do that she didn't deserve that fate or anything that happened to her before it. You were as guilty as the rest of us that Alexandre took her before we could get there."

"Be that as it may," Viktor says tightly. "The intent was for you to rescue her, Liam, to get her out of the hands of the Frenchman. Not to keep her for yourself."

"What did you think I was going to do?" I narrow my eyes at him. "You can't tell me that you didn't know I had feelings for her."

"Feelings are one thing," Luca says quickly, before Viktor can say something else to go along with the rapidly darkening expression on his face. "Acting on them is another, Liam. You signed a contract before you left for Russia. A *betrothal* contract with Saoirse O'Sullivan."

"Aye." I sit back, feeling the dread that I'd been keeping at bay these past weeks slowly crawl through my veins as a chill settles over the room. "A preventative measure, while I went after Ana, to keep civil war from breaking out in my absence. The Kings have not all put their full loyalty behind me since my father—"

"And you think breaking this contract will make them do so?" Viktor shakes his head. "Use your head, *mal'chik!* What do you think Graham O'Sullivan will do when you tell him you're setting aside your promise to his daughter?"

"I don't know for certain, but—"

"I know your customs well enough," Viktor continues sharply. "The girl might remain untouched, but a broken engagement, particularly when her husband was meant to be the head of the Kings, will come down unfavorably—and unfairly, I might add—on her. Her father will be hard-pressed to make a decent match for her after this— have you thought of that?"

"I have, and I feel terrible about it, but—"

"But what?" Luca interjects. "Liam, no one is telling you that you can't have Ana, if the two of you can come to some arrangement. If Saoirse is willing to be amenable to a more—traditional arrangement, and Ana is willing to continue a discreet relationship with you without the bonds of marriage, then there's no reason why you can't have both love and duty. But you can't *marry* Ana, do you understand?"

"No," I say tightly. "I don't understand. I've already told Saoirse—"

"And does her father know?"

"No," I admit reluctantly. "Not so far as I know, but—"

"*Bladya, mal'chik!*" Viktor swears aloud, his face tightening with frustration. I hear Levin say something quietly in Russian under his breath to Viktor, who lets out a long-suffering sigh.

"I thought better of you when we made this alliance," Viktor says tightly. "Your father was a traitor to both the Kings and myself, and I would have been well within my rights to demand that the Kings replace the McGregor lineage with a new one. If Graham O'Sullivan had a son, I might well have. But he doesn't, only daughters, and when he assured me that his place at the right hand of the table would continue, that his daughter had always been unofficially pledged to the McGregor heir, I let it lie. I see now that perhaps I've made a mistake—"

"This isn't about you, Liam," Luca says calmly. Ironically, I hear the echo of my own voice saying something very similar to Saoirse yesterday. *This has nothing to do with you.*

"I understand, wanting personal happiness," Luca continues. "But there is more at stake here than yourself, Liam. There is an alliance at stake, other lives, other futures. My business, Viktor's, the people who work for us, who depend on us. If the Kings' table fractures on account of this, what am I to tell all of those affected? That you were in love? I'm sorry, Liam, but a man of your stature doesn't get to have the luxury of making choices in a vacuum—"

"Both of you have married for love!" I lash out, snapping angrily as I look between the two of them. "Look me in the eye and tell me that your marriage to Sofia, yours to Caterina, are not marriages of love? You had a second bloody wedding to declare how much you loved each other," I add, glaring at Viktor. "It's because of the unions I've seen between you and your wives that I dared hope for something better than a cold, distant, loveless marriage—that I hoped for a partnership. A marriage made for love—"

"Saoirse is a good, strong woman." Viktor frowns. "She could be a partner to you, as much as Sofia is to Luca or Caterina is to me—"

"She's not the woman I love."

"Our marriages didn't start out as love matches," Luca says, his voice taking on a slight edge. "Think about what you're saying, Liam. I had no intention of marrying when Rossi told me I had to either wed Sofia or let him eliminate her. I was perfectly happy fucking my way through Manhattan and anywhere else that I happened to go. I'd spent all my adult life promised to a woman I never intended to wed, and I enjoyed being Manhattan's most notorious, wealthy playboy. But my father, and Sofia's father, made promises. Promises I was required to uphold, and I *did*, out of duty. At first, I didn't love Sofia, and she didn't love me. There was desire, plenty of it, but not love. That came later, after we were married—"

"I don't desire Saoirse, either," I say flatly. "Not in that way. I don't want to marry her or fuck her."

"Then you're fucking blind," Luca says bluntly. "I'm married, not dead, Liam. Saoirse is gorgeous. You could do far, far worse—"

"She's not Ana—"

"Do you hear yourself?" Viktor glares at me. "Droning on about love and desire, like a fucking woman—"

"Are you telling me you didn't desire Caterina?"

"Of course I did." Viktor snorts. "Caterina was beautiful from the day I first saw her, long before I could have married her. Sofia is, as well. I would have taken either of them and gladly. Sofia is the descendant of Bratva royalty on her mother's side; she would have solidified my position as *pakhan*, just as Saoirse will solidify yours. Had my plan worked, I would have taken Sofia, married her, fucked her, made her the mother of my children, and been happy to do so as I used that marriage to take over Rossi's territory."

"Easy," Luca mutters, glaring at him. "We're allies now, but Sofia is my wife and the mother of my—"

"So she is," Viktor says, smiling tersely. "And since you wed her first, I demanded Caterina instead, another mafia princess to make an alliance with. If I couldn't beat you by stealing Giovanni's daughter, I joined you instead, by making the Rossi girl my wife. I desired Caterina, certainly, just as I'd desired Sofia. But above all, it was their usefulness to me that made me want to marry them, each of them." He narrows his eyes at me. "This is the lesson you need to learn, Liam. These marriages—Luca's and mine, were not made for lust or love. They were made to keep promises, fulfill duty, and build alliances. They were business decisions, first. After that came lust, and later, love. The love was a fortunate byproduct of our marriages and one that I admit we are lucky to have. I gain a great deal from the love of my wife, as does Luca. But this is the part that you need to understand—even if I hated Caterina, and she me, as she did at first—*we would still be wed.*

Viktor sits back, looking at me with clear irritation. "I don't care if you hate Saoirse O'Sullivan to her very bones, Liam. I don't care if you have to flip her over on your wedding night and bury her face in the pillow so that you can imagine it's Anastasia's pussy you're filling instead. You need to marry her for the good of this alliance and for your own good as well. I don't care if you love Anastasia, or keep her as a mistress, so long as it doesn't threaten your marriage. But marrying the Ivanova girl is out of the question." He shakes his head. "You can't possibly think that the Kings would settle for a marriage with a Russian girl of no consequence, fucked by at least a dozen different men before she came to your bed, kidnapped and sold, with nothing to offer, unstable and damaged? When you have Saoirse O'Sullivan, an Irish princess if there was one in this modern age, contracted to marry you?"

"What Viktor is trying to say," Luca begins, but I shake my head, slamming my fist down on the table as I sit up straighter.

"This *intervention* is a waste of your time," I say tightly. "I have no intention of going through with the marriage to Saoirse or insulting Ana by telling her that the best I can give her, after I've asked her to love and devote herself only to me, is a place as my mistress."

"But you'll insult Graham O'Sullivan and his daughter by breaking a contract made in church." Luca shakes his head. "I'm more patient than Viktor is, Liam, but mine is being stretched as well. It's not just our business arrangement, but my personal life that you're straining with this nonsense. Unless you've forgotten, as I'm sure you haven't, my wife is Ana's best friend. So much so that she dropped everything and flew to Boston, barely asking me beforehand if I was alright with it, when Ana called her sobbing over Saoirse. So much so that she laid into *me* for not telling her that you were engaged and keeping her best friend in your home and likely in your bed, to boot. We haven't fought like that since before—" Luca shakes his head. "You're straining the goodwill of everyone around you, Liam. You need to think—"

"So everyone has said." I glare at him. "Is it right of me to drag Saoirse into a loveless marriage? It's not right of me to marry where I'll be happy, but it's fine for me to do that?"

"Saoirse knows that love isn't guaranteed where marriage is arranged," Luca says calmly. "She expects it. I'm certain of that." He lets out a long breath. "I know this is difficult for you, but it's for the good of the families—the greater good. You can depend on that."

"So that's it?" I look between the two of them, Levin and Alessio silent and grave just beyond them. Except for Niall at my back, I've never felt more alone. "You demand that I go through with the wedding, and I'm expected to just—go along with what you demand?"

"If you want the alliance to continue, yes." Viktor pushes himself to his feet. "There's nothing more to say, Liam. You've made a promise and signed a contract. Breaking it isn't an option, not without tearing apart everything we've built. I know you're better than that. At least—I hope so." He jerks his head in Levin's direction, who gives me a sympathetic glance before following his boss out.

Luca stands too, Alessio just behind him. "I'm sorry, Liam. I'd like to tell you to do as you please. I'm grateful that Sofia and I have what we have. Viktor and I have both experienced tension in the early days of our marriages. It's not easy when it's not wanted by all parties. But in this world, it is necessary." He pauses as he walks behind my chair, one hand settling briefly on my shoulder. "I wish I could tell you differently."

When he and Alessio are gone, the room otherwise empty besides the two of us, Niall comes to sit where Luca was.

"We need to talk, Liam," he says quietly, and I stifle a groan.

"Not you, too. I know what you think of Saoirse, Niall, and—"

"It's not that." Niall leans forward, his voice low as he links his fingers on the table in front of him. "I have news of a sort, Liam."

"Did you knock some woman up? Are we having a double wedding?"

"It's serious."

The expression on his face sobers me, and any hint of gallows humor immediately flees. "What is it?"

"I've heard rumors from the Dublin table. About your brother."

For a moment, I think I stop breathing. I've spent the past few years thinking about my brother in as abstract of terms as possible, not wanting to consider the ramifications if he were alive, unable to come to terms with the possibility of him being truly dead. And now Niall, the man I trust most, the closest thing I have left to a brother in the world, is sitting in front of me and telling me that he has news. Or, if not news, at the very least, rumors.

"Do you want to hear it?" Niall lets out a breath. "Ah, what am I saying? Ya *need* to hear it for the good of yourself and the rest of the table."

"Everyone today has an opinion about that." I press my lips together, steadying myself. Truthfully, I don't know if I want to hear it. Whatever it is, rumors or not, it'll change the way I think about Connor, what I hope for, in the rare moments when I allow myself to hope for something in regards to him.

But Niall is right. If there's news about Connor, I need to hear it.

"Tell me," I say simply, and Niall nods.

"One of the Dublin gangs is bragging that they killed Connor McGregor. Word of it made its way through the streets to the kings. It's not confirmed," Niall adds. "No body has been seen, not by anyone we'd trust. But all the same—" He pauses, looking at me squarely. "Rumors or not, true or not, this is your family's legacy that we're talking about, Liam. If your brother is dead, if he's even *presumed* dead, as many have already these past years, this right here—it's all that's left of the McGregors. *You* are all that's left."

Niall stands up then, slowly, his hand heavy on my shoulder where Luca's was before. In it, I can feel the weight of the burden I bear—the burden of my family's name and the expectations of every man who sits around this table.

"Ya didn't ask for my advice," Niall says quietly. "But I'll give it to ya anyway."

He pauses, and I feel his fingers wrap around my shoulder, squeezing in remonstration or sympathy, I can't tell which.

"If you keep making the wrong choices, Liam, it'll all be gone. You'll lose the Kings. And there will be nothing left of the McGregor name."

EIGHT
ANA

I woke to an empty apartment.

Part of me was grateful for it. After what had happened last between Liam and me, I've had difficulty facing him. We've kept some distance from each other—me out of embarrassment, him out of…well, that I don't know, exactly.

If I'm being honest, I'm afraid to ask.

The trust between us is tenuous right now, at best. I believe what he told me about Saoirse, for better or worse. I believe that he'd made the betrothal out of expediency, not love, and I believe he now intends not to go through with it. But that doesn't change the fact that he kept it a secret from me or that he's now technically engaged. It doesn't change the fact that every time he leaves the penthouse, I wonder if he's going to see her. If he's on a date with her, having lunch, having dinner, pretending to be her fiancé until he can find a way out of it.

I know it's not entirely fair of me to resent sharing him. After all, he still shares a part of me with Alexandre, one that I'm desperately trying to escape. But since the moment Liam came for me, I'd believed that I had all of him. He *said* I had all of him, that he doesn't want anyone else, and still, even after I found out about Saoirse, he still insists that's the truth.

I want to believe him, and I'm afraid to, all at once. Deep down, I know, too, that's how he feels about me—wanting to trust in my feelings for him, afraid that at some point, I'll run back to Alexandre, and he'll lose everything for nothing at all.

I understand it better now, but it still hurts.

The penthouse always feels too big without him. I start my day slowly, cleaning up the living room, eating a small breakfast in an effort to please him even though he's not there, and cleaning up afterward. Part of me, beforehand, would have thought that Liam "punishing" me the way he had would only make me want to disobey him more. After all, what girl doesn't want to be given endless orgasms by a devastatingly handsome man as he croons filthy things in her ear in his accented voice?

But I'd discovered that, while I absolutely want Liam to strip me bare and pleasure me endlessly again, I don't want him to do it as a punishment. I don't want it to be to teach me a lesson, even if it's done pleasurably. I want him to do it because he wants me, and for no other reason—to do it because he's happy with me, because he wants to reward me with pleasure, not torture me with it.

No matter how exquisite the torture had been.

Partway through the afternoon, as I'm curled up on the couch reading a book, there's a knock at the apartment door. I nearly jump out of my skin, as always, afraid of who it might be, but the knock comes once more before I hear footsteps going back down the hall.

I go to the door with mingled excitement and trepidation, opening it slowly, unsure of what's on the other side. But what's there, to my surprise, is a large box not unlike the one that Alexandre left for me, what feels like forever ago now.

This time, though, I'm almost certain it's from Liam. I realize, as I pick it up and carry it inside, that I *hope* it is, and not from Alexandre. *That feeling means something*, I think, as I lift the lid off of the long white box and see the card atop the tissue paper inside.

Anastasia,

I'd like to take you out tonight on a date—a real date. Our first date, and show you Boston. If you'd like that too, my driver will be there to pick you up at seven. I've enclosed some things for you—if you like them, I hope you'll wear them for me tonight.

Liam

My heart skips a beat as I see the last word, the confirmation that it was Liam who sent me this. I'd never, not in a million years, tell Liam that Alexandre had done something similar for me when he'd wanted to take me out. I want Liam to feel that this is something special between us—I want it to *be* something special.

Slowly, I undo the tissue paper. There's a pair of shoes tucked on one side, black strappy Louboutins with a diamond strap across the toes, and next to them, I know, is a dress nestled in more layers of paper. When I peel it back, I gasp softly.

The dress is bright emerald green, and when I pick it up, it falls in silky folds, slithering over my hands richly. It's a floor-length dress with slits up either side nearly to the hip, and a reinforced v at the neckline that cuts low enough that it'll stop just below my cleavage. The sleeves are nothing but thin spaghetti straps, fragile enough to look as if they could break with a touch.

It's a dress designed to highlight all of my best attributes—my sharp collarbones, my ability to wear a dress cut so low due to my lack of cleavage, and my impossibly long legs. It's as if Liam thought of everything about me that he found most beautiful and chose a dress that would point out all of those things specifically.

But that's not all. There's a sleeve with small, cushioned pads—one to go underneath the balls of my feet and another to cushion my arches and heels, and then next to it, a black velvet box bigger than my hand.

When I open the box, there's a gold necklace with an emerald teardrop surrounded by diamonds and a matching pair of emerald studs—teardrop-shaped with a diamond halo around each.

If you like them, the note had said, as if there were any possible way I could *not* like such beautiful things. It takes everything in me to fold the dress and shoes back into the box, setting it carefully on my bed until it's time to get ready. I want to put it on now, but I force myself to wait, letting myself savor the anticipation.

Finally, a half-hour before the driver is supposed to be there, when

I've showered and done a light face of makeup and dried my hair, curling just the ends so that they float over my skin, I slip on the dress.

It fits me perfectly, as if it were made for me. My pale skin glows almost translucent against the emerald green of the dress, the silk slipping over my figure, clinging to my waist, parting for the long stretch of my legs, the v of the neckline just barely showing the slight swells of my breasts on either side. The thin straps cling to my shoulders, so fragile that they give the impression that they could break loose at any moment, sending the fabric fluttering down.

The jewelry goes perfectly with it, the emerald teardrop hanging between my breasts, the earrings glinting from between the strands of my hair. I look like a princess, dressed all in emerald green—an Irish princess.

Liam's princess.

Something in my stomach feels faintly cold at the thought. Saoirse is that, without a doubt. Well-bred, rich, meant to be the wife of an Irish King. I don't want him to make me into Saoirse; I don't want to simply replace her. I want him to want me for *myself*, as I want him for himself.

You're putting too much thought into it, I tell myself as I look at my reflection, stepping carefully into the now-padded shoes. Liam bought me a beautiful dress, a color that would look lovely on me, the color of his eyes, and if it's Irish green, there's nothing wrong with him wanting to see me in that.

It doesn't mean anything more.

My phone buzzes, a text from the driver telling me that he's waiting. Hurriedly, I grab a few things and stash them in the slender gold clutch purse that I'd found wrapped in tissue, buried in the bottom of the box, and walk carefully to the elevator, conscious of my feet. The pads help a great deal, but I haven't worn shoes like this in a long time. I'm also conscious of the way the scars wrap around, a few of them on the sides and tops of my feet, and the gnarly appearance of my ballerina's toes. But the dress is long enough that you can barely see them, and since the pedicure Liam scheduled for me, they're not as embarrassing to look at. Still, there's a reason why ballerinas rarely wear open-toed shoes.

My days of pointe shoes and warped feet for ordinary reasons are far behind me, though. I try not to think of it as I go out to the waiting car, thanking the driver who holds the door for me as I slip inside. It still feels so strange to have something like this—a car waiting for me, someone who will take me wherever I please. I only have to ask.

I wonder if I'll ever get used to it, if it's something I even *should* get used to. Liam's life is a far cry from the one I would have had on my own or even with Alexandre. Alexandre was rich—a billionaire, probably, to be able to spend a hundred million on my purchase—but he'd lived more like an ordinary person, albeit an eccentric one.

I push Alexandre firmly out of my mind as the car pulls out into traffic, refusing to let him be a part of tonight. This night is about Liam and I, about what Liam has planned for us, and I want to enjoy it fully, without thoughts of anything or anyone else.

The car takes me to a gorgeous restaurant, something nestled away in a tall brick building with a garden patio out front. The hostess smiles at me when I tell her that I'm here to meet Liam McGregor. She whisks me away through a room full of crisp white tablecloths and mahogany booths to a table towards the back, with a candlelit chandelier above it and a string quartet playing faintly from the other side of the room.

Liam is sitting there, handsome in a tailored charcoal suit, his eyes bright with happiness when he sees me. He stands instantly, unfolding his tall body from behind the table, and pulls out the chair next to him, thanking the hostess as he waits for me to sit down.

"I'm glad you came, Ana," he says softly. He looks good in candlelight, his eyes softer than usual, the red in his beard glinting. "I was almost worried you might not."

"What were you going to do if I didn't?" I tease him lightly. "We live together."

"I would have waited for a while to see if you'd come." Liam lifts one shoulder in a shrug. "And then I would have gone from there, I suppose, if you hadn't."

The words sound casual, but from the way his gaze catches mine and holds it, I know it's not. If I hadn't come, it would have meant something about us, about him and me. It would have been saying that

I wasn't ready to move forward, not ready to put my trust in him, and I didn't want him the way he wants me.

But I do, and I think that I am. I *want* to be ready, to trust him. This is the first step in that direction.

"There are things I don't know about you, Ana, that I want to," Liam says, and my stomach knots at the thought of what those things might be. But then he slips the wine list out of the menu, and I feel myself relax.

"Like, what kind of wine do you prefer?" He scans the list. "Red or white?"

"Red," I tell him confidently. "Although it was mostly cheap blends back in my Julliard days."

"Well, there'll be none of that here, for sure." Liam crooks a smile at me. "Only the best for you."

The server appears, and he orders a bottle of wine, some pinot noir that I don't recognize. "It's a good one," Liam tells me confidently, and I smile at him.

"I trust you," I say teasingly, and both of us go very still as the words hang in the air between us for a moment, as if I were talking about something other than wine.

"I took the luxury of ordering an appetizer for us to come after the wine," Liam says. "A few things, since I wasn't sure what you'd like best. But order anything you like for dinner, Ana. Whatever you want, you should have."

The server returns with the wine, uncorking it and handing the cork to Liam as she pours a bit into each glass, handing them to us. Liam breathes it in, swirling it in the glass before tasting it. I try to follow his lead, although it doesn't mean much to me—as far as I can tell, wine is wine.

"Perfect," Liam tells her, and she adds to our glasses, leaving the bottle.

"I know not everything is right between us at the moment," Liam says when the server is gone. "I know we have things to work through, things to decide. But I wanted to have a normal night with you, Ana, a real date. I wanted to show you what life would be like when it's just the two of us, when there's no one else we're thinking of or beholden to, when it's just you and me, and the life I want for us to have together."

"I appreciate that." I take a sip of the wine, my eyes fluttering briefly closed at the taste of it. It *is* incredible, one of the best wines I've ever tasted, including the French wine I had in Paris. "But we can't ignore all of it, Liam. Even if it's just us, even if there's no one else, it's never going to be easy. It's not all going to be fancy nights out and hours of us pleasuring each other."

"Why not?" Liam grins at me, and for a moment, it looks almost boyish, despite the beard. "I can think of nothing I want more than to spend hours pleasuring you, Ana."

His hand slips under the tablecloth, finding my knee beneath the green silk, and a shiver runs through me at the warmth of his palm against my skin.

"I know, and trust me, I—I want that too." I take another sip of my wine, trying to steady my thoughts. "But Liam, there's more to this than that. You're—you're an Irish King, and I'm—"

"Did Sofia tell you to think about these things while she was here?" Liam's lips thin slightly. "You don't need to worry about that, Ana. Those things are for me to worry about—"

"She didn't," I tell him quickly. "Not everything I think is because someone else put it in my head, Liam—"

"That's not what I meant." He lets out a sigh, taking another sip of his wine. We're momentarily interrupted by the server reappearing with our appetizers—a delicate-looking bruschetta, caviar on toast points, and what looks like beef tartare with a runny egg on top. My stomach growls—I haven't eaten all that much today, although I'd made sure to at least manage something for breakfast and lunch. I reach for one of the toast points, gingerly taking a bite. I've never had caviar before, but I'm not sure if this is the appropriate time to bring that up.

"Luca and Viktor aren't overly pleased with my having you here either," Liam says. "I thought perhaps Sofia had thoughts about it as well, that she'd shared with you."

"Sofia just wants me to be happy," I say softly. "If I want to be here, then she'll support me. If I want to go to Manhattan and stay with her, she'll support me in that too."

"That must feel good to have that."

"She's my best friend." I set the toast on the small, delicate china plate in front of me. "Do you have anyone like that?"

"In a way." Liam frowns. "Niall is like a brother to me. He is, for all intents and purposes, my best friend. I know he'd do anything for me. But he doesn't always agree with my decisions."

"Is this a decision he doesn't agree with?"

Liam nods. "He thinks I should marry Saoirse. In fact, the overwhelming consensus seems to be that I should marry Saoirse."

"And yet here I am," I murmur. "Out on a date with you."

"Here you are." Liam's hand is still on my knee, his fingers rubbing over the rounded bone there. "I love you, Ana. I know that we haven't known each other for long. I know that it's not easy what we're doing here. But I want, more than anything, for you to believe that. To trust in it—that whatever comes, I love you."

"I do believe it," I say softly. "But I also know that sometimes, love isn't enough."

Liam looks at me as he takes a bite of the beef tartare, curiosity in his eyes. "Your parents?"

I nod. "Among other things. My mother loved my father very much, or at least that's what I remember. When we came to New York, I was young, but I never remember a raised voice between them. I only remember them touching each other, smiling. But my father got into trouble with the Bratva in Russia. He was murdered—and my mother and I fled here." I give Liam a sad, tentative smile. "They loved each other, but it wasn't enough to save him. He died, and she was never the same after. She never loved again, never married again. He was it for her, and I saw that she was somehow—less, when he was gone. Like a part of her had been carved away, a part that she needed."

"I would argue that her love for you saved you, though," Liam says, sipping his wine. "Her love for you was enough to get you both here, to give you a good life."

I nod. "In a way, I guess that's true. But the point remains the same.

If us being together causes problems with the Kings—are they really going to care that we love each other?"

Liam pauses, and I can see him thinking about what I've just said. I haven't said *I love you* to him yet, not in so many words, because of his insistence that I wait until I'm certain that it's only him that I love. And yet, I couldn't stop myself from saying that, at least—because it's true. I do love him, even if I can't say it to him yet.

"Let me worry about that," Liam says finally. "I should have told you everything sooner, Ana, I admit that. But you don't need to worry about the decisions and machinations of the Kings. That's for me to concern myself with once I've ended the engagement to Saoirse."

"You're going to do it? You meant that?"

"Yes," Liam says firmly. "It's been suggested to me that I should marry her anyway and keep you on the side—but I'm not going to do that," he adds quickly, seeing the shift in my expression. "I know that you may not believe me entirely, considering the secrets I kept from you so far, but I think infidelity is abhorrent. When I marry, I've always intended to be faithful to my wife—which is part of why I can't bring myself to marry Saoirse. She's a beautiful, tough, intelligent woman, but I don't *want* her, not in any way. Not in the way a man should want his wife. And I can't resign myself to a cold, loveless marriage any longer, not after—"

His eyes glow in the candlelight, heating with desire, and the hand that's on my knee slides a bit higher. "You've shown me things I didn't know I could feel, Ana," he murmurs softly. "I didn't know the depths that desire could reach until I was with you. I can't go back after that—not now, not ever. You're it for me, and you always will be. So no, I won't keep you on the side, and I won't marry Saoirse. But Ana—"

Liam takes a breath, and I can feel his hand tighten on my leg. "I need you to meet me there, too. I need you to fight for this as hard as I'm fighting for it. Because if I lose you, after risking everything else—"

The words hang in the air between us, and I don't know what to say. I want to promise him everything, to tell him that there's no one else but him, but I know that's not entirely true, not yet. I'm finding my way there, little by little. But after he's tried so hard to show me that he's telling me the truth, I can't bear to say anything to him that isn't entirely true, either.

The server appears to take our orders, and the moment is broken. I'm almost grateful for it, although I can feel Liam's eyes on me as he places his order of filet and lobster with gorgonzola sauce, and I place my order of lamb chops with demiglace and spring salad. As the server whisks away the remains of our appetizers, Liam clears his throat, and I know he's going to make an effort to change the subject.

"So, what would your ideal date be, Ana?" He smiles crookedly at me as he takes another sip of his wine. "I planned this one as best as I could, under the circumstances, but since I hope there'll be more, I want to know what you would pick, if you could do anything."

"Anything?" I frown. "I don't know Boston very well."

"*Anywhere*," Liam confirms. "Not just in Boston."

"Oh, that's easy, then." I laugh. "I'd be on a tropical beach somewhere in the sun, listening to the waves and drinking some kind of fruity drink. I love New York, really I do—the museums and the libraries and the art galleries and everything there is to do, and I'm sure Boston has so much of that as well—but god, I hate the cold." I shiver, laughing, and I see Liam's smile broaden, his eyes watching me intently as if he loves listening to the sound of my voice. "I'd go on a tropical vacation in an instant, if I could pick up and go anywhere."

"Then it's decided." Liam grins. "That's what we'll do for our honeymoon."

My heart skips a beat in my chest, but I manage to keep my voice even, light and teasing, as I raise an eyebrow at him. "Oh? Are you proposing to me?"

Liam's eyes darken just a little. "If I were, would you say yes?"

I can feel my pulse fluttering in my throat. *Yes*, I want to say, but I bite back the word, because I know he'll take me at it. I could end up married tonight if I'm not careful—I wouldn't put it past Liam to sweep me off to the nearest cathedral after dinner, his prior engagement be damned. And I'm not ready for that—not quite. Not yet.

"You don't even have a ring," I tell him teasingly, and Liam laughs, though I can hear a slight edge to it.

"Yes, I've been known to forget those."

The server reappears with our food and another bottle of wine, and we both dig in. The food is incredible, some of the best I've ever tasted. I force myself to go slowly, cutting each bit of lamb into tiny, respectable bites instead of devouring it the way I want to. I want to seem elegant, like Saoirse, composed and poised.

"Did you put me in green tonight for a reason?" The question slips off my tongue before I can stop it, and Liam looks up, startled.

"I—"

"Did you want to see me dressed like her? A princess in Irish green?" I don't mean to sound accusing, but I must feel it because the thought makes itself known that way. Liam sits back, and I can see his expression tighten, the mood darkening slightly. I feel bad instantly for saying it, but at the same time, I want to know.

"No," Liam says calmly. "I suppose I can see how it might seem that way, but no. I *did* like the color of the dress, I won't lie. I'm partial to that shade of green, I suppose. But there wasn't any intention behind it. I simply thought it would look beautiful on you. And it does," he adds. "You do look a bit like an Irish princess. But nothing like her. And I mean that in the best possible way."

I let out the breath I hadn't realized I'd been holding. "I'm sorry," I say softly. "I didn't mean to say it that way. I just—"

"It's okay." Liam shakes his head, taking another bite of his filet. "It's not always going to be easy navigating this. I can understand how you might feel that way. But Ana—" He sets his fork down, looking at me squarely, and his hand slides up my thigh again, pushing the silk aside. "I don't compare the two of you. But if I were to do so, it would always be you that I wanted, you that I found most beautiful. *You* are the one I want, and there's no one else."

I wonder how many times he'll say it before I can say it back in truth, before I can think of Alexandre without the slightest shiver down my spine or twist of desire in my stomach. Before the things that happened between us are just that—things that happened and not things that I miss.

We end up with a chocolate mousse topped with berries for dessert. Liam pulls my chair closer to his, dipping the silver teaspoon into the mousse and raising it to my lips as his hand finds its way higher up my thigh.

"I've thought about this before, when I've fantasized about you," he murmurs softly in my ear. "Feeding you a luxurious dessert at a restaurant, my hand on your leg beneath the tablecloth, where someone might see, although they probably won't. And even if they did," he whispers huskily as he raises a raspberry to my mouth. "They wouldn't dare say a word."

My heart is hammering in my chest. His fingers are almost to my inner thigh. In another moment, he'll discover the decision I made before leaving the apartment—one that I wasn't sure about, but dared anyway.

His fingers slip higher as he pushes the raspberry between my lips, higher still as he takes a small bite of the mousse. Then I see his eyes widen as he makes the discovery, his fingers sliding against the soft, damp folds of my naked pussy beneath the silk dress.

"Naughty lass," he murmurs, his tongue running over his lower lip to catch the bit of mousse clinging there, and I feel a fresh rush of desire between my thighs at the thought of that tongue between my legs, sliding over my clit, licking me to one of the fierce orgasms that Liam is so good at wrenching from me.

He feels the arousal, my flesh swelling and dampening, and he makes a noise low in his throat. "You did this on purpose, lass, just like those lace panties the night I spread you wide on the dining table." His lips lean close to my ear as he raises another bite of the mousse to my lips. "As the leader of the Irish Kings, I own this city. I could put you on this table, here and now, just as I did in our dining room at home, and no one would say a word. No one would dare. I could toss your skirts aside, spread your pretty thighs, and make a dessert out of you in front of every patron here, and they'd all watch."

I swallow hard, my clit suddenly throbbing, aching for his touch. "You wouldn't," I gasp softly, and Liam chuckles, his finger pressing between my folds as the teaspoon slips between my lips.

I taste chocolate at the same moment his fingertip grazes my clit, and I can't help the moan that escapes me. I see someone at a nearby table looking at me out of the corner of their eye with surprise, as if they can't believe the dessert is quite *that* good, and I feel myself flush.

"Ah yes, lass, blush just like that for me," Liam murmurs. "No better way for them to know what I'm doing to you than that." His fingertip strokes the slick, swollen flesh of my clit, and I shudder, gasping around the piece of strawberry that he slips into my mouth.

"I could make a show of it," he murmurs. "Every man in here would envy me. Every woman would wish they were you, with the Irish King's mouth between your thighs. Is that what you wanted, lass, when you came here with no panties on? For me to eat you out in front of this entire restaurant?"

"Oh god, no," I whisper, flushing even brighter. Liam's finger is circling my clit now, faster, and I can feel my arousal heightening, dripping, coating his fingers and my inner thighs. I squeeze my legs together around his hand, suddenly terrified I'll leave a wet patch on my dress, and then everyone here *will* know for certain what we've been doing.

"What were you hoping for, then?" His fingers dip lower into my entrance just long enough to make me gasp and clench around him before he drags them back up to my aching clit, pinching it gently between thumb and forefinger, just as he takes another bite and then feeds me one, muffling my tiny cry of pleasure. "For me to make you come while I fed you dessert?"

"I, I just—I didn't think, I—"

"We have the same fantasy," he murmurs in my ear. "I want to make you come, right here for me, with my voice in your ear and the taste of chocolate in your mouth. Every time you taste it, for the rest of your life, you'll remember this—this restaurant, and my fingers on your clit, making you come in front of everyone." Another piece of fruit, the sweetness bursting on my tongue, the same way I feel as if *I'm* about to burst, my desire trembling on the edge, his fingers rubbing my clit again, harder this time.

"Is that what you want, lass? To come right now, right here, with everyone watching?"

"They're not all watching—"

"They will be," Liam murmurs. Then his hand moves faster,

rubbing in the tight, quick circles that he knows will send me over the edge, and I grab his thigh, my fingers sinking into the tight fabric of his suit trousers as I gasp.

"Yes! Yes, Liam, please, let me come, make me come, ahh—" I whisper the words frantically, hushed next to his ear, praying that to anyone watching, it'll merely look like we're madly in love, pressed together, whispering over dessert, our hands on each other's legs.

"Then come for me, lass," Liam whispers, and with his fingers flicking expertly over the tight, throbbing bundle of nerves between my folds, there's nothing I can do but obey.

He slides one last teaspoon of dessert into my mouth. I gasp around it, sighing as the chocolate coats my tongue in the same instant that Liam's fingers are coated with the wash of my orgasm, crashing through me as I lean into him, ducking my face against his shoulder as my nails nearly dig through the fabric of his pants into his thigh. I try to hold still as the climax rolls through me, not to shudder or moan, and Liam turns his face towards my ear, whispering with a dark, wicked edge of laughter to his voice.

"Ah yes, little lass, come for me. So wet, so hungry—ah *fuck*." He moans lightly, not loud enough for anyone to hear, as I press myself against his hand, wanting more of the pleasure, even as I'm horribly, shamefully aware of how many eyes in the restaurant probably know what we're doing.

And then, just as the last tremors of my orgasm pass through me, Liam slides his hand out from beneath my skirt and from under the table. Deftly, he swipes his two fingers around the rim of the mousse cup, chocolate on his fingertips, as he raises them to his lips.

With my eyes on him—probably the whole goddamned restaurant's as well—he slides his fingers into his mouth, his eyes twinkling darkly at me.

"Delicious," he murmurs, and if I'd been standing up, my knees would have buckled at the sound of his voice. As it is, I'm not sure I can stand.

I can see everyone in the restaurant quickly looking away, back to their meals. "Do you think they know?" I whisper tremulously, and Liam laughs.

"If they do, they'll never let on. But what *I* know, lass, is that I'll need a moment before I can stand up." He chuckles, and I feel him against my hand as I slide it across his lap, hard and throbbing, straining against his fly. "Go clean up, lass. I'll tell the car to come around in a few."

Liam smiles at me, reaching for my hand and raising the back of it to his lips.

"The night isn't finished yet."

NINE
ANA

It takes me a moment in the bathroom to regain my composure. I clean up quickly, washing my hands, grateful to see that at least I hadn't made a mess of the back of my skirt. My knees still feel weak, my fingers trembling, but I take a deep breath, fixing my lipstick in the mirror, and looking at my flushed, glowing face.

I look like a woman who just had one of the best orgasms of her life. I look like a woman in love. The first I know is true, and the second—I'm almost certain of it.

How could I not love Liam? He kept secrets from me, it's true, but with a calmer head, I can understand his reasoning. I can see why he might have done so. He's crossed a literal ocean for me, given me everything I could desire, shown me that he wants me to distraction, and sworn his love to me. What else could I possibly want?

I feel almost giddy as I leave the bathroom, clutch in hand, heading for the restaurant's lobby, where I know he'll be waiting for me. *He'd said the night isn't finished, and I'm eager to find out what comes next and what he has planned for us.* It's already been everything I could possibly have dreamed—beyond that, even, and I can feel the butterflies in my stomach as I walk out to meet him.

He's standing there waiting for me, tall and handsome in his impeccably cut suit, his hair and beard burnished red beneath the lights. Liam smiles at me, taking my hand in his long-fingered one as he leads me out to the curb, and I shiver, thinking of those fingers between my thighs a moment ago. He opens the door to the car for me, and I glance at him as he slides inside, a sudden idea forming in my head.

"How far until where we're going next?" I ask softly, and Liam glances at me curiously.

"A few miles, though it'll probably take longer than it should, in Friday night Boston traffic. Why?"

"Put the divider up," I whisper, and Liam's eyes widen.

I wonder if he'll try to stop me. But the rule is no sex until I'm his and his alone, no *intercourse*, and he's made me climax numerous times between the last time we tried to sleep together and now. He just made me come in front of an entire restaurant, one of the most memorable orgasms of my life, and now I want to do something for him.

He opens his mouth as if to say something, but then closes it.

The divider between the driver and us darkens, and I lean over, my fingers reaching for his belt.

"Ana, you don't have to—"

"I know. I *want* to." I mean it, with everything in me. I've craved the taste of him, the feeling of him, to touch him and hear the sounds that he's sworn only I can elicit from him. I want to see him, and in the close, cool darkness of the backseat of the car, I undo his belt, dragging his zipper down and slipping my hand inside.

He's already hard again, just from the anticipation. I slip him out into the open air, every long, hard, throbbing inch of him, and as my hand tightens around his shaft, I hear him groan low in his throat.

There's no time to tease him. There might be traffic, but a few miles is a few miles. I push my hair to one side, bending my head to lower my lips to the damp, slick flesh of his tip, and when I swirl my tongue around it, lapping up his arousal, I feel Liam's fingers run through my hair.

"God, Ana, there's no fucking better feeling in the world than your mouth."

I moan softly, sliding my lips down, wanting to take all of him. I love the feeling of my lips stretching around his girth, the taut flesh sliding over my tongue, into my throat. I love feeling him pulse in my mouth as I go all the way down, the warm scent of his skin as my nose brushes against the dark reddish hair on his abdomen, and I choke slightly as he slips into my throat. The muscles convulse, tightening around him, and Liam groans again.

"Are you going to make me come, little lass? Like I did for you, just now?"

I nod eagerly, feeling him twist my hair around his hand, his palm against the back of my head gently as I start to slide up and then down again, lips and tongue reaching to caress every inch of his straining flesh, the taste and scent of him filling my senses. I slide all the way down again, choking on the thickness of him deep in my throat, and Liam's hips arch upwards as he groans again.

"Fuck, Ana—" I feel his hand tighten in my hair, his cock twitching between my lips as he pushes himself deeper. "Fuck, I love when you swallow my fucking cock, *fuck*—"

I want more. I want all of him. I slide my hand between his legs, cupping his taut balls in my palm, fingers stroking the tight skin as I come up for air, panting before I take his cock down my throat again. I can feel him tensing, the muscles in his thighs flexing, and I know he must be close.

"Ana, Ana, *god*—" Liam is panting now, trembling with pleasure, his hand knotted in my hair as I increase my pace, sucking his cock fast and hard. I want him to come, want to taste it, want him to fill my mouth, and I think he knows that, because I hear him groan again, this time loudly enough that there's no way the driver doesn't hear, but I think he's past caring.

"I'm going to come, Ana—*fuck*, Ana, I'm, *shit*—" The sound he makes is one of pure, strangled pleasure as I feel him throb between my lips, his cockhead rubbing over my tongue as the first hot spurt coats it, filling my mouth with the salty heat of him as I swallow convulsively, wanting to catch every drop. I tighten my lips around him, sucking harder, my other hand at the base of his cock, stroking every inch that I can't force down my throat as he keeps coming, his head thrown back now, hips pushing himself into my mouth as his cum fills it.

"Ana, Ana—" He moans my name repeatedly, his hand loosening in my hair, stroking the back of my head. "Oh god, Ana, that's enough. I can't take anymore—"

I come up slowly, licking away the last drops of cum on my lips as Liam tucks himself away. The look of half-astonished pleasure on his face sends a ripple of desire through me.

"God, Ana—" he murmurs, and then his hands are on my face, pulling me in for a kiss as if he didn't just fill my mouth with cum, his lips seeking out mine as his hands slide into my hair.

He kisses me, long and slow and deep, until I'm breathless and the car pulls up to the curb, and we finally slide apart.

"Where are we?" I ask when we've both fixed our clothes, and Liam opens the door for me, giving me a hand out.

"The Boston Opera House," he says with a smile, his fingers linking through mine. "Come on, I have our tickets."

Tickets to what? I want to ask, but I also want to let him surprise me. It could be anything—a concert, the opera, a play, and I lean into him as we walk in, savoring the feeling of my fingers laced through his, the warmth of his palm against mine, the scent of his cologne in my nostrils, the taste of him still lingering on my tongue. I'd imagined us so many times now as a couple, being together for real, doing all the things that couples do. Still, it's never felt as real as it does now.

This night, this date, has given me hope and assurance for us, for our future, like never before. I feel closer to Liam than I ever have, warm and happy, light as a feather, as he hands over our tickets without me really hearing what he says. I glide up the stairs next to him to our box seats overlooking the stage. I lean in close to him, feeling his fingers in my hair as we wait for the curtain to go up, tracing the back of my neck, his lips seeking out mine again as we sit there in the darkness, and I feel like I'm in a dream.

My dream, his dream. *Our dream.* It feels magical, better than anything I could have imagined. As the curtain rises on the stage, I turn eagerly towards it, wanting to know what Liam picked out for us to see together.

And then the first notes of *Swan Lake* fill the air, and I freeze in place.

No. No, no.

The music feels like it's assaulting my senses, the sight of the ballerinas on stage cutting into me, as if every one of them individually held a knife and drove it into my chest. I haven't been to the ballet since Franco, haven't listened to an orchestral soundtrack, haven't watched it or looked at my old videos, or so much as touched the pile of pointe shoes and tulle that was still in my closet before I left my old apartment.

I haven't been able to bear it, not any of it. Just the opening notes feel like a slap to the face, a searing reminder that the thing I once loved above all else, that I gave my heart and soul to, is lost to me forever. That no matter how healed I am, how far I move past it, how much acceptance I find, I will *never, never* dance on a stage like that again. I'll never slip my foot into a pair of satin shoes because they've been warped beyond anything that dance could have ever done to them. I'll never wind satin ribbons around my ankle, never feel the crush of tulle between my fingertips, the stretch of a leotard over my carefully honed body. Even the worst parts of it—the pain, the exhaustion, the anxiety, the backstabbing for parts, I'll never experience that again either.

I was meant to be on a stage like that by now. I'd be graduated, in New York, taking the place that I'd been told I was a shoo-in for as prima. I'd be dancing the part of Odette on a Manhattan stage, the crowd a blur as I danced, leaped, pirouetted, spun, as hands lifted me into the air, as the music overtook me, and I *became* her, just for a little while, lost in the magic of it all.

Never again. Never again. Never, never never, never—

"Ana? Ana!" Dimly, I hear Liam's voice, and I realize that I've clapped my hands over my ears, turning my head away from the stage so that I don't have to see them. He reaches for me, but I twist away, feeling my heart tear like paper as I look at his earnest, worried face and realize that he didn't do this on purpose. He didn't mean to hurt me. He simply—didn't know that it would. And somehow, that feels just as awful.

"I can't," I whisper. "I can't, I can't—" I push myself up from my seat, stumbling blindly towards the curtain leading out of our box, my feet suddenly aching in the strappy shoes. I nearly fall as I reach down to yank them off, clutching them in my hand like Cinderella fleeing the ball as I run from the box, down the steps, and out into the red-carpeted lobby, feeling eyes on me as I bend over, panting and trying not to burst into sobs and not caring.

"Ana!" I hear Liam's voice behind me, breathless, and I know he's caught up to me. I can't turn around to face him, not yet, but he's not giving me a choice. I feel his hands on my waist, turning me, and I feel the tears starting to come as I look up at his handsome face.

"How could you?" I whisper, the words breaking as they slip out. "How could you do that, Liam—"

"What?" He looks genuinely confused. "Ana, what's wrong?"

"What's *wrong*?" I stare at him, my heart suddenly hammering in my chest. "If you have to ask that, Liam—then there's no point." I swallow hard, pain and heartbreak and anger welling up all at once. It suddenly seems clear to me how little we know each other, how we couldn't possibly be in love, not if he couldn't grasp this one simple thing without me having to say it out loud. "You don't understand me," I whisper brokenly, backing away from him. "You don't know me at all—"

"Ana, that's not true!" Liam's eyes widen with alarm, and he reaches for my hand, the one holding my shoes. "Look, just put your shoes back on. You can't be barefoot out here. It's not good for your feet. We'll go home if that's what you want. We—"

"No." I shake my head wildly, feeling the panic welling up inside of me. "I don't want to go—it's not my home, Liam, it's yours. None of this is mine, not even you—"

"Not this again." Liam groans. "Ana, I've told you, the engagement—"

"You're hers. In every way that matters, you're hers—"

"No! Not in every way that matters." Liam raises his voice, and now I know for sure everyone *is* looking at us, but he doesn't seem to care. "In every way that matters, Ana, I'm yours. I love you, and I know you. You can't mean that I don't—"

"If you did," I whisper brokenly, "you wouldn't have given me shoes that show my feet. No ballerina wears open-toed shoes, but especially not one as destroyed as me. And if you knew me, *really* knew me, if you'd listened to everything I'd said—you would have never taken me to the ballet. You'd know how much it would hurt me to see it, how much it would hurt to remember that I'll never dance again, that I'll never be the prima I was meant to be—"

Liam's eyes widen. "Oh god, Ana—I didn't mean it. I thought—fuck—I thought you'd enjoy seeing it again, that it would bring back the good memories. I thought it would be something that reminded you of happier times—I—" He rubs his hand over his mouth, his eyes glistening. "Fuck, Ana, I'm so sorry. I didn't mean it—"

"You don't know me," I whisper, backing up, the shoes still clutched in my hand. "You don't, and it won't work. It can't work, Liam. I'm sorry."

And then, before he can say another word, before he can reach for me or try to stop me, I turn and flee from the opera house, out into the street.

TEN
ANA

I make it three blocks before a strong hand grabs my wrist, hauling me sideways and knocking me off balance, and a pair of arms go around my waist, pulling me back.

"Liam, let me go!" I shriek, swatting at the hands, writhing in his grasp. "I don't want to talk to you right now. I don't—"

"It's not Liam, *petit*."

I freeze in place, going very still as I hear that familiar French voice sweeping over my senses in a way that feels almost dizzying.

"Alexandre?" I whisper, and slowly, as the arms around my waist loosen, I turn in their circle so I can face the man holding me.

It can't be him. It *shouldn't* be. But it is. In the streetlights, plain as day, I can see his every familiar, handsome feature—the sharp cheekbones and jaw, the aquiline nose, the shining blue eyes that I'd once loved so much.

"Come with me, *petit*," he says, his hand closing on my elbow and pulling me into the alleyway. "Before he catches up."

"Alexandre, I can't—Alexandre!" I yank backward, struggling. "I'm barefoot. I can't go through an alley like this. My feet—"

"Then I will simply carry you, *petit*." He scoops me into his arms before I can protest, carrying me through the alley to the next street over, whistling for a cab as we emerge. "My little doll needs not walk, if she does not wish to."

"Alexandre, what are you doing? How did you?"

"I followed you to the opera house. Shh, *petit*, I know what you are thinking, the word going through your head. But it is not like that, not at all. I wanted to see that you were safe, that you were happy. And as far as I can tell, you are neither of those things from the way you were tearing down the street crying. So." He steps forward as a taxi pulls up to the curb, opening the door and depositing me inside as he slips in next to me. "We'll go to my hotel, and you can tell me what happened."

I blink at him, stunned into silence by how quickly everything has happened. Alexandre is giving the driver the name of a hotel, and it occurs to me that I could fight, kick, scream, beg the driver to call the police or scramble out of the cab. But I can't quite bring myself to do it. It's not just the shock of being suddenly grabbed by Alexandre out of nowhere. It's the fact that, at this particular moment, I'm not entirely unhappy to see him.

My night with Liam had gone from magical to horrific in a matter of seconds. I'd felt as if I were in a dream, as if everything were perfect between us. Then I'd been slapped in the face with how little he seemed to understand what would really make me happy and what would make me feel as if my heart were being torn out of my chest.

And now, sitting here next to Alexandre, seeing him for the first time in weeks, feeling his touch, breathing in his scent, I feel as if I'm being ripped in two all over again. I'm falling in love with Liam. I know that beyond a shadow of a doubt. But at one time, I *loved* Alexandre.

I'm not entirely certain that I don't any longer.

We ride in silence back to Alexandre's hotel. He doesn't ask me questions or try to touch me until we reach the curb, and he steps out to open the taxi door. He reaches for me then, sweeping me into his arms bridal style. I'm transported back to the Paris apartment in an instant, though we're still very much in Boston.

He ignores the looks we get as he walks through the black and gold tiled lobby to the elevator, some confused, others suspicious, and some adoring, as if we're some romantic just-married couple, the husband carrying his new wife up to their bridal suite.

I'd imagined marrying Liam just a little while ago, though it feels like ages now. I can't imagine marrying Alexandre. Despite all my feelings for him, it's not a dynamic I ever imagined—or one that I'm sure I would want.

He sets me down just outside his door, opening it and ushering me in. The room is large and luxurious, with a huge bed and a jacuzzi tub ensuite, an open door leading to a bathroom, and a small living area to the left side near the balcony, with a comfortable-looking sofa and lacquered coffee table.

"What do you think, *petit*?" Alexandre asks, seeing me look around the room.

"It's lovely. How—how long have you been here?" I look back at him, feeling my fingers start to tremble. I'm still clutching the shoes, and that hand feels slightly numb as if I'm not entirely sure I could uncurl my fingers any longer.

"Not long," Alexandre says vaguely. "Anastasia, what happened tonight?"

He only uses my full name when he's angry, serious, or full of emotion. I'm not sure which of those things he is, exactly, but I give him my full attention anyway, meeting his piercing blue eyes with my own.

"Liam and I were out on a date," I say softly. "And it was wonderful—the first part of it, at least. But—"

"But?" Alexandre urges, and I realize he's looking forward to this. He wants to hear how Liam has hurt me, upset me, disappointed me—not just for his own pleasure in seeing Liam fall, but because it could mean I'll come back to him. It could be the reason he gets me back.

I realize, at that moment, that it's not just a matter of money, ownership, or pride. Alexandre misses me. In his way, as much as he knows how, he loves me. And he wants me with him, not only because he sees me as *his*, but because he'd very much believed that he would never have to live without me.

I'd led him to believe that. I'd promised it to him.

"He took me to the ballet," I whisper. "And from the very first notes, I couldn't, I—" I feel a fine shiver go through me, making me tremble all over again. "I couldn't stand it, I couldn't, the memories, the—"

I feel the tears well up in my eyes, breaking the words, and Alexandre reaches for me, instantly pulling me into his arms. "Shh," he whispers. "Shh, *petit*, shh. There's no need to cry, now."

"I thought he understood me," I whisper against Alexandre's shoulder, conscious of his arms going around me, stroking along my spine, down to my lower back. "I thought he—I don't know why he did that, why—"

"He did not know, *petit*," Alexandre murmurs. "He did not understand. He does not see your soul, as I do, your beautiful, broken soul. My little doll, my *petit*, my Anastasia—"

He's crooning to me now, his voice thickly accented, his breath in my hair, on my cheek as his hand's rove over my back, pulling me closer, into the circle of his arms, against his chest. There was a time when I felt safe here, or at least, the safest I'd felt in a very long time, up until then.

There was a time when I wanted to stay here and believed that I would.

"Don't cry, *petit*," Alexandre whispers, tipping my chin up so that he can run his thumbs over my cheeks, wiping away the tears below my eyes, along my jaw. His hands feel strong, his fingers sweeping over my cheeks with firm strokes, and I lean into his touch without thinking about it, without meaning to.

It feels good to be held right now, to be touched. I sink into it, closing my eyes, and I hear his soft groan as he cups my face in his hands, his thumbs still skimming over my cheekbones.

"Look at me, *petit*," Alexandre whispers. "Look at your Alexandre."

I open my eyes, knowing even as I do that, he'll take it as an acknowledgment of his words, that he's still mine, that I'm still his. But I can't think, my head foggy with grief and pain and confusion, and a man that I once loved is touching me, holding me, soothing me.

It's so easy to fall into it again. To fall into *him*.

"That's it, *petit*," he whispers. "I knew you would remember us once you saw me again. I knew you would remember all that we were to each other."

And then, before I can stop him, before I can even breathe, his hands are drawing my face up to his, my lips up to his, and his mouth comes down onto mine, warm and gentle and firm, kissing away the pain.

My fingers open, unbidden, and the shoes drop to the floor.

I should push him away. I should tell him no. But instead, my hands press against his chest, against the crisp linen of his black button-down shirt, and Alexandre groans as he pulls me closer against him, his mouth slanting over mine.

"I've missed you, *petit*," he rasps, and I can feel it in every line of his body, taut with desire, in the hard line of his cock already pressed against my thigh. "I've missed all of this—your hands, your lips, your body—"

His own hands are sliding down, over the silk clinging to my waist, down to my hips as he pulls me against him. I feel him walking me backward, moving me towards the bed, and a part of my mind is screaming at me that I need to stop him, that *we* need to stop.

And another part of me only remembers Paris, only remembers our first night in his bed, the nights that came after, whispered promises of love and forgetting that he owned me, remembering only that I believed he loved me.

"You promised you would not leave me, *petit*," Alexandre whispers, his lips brushing against mine as he backs me against the bed, the soft duvet brushing against the back of my leg as my skirt sweeps aside. "But I can forgive you for that. You made a mistake, but you are here again, in my arms. Here with me—"

He lifts me onto the bed, following me down so that he's stretched atop me, and even as my mouth starts to form the words *no, I can't, we can't*, my fingers are pulling at the buttons on his shirt, undoing it so that I can touch the smooth muscle beneath, trace the lines of him that I'd nearly forgotten, pulling it out of the waist of his pants so that I can touch lower still.

"Yes, *petit, mon Dieu*, I forgot how good your touch feels. *Merde*, ah!" Alexandre moans as my fingers skim along the waist of his pants, toying with the hair there, my lips upturned to his as he kisses me, hard and firm, devouring my mouth.

"It's only you, *petit*, only you—"

It could only ever be you. I hear Liam's voice in my head, clear as day, and I jerk backward, reality crashing back in on me as I realize what we're doing. "Alexandre—"

I go to push at his chest, but he clasps my hand in his, his other hand stroking my cheek as he kisses me again. "I want to be inside of you, *petit*. I need it, after so long. Say yes—"

His hand is drawing mine down, down to the thick ridge of him, pressing against his fly, and my fingers unconsciously close around it, stroking him lightly as my head tips back for his lips to skim across my throat. It feels almost impossible to stop, impossible to tell him no. I feel as if I'm being ripped apart, a voice in my head screaming that I have to stop, that I'm being unfaithful to Liam in every way that matters, that I can't let this go any farther, that in another few minutes I will have gone so far that I can never take it back, and I'll lose Liam for good.

And another part of me wants to pull Alexandre down atop me, to devour his mouth with mine, spread my thighs for him and let him sink into me, feel the pleasure again of losing myself in him, of knowing that I don't need to do anything other than please him, anything other than be his, and that will be enough—

I'd run from Liam's mistake tonight and fallen straight into Alexandre's arms. It's either fate or terrible luck, and I don't know which, but I know one thing for sure. There's no other woman for Alexandre. There is no one for me to compete with, no one for me to feel guilty over, no one for me to compare myself to. No one else.

What about Yvette?

He doesn't love her—

The memory burns through me, sharp and cutting, of Yvette with a gun to my head as Liam miserably took his place between my thighs. Her evil smile as she watched Liam make me come, knowing that it might mean my death, *hoping* that it would. And Alexandre standing there, letting it happen. *Encouraging* it even, to a point.

"You betrayed me," I whisper it at first, then louder. I pull my hands away from his cock, reality crashing in over me as I shove at his chest, trying to push him away from me. "You said you'd protect me, and you *lied*. You gave me to Liam, you almost let Yvette kill me, you—"

"Mistakes were made on both sides, *petit*." Alexandre looks flustered, his dark hair falling messily over his face. It always makes him look younger, more innocent, more like the boy he'd once been before his father's cruelty had warped him. "I'm sorry, I should never have let you go—but you've come back to me, Anastasia. You're here, now, and I need you—"

"No." I push at him harder, trying to squirm out from under him, and real fear shoots through me as I consider where this could go. "Alexandre, please, let me up. I don't want this. Please get off of me, please—"

He pulls back slightly, confusion written across his face. "*Petit*, no. Don't do this. Let me love you, let me *make* love to you, please—"

"Let me go!" I shove at him, my eyes widening with fear. "Alexandre, don't hurt me again, please. Please let me go—"

We're both begging each other for different things. He realizes that, I think, his face going very still as he suddenly pushes away from me, kneeling between my open legs, my skirt tangled around my thighs. He's hard as a rock, his erection nearly bursting the fly of his pants, but he seems momentarily unaware of it.

"*Petit*—"

I scramble out of the bed, fixing my dress hurriedly and grabbing for my fallen shoes and clutch. "I have to go, Alexandre. I never should have let you bring me here—"

"No! Don't go, Anastasia, not again." Alexandre crawls off the bed, coming towards me, but I back up in a rush, holding my hands and clutching my things out in front of me as if I could ward him off with shoes and a purse. "Stay with me, *petit*, please."

"I can't. I'm sorry." I bolt for the door, praying that it will be unlocked, and it is. I don't know if he'll follow me as I rush out into the hall, but I run towards the elevator, grabbing my skirt up in my hand as I make a mad dash for it.

I don't hear his footsteps behind me. It's as if, now that I've told him no once again, he's actually listened to me. I look back once as I slam my hand against the button for the elevator, and my heart drops as I see him standing there outside his door, his shirt still unbuttoned and open, staring after me.

But he doesn't come after me. He stands there, watching me as I step into the elevator, and he doesn't say a word. He doesn't move, and as the elevator doors close, I wonder if that will be the last time I ever see him.

ELEVEN
ANA

I called Liam.

There was nothing else I could do. Out on the sidewalk, my hands shaking, barefoot in an emerald green gown that I would have bet cost three months rent on my old apartment, I didn't have a cent to my name. No cash, not even the card Liam had given me to use. We'd been going out together tonight, so I'd assumed I wouldn't need it.

Every footstep, every sound of a door opening behind me makes me jump, certain that it's Alexandre coming down to drag me back up to his room to finish what we started. I can't even blame him entirely for it—I'd participated, too. For just a moment, I'd lost myself in it, in what we'd used to have, and I'd almost made a horrible mistake.

One that I'm sure I would have regretted forever because it would have cost me Liam.

I don't know how to reconcile what happened earlier tonight. I'm not sure if I overreacted or if I was right to be upset. I can't help feeling that he *should* have known, that he should have thought better of taking me to the ballet, when all I've ever told him about it has been laced with pain and hurt.

But the one thing I know for certain is that I shouldn't be here. I shouldn't be with Alexandre. Not now—and probably not ever again.

When Liam's car pulls up to the curb, and he gets out, my heart lurches in my chest, my stomach knotting as he wordlessly reaches for my elbow, helping me into the car. He's absolutely silent, but I can see the hurt written across his face, and I'm dreading everything that's to come, everything that I have to tell him.

Was it really just earlier tonight that I went down on him here, on our way to the second half of our date? It feels like an entirely different night, like it happened to someone else. Like I watched it in a movie.

I sit in silence, as far from Liam as I can get on the opposite side of the car, and he makes no effort to reach for me, touch me, or move closer. The quiet of the car feels thick and oppressive. It doesn't break until we're all the way into the penthouse, not in the elevator or the hall, not until Liam has unlocked the door and ushered me in, closed and locked the door behind him, and turned to face me.

"Where was that I picked you up?" he asks, and his voice is deadly quiet. "Whose hotel was that?"

I know before I answer that he already knows the truth. There's no point in lying. "Alexandre's," I say softly, and I see something crumple in his face, though he's obviously trying not to let me see.

"Tell me one thing, Anastasia," Liam says, and there's a warning edge to his voice. "And don't lie to me."

He never uses my full name. It sends a shudder down my spine, fear and a thrill all at once, and I know I'm on a knife's edge with him. What happens in the next moments will determine everything.

I have to tell him the truth. It's all I can do.

"Did you call him?" Liam asks, his voice low and dangerous, and I shake my head.

"No," I whisper, and I see him narrow his eyes as he steps toward me with the deadly grace of a panther, his green gaze fixed on mine.

His hand reaches out for me, but it's not gentle. He doesn't hurt me, not exactly, but his fingers close on my chin, holding my face still as he looks down at me with an expression so dark that for the first time, I'm a little afraid of Liam McGregor.

"You've pushed me to the very edge tonight, Ana," he murmurs.

"Don't lie to me."

"I'm not lying," I promise, my voice trembling. "I didn't call him. I was running away from the theatre, and he came out of an alleyway and grabbed me. He was following us. He picked me up and put us both into a taxi, and—"

"And it didn't occur to you to scream? To tell the driver he was abducting you? To shout for help?" Liam glares down at me. "You just —went back to his hotel?"

"I thought about it," I admit. "But I—"

"But part of you wanted to. Tell me the truth, Ana, all of it. You wanted to go with him."

For a moment, the words hover between us, his fingers tight on my chin as he stares down at me, and I feel myself trembling in every part.

I'm terrified. And I'm also terribly, terribly aroused.

"Yes," I whisper, looking up at him. "Part of me wanted to go back with him."

"Because a part of you still loves him, even now. And you were angry with me."

"Yes."

"You wanted to hurt me."

My eyes flutter closed, my heart tearing open yet again at the words that I hadn't known were true until right this second.

I'd thought Liam didn't know me, but he does. He might not have known that the ballet would upset me, but he knows something deeper. He knows a part of my soul that even I'm ashamed to see.

That part of the reason I went to Alexandre's room, part of the reason I came so close to making that terrible mistake, was that Liam had hurt me tonight, unwitting as it was.

And I'd wanted to hurt him in return.

"I'm sorry," I whisper, my eyes still closed. I don't want to open them and see the expression I know must be on Liam's face. I don't want to see that I've hurt him, see the possibility of ending everything there in his eyes.

His hand is still on my chin, holding it. "Did you fuck him?" His voice is dark, angry. "Tell me the truth, Ana."

"No," I whisper, squeezing my eyes tighter against the threatening tears. "I swear—"

"Look at me and say that again," Liam growls, his fingers tightening on my jaw. "Tell me you didn't fuck him."

"I didn't—"

"Open your eyes, Ana!"

His voice rumbles over my skin, and my eyes fly open, staring up into his brittle green gaze, glittering darkly in the shadowy entryway.

"Tell me."

"I didn't have sex with him, Liam. I swear. I promise you. He didn't—we didn't—"

"But you wanted to." It's not a question; I can hear the surety in his voice. "You still have feelings for him. That's why you let him take you back to his hotel without screaming or throwing a fit."

"I—" I swallow hard, trying to think of how to explain it to Liam, how to make him understand. "I thought that maybe I did. I didn't know—I was upset. With you, with him—with all of it, but I stopped him! I didn't let it go that far because I thought of you, and I knew I would lose you, and I didn't—I couldn't—"

I'm stumbling over my words, trying to find a way to make Liam understand, and I'm almost certain that I'm failing horribly. I don't see any understanding or forgiveness in his green eyes, only pain and hurt. I feel like I'm cracking into a million pieces knowing that I've caused it.

"Did he kiss you?" Liam's voice is harsh, rasping. "Did he?"

"Yes, he—"

Liam's hand tightens on my jaw, dragging me up against him, my lips up to his as his mouth comes down on mine. I gasp with shock, and that's all he needs. His other hand goes to my lower back, crushing me against him in the same way his lips are crushed to mine, his tongue plunging into my mouth, tangling with mine as if to erase any lingering taste of Alexandre. It's a kiss more possessive than any he's ever given me before, violent and hungry, and I can feel my heart pounding wildly as I lean into it despite myself wanting him. I want the taste of his mouth and the heat of his body. I want him to take this all the way, to make me his completely, to show me that it's really me he wants, and not Saoirse.

I can't help but wonder, as the pleasure of the kiss races through my veins and heats my blood, if I'd subconsciously wanted, in some way, to make him jealous. It's a horrible thing to think, and not a game I'd meant to play. But inadvertently, I had. And I can't help but think I'm about to see a side of Liam that I haven't seen before.

Just that small thought is enough to send a pulse straight down between my thighs, an ache of need spreading through me as Liam kisses me hungrily.

"There," he says darkly when he finally breaks the kiss. "Now you can tell me, for certain, which of us is better. Who do you prefer to kiss, Ana? Me, or Alexandre? Should I send you back to him to try again, just to be sure?"

"Liam—"

"I'm not giving you back to him." Liam's hand drops from my jaw, both of his hands on my hips now, holding me against him. I can feel how hard he is already from the kiss, thick and rigid against my thigh, and I can't help but arch against him. I'm still upset with him, but I want him, too. I want to go back to how we were before his trip, before I found out about Saoirse, before the ill-fated date. I want—

"I don't want you to," I whisper. "Liam, tonight hurt me for a number of reasons, but I shouldn't have run away. I should have stayed, so we could talk about it. I *want* to talk about it with you, to work through these things like a normal couple, to fight and make up and make mistakes and make up again—"

"Except you did run. Straight back to him."

"I didn't! He was following us, watching me—"

"So you say." Liam's gaze holds mine, darkly, and I see then and there that he doesn't entirely believe my story of how I ended up in Alexandre's grasp. "You have to let him go, Ana. If you can't let him go, then there's no future for us—"

"Liam, please," I beg, my hands going up to his chest, fingers sliding against his skin in the open v of his button-down. "I swear, I didn't call him. I didn't ask him to come to get me. I didn't have sex with him. We kissed, and there was some touching, but it didn't go further than that, and then I left. I ran *from* him, and I called *you*. Liam—"

I take a deep, shuddering breath, forcing myself to hold his gaze even though what I see there—a depth of pain that I'm afraid I can't rescue us from—tears me apart. "I'm sorry," I whisper. "I know I was a bad girl. I know I hurt you, even if I tried not to. Please, Liam, don't stop loving me. You can punish me if you want. You can do anything you want to me; I deserve it. Just don't tell me this is over, not when I finally feel so certain that it's you, that it was always supposed to be you—"

Liam's hands tighten on my hips as he looks down at me. "You want me to punish you?" he asks darkly.

"Yes, please," I whisper, trying to keep my voice steady even though deep down, I'm both terrified and so turned on that I can hardly stand it. What Liam had done to me the other day for punishment was a torturous pleasure beyond anything I'd ever imagined, but I know right now that's not what he means. Right now, he's hurt, and I can see the darkness gathering in him, a side of him that he's never shown me before. *I won't hurt you,* he'd promised me before, but now I think he might need to, if only a little, for both our sakes.

"You can make it hurt, if you need to," I whisper, and Liam's eyes widen. "You can spank me, you can fuck my throat, you can do anything you want. Anything you think is best for me—and for you. Whatever will make you believe that I'm yours, Liam, whatever you think I deserve for letting him take me back tonight, for letting him touch me, kiss me—"

"Ana, I—" There's a faint protest in his voice, but from the way his hard cock throbs against my thigh, I can tell the idea turns him on— that maybe he knows what he would do, even now. That maybe he's—

"Have you thought about it?" I ask softly, reaching up to push a lock of auburn hair out of his eyes. My heart is pounding in my chest, adrenaline pulsing through my veins. "How you would *really* punish me, if I were ever that bad?"

Liam swallows hard, and underneath my palm, I can feel his heart pounding, too. "I—"

"It's okay," I murmur softly. "I wanted you to reward me when I was a good girl for you. So you should punish me now when I've been bad. Please, Liam. I think you need it to get past this, and if I'm being honest—" I take a deep breath, feeling a tremor of desire run through me. "I need it too. Please."

I *feel* the shudder that goes through him, feel his cock swell against my thigh, the way his entire body stiffens with desire. His hands slide from my hips to my waist, and I see something dark and commanding in his gaze that turns my knees to water.

"Then go to my room, Ana," he says hoarsely. "And wait for me there by the bed."

I nod, turning away from him with my heart pounding. I want this—want him, and in a way, I almost feel as if it could be a new beginning for us. I walked away from Alexandre, back to Liam. I have to trust that Liam is going to walk away from Saoirse and stay with me. And tonight, Liam can show me that he can make me his, that he can satisfy that darker side of me that my trauma seems to have brought out, the part that Alexandre fed into.

Slowly, I walk into his bedroom, remembering all too clearly what we did the last time I was in here, the pleasure Liam had wrung out of my body, over and over again until I'd cried from the sheer overwhelming exhaustion of it. I know tonight won't be the same, but I know there'll be pleasure. Liam can't touch me without giving me pleasure, even if there's pain too. I can feel myself trembling with anticipation, wondering what he'll do and how it will feel for Liam to take complete mastery of my body.

I wait for him next to the bed as he'd asked—no, *commanded*—barefoot with the plush rug between my toes, soft against the scarred bottoms of my feet, with my hands clasped in front of me and my head bowed. I can feel my blood racing through my veins like a second heartbeat. I want him so intensely that it's almost painful, my breath catching in my throat as I hear the bedroom door creak open and see his black Italian leather shoes crossing the darkly gleaming hardwood floor towards me.

Liam stops in front of me, and I feel his fingers slide under my chin, tilting my face up so that I'm looking at him. He reaches around, switching on the lamp by the bed so warm light floods out, softly illuminating the room. I can see an expression on his face that I've never seen before.

"Tell me again that you want this, little lass," he says softly. "That you want whatever punishment I choose to give you."

I nod, my mouth so dry that I barely feel like I can speak, the words catching in my throat. "I want it, Liam. I *need* you to punish me, so we can wake up tomorrow and try to start fresh. So there's no lingering resentment. You'll punish me for having been a bad girl, for letting Alexandre touch me, for wanting him. You'll take my body back from him, and then it'll be only us. I want this, Liam. And you do too, I think."

"Oh, lass, you have no idea." Liam's voice is hoarse with need. "I've not done something quite like this before—but I've thought about it. I've thought about doing it to *you*." His fingers stroke along my cheek. "I won't be fucking your sweet pussy tonight, though, lass, if that's what you're hoping for."

My eyes widen, and I know he can see the disappointment in them. "Liam—"

"Shh." He presses a finger to my lips. "When we do that for the first time, Ana, it won't be a punishment. It certainly won't be on the same night I almost lost you to another man, even if it's to make you mine. But that doesn't mean I won't be inside of you, lass." He looks down at me; his eyes are so full of dark desire that it sends a shiver down my spine. "You'll take whatever I choose to do to you?"

I nod speechlessly, my throat so choked with need that I can't speak.

"You'll need a word, I think, if it gets to be too much." His gaze turns thoughtful, and his other hand strokes down my side, gathering the rippling material of my dress in his fist. "Emerald, I think. That's your word, Ana. Say it, and I'll stop. But I can't promise you'll stay if we don't bring this night to its conclusion." Liam's green eyes search mine, and I can see that under the desire, the hurt is still there. "I can't keep loving you if you still love another man, Ana—if you're not entirely mine."

"Okay," I whisper. "I understand."

"Good," Liam murmurs the word throatily, his hand drifting up my spine. He finds the zipper of my dress, his fingers tugging at the delicate pull. "Then, little lass, it's time for your punishment."

TWELVE
ANA

Slowly, Liam pulls down the zipper of my dress. I can feel in his touch that he wants to make it last, that he's drawing this out on purpose. Part of me wonders if he thinks this could be our last night together, and just the thought of that makes my heart ache.

If you use it, I can't promise that you'll stay. Liam is tired of waiting, and I can't entirely blame him. If what he said about Saoirse is true, if he never planned to marry her, then he's been risking a great deal all this time waiting—mostly patiently—for me to get over Alexandre, to put him in the past, something that I'd shown tonight I haven't yet done. Not completely.

So this is my chance to show Liam that I'm his entirely, that I trust him not to take it too far, not to push me further than I can manage. A chance for him to show *me* that even if he misstepped with the ballet, he does understand me. That he understands my core, what I need right now for us both to start again.

His fingers skim down the warm, bare flesh of my spine as he pulls the zipper down, and I shiver. I feel like I can't breathe, my heart racing, my skin tingling with anticipation. I'm already wet—I can feel it on my bare pussy beneath the dress, on the soft inner flesh of my thighs. Liam fingering me to an orgasm in the restaurant feels like it happened in another lifetime, but I remember how good it felt. How a part of me wanted him to do exactly what he'd threatened and spread me out atop the table for the entire restaurant to watch him pleasure me.

"You're trembling, lass," Liam murmurs hoarsely. "You're frightened, but you want it, too. I can *feel* how much you want it."

He reaches up, pushing the fragile straps of the dress off of my shoulders, letting them slip down my arms as his fingers caress the soft skin there, tracing my collarbone, down the v of the neckline to my cleavage. "I won't do more to you than you can bear, Ana," he says softly. "You asked for pain, but it will never be too much." His hands fist in the satin on either side of my waist. He jerks downwards, stripping the dress from me in one smooth motion so that it pools around my feet, leaving me completely and utterly bare. "Do you trust me, Ana?"

"Yes," I whisper, swallowing hard. "I do, Liam."

"Good." His hands skim over my bare waist, over my slender, trembling body as I stand there nude, looking up at him. Once again, I'm completely bare while he's still fully dressed, and I can't fully describe how arousing it is to me, how intensely, vulnerably erotic it feels.

He unbuckles his belt, and my breath catches in my throat as he slides it out of the loops, at the whisper of leather on fabric. "Give me your wrists, lass," Liam says, and I raise my hands mutely, palms pressed together, wrists outstretched. He loops the leather around them, and I gasp at its feeling against my skin as he pulls it taut, not tight enough to hurt, but enough to bind my wrists together.

"Lay across the bed," he instructs. "Face down, and spread your legs for me. I want to see how wet you already are for me."

I blush when he says that, because *I* know how wet I am, how deeply aroused, and in a moment, he will too. But unlike in the past when I've wished I could hide it from him, tonight I want him to know. I want him to see the evidence of how much I want him, to let my body be the proof of how I feel.

"I'm not going to tie you to the bed, Ana," Liam says. "Your wrists are bound for my pleasure, so you can't be overcome and touch yourself or me, but I'm not going to restrain you otherwise. I want you bent over this bed of your own volition, willingly taking your punishment. I want to see that you're here because, deep down, you want this. Because you've asked—*begged* me for it, not because I've tied you down."

His voice is deep, his accent thicker than ever, sending desire rippling over and through me. "You're going to display yourself for your punishment, Ana, and you're going to do it now."

I can feel myself trembling all over with need as I obey, turning to face the bed so that the front of my thighs are pressed up against it and bending forward, my wrists dangling over the other side. Unless I turn my head from this angle, I can't see him. That only heightens my arousal, wondering when his first touch will come, what it will be.

Obediently, I spread my thighs open as I hear him step towards me, and I hear the noise he makes deep in his throat as I'm displayed for him, wet and swollen, waiting for his touch. I feel his hand stroking up the back of my thigh, making me tense with anticipation. I hear the light moan that slips from Liam's lips as his fingers rise higher, feeling the sticky flesh of my inner thigh, stroking along the soft puffy flesh of my outer pussy lips.

"I can see you glistening for me," he murmurs. "So wet, so needy for your punishment. You've been a bad girl, but you're always so good for me here. Wet and wanting, just like I like you."

I moan softly, my back arching as I push myself into his hand, wanting more. I want him to slip his fingers between my folds, stroke my throbbing clit, and thrust them into me. Still, he keeps his touch light, teasing me without ever delving inside before his hand returns to my thigh, and I whimper in protest.

"So needy," Liam murmurs darkly. "But this is a punishment, Ana, not pleasure. Not yet." His hand squeezes my thigh, his fingers applying just a little more pressure than usual, and then up to my ass, his palm sliding over the slender curve.

"I wanted to spank you the other day when I punished you." His voice is low, smoky, winding its way around me as he tells me his darkest desires. "But I chose to punish you with pleasure instead.

Tonight, though, you asked for pain. So I think this is how I'll give it to you."

His hand smooths over my ass cheek, squeezing lightly. "I thought about using the belt. But I want you to feel my hand on your bare skin, Ana. I want there to be nothing between us when I do this to you."

I hear the rustle of fabric and look over my shoulder to see him unbuttoning his shirt. Liam catches me looking and slaps me lightly on the back of the thigh, not enough to truly hurt, but enough to sting.

"Face forward unless I tell you otherwise, lass. Part of your punishment is not to get to see me as I do this to you, not to know what's coming next." He chuckles darkly. "I think that may be a pleasurable torment, though."

He's not wrong. It's torture not to be able to see his handsome, muscled body as he strips down, to hear the sound of his zipper and the rustle of his pants being pushed down over his hips, and not see his thick, hard cock springing free. It's like him not allowing me to touch him magnified a dozen times over. I bite my lower lip as I hear him move towards me again, knowing this time that he's naked and hard, just out of my view.

I want him so badly. I'm aching for him, and I know it will only be more intense by the time he's finished. I feel his hard cock brush against my thigh as he stands behind me, smooth and hot against my skin, and I want him inside of me. My back arches, a small gasp slipping from me when his hand smooths over the curve of my ass, and Liam makes a noise deep in his throat.

"Tell me you want it one more time, lass."

"Please," I whisper, my voice choked with need. "Please punish me, Liam."

The first crack of his hand against my ass sends a shock across my skin, making me stiffen and cry out. It's not even a real pain at first–especially not compared to some pain I've experienced–but the sensation is startling. I can tell that he's going slowly, building up, his hand rubbing over the stinging, warm spot where his palm struck me a moment before.

The second comes on the other side, his hand connecting with the curve of my ass, and I stiffen again, the sensation burning across my skin and directly between my legs. It hurts more the second time, and then the third as Liam increases the firmness of his spanks. Still, it feels as if each jolt goes straight to my pussy, heating my skin and spreading out over my ass, my thighs, increasing my arousal until I'm so wet that I can *feel* myself starting to drip down my inner thighs and onto the edge of the bed.

"Liam–" I moan his name, my back arching, my ass tilting up for another, and he knows as well as I do that I'm enjoying this punishment far too much. It hurts, it does–he builds up the intensity of the spanking, his palm coming down again and again with an increasing strength that's multiplied by the sensitivity of my reddening flesh, but it also feels so fucking *good*. I can feel myself starting to grind against the bed, wanting any friction against my throbbing clit, and I hear Liam chuckle behind me as he brings his hand down again, making me cry out.

"You're enjoying this a little too much, lass. Maybe it's your sweet pussy that needs to be reminded of who it belongs to." He reaches between my thighs, cupping me, and I moan with helpless need. "No coming until I give you permission," he warns. "Spread those thighs open, lass."

I'm already spread wide for him, but I open my thighs a little further, pushing back so that he has full access to my swollen, wet pussy. I grind against his palm, moaning as he takes his hand away. Then I gasp aloud when he slaps firmly between my legs, his hand connecting wetly with my aroused flesh, the slap stinging my clit.

"Liam!" I cry out, and he chuckles, spanking my pussy again.

"Does that feel good, lass? My hand punishing your sweet pussy?" He slaps again, and my thighs tremble.

"You're going to make me come, Liam, please–please–"

He slaps again, harder this time, and I'm shaking with trying not to come. He hasn't given me permission, but I'm so close, each stinging, pleasurable smack of his hand against my folds and clit pushing me closer to the edge. "Liam, I'm going to come. I can't stop it–"

His next slap lands on my ass again, the hardest one yet, and I scream with frustration and pleasure and pain all at once. The spank feels as if it jolts directly between my legs, but it's not enough to make me come, no matter how close I am. "Liam, please—"

"Not yet, lass. This *is* a punishment, remember? You'll come when I give you permission and not before."

I lose count of the slaps against my ass. With each one, I can feel my ass reddening, feel the frustrated pleasure building even as the slaps become more and more painful, my ass throbbing with the heat of his palm.

"Fuck, Ana—" Liam groans, his left hand resting on my ass as I feel him shift, hearing his right hand moving along his shaft as he strokes himself briefly. "I need to be inside of you, lass. You're driving me fucking insane. I wish you could see how beautiful you look right now, my handprints on your ass and your skin so red–*fuck*."

And then I feel the swollen, hot tip of his cock pushing against my clit, and I lose every last shred of control that I have over my own orgasm.

I'm so wet, slick and drenched, and dripping with arousal. I can feel it even more as I throw my head back, my bound hands clutching at the bed as my back arches hard, Liam rubbing his cock against my clit and pussy as I come hard. I can feel myself clenching, desperate for him to fill me, pushing back and grinding against his cock in the hopes that he'll slip inside of me, but he doesn't. He just rubs against me, sliding his shaft between my folds, bumping the head of his cock against my clit as I scream with the built-up pleasure, my own arousal lubing his cock until he's as slick and wet as I am.

And then, as I lie on the bed still shuddering with pleasure, I feel the head of his cock between the cheeks of my ass, and I know exactly what he's doing.

"Such a bad girl," Liam says, one hand still stroking the curve of my burning ass, and the satisfaction in his voice tells me that he did it on purpose. Somehow that arouses me even more, even as the head of his cock rubs against me, and I feel a small shudder of nerves. "You came without permission, little lass."

"You made me come," I whisper, but I'm already arching against him, wanting him inside of me anywhere, filling me up however he's willing to.

"Maybe." Liam's voice is raspy with desire, dark and full of need. "I'm going to fuck you now, lass, and this is how I'm going to do it. To punish you, yes, but also to take something for me, depending on how you answer my next question."

"What?" I ask breathlessly. I can barely think, my pussy aching with the need to be filled, my clit still throbbing from my orgasm, my ass clenched with nervousness at the imminent intrusion. Liam is pressed against me there, his slick cockhead pushing ever so slightly against my entrance, just waiting.

"Did Alexandre fuck you like this?" Liam rocks forward, the head of his cock pushing against me, and I cry out. "Did he fuck your ass, Ana?"

"No," I gasp, my thighs spreading involuntarily wider as my pussy gushes with arousal, my body trembling with need. "No, he never did, I swear."

"Then I'm going to do it now, Ana, and take that for myself. I'm going to fuck your ass, and come in your ass, and you're going to beg me for it." He squeezes my ass cheek with his left hand, slapping me lightly on the still-stinging flesh. "Beg me, lass."

The words spill out without my even having to try. I'm desperate for it, for anything that means he's inside of me, desperate for more pleasure, for *Liam*. "Please," I gasp, pushing back against him. "Please fuck me, Liam, fuck my ass, please, please–"

"*Fuck–*" Liam groans, and I feel the shudder of pure pleasure that goes through him, his cock throbbing against the entrance of my tight, sensitive hole as he hears me beg. "Fuck, I love hearing you beg for me, lass."

I've never done this before. I don't know whether he realizes it or not, whether I should tell him that not only did Alexandre fuck my ass, that *no one* ever has, but it's too late. He's pushing forward, the thick head of his cock pushing past the tight ring of muscle, and even as slick as he is, it's an effort for him to get inside.

"Relax, lass," Liam grunts.

"I'm trying," I whisper, my back arching. I cry out as his head breaches me, stretching as he pushes the first inch inside, and the groan of sheer pleasure that slips from him sends a wave of arousal through me, relaxing me a fraction.

"God, your ass feels so fucking good," Liam groans. "Tight and hot–" he rocks forward, his hand slipping between my legs as he pushes forward another inch. He starts to stroke my clit as he pushes into my ass an inch at a time, making me cry out with pleasure.

He feels fucking *huge*. He's well-endowed, but inside of my ass, his cock feels monstrous, filling me in a painful and pleasurable way all at once. But each jolt of pain is mingled with the feeling of his fingers stroking my clit, rubbing it in tight circles, and Liam moans as he gets half his cock in my ass, still pushing forward.

"I won't last long," he murmurs. "God, you feel so good." He pushes forward again, and I claw at the bed, crying out with pain and pleasure as he thrusts again, in one hard, swift motion that seats him fully inside my ass. In the same moment, he pinches my clit, rolling it between his fingers in a way that sends bursts of sensation over me that I can't control.

"Oh god, Liam! Liam, I'm going to come again, I can't stop it, I'm coming, I'm coming–"

It's like nothing I've ever felt. I'm so full of him, my ass arched against the smooth, hot, muscled flesh of his abdomen and groin, his thighs pressed against mine, his cock stretching my ass as he rubs my clit fiercely, and an orgasm unlike anything I've ever experienced crashes over me as I throw my head back, straining at the belt holding my wrists together as Liam pushes himself as deeply into my ass as he can go.

"Good girl," he whispers, and I moan helplessly, still coming hard. "Such a good girl, Ana, coming with my cock in your ass. It feels good, doesn't it?" He rocks against me. "You take it so well, my good little lass."

And then he starts to thrust.

His hands squeeze my hips as he fucks my ass, his groans of pleasure mingling with my gasps and moans as he thrusts into me again and again, his thighs flexing against mine, and the sounds he makes are of such intense pleasure that it has me on edge again in a matter of minutes, grinding my pussy into the blankets as Liam takes me in the ass. I can feel his cock hardening even more, feel him going faster, harder, until he lets out a sound of such absolute ecstasy that I know he's close.

"Fuck, Ana–" he gasps. "I'm going to come. I'm going to fucking come in your ass." He reaches between my thighs again, teasing my clit, rubbing it in quick, fast motions that make me cry out with pleasure. "Come again for me, lass, that's my good girl, once more, and then I'm going to make you come again while I fill your fucking ass–"

The orgasm crashes over me, swift and hard, Liam's cock pounding into my ass as he rubs his fingers over my clit. I feel him stiffen against me, shoving into me so hard and deeply that it pushes me forward on the bed. My back is arched so deeply it feels as if it could snap, my ass grinding back against him, and I'm gasping with pleasure, hardly able to speak.

"Again, again," I beg, and Liam groans.

"That's right, lass. Good girl. Beg for it, beg for my cum in your ass, beg me–"

He slips two fingers into my pussy then, stroking the inside of me while his thumb rubs against my clit, and I can feel his cock throbbing inside of my well-fucked ass.

"I'm going to come, lass," he groans. "I'm going to come, beg me, beg for it like a good girl, and I'll make you come again–"

"Please," I gasp, writhing against him, against his cock and fingers, desperate for more of it. "Come in my ass, Liam, please, please come for me, make me come too–"

"Fuck! Oh god, Ana, *fuck*–" He nearly shouts it, his fingers thrusting into me as he slams his cock deep in my ass once more, his entire body going rigid as he groans aloud. "I'm going to fucking fill your ass with my cum, *fuck, fuck*–"

"Liam!" My throat is hoarse as I nearly scream his name, the first hot rush of his cum in my ass mingled with the thrusting of his fingers and the friction on my clit sending me into spasms of pleasure so intense my vision blurs, my entire body stiffening, jerking, grinding against him as he shudders against me, our cries of pleasure mingling as we come together for the first time, and though part of me wishes he'd been making love to me a different way this first time, I know this is right. He's taken something I've never given to anyone else. I'd never thought *this* could be so intimate, but it feels like a beginning, a promise, like I've given him a part of me that will only ever be his.

He pitches forward, his chest pressed to my back, both our bodies slick with sweat as we arch against each other, his cock still spurting inside of me in hot throbs that trigger another spasm of pleasure in me with each one. His hands slide up, wrapping around mine, his hips still grinding as he pushes himself as deeply inside of me as he can, his breath against my ear and neck, both of us skin to skin until we're lying there, pressed together on the bed.

When he slips out of me, I'm crying, the last aftershocks of my orgasm mingled with my shoulders trembling as tears slide down my cheeks. Liam is leaning forward on the bed over me, panting, and it takes a moment before he realizes.

"Ana!" There's alarm in his voice, and he moves to kneel on the bed next to me, still naked and half-hard, as he undoes my wrists. "Lass, are you okay? You didn't use the word, so I assumed—"

"No, I'm fine," I manage to choke out through my tears. "Really, I—"

"You don't sound fine," Liam says doubtfully, pulling me into his arms. I curl against his chest, and he strokes my hair, his fingers running through the sweat-dampened tangles around my face. "Ana, what's wrong?"

"It's not—it was just intense. I never—" I gasp back another sob, and Liam groans, his hand pressed to the back of my head as he holds me.

"I didn't realize you'd never done that before at all, lass. Just not with him. I'm sorry, I should have—"

"You couldn't have known. I didn't tell you." I press my face against the smooth skin of his chest, breathing in the faintly sweaty, masculine scent of him. "I didn't think I'd cry. I'm sorry, Liam."

"There's no need to apologize, lass." Liam presses a kiss to the top of my head. "I'll get something to clean us up with, and you'll sleep here tonight."

I look up at him, startled. "What? Are you sure—"

"If you want to, then yes." He tilts my chin up, wiping away a falling tear with his thumb. "Your punishment is done, Ana. I'm not going to send you back to your room to sleep alone. You're mine, aye? You proved that tonight."

"Yes," I whisper. "I'm yours, Liam. I swear, I only want you. I knew—when Alexandre touched me tonight, I knew. There are parts of me that will always be grateful that he took me away from Alexei, who treated me mostly with kindness and probably spared me something much worse. But I don't have a future with him. My future is here, with you."

"And mine is with you. Not Saoirse." Liam brushes his lips gently over my forehead. "I'm yours as well, lass. I'm sorry for my mistake tonight when I took you to the ballet. I'll be more careful in the future, to think instead of rushing headlong into what seems like it might make you happy at first, without thinking it through."

He leans me gently back against the stack of pillows on the bed, gracefully sliding off as he strides towards the bathroom. I have a moment to appreciate the long, lean lines of his body, the muscled swell of his ass before he disappears into the room only to emerge a few minutes later.

Liam joins me on the bed again, gently taking the warm cloth he brought back with him and sliding it over my inner thighs, between them, cleaning me up carefully before turning me on my side. I don't catch a glimpse at what he's doing, but then I feel something cool and thick against my skin, and I realize he's smoothing lotion over the still-stinging flesh of my ass cheeks.

"How's that, little lass?" Liam asks gently, his hands massaging my flesh, and I let out a sigh.

"It feels good," I tell him quietly, and when I roll back over onto my back as he moves his hands away, I can see a faint smile on his face.

He takes the cloth and lotion back to the bathroom and then rejoins me, pulling the covers over us both as I sink into his arms, snuggling down into the soft warmth of the bed.

"If you believe me," I ask softly, "Why did you—choose to fuck me the way you did tonight? Why not—" I bite my lower lip nervously. "Was it just because you were punishing me?"

"That was part of it," Liam says quietly, his fingers still running through my hair. "And part of it was because I wanted to take something tonight that he'd never had. Just as you needed to be punished to feel absolved, I needed that. I needed to know I had something of you for my own, that he didn't."

"What if I'd said he had?" I whisper, my heart suddenly skipping a beat in my chest. "What would have happened?"

"I don't know," Liam admits. "I needed something, Ana. Maybe I wouldn't have been able to continue—I don't know. But that's *not* what happened, so we don't need to talk about it. It doesn't matter." His arm tightens around me, and he gently brushes another kiss over my forehead. "I want to make love to you, Ana. That's what I want it to be when I'm in your pussy again. That couldn't be tonight. But it will be soon. I'm going to deal with breaking my engagement to Saoirse in the next few days, and then—"

"Then?" I look up at him, wanting to see the expression on his face. He looks tired, but more peaceful than before.

"Then there will be nothing between us and our happiness, Ana. Not Alexandre, not Saoirse—nothing to stop you from being mine entirely, and me yours. We'll begin our lives together, with nothing standing in our way." His fingers brush lightly over my cheekbone. "I love you, Ana."

I want to say it back so badly, but I know instinctively that it's not time yet—not tonight, with what happened still so fresh. Instead, I snuggle into his chest, one arm over his muscled abdomen, breathing in the scent of him as I feel his heartbeat beneath my cheek.

We both fall asleep like that, curled in each other's arms for the first time, and it feels like a step forward. It feels like progress, like a new step in our relationship, and as I drift off, I realize that I feel something else I hadn't expected to feel tonight.

I feel *happy*.

I don't know what time it is when I wake up again, my stomach churning with such an intense nausea that I throw the blankets back, scramble out of bed, and rush towards the bathroom. I fall to my knees on the cool tile, grasping the sides of the toilet as I heave up everything I ate and drank tonight, convulsing with tears running down my cheeks.

I don't hear Liam come to the doorway, but when I finally look up, wiping my mouth with a tissue, he's standing there with his eyes bleary and hair tousled, looking so endearing in his sleepy state that I wish I felt well enough to appreciate it.

"Are you okay?" Liam's forehead is creased with concern. "Did something you ate tonight not settle well?"

"Maybe?" I frown. "I felt sick this morning too. Maybe I just picked up some kind of stomach bug—"

Liam's eyes narrow suddenly. "Ana—when was your last period?"

"I—why?"

"I haven't seen tampons in your bathroom or any kind of feminine product. You've been here for over a month—you should have bought some or asked me to pick them up for you because you needed them. Ana—"

My stomach drops in an entirely new way, fresh nausea bubbling up. I bend over the toilet again, my eyes squeezing tightly shut. *No, no, no—*

"There are all kinds of reasons why I might not have gotten my period," I say weakly. "I've lost it before from low body fat when I was dancing. I was malnourished for a while before now. I've only just started putting on weight—stress can make it stop too. There are all kinds of reasons." I trail off, seeing the doubtful look on Liam's face.

"Being pregnant can make you lose it too," he says grimly.

"It's not that." I shake my head. "It can't be—"

"It certainly could be." Liam frowns. "We've had sex twice without protection, Ana. Did you and Alexandre—"

I feel sick all over again. I'd wanted to put Alexandre behind us tonight, to not talk about him again, especially right now. But it seems to be impossible, and what Liam is suggesting feels like a fresh horror, a new reason to feel hopeless all over again.

Not Alexandre. It can't be.

But Liam is right—it *could*.

"I'll buy a pregnancy test and bring it home tomorrow," Liam says firmly.

I shake my head, my eyes widening. "No," I whisper. "No, let's wait—maybe it's a stomach bug. Maybe I'll get better—or I'll get my period—"

If it's true, I don't want to know. I don't want to face that, to deal with what could happen because of it. I don't want to have to think about it.

"I'm getting a test tomorrow, Ana," Liam says firmly. "We need to know, one way or another. Come on, now." He walks towards me, gently helping me up off of the tile and to the sink, filling a glass with water and a tiny cup with mouthwash so I can rinse my mouth out. "Let's go back to bed."

It's comforting to curl up against him again, to feel his warmth next to me as I try to fall asleep. But I don't, not for a long time.

Because now there's something new to be afraid of.

THIRTEEN
ANA

When I wake up the next morning, it's next to Liam. The sun is just starting to filter through the curtains, and his alarm hasn't gone off yet, so I can just look at him for a moment. He looks different when he's sleeping—more boyish, less weighed down. His auburn-red hair is falling over his forehead, his long lashes brushing against the tops of his cheeks, his shoulder rising and falling with each breath. He looks relaxed. Peaceful.

I know, of course, that he's not. Deep down, he must be thinking the same thing that I am—if I'm pregnant, it changes *everything*. If I'm pregnant, there's a new obstacle between us. A new obstacle for *me.*

I barely slept at all after Liam woke up to find me puking in the bathroom. I lay awake, thinking about the possibility, trying to come up with all the reasons why it can't be true. I ticked off on my fingers all the other times I'd lost my period for various reasons—staying ballerina thin, stress, lack of proper nourishment. But my mind kept circling back to the one time it *wasn't* that, in my first year at Juilliard, before I'd met Sofia.

Those pink lines, crouched in a tiny apartment bathroom, shoving it into my purse so my roommates wouldn't tell on me to our teachers. Finding the one I trusted, telling her, hearing her advice, calling my mother in tears, and hearing her say the same thing:

"You have your whole life ahead of you."

"You have such talent."

"Potential to be the youngest prima in the history of the New York Ballet."

"Such a shame to squander it—"

"You'll have plenty of time later."

It hadn't seemed like a real thing, then. Just a concept. I wasn't against the idea of ending the possibility of a baby before it even really began. The guy who had probably been the one responsible would *definitely* have been for it. Based on timing, I'd always been pretty sure that the potential father of that baby was Michel Alazar, one of the lead male dancers, and a guy who occasionally fell into my bed or his. Dance is intimate, full of hands and bodies touching, warm breath on a slender neck, taut spandex, and graceful, beautiful movements full of gorgeous athleticism that make a handsome man something almost godly. I'd always found male ballet dancers to be art in human form, and Michel was no different. He was headed for an illustrious career too. He had no interest in a permanent relationship, let alone a child. We'd been the same in that way.

I'd gone alone. I hadn't been upset so much as embarrassed for being careless, for putting myself in that position at all. It had just been that one night, Michel too drunk to get a condom on and me too drunk to care, and he'd pulled out. But not fast enough.

Afterward, I'd been out of class for two days, and then I'd gone back as normal. It had been simple, easy. And deep down, I'd questioned whether I would have made a good mother at all, my career aside. My own mother had done her best, but fleeing Russia after my father's death and struggling to make a living here had left her tired and strained, less able to give me the love and attention I'd been used to as a child. I'd want to give any child I had something better than that, but how? I certainly wouldn't be able to if I had to drop out of Juilliard. As a scholarship student, I was always very aware of how lucky I was to be there at all, that it was my talent that kept me there. A baby would have ended everything. I didn't even know if I *wanted* children.

As I lay there all night, and as I roll onto my side to look at Liam, I have to admit that I still don't. I'd never had a chance to really consider it. I'd never had a serious enough relationship to think about marriage, family, and children. When Sofia had been swept away by Luca, when Franco had destroyed everything for me, I'd been on the cusp of *beginning*. All of that was still very far away. I'd always thought of children as something I'd figure out later, if I got into a serious relationship down the line. I'd decide then if it was something I wanted.

Would I, if it were just Liam and me? No Alexandre, no Saoirse to muddle things up. I honestly can't say. Liam and I haven't had a chance to be that. We haven't even had sex, really, just the two of us in some way that isn't fucked up.

But he has been inside of me, and that means there's a non-zero chance that if I am pregnant, it's his. But more likely—

No. No, no. I can't let myself even think it. *I'm not pregnant. I can't be.*

Liam stirs next to me, opening one eye and looking over at me. "Good morning," he says raspily, and my heart turns over in my chest. It's the first time we've woken up like this together, and at this moment, I want to do it every day forever. I want to see him look up at me, tousled and sleepy-eyed, his voice edged with that accent that fades sometimes and comes back in others, and I want to know that I'll get to do it over and over again.

He made a mistake last night. So did I. But surely we can start fresh again. One more time.

Liam leans over, cupping the side of my face in one hand as he kisses me quickly, and I feel my heart skip another beat at the feeling of his lips on mine. They always feel good—*right*, as if he's the person I've been waiting my whole life to kiss, and it was never quite right until now. I lean in, wanting to savor it, and he lingers for just a second before pulling back.

"I have to head straight out this morning," he says, swinging out of bed. The black pajama pants he's wearing hang low on his hips, letting me see all the smooth rippling muscle of his chest and abs, the deep cut lines disappearing into the gathered waist of the pants. He slips them off without a thought as he reaches the dresser, and I catch a glimpse of his rounded, muscled ass before he slips on a pair of dark grey boxer briefs.

It's so casual, so domestic, that my breath catches for a moment. This feels *normal*, more normal than anything has felt for me in a very long time. It's very easy to imagine this being our every morning, easy to forget all the obstacles still in our way.

But I told Alexandre last night I was done. I did everything I could to prove to Liam that I'm his—that I want *him*. My still-sore ass is proof of that, although whenever I shift and feel that lingering soreness, inside and out, it sends a pulse of desire through me. What Liam did to me was a punishment, but it also felt *good*.

Liam will deal with Saoirse and their engagement soon. I believe that, and I cling to that thought to keep my spirits up, long past when Liam has left for the day, and I've eaten breakfast and done my stretches in the living room. I'm just getting up from my yoga mat, tucking strands of hair that fell loose back into the bun on top of my head—far messier than anything I would have gotten away with in my ballerina days—when I hear a knock at the door that sends my heart plummeting to my toes.

Liam wouldn't knock, and I'm not expecting anyone. So unless he's sent someone here to check on me or to pick something up—not entirely outside the realm of possibility—whoever is on the other side of that door is no one I want to see.

The knock comes again, harder this time. "Anastasia? I know you're here. Open up." Another hard, insistent knock.

It's a woman's voice. Saoirse. I'm certain of it, and I feel my stomach turn over with anxiety. I don't want to let her in, but I'm pretty sure she's going to stay there until I do.

So reluctantly, I walk to the door and open it, swallowing hard. I have a vague hope that it's someone else—*anyone* else, but it's not. The moment I see her delicately pale face and dark strawberry hair, I know it's Saoirse.

She pushes her way into the apartment, barely looking at me until she's in the living room. When she finally turns around, it's to sink down onto the couch, folding her hands in her lap. The diamond and emerald engagement ring is still on her finger, glittering in the sunlight, and my mouth feels dry as I look at it. As long as it's there, it feels like a symbol of the claim she has on Liam. A reminder that no matter what Liam says to me, no matter what he promises, he isn't fully mine right now.

"We need to talk, Anastasia," Saoirse says. Her voice is light and elegant, her bearing almost royal, her accent cultured despite the hint of Gaelic. She's wearing crisp black trousers with a slim leather belt and a cream silk shirt tucked in, the sleeves buttoned neatly at her wrists and her red hair falling over her shoulders and down her back. She has small diamond earrings on her ears and no other jewelry, a slim black shoulder bag next to her, turned inwards so that I can't see if it's designer or not. Everything about her is understated but polished, elegant but unassuming. The latter, I can tell, is a façade—Saoirse knows exactly what she's doing.

"It's Liam's business to talk to you," I say simply, standing next to one of the armchairs with a hand on the back. I don't want to sit down. I have the feeling that I need to stay on my feet, ready to flee, though I don't know really where I would go. "There's nothing for *us* to talk about, Saoirse. It's between you and Liam."

"See, there we disagree." She smiles politely at me. "I don't think you fully appreciate the situation Liam has put himself in for you, Ana. Can I call you Ana?"

"I don't think my saying no is going to stop you."

Saoirse raises an eyebrow. "There's no need to be impolite. Here you are, fucking *my* fiancé in his home, and I'm not being impolite to you. I simply think that you don't understand the gravity of the situation, Ana."

"And you're going to explain it to me?"

Her lips press together in a thin line. "Liam is an important man, Ana. I don't think you're overly familiar with the Irish Kings—or the rest of them, at least. But Liam is at the head of the table. That means something. And what it means—"

"Is that you think you're owed him?"

Saoirse blinks. "Well—no, although it's always been assumed I would marry a McGregor son. I just—" She clears her throat. "I'm not owed Liam, though marrying the head of the Kings is my birthright, as much as that seat is his. But what it means, Ana, is that he's putting a great many lives, businesses, finances, the trust of his men, and even his own life in danger by insisting on being with you. By insisting he's going to set *me* aside. And I don't think you realize that, or at least haven't fully grasped it."

I stare at her. *His life?* I don't want to believe that. I *can't*. It seems so archaic, so insane to think that Liam could risk his life or anyone else's by choosing to be with someone different than he was meant to.

"He's breaking a vow, Ana," Saoirse says calmly, and I wonder if I said some part of that last thought aloud. "A contract, signed in church, before a priest, my father, and uncle. That matters to the Kings. A man who can't keep his word is no man at all."

"He's kept his word to me," I say faintly. I don't mean for it to hurt Saoirse, but I see the flash of it there in her eyes anyway.

"You don't matter," she says matter of factly. "Not to me, not to anyone in the Kings. Here you're no one, Anastasia Ivanova. It doesn't matter who you used to be. And it doesn't matter what Liam has dreamed up to make himself believe you can be accepted here. You can't."

The throb of hurt that pierces my chest cuts just as deeply as Saoirse intended because I know she's right. I don't belong here. I have no one but Liam, and things have never been easy between us. If Liam decides that he's risking too much, I'll have nothing here at all.

"You should go back to New York." Saoirse's voice is almost gentle, as if she's really just trying to help me do what's best, as if she's actually my friend. "You have friends there. If you care for Liam, you won't keep putting him through this. You'll let him go, so he can live the life he's meant to, the life he was perfectly happy with before he met you. And you can go on to do—something else. Whatever will make *you* happy. Just as long as it's not here."

I swallow hard, gritting my teeth to stay calm. "I'm not making Liam do anything, Saoirse. He's a grown man. He doesn't need me to make his decisions for him. He certainly can make those choices for himself and tell me what they are, which he has. Anyway," I add, taking a deep breath and steeling my nerves. "I don't know why you want a man who doesn't want you. Isn't it embarrassing for you to have to try so hard to get him to marry you?"

If Saoirse registers my insult, it doesn't seem to faze her. She seems nearly unflappable this time, her expression calm and poised. "It's not about love or desire, Ana. I'll admit that I find Liam to be very handsome, and I want him as my husband. Out of the McGregor brothers, he was my preference, though I hadn't thought he would be the one I would marry. It was a pleasant surprise. And I could love him in time, I think. Deep down, he's a good man—just a confused one right now." Saoirse smiles tightly at me, and there's no humor in it. "But this isn't about any of that, Ana. It's about duty. It's about what I was raised to do. Liam *wasn't* raised for this. He wasn't brought up to be the heir, to fill that seat, but now it's his, and he's trying to make a go of it. *I* can help him with that. My father has been the right hand to the reigning Irish King all his life. It's all I've ever known. I was raised to be the wife of *the* Irish King. Liam *needs* me and what I can offer him."

"He needs me too," I whisper, wishing I hadn't said the words as soon as they slip out. They feel too intimate, too vulnerable. But Saoirse has already heard, and she gives a short, bitter laugh.

"For what? The way you look on your knees? You're not the kind of woman who marries a man like Liam, Ana. You have nothing to offer him except a pretty face and what I'm sure is a lovely, talented body, but that won't help him keep his spot at the head of the table. It could well make him lose it—if not his own head entirely." Saoirse pauses, her bright green eyes fixed on mine keenly. "What can you do for him, Ana, other than tear him apart?"

The silence that fills the room is poignant. In a way, I know she's right. Everything I have to offer him—pleasure, love, devotion—is nothing when it comes to the other part of his life that involves the Kings. There, I'm only hurting him, not helping him. But I feel, deep down, that I spoke the truth when I said I can't and shouldn't make those decisions for Liam. He's capable of making his own choices, of choosing what's most important to him, and telling me.

"True love, Ana, would be walking away from this and letting Liam live the life he was meant to have." Saoirse's voice floats across the room towards me, and I meet her gaze, refusing to let the tears that I can feel shimmering in my eyes fall.

"The life he was meant to have." I let the words slip off my tongue, considering them. "With you."

"Yes," Saoirse says, and I think I detect the slightest thread of sympathy in her voice. "With me."

There's silence again, one that stretches out, and then Saoirse takes a deep breath. "Think about it," she says quietly as she passes me. "Liam says he rescued you. It might be time for you to rescue *him*—from himself. Before he tears everything down."

And then she's gone, slipping out of the front door almost as quickly as she showed up. The clock says she was here less than twenty minutes, but it feels like it was a lifetime. I sink into the armchair, my hands shaking, squeezing my eyes tightly shut against the tears.

I don't want to cry. I *won't*. I swallow hard, trying to force the swirling emotions down. Still, they're bubbling up too strongly, making Liam's huge luxurious penthouse feel small and claustrophobic. Without thinking too clearly about it, I grab my phone and shove my feet into a pair of flats, heading out of the front door and to the elevator still in my sweaty messy bun, yoga pants, and baggy t-shirt, too upset to think about how I'll look walking down the street. I just need to get outside, to get some air—

The fresh, warm air in my face, sucked into my lungs when I step outside, helps calm me a little. I breathe in deeply a few times as I go out to the sidewalk, turning left for no particular reason and starting to walk. I just need some space, some time to think—

My feet start hurting barely a block in, but I force myself not to think about it. I'm not ready to go back in yet, into a space that's more Liam's than mine, where I'm made to think about the life he had before I suddenly appeared in it. Saoirse had said he was happy with the direction of his life before I showed up, and I have no reason to think that's not true. If he hadn't met me, he would probably have married her, no questions asked. Maybe she would even have made him happy—she seems nice enough, objectively, someone who fits into his world.

Whatever happens, because Liam and I love each other, it's my fault because he met me.

Saoirse said that the consequences of that could be very bad, and I'm not convinced that she's not telling the truth about that, too.

My thoughts are a mess, so much so that I don't even hear the footsteps behind me until it's too late. I barely register the hand gripping my elbow and dragging me sideways until I'm nearly in the car. By then, I'm so off balance that when I stumble and fall, the hands on me take advantage of it to pull me into the waiting car idling at the curb, some nondescript sedan with a cloth interior that smells like upholstery cleaner.

I know it's Alexandre before I register his face. I know his touch, his scent, the way he feels next to me. For a brief time, we were that close. I haven't forgotten, even if I want to put it behind me.

But there's another scent in the car, too, one that makes my heart nearly stop with shock. Cigarettes and lipstick, a scent mingled together, take me back to a feeling of a sick pit in my stomach, a posh French accent insulting me, a sharp nail against my nipple, a gun to my head. I know who's in the front seat of the car, taking us wherever Alexandre has decided we need to go.

Yvette.

For a moment, the world is entirely out of focus. The only things I see swirling colors, making me dizzy and nauseous, my senses swamped with the scents of Alexandre's skin and Yvette's cigarettes and her lipstick and his warm, chocolate-scented breath. And then it all snaps back in, and I sink dizzily against the back of the seat, Alexandre's hand still firmly holding my elbow as if I might throw myself from the moving car.

I dare to look at the driver's seat, not wanting confirmation of what my senses are telling me but still needing it. I see her, Yvette, her dark hair still in that stylish bob, her ubiquitous red lipstick perfectly applied, but with a new feature to her pretty sharp face.

A half-healed wound on the corner of her forehead, creeping into her hairline, the healing scar where she likely had stitches ugly and red. It mars her beauty and adds to it in a way. Still, I remember all too well where that's from—Liam pistol-whipping her to the floor as he tried to get me out of Alexandre's apartment.

I might have hated what he had to do to Alexandre to get me out of there, but I've never for a moment wished he did less to Yvette.

She doesn't so much as look in the rear view mirror at me. Her presence makes my heart beat erratically in my chest—if she's here, it can't be good. I'd thought she was dead, and just the knowledge that she's not makes me feel sick to my stomach, mingled with a steadily growing panic over what she and Alexandre have planned for me. *Did my rejection last night hurt him that much? Is he just going to get rid of me now, once and for all? If he can't have me, no one can?*

"Alexandre—" I try to speak up as we drive, but he shushes me, his grip on my arm tightening as he does so. He doesn't allow me to speak until we're out of the car and headed up to the hotel room, Yvette leading the way like some kind of angry bodyguard, her huge dark sunglasses obscuring a good bit of her face.

"Be quiet, Ana," he says again when I try to protest as he pulls me into the elevator. "Don't think of screaming for help, either. You and your Irish lover will regret it. We'll talk in the room."

I know I should fight back, try to prevent him from taking me up there, where there's no one to see, hear, or save me. But I feel panicked, frozen, and unable to decide what to do or what course of action might get someone to come to my aid instead of pretending to look the other way.

"Alexandre, please—" I beg when we're in the room, the door shutting with a finality that sends a shudder down my spine. "I'm sorry I upset you last night, but you have to be reasonable. I don't want—"

"I am being reasonable," he says coldly. "I stopped when you asked me to last night, didn't I? Let you run off as if you don't belong to me."

"Bought and paid for," Yvette says archly. "A naughty pet. A very bad girl. I wish you'd let me teach her some manners, Alexandre—"

"Enough," he says curtly. "Anastasia, that goes for you as well. I've been patient, let you gallivant around Boston with this Irishman, and trusted you'd come to your senses, but it's clear that you need a firmer hand, someone to guide you. You've done nothing but play games with me, lead me on, and toy with the emotions I have for you—"

"No!" I exclaim pleadingly, shaking my head. "Alexandre, I'm not playing games, I swear. I care for you. I do. I have since Paris. I'm grateful to you for everything you did for me."

I can see a look cross Yvette's face at that, as if she smelled something bad, but I ignore it, plowing ahead. "I meant everything I said to you in Paris, I swear. But things have changed—"

Something in Alexandre's angry expression falters, but Yvette takes a step forward, her pretty face twisted with irritation. "So flighty," she hisses. "So capricious. Her feelings just *changed*. This is why you can't get attached to pets, Alexandre. Their emotions are so all over the place. I'm glad you called me, so that I could help you come to your senses about this. We'll get her back to Paris together, and then—"

My mouth goes dry. *So it's Yvette's fault.* Alexandre must have called her last night after I ran away—to vent, to commiserate, maybe even to ask advice. Clearly, she'd come right away, seeing her chance to dig her hooks into him further. But of course, he doesn't see it like that. He never has—for the brief time I've known Alexandre, he's always been mostly blind to Yvette's flaws and tolerant of the rest.

"I'm going to call Liam," Alexandre says calmly. "He's going to come here, and we're going to—discuss what's to be done about this. You will be leaving here with me, Ana," he adds, his voice cold as he digs his phone out of his pocket, heading to the door to step out into the hallway to make the call.

The last thing I want in the world is to be left alone with Yvette, but that's exactly what happens.

"Miserable little bitch," she hisses. "I should have shot you."

"I'd hoped you were dead," I snap back, my fear momentarily turning to anger and bubbling up. "I wanted Liam to kill you. You're poison to Alexandre, you—"

I don't see the slap coming. Yvette's hand cracks sharply across my cheek, burning as my head snaps to one side. "He's never going to love you," I spit out, gritting my teeth against the bloom of pain and forcing myself to look directly at her. "Never—"

This time the slap comes from the other side, wrenching my neck to the left, my face now nothing but stinging heat. "Little *cunt*," Yvette hisses. "*Chien—*"

"Stop! *Non,* Yvette." Alexandre's voice is sharp and commanding when he steps back into the room, and even Yvette draws back, her hand dropping to her side. "I told you she wasn't to be harmed."

Yvette frowns, but steps back.

"Did you call Liam?" I whisper in a small voice, and Alexandre nods.

"He is on his way. When he arrives, we will deal with all of this then."

Fear snakes its way down my spine, cold and icy. "Don't hurt him, Alexandre, please! Whatever you want from me, I'll do it. Just don't hurt Liam—"

Alexandre says nothing, only turns away from me, watching the door with his arms crossed over his chest and his jaw set. On the other side of the room, Yvette is wearing a triumphant smile, and I can feel my heart sinking to my toes.

I'm almost certain Liam is walking into a trap.

And there's nothing I can do.

FOURTEEN
LIAM
ALEXANDRE HAS ANA.

The fear I felt when I heard his voice was sharp and immediate, chilling me to the bone. He hadn't sounded angry, but somehow that felt even more terrifying, as if the calm, cold tone meant something far more ominous. Anger and passion I could deal with, but if he's ceased to care about Ana, if all he wants is his revenge on us both, that's a far more dangerous situation.

I was walking out of the drugstore when he called. Now, with the phone clutched in one hand and the bag holding Ana's pregnancy tests in the other, I'm standing at the curb in the warm early summer air, feeling a dark sense of dread growing until it nearly overwhelms me.

I'm in such a daze that it takes me a second to realize that my driver has pulled up to the curb. He steps out, his wrinkled brow creased as he peers over the top of the car at me. "Mr. McGregor, is everything alright?"

I blink, snapping out of the fugue that Alexandre's call had left me in. "Yes. Just a slight change in plans, Ralph. I have another stop to make."

"Of course, sir."

I give him the name of Alexandre's hotel, leaning back against the cool leather of my seat and closing my eyes as Ralph pulls out into traffic. My heart is hammering in my chest. Every second that ticks by reminds me of the hours and days and weeks that I'd worried over Ana, trying to find her, wondering what was happening to her while I was searching. Now Alexandre has her again, and my imagination runs to all the worst places as the car stops in the lunchtime Boston traffic, again and again, panic rising into my throat in a hard lump.

"Can we get there any faster, Ralph?" I lean forward, looking at the gridlock ahead of us, and Ralph glances up, looking at me in the rearview mirror.

"Going as fast as I can, sir."

Shit. I grit my teeth, forcing myself to remain as calm as I can all the way until we're two blocks from the hotel. When the traffic slows to a dead halt again, I can't take it any longer.

"Stay in the area, Ralph. I'll call you if I need you."

Before he can ask unnecessary questions or protest, I'm out of the car, still clutching the bag as I start to jog the two blocks to the hotel, dodging passersby as I go. It's not overly hot out yet, but my button-down is still clinging to me with sweat by the time I reach the doors to the lobby, and I'm faintly out of breath.

Clearly, I need to swap out some of my weightlifting for cardio.

I push the door open, ignoring the concierge asking me if I need help as I head straight for the elevator. Alexandre gave me the room number on the phone. Nothing in the world can slow me down or stop me as I head up, gripping the elevator railing as if I could somehow make it move faster with sheer will.

If he's hurt her, I'll kill him.

When the doors opened, I burst out of the elevator and headed straight for 546, the number Alexandre gave me. I have a brief, momentary fear that he might have given me the wrong information and sent me on a wild goose chase while he spirits Ana away to wherever he might want to take her, but logic tells me that's not true. *Come here straightaway,* Alexandre had said. *We'll settle this then, the matter of who Ana belongs to. No more of this nonsense.*

If he was telling the truth, then Ana is here. And he is, at the very least, done with playing games.

I can only hope.

When I reach 546, I knock on the door firmly, my heart in my throat but trying to appear as composed as possible. I can't throttle the man the minute the door opens, no matter how much I want to—but when it does swing open, and I see Alexandre's face, grim and quiet, it takes everything in me not to do exactly that.

He looks *hurt*, as if he's enduring the same pain that Ana has, that I have, as if he's a brokenhearted man struggling with the potential loss of his love. *How dare he think of Ana like that*, I fume inwardly, shoving my way into the room and pinning him with an angry glare.

"What the fuck is going on—"

The words die on my lips as I see Ana sitting on the edge of the bed, her face so pale that the red marks on both cheeks from where someone has struck her are brightly visible, looking nearly painted on. I pivot towards Alexandre, a black fury rising up in me as I take two strides towards him, and it's only Ana's voice that stops me in my tracks.

"Liam, no—he didn't hit me. It was Yvette."

I whirl, instantly catching sight of the dark-haired bitch on the other side of the room. I can see a red scar on the side of her face, marring her otherwise model looks, but it's not enough to make up for the fact that she's still breathing.

"I thought I killed you," I growl at her, clenching my teeth.

Yvette gives me a cold smile. "I don't die easily."

"Clearly. But it's a mistake I can rectify. Especially after you *dared* to put your hands on Ana again—"

"Liam, we have things to discuss." Alexandre's voice cuts through the air, sharp like a knife. "Or are you more concerned with Yvette than the woman you claim to love?"

"Of course not." I round angrily on him. "But *you* can't even protect her from this cunt, so how dare you suggest to me that you should have any say in—"

"What is that?" Alexandre points to the bag in my hand, and I feel everything in the room come to a screeching halt.

I glance over at Ana, who has somehow gone even paler, as impossible as that seemed. Her blue eyes are wide with terror, and I want nothing more than to go to her and hold her, pull her into my arms and promise her that everything will be okay. But from the way Alexandre has angled himself between us, it's clear that he's not going to let me get to Ana so easily.

Ana shakes her head, the expression on her face fearful, but from the way Alexandre's eyes have narrowed, flicking from the drugstore bag in my hand to my face and back again, it's clear that he's not going to let this go so easily.

"What. Is. In. The. Bag?" Alexandre repeats the question through gritted teeth, his sharp jaw clenching tightly with irritation that I didn't immediately answer his question. "I don't like to be kept waiting, Liam—"

"I'm not one of your pets," I snap at him. "I don't have to jump when you say jump, and I certainly don't have to divulge personal information to you—"

Alexandre snatches the bag out of my hand before I can stop him, before I can even react, with one surprisingly fast movement. "I'll find out myself," he hisses, and I hear Ana's small cry of fear as he opens the bag, peering inside.

I see his face go pale too as he registers the contents, shock written across every feature as he slowly looks up, first at me and then at Ana, and then at me once again.

"What is the meaning of this?" he asks quietly. "Is this for your fiancé, Liam? Saoirse? Did you take her precious virginity ahead of the wedding after all, lying to sweet Ana about your involvement with this other woman?"

I can hear the faint hope in his voice, that it's something so salacious, something that would divide Ana and me forever. It would possibly send her back into his arms, and that's exactly why I can't use that lie. It's a convenient one—it would get us out of having to admit to Alexandre that Ana is pregnant. But if I say out loud that I've been with Saoirse, I feel as if Ana won't ever be able to completely forget my saying that, even if it's not true. The trust between us is fragile, still building, and I can't bring myself to say anything that might damage it in any way, especially after my error last night when I'd taken her to the ballet.

But I also can't bring myself to tell Alexandre the truth, to give him anything that might make him think he has a claim on Ana more than he already does.

"Tell us the truth, Liam." Alexandre's mouth is curling on one side in a smirk as if he's certain that my hesitation is because of Saoirse and not because of the truth—that Ana's pregnancy will complicate things so much more.

"I—" I swallow hard. "This is a personal matter, I—"

"I threw up last night." Ana blurts it out, her voice strangled, and my head instantly whips in her direction.

"Ana, don't—"

"He's going to get it out of us," she says miserably. "We'll stay here until we tell the truth, so we might as well. And he deserves to know. I know you hate him, Liam, but he wasn't—he wasn't cruel to me. In a way, he saved me, too, from Alexei. So I can't sit here and lie. My period is late," she adds, looking at Alexandre. "But that doesn't mean anything. I'm too thin. It could be—"

"You are too thin, *petit*. I tried to feed you." His expression is gentle when he looks at Ana, concerned in a way that makes me prickle with anger. I don't want anyone but me looking at Ana in that way.

"It's not pregnancy, Alexandre, I'm almost certain of it—"

"Oh, *merde*," Yvette spits out, her eyes narrowing as she looks at the three of us. "Now the little bitch is whelping, after all of this? Who would want a child with this–" She wrinkles her nose, and Alexandre shoots her a sharp, angry look.

"Hold your tongue, Yvette," Alexandre says sharply.

"I'm not pregnant!" Ana gasps the words, sounding desperate. "I'm not–"

"Clearly, that's not what Liam thinks." Alexandre shakes the bag containing the tests. "Clearly, Liam thinks that there's a good enough chance—"

"He's overreacting!" Ana's voice is pleading. "Alexandre, let's just discuss what you wanted to talk to Liam about, and then we can go. This is over between you and me. We can't do it anymore. I told you—"

"You're not going anywhere. There's an easy answer to this."

Alexandre digs out one of the boxes and holds it out to Ana. "Take the test, *petit*. And then we will know."

Ana is bone-white by this point, as if there's not a drop of blood left in her face. "Alexandre, please. I don't want to do this here."

"It could be either of our baby, *petit*, if you are pregnant. You should do it here, with both potential fathers present. Or—" a new thought appears to cross his face. "Has Liam not—"

"I haven't come inside of her," I speak up quickly, hoping that it will deter him. "And it's been a few weeks since she was in Paris. Surely you used protection with her. Ana is right. There's some other explanation for her illness."

I'm bluffing, of course. I haven't finished in Ana, but I've been inside of her twice, for a good amount of time, without a condom. Anyone who's gone through basic sex ed knows that while that might not be enough to *try* to get pregnant, it can certainly result in an accident. And the second time, I'd pulled out of her just as my orgasm had begun. I remember all too clearly the sight of her cum-stained thighs—and just a few days ago, I'd stroked myself to completion on her pussy, coating her with my cum without thinking of the potential consequences. That last can't be the culprit of Ana's likely situation—but I haven't been careful. Neither of us have. Not as cautious as we should have been if we were trying to prevent Ana from getting pregnant. But truthfully—I hadn't thought about it. The idea of Ana being pregnant with my child, while terrifying in a sort of abstract way, is also an exciting one. I've always known I would have children if my wife and I were able. I just hadn't thought about it in any real, concrete way yet. I hadn't had any reason to.

It's not Ana's pregnancy that upsets me in and of itself. It's the possibility that it could bind her more tightly to Alexandre—and very well could, here and now, if he forces her to take the test.

Alexandre smirks, a look of satisfied glee crossing his face—likely at the thought that I haven't enjoyed the same pleasures with Ana that he has. "Oh, I did not use protection, *monsieur*." His cold, terse smile only grows. "You may not have come in her sweet pussy, but I most certainly have. More than once. Which only makes me all the more insistent, *petit*. You will take the test here."

I round on him, black fury rising up in a storm cloud of nearly uncontrollable anger at the thought of him inside of Ana, filling her–

"You didn't take any precautions?" I snap. "Were you *trying* to get her pregnant?" The thought of it makes me feel sick.

Alexandre chuckles darkly. "Not trying, *monsieur*, no. But why would I not? Anastasia was–*is*–mine. And she certainly didn't have a word to say otherwise."

Ana goes very pale at that, her eyes flicking nervously to me. "Liam, I–"

I hold up a hand, unable to listen to any more of it. "Ana, no. I don't want to hear about it. I understand–it happened. But I can't–" I take a deep breath. "It doesn't matter," I manage to say, as difficult as it feels. "He'll never touch you again."

"We'll see, *monsieur*," Alexandre snaps. "The test, Anastasia?"

"It's best taken in the morning," Ana protests. "It might not be accurate—"

"Your Irishman was very thorough." Alexandre shakes the bag again. "There are five more boxes in here. Twelve tests in total, including what's in my hand. All twelve cannot be wrong. You will take them until we know for sure. Until we see a clear difference between results."

"I can't." Ana shakes her head, visibly on the verge of tears. "Not with Yvette here, please, Alexandre. I can't do this. It's too personal, it's—I'm going to have a panic attack, and I know how much you hate my fits. Please just let me go home, and I'll call you. I promise."

"You left me, *petit*. I am sorry to say that I do not trust you as I once did." Alexandre does look as if he's sorry, his mouth twisting sympathetically. "I do not trust you not to tell me a different result than the truth."

"But—"

He holds up his hand, ignoring me entirely now in favor of Ana. "But if it will make you more comfortable, *petit*, I will ask Yvette to leave."

"You will not!" Yvette starts to protest, her eyes going wide with shocked anger, but Alexandre pins her with a cold glare. It's in that moment that I see that perhaps she doesn't have as much of a hold on him as I'd believed—or at least not always. There are things more important to him than Yvette's approval.

"You will leave, Yvette, so that we may conduct this matter in private. Ana is right about one thing, it is deeply personal and among the three of us. Please go down to the lobby, go to the bar, have a drink, have tea in the restaurant—I don't care, so long as you are not within earshot of this room. I'll call you when we are finished here."

"Alexandre—" Yvette starts to protest, looking both shocked and more than a little hurt that he's kicking her out. Still, Alexandre's expression is as cold and impassive as I could have hoped it would be in this situation.

"Now, Yvette."

"I won't forget this," Yvette hisses in Ana's direction as she leaves, but she *does* leave, the door slamming behind her as she goes. Alexandre waits for her footsteps to recede down the hall, and then he holds out the box to Ana.

"There are no more excuses, *petit*," he says. "Take the test."

Ana looks up at me sorrowfully, but we both also know that there are no more excuses either of us can make. Alexandre is motionless, his hand outstretched. When a beat passes and then another without him flinching or moving away, she finally grabs it out of his hand, her fingers tightening around the box as she takes a deep breath.

"Fine," she whispers. "We'll do it your way."

"I am glad you see reason, *petit*." Alexandre steps back, setting the bag of remaining tests on the nightstand next to the bed. "Soon, we will all have answers."

FIFTEEN
ANA

Answers, indeed.

Some time later, I'm staring at a row of ten pregnancy tests lined up on the luxurious bathroom counter, their flimsy plastic in stark contrast to the dark grey granite of the countertop. All but one has the same result—two pink lines or a plus sign showing in the tiny window.

Positive. All but one has a line and then the faintest glimmer of pink next to it, so light that it's impossible to tell if it's an actual second line or just a mirage. Still, I cling to that fragile thread of hope, even as Alexandre holds out the last box insistently.

"Two more, *petit*."

"Just—give me a minute." I press my fingers to my temples. "I don't have to pee again yet."

"Get her more water." Liam is nearly as anxious as Alexandre now, hovering near me and looking over my shoulder at the row of tests.

"Just, please—" I press my hand to my mouth, trying to breathe. Trying not to panic. Alexandre slips out of the bathroom, and it gives me the briefest moment alone with Liam as I stand there, looking at all the evidence that I am, in fact, pregnant. "I can't do this," I whisper. "I can't be pregnant, Liam. I just can't. I don't know if I can be a mother, if I would even *be* a good mother—"

"Shh." Liam drops a kiss on the top of my head, his hand resting comfortably on my lower back for a brief moment. "You'll be a fine mother, Ana, if that's what you want. You have choices in this, and I'm not going to take them away from you. But first, we need to deal with Alexandre. Let's figure this out first, and then we'll discuss the baby."

"*If* there's a baby. Maybe they're defective, maybe—" I'm hoping the last two will show clearly negative, to sow real, definite doubt. *Nine* pregnancy tests out of ten can't be wrong, but maybe out of twelve—

That would be enough doubt to push off any real answer until I could see a doctor, at least. I could insist that I want to go back to Manhattan to see *my* doctor. Liam could come with me, even. Anything to get away from Alexandre while we sort this out.

Alexandre brings me the water bottle, the top already unscrewed, and Liam's hand leaves my back instantly. I miss his touch as soon as it's gone. I know we can't afford to antagonize Alexandre more than he already is. Still, at the same time, I want so badly to show Alexandre how things have changed, that I'm not the girl who was in Paris with him, that this can't work anymore.

Two more tests.

I half expect the men to insist on waiting in the bathroom while I pee, but thankfully they at least give me privacy for that. It's a few minutes alone to gather my emotions and thoughts until both plastic sticks join the other ten on the counter, and we wait for the displays to change. Behind me, I can feel how agitated both men are, and it makes me feel sick to my stomach.

Or maybe it's the baby doing that.

The wait feels agonizing. I stare at the little windows, praying that as one pink line develops in each that there won't be another. But sure enough, a second starts to clearly show in both, and I feel tears swimming in my eyes, dizzy nausea swamping me until I have no choice but to run to the toilet, falling to my knees as I sob, heaving into it again and again.

I'm pregnant. There's no question about it. Eleven clearly positive tests and one inconclusive. There's no way to argue with it. Behind me, over the sounds of my puking, I can hear Liam and Alexandre starting to argue.

"It's mine, *monsieur*," Alexandre snaps. "Not only *could* it be mine, it almost certainly is. I've slept with *petit* on several occasions—twice the first night, again the next day, and many nights after that, in her room before the dinner party—"

"I don't need an itemized list of every time you fucked her!" Liam's voice rises, thundering in the bathroom that suddenly feels far too small for the three of us. "I've fucked her too, Alexandre. Your French cock isn't the only one that she's had since—"

"Please stop. Please—" I sink onto the soft mat at the edge of the toilet, dabbing at my mouth with a tissue, but the men are far too busy arguing to listen to me. "Please—Alexandre, Liam—"

"You didn't come inside of her. You said so yourself—"

"I started to!" Liam snarls. "And anyway, you know as well as I do that you don't have to stuff a woman full of it to get her pregnant. It could very well be mine—"

"Oh, I've stuffed her full of my cum, *monsieur*," Alexandre smirks. "The odds are, after how much of my cum she's taken—"

Liam swings before Alexandre can see it coming. His fist connects squarely with the Frenchman's jaw, the sound reverberating in the room as Alexandre recovers, lurching forward to throw his own punch toward Liam. But Liam is a trained boxer—Alexandre might be fit and muscular, but he's not a fighter. He doesn't know how to move or dodge, and he misses both of the blows he tries to strike before Liam grabs him by the front of the shirt and throws him against the counter, the pregnancy tests scattering everywhere as the two men tussle. A soap dish goes flying, cracking against the tiled floor and shattering. I gasp, inching backward, away from the fight as Liam throws Alexandre into the shower doors, the glass shuddering so that for a moment, I think it might splinter.

"Stop!" I scream, my hands covering my mouth as I try not to burst into tears. Alexandre manages to land a hit, his fist connecting with Liam's jaw, and I cry out, scrambling to my feet and flinging myself towards the two men. "Please, stop! Stop it! Stop!"

I'm screaming it over and over, and Liam gets one more blow in, sending Alexandre sprawling to the tiled floor before he realizes that I've thrown myself into the fray and steps back, panting as he looks down at the bruised man on the floor.

"Get up, Alexandre," I say faintly, feeling overwhelmed with how quickly the situation has escalated. The plastic tests are scattered across the floor, the detritus of this awful nightmare we've found ourselves in.

"I should have killed you in Paris," Liam snarls at Alexandre. "I should have made sure you were fucking dead, you—"

"Stop!" I shout it again, looking between the two men. "Alexandre, *get up.*"

"I'm trying," Alexandre says tersely, pushing himself up with the slowness of a man who hurts in every joint. "Your Irish lover shot me in Paris, or don't you remember? Those wounds are still healing, and now he's injured me again."

"And yet you keep surviving. Like a cockroach, you and that chain-smoking bitch—" There's no mistaking the black fury in Liam's voice and on his face. "I'll rip you both apart—"

"Listen to me, both of you." I step between them as Alexandre stands shakily, holding onto the wall for balance. "Either of you could be the father. I don't like that, but it's true. Whether one is more likely than the other—that's not something we're going to talk about right now. *I'm* the one carrying your potential child, which means *I'm* the one you don't want to upset right now. I need you both to stop—I need to think. I need a minute."

To my surprise, both men actually go silent. I take a deep breath, pushing the heels of my hands into my eyes as I try desperately not to cry. Slowly, I make my way past them, scooping test after test off the floor and depositing them in a pile on the countertop. Then, just as slowly, I turn to face the two men again, using every bit of strength I have left not to collapse into a panicked, melting puddle onto the floor.

I need someone right now, and no one seems able to be there for me. I suddenly, desperately want Sofia, my best friend, the person who doesn't have any interest in this fight except for what's best for me. But she's not here, and I know that both Liam and Alexandre, at this moment, are too caught up in their own emotions to pay attention to mine.

"I need to talk to both of you," I say quietly. "But separately."

"I—" Alexandre starts to speak up, but I shake my head firmly, gritting my teeth in an effort to stay calm.

"Liam, can you please step out for a minute?" I ask it as calmly as I can, gripping the edges of the countertop as I lean back against it. "I want to talk to Alexandre."

The look on Liam's face is instantly one of shocked hurt. I know he wasn't expecting me to send him out first. But I want to get the conversation with Alexandre over with before I talk to Liam. Of course, I can't say that out loud, so I give Liam a pleading look, hoping he'll understand. I *need* him to understand.

He pauses for a moment, but then he nods. "Alright, Ana," Liam says softly. "Whatever you need." He strides towards the bathroom door and then pauses, his hand on the knob. "I won't listen in," he assures me. "But if you need me, Ana, I'll be just outside."

Liam gives Alexandre one more piercing look, his mouth thinning as he does, and then he steps out, closing the bathroom door firmly behind him.

It's only Alexandre and me, alone.

SIXTEEN
ANA

The moment Liam leaves, Alexandre starts to walk toward me, hands outstretched. "*Petit*," he murmurs, his voice low and sweet once again. "This is wonderful news. I—"

"Stop." I hold up a hand, shaking my head. "This isn't some kind of celebration, Alexandre. This—" I swallow hard, sinking down to sit on the edge of the jacuzzi tub as I look at the pile of pregnancy tests on the sink. "This is insane."

"It is wonderful, *petit*," he insists. "We've made a baby together. You must see that you have to come back to Paris with me, now, so that we can experience the pregnancy together, so that we can raise our child together—"

"You don't know that it's yours. Not for sure." I drop my head into my hands, rubbing them across my face as I try to fight back frustrated, frightened tears.

"*Petit*, please—" he takes another step towards me, reaching out as if to touch my shoulder, but I pull away.

"Stop, Alexandre. I don't want to be touched. Not right now. Just— we need to talk this out. We don't know if it's your baby. But if it was —" I take a deep breath, unable to look directly at him. I can't stand the happiness on his face, how enthused and joyful he looks at the possibility of us having a child together.

"I know you say you don't want to discuss the odds, *petit*, but you must understand, you and I—"

"What sort of life, exactly, do you think the two of us would have with a child?" The words burst out of me, and I finally look up at him, glaring with frustration. "How could a baby possibly fit into your life, into how *our* life was back in Paris? We didn't have a normal relationship, Alexandre! What, are you going to *date* me now? Make me your girlfriend or your wife? You can't have a baby with your *little doll,* your *broken toy.* You can't keep me as a pet and have me give you a child! You can't make me eat off of the floor and dress and bathe me, control my every waking moment when I have a baby to care for!" Tears are brimming in my eyes, and I wipe them away angrily. "Our relationship wasn't that kind of relationship, Alexandre. It was all about ownership, trauma, pleasure and pain, and humiliation and yes, a twisted fucked up kind of love, but not the kind of love that makes a healthy childhood!"

I shake my head, sucking in a breath as I try to calm myself down before I start to spiral out of control again. "We're both fucked up, Alexandre. We've both been through so much, been so traumatized by others. I don't even know if I *can* be a mother or if I'll just ruin this child's life the way mine's been ruined. But I do know that if I choose to bring this baby into the world, *two* broken people can't be good parents to another person. *We* can't do this, Alexandre, you and I. We just can't."

"Is Liam not broken?" Alexandre's voice is sarcastic, almost vicious. "Your Irishman is whole, then? Not hurt by anyone? Clean and pure of all damage?"

"If he's damaged, you did it to him," I snap back, narrowing my eyes. "You forced him to fuck me in front of strangers with a gun to my head. Told him it was his fault if he refused, his fault if he did it, if I died either way. *You* did this to him. So don't suggest that it's anyone's fault but yours. You wanted to destroy any chance of Liam and I being together by making him all but rape me. Instead, you just destroyed *our* chances—yours and mine. It doesn't matter how much I once loved you; I can't look at you without remembering that. Without remembering how you let Yvette use you because she was jealous."

Alexandre is very quiet for a moment. "You said *loved, petit,*" he says after a few seconds of silence. "Do you not love me still?"

I hesitate. I shouldn't have. I should have sworn to him, instantly, up and down and to my grave, that all the love I had for him is dead. But instead, I pause, my heart leaping into my throat as I try to say the words that aren't entirely true, and Alexandre grabs onto them like a life raft for a drowning man.

"So long as I believe you have a shred of love for me, *petit*, so long as there's a chance the baby is mine, I won't leave. I won't go back to Paris, and I won't abandon you. You are *mine, petit*, and I will not leave so long as there is a breath of a chance for us."

"I'm not a book or a painting!" I get to my feet unsteadily, my heart racing in my chest. I know he meant the words to be romantic, but in my current emotional state, all I feel is panic. "I don't belong to you, and neither does *my* baby, no matter how much you paid for me!" I'm breathing hard now, feeling myself flush red. "I don't belong to Liam, either. If I choose either one of you, it'll be for myself and possibly the baby. I won't be *owned*, not by anyone. Not after everything I've endured."

Alexandre's brow furrows, and I see a flash of anger mar his handsome, artistic features. "What do you mean by this, *petit*?" he asks, his voice taking on a dangerous edge. "Are you considering not keeping this child?"

I throw up my hands in frustration, letting out a sharp, angry breath. "I've known I was pregnant for less than an hour, Alexandre," I retort. "I couldn't possibly know right now one way or another what I'm going to do."

"You will not choose anything other than this baby!" Alexandre roars, and I stumble back, nearly falling into the tub in my sudden, frightened shock. I regain my balance, but tip forward, falling to my knees on the tile, and the impact takes the wind out of me. I start to cry, tears trickling down my cheeks as I shudder with a few sudden, gasping sobs. Before I can push myself back up, Alexandre is on the floor next to me, reaching for me, gentle all over again.

"I am sorry for my outburst, *petit*," he whispers, his voice cracking, and when I look up, I see tear tracks on his cheeks, too.

"Alexandre—" I blink at him, reaching out despite myself to touch the damp line on his cheek, just below the sharp bone. "What—"

"I am sorry," he repeats. "I—my stepsister, Margot, who I loved and had an affair with as a teenager. She—" He swallows hard, and I know what he's going to say before it comes out of his mouth.

"You got her pregnant?" I whisper, and Alexandre nods, his blue eyes brimming with fresh tears.

"Our father discovered it," he says in a hushed tone, his hands curling into fists. "He forced an abortion on her. He wouldn't take her to a doctor, either—he said a slut like her didn't deserve it. He did it, out—out in the barn. He made me watch." Alexandre's face crumples at that, his head dropping forward onto my shoulder.

I'm frozen in shock, unable to move. The horror of it feels like ice in my blood, Alexandre's pain softening me towards him despite myself. Whatever there is between him and me—whatever pain and hurt and history—has nothing to do with this. His stepsister certainly didn't deserve it, and I can see that Alexandre's pain is real. His shoulders shake as he cries, his Adam's apple bobbing as he finally looks up at me, swallowing convulsively, his eyes reddened.

"It was only a few days later that she died," he murmurs.

"I'm so sorry," I whisper. "Alexandre—I can't begin to explain how sorry I am, truly—"

He shakes his head, sitting back on his knees as he wipes at his face, giving me a tight, sad smile. "It was long ago," he says quietly. "And not your fault. But you see why the idea of you not keeping this child is so—difficult for me."

"I do," I say quietly, and I mean it. My personal choice aside, I can understand his pain. "Did you want the baby?" I ask delicately. "You and Margot, I mean. Did you talk about it, before—"

Alexandre nods. "She told me the morning she was certain, alone. Before our father discovered it—discovered...us. She was overjoyed. We made plans together—plans to run away, be married, and escape him. It was the last time we ever made love, before—" His voice breaks again, and he looks away.

"We were going to be a family," he says finally, looking back up at me. "We were going to be together, the three of us, and that was stolen from me." His jaw tightens, his blue eyes burning into mine. "I will not allow that to happen to me again, Anastasia."

My heart lurches in my chest. "I'm sorry," I whisper. "I'm so sorry that happened to you and your stepsister. It's horrible. What happened to her—it's the worst thing I can imagine. But I don't *know* what I want to do, Alexandre. I haven't had a chance to even process this yet, let alone make decisions and choices for my future—and it *has* to be my choice. *Mine.* Not anyone else's."

Alexandre's face smooths, and he smiles at me, reaching up to touch my cheek gently. We're both still kneeling on the floor, very close, so close that I can feel his warmth and smell his cologne and the scent of his skin. Familiar smells, smells that once made me feel safe. *Loved*, even. Protected.

"That is why you loved me, *petit*," he murmurs. "I made all the choices for you—all you had to do was obey. It could be like that again."

"No," I whisper, shaking my head, and I can feel tears rising up in my eyes again. "It can't, Alexandre. It really can't."

"So long as you love me even a little, *petit*, I don't believe that." Alexandre shakes his head. "Come back to Paris with me. We'll be together. If you want to make choices, *petit*, if you want to be Anastasia and not my little doll, I will try to learn to live like that again. It can be different for us. We will be a family, just as—"

"Alexandre—" Tears spill over my lashes, and I shake my head, feeling as if he's cracking my heart open all over again. "I don't believe you. I *can't*. Maybe the Alexandre who loved Margot, maybe that man could have been a husband and a father, maybe he could have lived that life. Maybe–maybe you could, still. But not with me. We began things a certain way–and I don't think we can change that. Perhaps there's someone out there who could heal you the way Liam has helped to heal me–but I can't, Alexandre. I wanted to so badly. I did." I try to stop the tears, but I can't. They're falling harder now, and I lean forward, pressing my forehead against his. "There's no future for us that makes sense."

I reach for his hand, feeling his long fingers brush against my palm. Artist's fingers, pianist's fingers, the hands of a man who loves beautiful things. "You love everything that is beautiful and broken, Alexandre," I whisper. "And I'm starting to heal, here. You're right that I do still love you. I think a part of me always will. But I'm starting to believe, more and more, that this is where I belong. That Liam is who I belong *with*. I felt that before the baby, and this baby won't change that. No matter whose it is—"

There's a hard, heavy knock on the door and Liam's voice from outside. "Ana? Are you alright? It's been a while—I think it's time we talked. You and I—alone."

Slowly, feeling shaky, I stand up. I hold out my hand for Alexandre, to help him up too, and he looks up at me from where he's kneeling with wet blue eyes. In that moment, it feels like something has shifted between us.

He takes my hand, his palm warm against mine, and gets to his feet. He holds my gaze for a long second, and I expect him to say something else, but he doesn't. He simply turns away, walking towards the door. As he steps out, Liam pushes past to enter the bathroom, and Alexandre looks back at me once, sorrowfully.

And then the door closes once more, and it's Liam and me.

SEVENTEEN
ANA

I feel calmer with Liam standing there. Alexandre isn't that much taller than me, but Liam is inches taller, so he looks down at me, his face creased with worry.

"He didn't hurt you, did he, Ana?"

"Do I look hurt?"

"I mean with words. Emotionally. Shit, I don't even know what I mean now, lass. It was torture leaving you in here with him. But you asked, so—"

"I appreciate it," I say softly. "I know you don't want to hear it or even think it, and neither do I—but there *is* a chance that the baby is his. And so I needed to talk to him alone."

"He's right." Liam lets out a sharp breath, evidently able to admit it without Alexandre present. "The odds are that it's his. The two of you had unprotected sex, to completion, often. You and I—"

"You don't need to say it again." I lean back against the counter, gnawing on my lower lip. "Alexandre wants me to go back to Paris with him, of course. He says we can raise this baby together."

"And what did you say?" Liam's expression is carefully guarded, as if he's afraid of my answer.

"I told him no." I see the relief that flashes across Liam's face, though he hides it quickly. "He and I can't raise a child together. What he and I were to each other—it wasn't that kind of relationship. It couldn't ever be. I can't go back to Paris with him, but—"

"But what?" Liam prompts, his expression concerned again.

"The baby might not be yours. If I'm not going with Alexandre—do you want me to go back to Manhattan? You can't possibly want me now—I might be carrying another man's child, and after all of this—"

Liam crosses the space between us in two strides, shocking me into silence as he reaches for me, one hand on my waist and the other cupping my cheek. He looks fiercely down at me, his green eyes glistening with emotion.

"I don't care whose baby it is biologically, Ana, his or mine," Liam insists, his voice full of passion. "I *love* you, and if you want this baby, if you want me, then I am yours. We'll be a family." His voice deepens, taking on a darker edge. "I'll kill Alexandre for you or have Niall do it if you don't want the blood on my hands, and you'll be free of him. He and Yvette both. I'll—"

"No!" I gasp, pulling back and shaking my head. "No, Liam, please. I don't want that. I—"

Liam pulls back, too, defeat creasing his features, making him look older, exhausted. "You still love him," he murmurs. "After everything—"

"It's not that," I insist. "I just don't want him *dead*, Liam. There's a middle ground between *I want to go back to him* and *I want him murdered*. I *need* you to understand that." I reach for his hands, enclosing his broad palms in mine. "This isn't all Alexandre's fault, Liam. He's broken too, in so many more ways than you know."

Liam reaches up, pulling one hand free to push a lock of blonde hair out of my face, his fingers tracing my jaw as they slip down. "As long as he's alive, Ana, he'll haunt us."

"If he's dead, he'll haunt us too," I say quietly. "This—all of this—comes back to me and my choices from the very beginning, to go infiltrate Viktor's Bratva to try and help Sofia. I can't live knowing I'm the reason for his death. I just can't."

Liam frowns, clearly upset. I can see it on his face, the way his forehead is creasing, the frustration in his eyes. "You wouldn't be, Ana," he says firmly. "This is *your* choice. To keep the baby or not, to go with Alexandre, to stay with him, even to leave us both and do this on your own—you can choose whatever you want. All of it is your choice, and as for Alexandre—he chooses for himself, too. If he stays and fights for you, after you have told him no, the consequences of that are his. Not yours."

He pauses, his thumb passing softly over my lower lip. "You know what choice I want you to make, Ana. But it's yours. Only yours."

I look up at his green eyes, so full of emotion, full of *love* for me. He bends down, his lips brushing over mine softly, and I suck in a breath, leaning into the kiss. The soft press of his mouth against mine is enough to send tingles rushing over my skin, heat building in my stomach. My hands go to his hips, pulling him against me so that I can feel the heat of his body, burning through his clothes and into mine.

"I love you, Ana," Liam whispers against my mouth. "Nothing and no one can change that. But you *will have* to choose."

"I know," I whisper, my eyes fluttering closed against fresh tears. "But for now, Liam, I just want to go home."

"To the penthouse?" he asks softly. "Or Manhattan?"

"The penthouse." I look up at him, wanting him to understand what I'm asking. "Our home."

Understanding dawns in Liam's eyes, and he nods. He takes my hand, his fingers threading through mine. Together we walk out of the bathroom and into the main room of the hotel suite, where Alexandre is sitting in front of the fireplace, his head bowed. He looks up instantly at the sound of our footsteps, his face pale and drawn.

"I'm leaving, Alexandre," I say firmly. "Please don't try to stop me. If I want to talk to you, I'll call you. If I change my mind, you'll be the first to know. But—" I take a deep breath, my hand tightening in Liam's. "I won't."

The pain in Alexandre's face, the heartbreak, is difficult to see. He'd had a strange way of showing it, but if I'd ever wondered before then if he'd loved me, I know at that moment that he did. The look on his face isn't one of a man losing a possession or an investment. It's the look of a man whose broken heart is shattering all over again.

But I can't be the one to heal it.

"You're letting them go."

It's a statement, not a question, said in Yvette's voice. None of us heard her come in, too caught up in the tension ricocheting among the three of us. But now Liam and I turn towards her, still hand in hand.

"Get out of the way," I tell her sharply. She's standing in front of the door, blocking my path.

"Do you want me to kill them both, Alexandre?" Yvette's hand twitches towards the back of her cigarette-leg capris, under her blazer, and I know in that instant that she's armed. I don't know why I'm surprised.

"Stop, Yvette." Alexandre's voice sounds dead, flat—emotionless. "Let them pass."

"But—" Her eyes widen. "No! You said you were going to keep her, make her pay for leaving you, that you'd make him pay for what he did to me—"

"Let them pass," Alexandre repeats. "Don't make me say it again, Yvette, or it will be you on your knees, and you won't enjoy it."

Her face pales, but she steps aside. Liam's hand tightens on mine, and he strides forward, obviously trying to get us both out of the room as quickly as possible before Alexandre can change his mind. And I don't disagree.

Not even once we're in the elevator do I feel like I can breathe. If I'm being honest, I'm not sure if I'll ever be able to relax fully again.

Our ride home was quiet. But the instant we're inside the penthouse, Liam shuts the front door and locks it, his hands on my waist as he grabs me and turns me, pushing me back against it so fiercely that the air rushes out of me in a gasp.

When his mouth crashes down on mine, it steals every last bit of breath in my lungs.

Liam's hands bury themselves in my hair, dragging my lips to his, as he kisses me like a starving man. His hips press against mine, his cock rock hard and throbbing against me, and I gasp with pleasure as his tongue thrusts into my mouth, tasting me, devouring me as his hands cup my face, slide to my breasts, over my ribs, and waist, as if he can't get enough of me.

"I have to make you come," he gasps. "I have to fucking feel you come, Ana, *god*—" His hands are on the waist of the yoga pants I'm still wearing from earlier, dragging them over my hips with my panties, yanking them down to mid-thigh so that I can't get my legs more than a few inches apart, but Liam doesn't seem to care. He's still kissing me, his tongue in my mouth, sucking my lower lip, his teeth grazing against the edge as his fingers thrust between my legs, sliding between my folds and into me instantly.

"Christ, you're sopping wet," he groans, his fingers pumping into me hard, his thumb finding my clit and rolling over it, pressing, rubbing, until I'm moaning into his mouth. "Fucking come for me, Ana, come as hard as you can—I need to feel that pussy around my fingers, *please* fucking come for me—"

It bursts over me so hard and fast that it takes my breath away. I've never orgasmed so fast in my life. Liam's mouth is relentless on mine, his fingers fucking me as hard as his cock ever has, curling and pressing against that sensitive spot, rubbing, his thumb circling the slick nub of my clit, and he groans against my mouth as I clench tightly around him, my pussy squeezing his fingers in a death grip. His other hand fists in my shirt, dragging it upwards until I think he's going to actually rip it. However, he breaks the kiss, yanking it over my head with his fingers still buried inside me.

"Not enough," he groans against my mouth. "Not ever enough—"

For a split second, I think he's going to fuck me there, against the door. But he drags his fingers out of my pussy instead, sweeping me into his arms and carrying me the few yards to the sofa in the living room before depositing me on it upright, kneeling in front of me on the hardwood.

His hands slide under my sports bra, pulling it off, his thumbs brushing over my nipples and making me moan as he yanks it over my head and throws it aside. "I have to taste you," Liam groans, his hands going to my inner thighs, spreading my legs so far apart that I'm nearly doing the splits as he stares at my pussy, opening in front of his eyes like a wet, swollen peach, my clit throbbing as he looks at me spread open for him.

"You have the most beautiful fucking pussy," Liam murmurs, reaching between my thighs with one hand to rub his thumb from my entrance up my slit, dipping inside momentarily before going all the way up to my clit and circling it. "And I'm going to eat it until you scream, Ana."

And then he leans forward, his head delving between my thighs.

I gasp aloud when his hot tongue runs over my folds, lapping up the arousal dripping from my entrance before he slides it up to my clit. His hands hold me firmly open as he devours my pussy, my already oversensitive clit pulsing at the onslaught of his tongue. It feels so good. I'm not sure if anything has ever felt as good as Liam going down on me, except his cock inside of me. I'm already gripping the edges of the sofa, panting as his tongue circles my clit, laps at it, sucks it into his mouth, and I know he's going to make me come just as hard as the first time when he squeezes my thighs, pressing his mouth as tightly against my pussy as he can as he groans, the vibrations running over my swollen flesh and sending me tumbling over the edge.

"Liam!" I scream his name aloud, one hand going to his hair, tangling in it as my hips jerk upwards, grinding against his face as my head falls back, and I gasp. I feel like I can't breathe, can't think, can't do anything other than gasp and writhe against him as he keeps going, one hand sliding between my legs and two fingers thrusting into me to prolong the orgasm, keep it going as I shudder and grind against his mouth, coming hard on his tongue.

It feels like it goes on forever. He doesn't come up for air until I'm limp against the couch. I watch dazedly as he slips his fingers out of me, lazily licking them clean like a fucking housecat as he looks at me.

"You're delicious, Ana," he murmurs. "And I'll make you come like that every day for the rest of your life if you want, if you stay with me." He slides up onto the couch next to me, pulling my naked body into his lap, against him, his lips pressed against my hair.

"Just stay with me," he whispers. And at that moment, more than anything else in the world, that's what I want to do.

EIGHTEEN
LIAM

The next morning, I'm on my way to the O'Sullivan estate.

I'd known already, of course, that I couldn't marry Saoirse. I'd tried to tell her that. But yesterday, seeing those pregnancy tests with their near-identical result lined up, the gravity of the situation had hit me all over again.

Ana is pregnant. And regardless of the child's true parentage, one way or another, the baby is mine, if Ana wants to stay. I want to marry her, raise the child together, and make the family I never had. To do everything differently than my father did.

I leave her sleeping in my bed—*our* bed, it's starting to feel like, after sharing it with her the last two nights—and have Ralph drive me out to the O'Sullivan property, where I'd arranged with Saoirse over text to meet her in the back gardens again to talk.

Except when I walk through the back gate, making my way down the cobblestone path to the fountain where I'd last had a conversation with her, it's not Saoirse's tall, slender figure and strawberry hair that I see waiting for me.

It's a broader figure, with shoulders set, sunlight gleaming off of hair that has gone the buttery white that redheads so often do in old age.

Graham O'Sullivan.

She'd sent her father to deal with me.

It's hard to blame her, I suppose. But as Graham turns to face me, hands in his pockets and his lips pressed thinly together in his thick beard, I steel myself for the conversation to come. Saoirse isn't *easy* to deal with, but in the present situation, I'd have rather had this conversation with her than with Graham.

For all intents and purposes, Niall is my right-hand man, the one whose input and advice I value. He's my enforcer too, whose penchant for violence and more brutal nature I often rely on, but as far as the table is concerned, he's *only* that. Graham is my advisor, as he was to my father. The position he holds at my right hand is the closest he can get to my seat without a son, and he has only Saoirse to marry off to maintain his position. Part of the agreement to allow me to take my father's place with my brother gone was that Graham holds that position, an elder advisor to help me pave my way as the unexpected new head of the Kings.

If I can set Saoirse aside and marry who I please and minimize the fallout among the other members as a result, I can make other changes, too. It will set a precedent that I make my own choices as the reigning Irish King. I can replace Graham with Niall, in time.

Graham knows that. If he'd had a son, everything might have been different. But with only Saoirse to keep me from going rogue and bending the table to my will, he's not going to let me walk away from this easily.

I'd known he wouldn't. But I *will* walk away.

"Graham." I greet him tersely, and he surveys me.

"It's come to my attention, Liam McGregor, that it's your intention to disgrace my daughter. What do you have to say for yourself?"

"I've no intention of disgracing her, I assure you. In fact, I've been very careful to avoid harming Saoirse's virtue—"

Graham turns his head, spitting angrily on the cobblestones. "I'm not talking about her damnable *virtue*. If I thought that was in danger, I'd be bundling the two of ya off to the priest this minute for a wedding without any pomp or circumstance. No, it's my concern that it's the complete opposite. Saoirse tells me you think you can break a contract made before God and witnesses and not marry her at all."

"I can," I say simply. "And I will." I step back, out of range of Graham's fists, just in case he decides to start swinging. "I can't marry Saoirse. I shouldn't have agreed to it in the first place—"

"So you can marry the Russian girl you've been keeping under lock and key?"

I can't stop the look of surprise that crosses my face, and Graham chuckles. "Aye, lad, my daughter told me everything—your disinterest in the marriage, her failure to keep your attention, the little Russian whore you're keeping in your penthouse that she found. There are no secrets now, aye? So let's have a conversation like men, and discuss what's to be done. You'll tell me the truth since I know a good deal of it already, at any rate."

I'm momentarily speechless with shock. "She told you all of it?"

Graham laughs. "Is that such a surprise? My daughter is loyal. She understands duty and family. It's just one of the qualities that will make her a fine wife for you once you're married."

"I won't be marrying her." I do my best to keep my voice even and cool. "Ana is pregnant."

Graham's eyes widen momentarily, but he quickly gets his expression back under control. "And are you certain it's yours, lad? I hear she went through a good number of hands before she ended up in yours."

My teeth clench at the insult to Ana, but I wrestle my emotions quickly under control. I can't hesitate, can't give Graham the slightest inclination that there's a chance the child might *not* be mine. As far as I'm concerned, the question of biology aside, the baby *is* mine—and I'm not about to stand here debating DNA with Graham O'Sullivan. "Yes," I tell him coldly. "The child is mine. I am sorry for the insult to your daughter, Graham, and for any pain I've caused her. But you see that I can't marry her—nor would I think that Saoirse would want to marry *me* any longer, given these circumstances."

"My daughter will keep her word as long as you keep yours." Graham fixes me with a glare. "Saoirse admits that her feelings towards you have changed, but she's still willing to do her duty."

I stare angrily at him, my frustration reaching a boiling point. "My answer is no, Graham. I am not your subordinate. I am your King. You sit at *my* right hand. I will not marry a woman I neither love nor desire when I have one who I both want and love deeply. I *cannot*—"

"Marriages aren't about love for men like us." Graham shakes his head with disgust. "The idea of love is for women and novels. Even Saoirse is intelligent enough to know that a good marriage doesn't need love, only a commitment to duty. But—" he narrows his eyes at me. "My daughter—and I—have conditions for the marriage."

"This ought to be good." Frustration laces my tone, but we might as well get it all out in the open. It's as if Graham hasn't heard a word I've said—or if he has, he refuses to listen, believing, of course, that he knows better. As long as I'm here, I might as well hear all he has to say, though, because once I leave, I have no intention of retreading this ground again. "Go ahead. What *conditions* do you have?"

"You'll send Anastasia back to Manhattan immediately."

I snort. "I'll do no such thing—"

Graham continues as if I hadn't spoken at all. "You'll send her back to Manhattan until the baby is born. If it's yours, then you may support it financially. However, my daughter wishes that your involvement be minimal to none. It will be a bastard who won't inherit—unless you wish to repeat the mistakes of your father. Your emotions and inheritance will be for the children you sire with Saoirse."

"The child is mine. I won't hear this—"

"Do you think the table will accept the Russian whore as your wife?" Graham sneers at me. "Do you honestly think they'll countenance you setting Saoirse aside and accept this Anastasia Ivanova—"

"I sit at the head of the table!" I roar, my voice finally rising as my anger bubbles over, the tension of the past days reaching a breaking point. "*I* say what my decisions will be—"

"That seat is earned, not owed." Graham's green eyes are dark with anger. "Your father sat there for years because he *earned* that spot, not just because his father did. Do you think Viktor Andreyev *took* him to punish him for his deceptions? Do you think we let him take your father out back and shoot him like a dog because we are all toothless wolves when faced with the might of the Bratva?" Graham shakes his head. "No, lad. We gave Viktor your father because he earned his end, too. He lost his way. Your brother should have been there to inherit, but he renounced the folly of his family before that—leaving you. Your position is tenuous, Liam McGregor. You see my daughter as a shackle, but if she is, she's one that will bind you to that seat in the eyes of every man there."

"Graham—"

"Fidelity is not a condition of this marriage, lad. Desire and passion don't have to be found in the marriage bed. You want mistresses? Keep them—no man at the table will fault you for that, least of all me." Graham chuckles wryly. "Just not in your own house, lad. You need to be discreet about these things. And not Anastasia. *That* is not negotiable. The Russian girl has to go back to Manhattan—"

"None of this matters." I cut him off, unable to listen any longer. "This isn't about me wanting to fuck around, Graham. This isn't even about my lack of desire for Saoirse—under other circumstances, I could learn to be happy in this marriage. It's about Ana, and only her. I love her, and I want her and our child. I made a mistake in signing that contract at all. I can't make that mistake again and stand up and marry Saoirse. I *won't*. I'll break one vow, aye, but I'll break it to avoid making another that I can't keep. My decision is made, Graham. It won't change."

"You're a fool like your father, then, and to the devil with both of you." Graham's hand slips into his pocket, and he pulls it back out in a fist. "Saoirse thought that might be your answer, though I insisted I'd make you see reason." He opens his hand, and I see the diamond and emerald ring, glittering in the sunlight. "She took this off, saying you could put it back on her finger when the Russian girl was gone. But it's clear you're so enamored of her that you're willing to give that girl a corpse to cry over instead of a breathing man to miss." He shoves the ring back into his pocket. "You're making a mistake, lad, and digging your own grave. This will have to come to the table, and you'll be given cause to regret this decision."

"I have every intention of telling the Kings my decision," I say coolly. "And I will, once I've dealt with other matters and can call a meeting. But I can guarantee you, Graham, that I will not regret my decision. And it *is* made."

I turn away from him then, stalking back down the cobblestone path. I hadn't meant to have it out with Graham today, but something about having it all in the open makes me feel lighter, though I can still feel the gnawing dread in my stomach.

My bravado about the Kings was little more than a bluff. I know very well how they will feel about my new choice of bride, and I know that Graham holds more than half the table under his sway. But I intend to make it all but impossible for them to force me to change my mind—and to test their loyalty to me and my position.

To hold the Kings requires strength. My brother had said that to me, too, once. I'll show them strength and resolve.

At the end of the day, it's only Ana that matters.

Nothing else.

NINETEEN
ANA

The minute I wake up alone in Liam's bed, I reach for my phone and call the person who, after the events of yesterday, I want to talk to more than anything else in the world.

Sofia.

It's not overly early, and she picks up on the second ring. "Ana?" she asks, a little breathlessly. "Are you okay?"

"I'm—well—I don't know. I—I needed to talk to you. I'm sorry if I interrupted something—"

"No, you're fine. I was just doing what passes for a workout when you're pregnant, which apparently still wears me out these days. What's going on, Ana?"

Just the word *pregnant* is enough to make me burst into tears. *Hormones, I guess. Or stress.* God knows I've been through enough of it in the past months. "Sofia, I—*I'm* pregnant."

There's a moment of stunned silence on the other end of the line. "Are—are you sure, Ana?" Sofia's voice is gentle, and I can hear a rustling as if she's sat down suddenly.

"I took twelve tests." I laugh a choked sound through my tears. "They were all positive but one, and it had a very faint second line. So yeah, I'm pretty sure."

"Oh, Ana." Sofia is quiet for a moment. "Is it—is it Liam's?"

"I don't know," I admit through another wave of sobs. I start crying harder, pulling my knees up to my chest under the blankets. "I—I—"

"Ana, breathe. We'll figure this out, okay? Just breathe—whose else could it be? Alexandre?"

I nod, forgetting for a moment that Sofia isn't here and can't see me. "Yes," I manage to choke out. "I feel so broken, Sofia. I don't know what to do. I didn't even want to believe it was possible until I saw the tests and—"

"Does Liam know?"

"Yes," I whisper. "And Alexandre. They were both there when I took the tests."

"How in the fuck—" Sofia sounds aghast. "What happened, Ana?"

"It's a long story. It doesn't really matter, except that Alexandre wants the baby if it's his, and Liam says he doesn't care *whose* it is, as long as I want to be with him, he considers it his."

"That sounds like Liam." Sofia goes silent for a moment. "Ana, what do *you* want to do?"

"I don't know," I whisper brokenly. "I really don't. I can't envision raising a child with Alexandre. It's ridiculous. It's *insane*. Alexandre and I can't have a baby together. But I don't know how Liam can really love this baby either way—how he can love *me* with that permanent reminder that I was with another man, that our child might not really be his. He'll look at us every day and—and—" I start crying again. I can't help it—I feel as if I'd gotten so close to what I wanted, so close to beginning to heal, only for all of the wounds to break open all over again.

"These men are stronger than you know," Sofia says gently. "Ana, you remember how Luca felt about marriage, and especially about children. Our contract specified we *couldn't* have children, and he was fine with that. He didn't want them at all. And now you should see him, Ana. He can't wait for our baby to get here. He dotes on both of us, and it isn't even here yet."

"Luca knows your baby is his," I say softly. "Do you think he'd feel the same way if there was some question about it?"

"I can't speak for Luca," Sofia says quietly. "Not in that circumstance because I truly don't know. And I believe that Liam is telling you the truth, Ana. You've been through so much, and all of your decisions were shaped by that. He sees that. He sees *you*, and I believe that he loves you. I believe that he will shape your family in whatever way is necessary to have you with him. But Ana—"

"Yes?" I wipe at my face, trying not to cry again. I'm so tired of crying, so tired of feeling as if I'm going to fall to pieces at any moment.

"You have to think about what *you* want too, Ana. And if you don't want to stay, or if you need space to make your decisions, you're always welcome here with us. You don't have to be with either Liam or Alexandre if you don't want to. You always have a place in my home, and I know Caterina feels the same way." Sofia pauses, and I can hear the hesitation in her voice.

"What is it?"

"You should know—Ana, Luca and Viktor aren't happy with Liam. They're angry about his choice to be with you instead of Saoirse—they feel that he's putting love ahead of duty and putting their alliance in danger. But none of that matters to me," she adds quickly. "You're my best friend, Ana. All I want is for you to be happy. Whatever that means."

I think about what she said long after we hang up, as I get dressed and eat breakfast. It doesn't stay down for long, but once I'm out of the bathroom, I make myself a smoothie, hoping I'll be able to keep something liquid down more easily. I'm gingerly taking the first sip when there's a knock at the door, and I walk tentatively towards it, hoping against hope that it's not Saoirse again. I can't deal with her today, and I'm sorely tempted to slam the door in her face if it is.

To my relief, it's Max. I let out the breath I'd been holding as he steps inside, flinging myself towards him and giving him a hug the moment he steps through the door, nearly spilling my smoothie in the process. I feel like I'm on a roller coaster of emotions this morning, and right now, I feel overwhelmingly happy that I didn't have to deal with Saoirse.

"Thank God," I mumble, and Max laughs, delicately detaching me as he walks into the living room.

"Not the first time I've heard that," he says wryly. "Liam asked me to check on you, said the two of you were in a bit of a—situation. Care to elaborate?"

I sink onto the other side of the couch, tucking my feet under me and reaching for a blanket. I'm cold suddenly, the events of the day before rushing back, and I bite my lower lip. "I'm pregnant."

It's the second time I've said those words this morning, and they still don't feel entirely real. It feels like something should be happening to someone else, like I'm living out someone else's nightmare. I can't help but wonder how I'd feel if there were no question that my baby was Liam's, if I'd still feel terrified and unsure, or if I'd just be happy and a little scared.

"And it could be Liam's or Alexandre's? Or definitely Alexandre's?" Max looks a little uncomfortable as he asks the question, and I can't exactly blame him. I'm sure he doesn't know the most intimate details of my relationship with Liam.

"Either. I don't know." Every time I say it, it feels just as awful. "I really don't."

"How would you feel if you knew it was Liam's?" Max asks gently, cutting immediately to the heart of the same thing I was thinking. "If it was a surprise, but one that you knew where it came from?"

"I don't know," I whisper again. "I wish I did. I'm so scared, Max. I'm terrified. And maybe if I knew it was Liam's baby, if I knew it was the product of how we feel for each other, I'd be just a little scared, but excited too. But I can't know. Maybe I'd be terrified either way."

"And Liam? What has he said?"

I give Max a small, sad smile. "That he wants it. He wants *us*. He doesn't care whose baby it is biologically. If we say it's his, it's his."

"So if you stay with Liam, you'll have a family. And later, perhaps you'll get the chance to find out how you feel when you know the pregnancy is Liam's, to experience that together."

"I just don't see how he can—how he can really feel that way. And I don't know if I'll be a good mother, if I *can* be—"

Max looks at me keenly. "Why would you think that?"

I pause, chewing on my lower lip. "I was pregnant once before," I whisper. "I didn't keep the baby. I was just starting at Juilliard—it would have ruined my whole career. The father was another dancer; he *definitely* didn't have any interest. Everyone encouraged me that it was the right decision, and it felt like it. So I made that choice. I'm sure you of all people have thoughts about *that*."

I expect Max to lecture me, but instead, he just sits quietly for a moment, as if taking in everything I've told him. "Do you regret it?" he finally asks gently. "The choice you made back then."

"I—" It takes me a moment to think about it. "Sometimes I think I do," I admit softly. "I lost my career in the end anyway, after all, for an entirely different reason. I wonder if it was all worth it, if I might have had a different life that made me happier, if I might have escaped all of this pain. But in the end–no. I don't regret it." As I say it, I realize that it's true. "It wasn't the right time. I'm not prepared now, but I *definitely wasn't* prepared then. I had very little support and even less money. The father wouldn't have been involved at all. I would have been almost all alone. I wouldn't have been able to do it. And if I'd made that choice–yes, a lot of the awful things that have happened to me might not have. I wouldn't have met Sofia, lived with her–I would have been living somewhere else with my child, a single mother. An entirely different life. But I also wouldn't be here now. I never would have met Liam."

"And now? If you made that choice now, do you think you would regret it?"

I look at Max in surprise, and he smiles. "Ana, I'm not here to judge you. I'm not actually a priest any longer, remember? And anyway, I'd like to think I wouldn't have judged you even then. I'm here to listen to you and help you find your way."

"I think I might," I whisper. "But how do I know if I'll be a good mother? My own mother tried, but she struggled so much. I don't even know if I would have chosen to have children if this hadn't just—happened. Now I think I want it—but what if *not* wanting it before means I'd be a bad mother? I wasn't sad the first time. I just felt relieved that it was done, and I could move on and go back to the life I'd worked so hard for."

"The choices you made in your old life don't mean anything for your life now," Max says gently. "You're not the same person, Ana. I think the fact that you're so worried about being a bad mother means that, truthfully, you're probably more likely to be a *good* one. You want this baby to have a good life. You want to make the right choice for you and for this child. You're already a good mother, Ana, because you're putting so much thought and effort into that. And whatever that means—going back to Manhattan and doing it on your own or staying here with Liam—you'll make that choice with your baby's best interests in mind as well as your own. But," he adds, grimacing, "I will say that I don't think you should go back to Paris with Alexandre."

"No!" I shake my head emphatically. "I'm not going to do that. I've already told Alexandre we're done—that I can't raise a baby with him. What was between us—I've tried to do what you said and held on to the good parts, the parts I needed while letting go of the rest and moving forward. I didn't expect him to come here after me. But what we had together can't turn into this. It just can't."

"I'm glad you've come to that understanding." Max hesitates. "Do you love Liam, Ana?"

The question is plain and simple, and I know the answer the moment I hear it.

"Yes," I answer, just as simply. "I do."

"He loves you." Max looks at me kindly. "I would give him a chance to show you that he can do what he says, Ana, and love you both no matter the true parentage of your child. After all, Joseph loved a child that wasn't his, and the world was better for it."

"I'm no Virgin Mary," I say with a laugh, and Max chuckles.

"No, that's true. And I'm not here to deliver a sermon to you, just as I'm not here to take your confession. I'm here to listen, and that's all. But Ana—"

"Yes?"

"I believe that Liam means what he says. I believe that given a chance, he will do everything he can not to make the same mistakes his father did. And that includes loving this baby, no matter what."

I feel tears rising up again, clogging my throat and burning behind my eyes, and I can't speak. I just nod, and Max reaches out, squeezing my hand.

"If you need anything, I'm here," he says gently. "Just a phone call away, for either of you."

"Thank you," I whisper.

It's barely noon, but I get into the bath anyway once Max leaves. I feel exhausted, aching all over from the stresses of the last twenty-four hours, and I sink into the hot water, closing my eyes.

I don't want to leave Liam. New York, the place I'd called my home for so long, feels a million miles away. *This* feels like my home now, not just Boston, but this penthouse, this space that I've shared with Liam. The thought of leaving it breaks my heart every bit as much as when I'd had to leave the apartment I'd shared with Sofia, the last real home I'd had.

I love Liam. Down to my bones, I know it's true. I haven't been able to tell him yet, by his own request, but I've known it for days, weeks even, and yesterday's events only confirmed it for me. The feelings I'd had for Alexandre—the feelings I still have, in a way—are a thing of the past. They belong to another girl, another Ana, just as the life I'd lived before the tragedies of the last few months belongs to another girl, too.

Here, in Boston, it feels like I've started a new chapter, a new life. I can't go backward. I know that for sure.

All that's left is to figure out how to go forward.

I lay in the bath for a long time, running through everything in my head. What finally jolts me out of my thoughts is the sound of my phone ringing. I sit up, water and suds sloshing as I reach for it, hoping it's Liam calling me to tell me he's coming back home early.

It's Caterina instead, and I answer it quickly.

"Cat?"

"Hey, Ana. Don't be upset at her for this, but—Sofia talked to me."

I have a brief pang of hurt. I would have wanted to decide when to tell Caterina myself—but I understand, too. Without me there, Cat is all Sofia has besides Luca. If Luca and Viktor are upset with Liam's relationship with me, I know it's probably put a strain on Sofia and Luca. I can't blame her for wanting to talk to Cat—especially since this affects Cat and Viktor, too, via Liam's alliance with them.

Not for the first time, I wish more than anything that Liam was just a normal man. Not an Irish King, not part of a huge crime family—just a man who could choose to be with me and not have so many consequences arise because of it. Someone who could make choices freely without having so many things to consider.

"Ana?"

"I'm here." I clear my throat. "She told you the—um—news?"

"Yes." Caterina laughs a little nervously. "I want to say congratulations, but I'm not sure that's the right thing to say under the circumstances."

"I don't know if I feel like it's something to celebrate either," I admit. "But it's happened, and Liam has promised me he wants us both. So we're going to figure this out together—"

"Is that the decision you've made?"

I hesitate, feeling suddenly put on the spot. "I—we still have to talk some things out, but I think yes, that's the decision we want to make—"

"Ana, come back to Manhattan." There's an almost pleading note in Caterina's voice as she says it that startles me.

"I—I think I want to stay here. I feel at home here, and Liam—"

"I know Sofia mentioned to you that Luca and Viktor are upset with the situation."

"Well, yes, but—"

"Ana, I love you. I consider you a dear friend. But I need you to listen to me carefully. Sofia won't tell you things as plainly as I will because she's your best friend, and she wants you to be happy, no matter what. She encouraged Liam to go after you. She's encouraged this relationship all along because she thinks the two of you are good for each other—and maybe that's true. But Ana—that's all that this relationship is good for. The two of you."

The water in the bath is still warm, but I suddenly feel terribly cold. "That's all it needs to be good for," I say faintly. "The two of us. Me and Liam."

"In this life that we live, Ana, that's not true. When it first started, Viktor's and my marriage wasn't good for either of us. I hated him, thought he was beneath me and didn't even want him to touch me. He was infuriated by me. We fought, we didn't get along, it wasn't a good match—but we married each other because it was best for *others*. For Luca's interests and the people who depend on him, for Viktor's interests and the people he's responsible for. Terrible things happened because of it, but good things came of it too, Ana. And now our marriage has turned into one of love. In this world, Ana, marriages don't start out that way. It doesn't matter that Liam loves you and not Saoirse. She's what's best for—"

"Don't you dare say she's what's best for him. You don't know that—"

"I do."

"Did Viktor tell you to say this?" I can feel my throat closing over again, anxiety and fear rising up to clog it.

"My opinions and Viktor's are aligned in this, Ana. You've been through so much already. If you stay with Liam and he keeps pushing forward to be with you instead of marrying the woman he promised to marry, it could have far-reaching consequences. He's putting himself and you in danger by continuing this relationship. Please, Ana, just come home."

I wrap one arm around myself, fighting back the tears. "I don't know if Manhattan is home anymore—"

"You have people here who love you. Sofia, me—"

"This doesn't feel like love. This feels like an intervention."

"Sometimes that's love," Caterina says gently. "Ana, Luca and Viktor aren't going to back Liam on this. The Kings aren't going to stand for him setting Saoirse aside. They care about business, loyalty, alliance, and promises Liam has made. His father was a traitor, and they are looking for those signs in him too, always watchful. If Liam goes against the other Kings, he won't have any backup. Luca and Viktor will stand with the alliance, not with him. Saoirse is practically Kings' royalty, Ana, Irish through and through, the eldest daughter of one of their most preeminent families. That she marries Liam and makes little McGregor/O'Sullivan babies is what matters to them. Not Liam's feelings, not yours, not love or desire. Duty. Keeping his word."

"He made promises to me, too," I whisper. "What about those?"

"The promises he made to a Russian girl of no consequence mean nothing to them," Caterina says, and her tone is gentle, but her words slice at me like knives. "I'm not trying to be cruel, Ana. To the people here who love you—to Sofia, to me, even Sasha, you mean everything. But to these men, you are nothing. They could kill Liam before they see him with you. Marrying you means that your child will inherit—*this* child, if it's a boy. If they believe the child is Liam's, they will see a half-Irish, half-Russian child as the future of the Kings. They won't stand for it. And if they think for even a second that there's a chance the child *isn't* Liam's?" Caterina sighs. "Oh, Ana, it will make everything so much worse."

"Liam is going to claim the baby as his. No one has to know that there's a possibility it might not be. To everyone else, this baby *is* Liam's, unquestionably—"

"Things have a way of getting out. Ana, everything about this is wrong. Everything about it is as likely to get Liam, and even you killed as work out—more likely, even. Please, please, just come back to New York—"

"I can't," I whisper, and I know that I mean it down to the very depths of my soul. "I can't leave Liam. Since the day I met him in Russia—there's been something there. I can't ignore it or walk away from it. He saved me and brought me here, and it's been healing me, one step at a time. I think this is where I'm meant to be, Cat, who I'm meant to be with. He crossed an ocean, countries, a continent to find me. I can't abandon him now."

I take a deep breath, closing my eyes. "I'm sorry, Cat. I hear what you're saying. But Liam's mind is made up—and mine is too. I love him. I'm staying."

I hear her intake of breath as she starts to speak, but I don't wait to hear what she's going to say. I end the call, dropping the phone to the tiles as the magnitude of what I've done, what I've chosen, begins to sink in.

My hands cover my face, and I lean forward, curling in on myself in the cooling water.

And then, all alone in the luxurious bathroom, I start to cry.

TWENTY
LIAM

Once I'm back in the car, all of the anger I'd forced down while talking to Graham comes rushing back to the surface, heating my blood. There's nothing I can do about Graham other than refuse his demands. I can't fight him. I can't hurt him. I can't remove him from the table, not yet. I can't *do* anything, and the sheer helplessness of the situation, the fact that I could stand before the table and tell them that I choose Ana and still have them rise against me, has me so furious that I desperately need some place for my anger to go.

Usually, I'd take it out in the boxing ring. But today, that anger *does* have somewhere to go. And it narrows in on one man—the one person I do have the power to do something about.

Alexandre.

I give Ralph the name of Max's hotel and reach for my phone, dialing Niall's number. "Meet me at Max's hotel room," I tell him. "The three of us need to talk."

I'm not sure, exactly, what it is I plan to do at first. But as the car winds through traffic, I can feel it all coalescing into one firm point, one idea that I can't shake.

Alexandre needs to die. As long as he lives, he's a threat to Ana and now to the child that could biologically be his. I feel that I have very little control over anything right now—but that I can control.

That, I can do something about.

I don't know exactly why I chose to go to Max's. Maybe some small part of me hoped that he would talk me out of what I planned to do, that he would be my conscience. Niall and Max, the devil and angel on my shoulders, respectively.

I know what Niall would say. And maybe I'm hoping he'll convince Max of the course I'm choosing, so that I can have both of the men I trust at my back.

"The look on your face tells me you're not here for a drink and a chat," Max says when he opens the door of his room. "I talked to Ana earlier today—"

"I'm not here to talk about Ana. I'm here about Alexandre."

"Oh." Max frowns. "Liam, maybe we should sit down and talk about this—"

"We'll talk when Niall gets here."

Niall arrives only a few minutes later, motorcycle helmet in hand and looking as unflappable and composed as always. "What d'ya need, Liam?" he asks, setting the helmet on the side table and leaning against the couch. He looks at my face, taking in my grim, angry expression for a moment. "Are we paying someone a visit?"

"Aye. Alexandre."

"Ah. Well, he's about due for one, I'd think." Niall smirks. "The priest coming along? He handled blood alright when it was time to do for Alexei."

"Let's think this through." Max looks slightly alarmed. "I know he's done terrible things, Liam, and I know you're angry that he's here again, trying to get to Ana. But think of *her* right now, Liam. Did she ask for this? She's the one who has suffered through all of it."

"No," I bite out. "She doesn't want him dead. But I'm doing her a favor by dealing with this, by eliminating him from the picture altogether. She doesn't see it now, but she'll realize it one day when we're not fucking *haunted* by him constantly. When we don't have to fear him stalking her or coming after our child. She's not asking me to do this, but I am making this choice. We can't live our lives with the specter of Alexandre following us everywhere."

"Did you come here for counsel or help?" Max asks bluntly. "Because that changes what I say to you next, Liam. You know I have your back in anything that I can do. But if you want my counsel—"

"Can it be both?" My voice is laced with irritation as I run one hand through my hair, feeling as if I'm nearly vibrating with anger from the inside out. "I made a mistake before, in Paris, going after Alexandre alone. I won't make that mistake twice. I'm not going into that hotel alone—I need men I trust at my back. You and Niall."

"You and I will do it on our own if we have to," Niall says sharply. "I'm with ya, Liam. Alexandre needs to die. He's done enough damage to you and yours."

"Killing him is a permanent solution—" Max starts to say.

"Aye, and that's why he's choosing it," Niall snaps back. "A permanent solution is what's needed here."

"I don't know if I'm the man you want at your back for this, Liam," Max says quietly. "I can't say what the right choice is."

"You've killed a man and helped cut the fingers off of another," I say flatly. "What's a little more blood?"

"A little more, and then a little more, and then there's a river of it," Max says. "But I told you I'm with you, Liam, and I meant it. I can't say I agree with your assessment of the situation, but if you truly believe this is the right path—"

"I do," I say firmly.

"Then I won't abandon you now." Max looks at me evenly. "Let's go find Alexandre."

"Aye." Niall steps forward, grabbing his helmet and opening the hotel room door. "After you, lad. Let's spill that blood."

It only takes one heavy knock for Alexandre to open the door. "Ah, Liam. And friends." He smirks. "I suppose I should invite you in."

"You don't look surprised," I observe. "Even though I've brought company."

"And we're not vampires, aye?" Niall growls. "To need to be invited in. We'll come in if McGregor says we do, and just now, he's decided that's what needs to be done."

"I knew you would come," Alexandre says, stepping to one side as I enter the hotel room, Niall and Max at my heels. "You pretend to be a gentle man for Ana, but at your core, you are a ruthless killer, just like all of the others. Luca, Viktor, Alexei, Vladimir, Levin, Kaito—you are all the same. Eager to shed blood over perceived slights, to claim what you believe is yours."

"How the fuck do you know about any of that—about any of them?" I narrow my eyes at him, feeling Niall bristling at my right. "So now you're not just stalking Ana, you're stalking me as well?"

Alexandre shrugs, a half-smirk curling one side of his lips. "I thought I should know more about the man who could take my little doll from me. I wanted to know, too, how it was that you found me. It wasn't hard to guess that the man who gave you the information that led you to me was Kaito Nakamura, who I made my last purchase from before I bought Anastasia from Alexei. All I had to do was pay Kaito a visit under the pretense of another acquisition and give him a handsome sum for what I wanted to acquire instead—information." He laughs. "He was happy to tell me about you, Levin, and Maximilian here, for a price that I was more than willing to pay. After all, I had already paid a hundred million dollars for Anastasia; I was willing to pay more to have her back."

He glances from me to Niall and Max and back again. "Kaito said to tell you, by the way, not to be angry with him—that he had told you the Yakuza have no loyalty but to themselves. He gave you information on me, and me information on you in return—fair is fair."

I grit my teeth angrily, but Alexandre isn't finished.

"From there," he says, the smirk still twitching on his lips, "it wasn't difficult to find out the rest of what I needed to know about you and your compatriots. Your identity, your family, your position—your *secrets*—I know it all, Liam McGregor. You should tell Anastasia the rest before she finds out on her own. Or have you told her already about your deceased half-brother?"

"You're obsessed," I snarl, taking a threatening step toward him. "Deranged. You're a madman—"

Alexandre shrugs. "Perhaps," he says coolly. "But I would have protected Anastasia better than you can. Loved her better, even. I kept no secrets from her by the time you came for her. She had all of me—the worst and the best. Can you say the same?"

"Enough of this." I reach for my gun in the holster at my back, beneath the blazer I have on, despite the heat of the day, meant to disguise exactly that. "I've heard enough, Alexandre—"

"Stop!" A feminine voice echoes across the room, thickly accented with French, and I know who it is without even looking.

"Call off your bitch, Alexandre," I growl, my hand on the butt of my own gun. "Now, before I shoot her first."

"I wouldn't try it," she says casually. "I'll pull the trigger before you can even get your gun free. There's a bullet pointed at your head right now, Liam."

My gaze flicks sideways, my blood running cold as I see that she does, indeed, have the drop on me. Only Alexandre had been in the room when we'd walked in—Yvette must have been hiding somewhere. We'd been so focused on him that none of us had seen her until it was too late, and now she has a gun pointed at my head.

Niall instantly reaches for his own weapon, and Yvette *tsks*, the click of the hammer sounding through the room.

"Don't even think about it," she says sharply. "You're the enforcer, right? You might draw fast, but I'll shoot before you do. Who will you work for then? Perhaps some third-rate gang might need you to chop heads for them. But it won't matter, actually, because you'll be dead." Her gaze holds steady on me. "You might as well have the priest say last rites for all three of you, because you won't be leaving here alive."

"Yvette, lower the gun," Alexandre says, and I glance sharply at him, shocked. "This is between Liam and me. I did not ask you to come in here, guns drawn. I am trying to convince Liam to handle this in a more civilized manner than *guns*, and then you—"

"Stop telling me what to do!" Yvette's voice rises a notch. "It's bad enough that you got your little Russian bitch *pregnant*; now you won't even let me protect you. *They* have no interest in being civilized, Alexandre, so why don't you just—"

A knock at the door startles all three of us, including Alexandre. "Who is it?" Yvette snaps, and for the first time, I see Alexandre look uncertain.

"I'm not sure," he says carefully. "If it is hotel staff, I will ask them to come back at a better time. Just—Yvette, hold your fire, please. This is not necessary."

He walks past me, Max and Niall, carefully, as if all three of us and Yvette were bombs that might explode at any moment. He opens the door, and I hear his sharp intake of breath. "What are you—no, this is not a good time. Anastasia!"

I hear someone push past him, coming into the room, and my stomach curdles. *Ana.*

"I came to talk to you, Alexandre, to ask you to please leave Boston, to please—"

Her words die off, and I pivot, unable to stay still. My hand is still at my back, though I don't draw my gun, counting on Yvette to be distracted enough not to shoot me. I have to see Ana, have to tell her to leave—

But I hadn't needed to worry about Yvette shooting me. The instant Ana barges into the room, her pointed chin tilted up as she speaks hastily to Alexandre, Yvette's focus swivels in a second. She turns, too, her pistol no longer pointed at me.

At that moment, every single person in the room is focused on Ana.

Including Yvette and her gun.

"Yvette, *no!*" Alexandre's voice is sharp, cracking through the air like the snap of a whip, but Yvette doesn't so much as falter. "Yvette, you will *not* hurt Anastasia. In fact, you will hurt no one here. We can have a civilized conversation about this—"

"No, we can't," Yvette says evenly, her gun still trained on Anastasia's head. "The time for civilized chats is passed, Alexandre. It passed when Liam came here, and you realized this little ballerina cunt was pregnant, and you let them *leave.*" She shakes her head in disgust, still keeping the gun level. "This girl has some hold over you, and there's only one way to put an end to this."

"Yvette, this is enough. You've lost your senses. Every decision I've made for and with *petit* has been my own. You are a part of my life—an important part—but you threaten that with your actions. I will not have you harming *petit*—or the baby. You threaten both Ana and our child with this—"

"*My* child," I growl angrily at Alexandre, but neither he nor Yvette appear to pay the slightest attention to me, focused entirely on each other and on Ana, who has gone bone-white with fright, her blue eyes wide and glimmering in her face.

"How the *fuck* do you think you can be a father, Alexandre?" Yvette spits, her face flushing red. "This girl was supposed to be a toy, a-a *pet*! But somehow, she got under your skin and into your head—both yours and Liam's heads, apparently," she adds, her voice laced with disgust. "I don't understand why or how. Look at her, the skinny, damaged little thing. She's *nothing*. But both of you—willing to sacrifice so much for her."

Yvette shakes her head, her finger sliding towards the trigger. "I'm going to do what no one else seems to be able to and put a stop to this once and for all. You'll all thank me for it, eventually, once it's done."

"*Non! Mon amie,* Yvette, *non!*" Alexandre's voice rises, his words a shout as he flings himself towards Yvette, as her hand twitches on the gun. Ana is frozen, visibly shaking but seemingly unable to move, but it doesn't matter. Alexandre lunging for Yvette is enough to throw Yvette off guard and delay her shot. Before she can recover, Alexandre wrestles her to the ground, her gun spinning away across the floor as he pins her down, his hands going to her throat.

I can hardly believe what I'm seeing. On my other side, Max goes for the gun that Yvette dropped, grabbing Ana and moving her away from the two figures tussling on the floor as Yvette tries desperately to get out of Alexandre's grasp. "*Mon amie, amour, non, non, s'il te plait*—"

Her words are strangled by Alexandre's fingers digging into her throat, and I see Niall start to move towards them, but I stop him, staring in horrified fascination. Yvette had blamed Ana for having a hold over Alexandre, but it was really her who had had a hold over him all along—egging him on, pushing him to depravity, to violence.

And now, in this final act of violence, I can see Alexandre breaking that hold.

At first, I think he's only going to knock her out. But as Yvette flails under him, grabbing and kicking and scratching, held down by the weight of Alexandre's body straddling hers and his hands gripping her slender neck, I realize that it's going much, much farther than that.

And I'm not inclined to stop it.

He's going to kill her, and I can't think of a single reason to save her, other than the fact that I'd like to do it myself. But asides from that, I can't think of any cause for Yvette to live.

"Alexandre—" Yvette chokes out his name, her eyes bugging as he tightens his grip. "Alexandre—*amour*—"

Her voice rattles, breaking off, and I can see the tendons in Alexandre's throat straining with the force of what he's doing, the sheer violence of it. It feels shocking to watch, even considering the things I've seen, intimate in a way that suggests none of us *should* be seeing it, this moment when Alexandre has finally snapped.

It feels as if it goes on forever, but in reality, it's only a few minutes. Yvette's struggling slows, then stops, her hands dropping away from Alexandre's arms and flopping heavily to the carpet at her sides. Alexandre doesn't let go for a moment, his shoulders heaving, his hands still locked around her neck.

Max is the first to speak up, stepping away from Ana and gingerly towards Alexandre. "It's over now, man," he says quietly. "You can let go."

The words seem to hang in the air, holding more weight than just the physical act of prying his fingers loose from Yvette's throat. Slowly, Alexandre takes his hands away, the prints of his fingers dark against her pale skin.

He gets up slowly, turning towards me as if to say something. But my rage boils up again because all I can think about is that evening when he'd forced me on Ana, when he'd let Yvette whisper in his ear and talk him into committing that heinous act that could have ruined Ana and I forever, and he hadn't killed her then.

Before he's all the way up from the floor, I'm already aiming at him, my gun pulled free of the holster at my back and leveled at his head.

"You're done," I growl at him, my voice rasping with anger as I step forward, not wanting to risk missing the shot. "I won't keep letting you get between Ana and me. Not now, and not ever again."

I'm so close to pulling the trigger—only a millisecond away. I can feel my finger twitching towards it, the blood rushing in my ears as I make the decision to end this once and for all—even in front of Ana.

I can't let it go on any longer.

And then I feel her, the slender weight of her flung into me as she screams my name. "Liam, stop!" Ana shrieks, grabbing for my arm and the gun as she throws herself against me. In the same second that my finger pulls the trigger, my arm is knocked to one side, the bullet going awry as Ana nearly knocks me into the nightstand next to the bed.

There's the heavy sound of a body falling, the dull thud of it on the carpet. For a brief moment, I'm afraid that I've hit Niall or Max, but when I look, it's Alexandre, crumpled and bleeding on the carpet next to Yvette.

The only thing I can't see is whether or not he's still breathing.

TWENTY-ONE
ANA

For one terrifying moment, I think Alexandre is dead.

He's on the carpet next to Yvette's dead body, bleeding from a gunshot wound in his upper chest, close enough to the shoulder that it might not have hit anything vital—but then again, it's impossible to know. I fling myself away from Liam, momentarily suspended between the two men as I have been all along. Then I'm on my knees on the carpet next to Alexandre, my hands pressed against the wound, trying to staunch the bleeding, to feel if he's still breathing, if his heart is still beating.

It is. I can feel the faint rise and fall of his chest, the faltering beat of his pulse in his throat as it sends the blood pumping out of the wound, and I feel as if I'm shattering all over again. I'd wanted to move on from my relationship with Alexandre, to start a new chapter, but I'd also known a part of me would always love him and what we'd shared. I didn't want him to *die*. I *don't* want him to die.

"Ana—" Liam's voice reaches me as he staggers up from where I'd knocked him into the nightstand, Niall helping him up.

"No!" I glare at him, tears streaming down my cheeks. "I asked you *not* to do this, Liam! I asked you *not* to hurt him! I wanted to *choose* you, but I can't make a choice if you've made yourself the only option!"

Liam stops in his tracks, pain etched over every feature as his eyes widen, locking with mine. "Ana, I'm sorry," he says. His voice suddenly contrite, but I'm already turning back to Alexandre, tears streaming down my cheeks as I feel his blood streaking my hands, hot and sticky between my fingers. Max moves between Yvette's body and Alexandre, reaching out to help me.

"We need to get him into the bed," Max says. "Someone grab cloths, hot water, anything you can find to stop the bleeding."

Liam is frozen in place, his expression startled, as if things had taken a turn he didn't expect. "Someone move, now!" Max snaps, and then he looks back at me. "Can you help me get him into bed, Ana?"

I nod, feeling dizzy, but determined not to let Alexandre die if I can help it. "I'll try," I say softly, but Niall is at my shoulder, gently steering me away.

"I'll do it, lass," Niall says in his raspy voice, his hand soft on my arm as he nudges me away from Alexandre. "It won't help him if he's jostled too much getting him up. Grab towels to keep the blood from getting on the bed, lass, and those cloths and water, if you want to help."

I nod numbly, stepping back as Max and Niall lift Alexandre up. He groans faintly with pain, a sound that goes straight to my heart as the two men step around Yvette's body, no one caring to move it as they carry Alexandre towards the bed.

I push past Liam, who grabs for my arm. "Ana, I'm sorry," he whispers. "I wanted to get him out of our lives. Every second I've spent with you since we were reunited, he's been there, haunting us. He's always fucking there, and I didn't think he would ever leave you alone, the baby—"

"No." I shake my head, pulling away. "You wanted revenge. At least be honest with yourself and me, Liam—"

"I wanted to protect you!"

"And I want to feel safe!" I stare at him, biting my lip hard against more tears. "But I also need to trust that you won't go behind my back and make my choices for me." I move away from him as he reaches for me again, shaking my head. "We'll talk about this later, Liam. I need to help Alexandre right now to fix what you've done."

Niall and Max are getting him settled in the bed when I come back with my arms full of hotel towels and a few hot wet cloths in my hand. Max is leaning over Alexandre, a vial of oil in one hand and his thumb swiping over the pale-faced man's forehead with the other, murmuring quietly. A few of the words drift towards me—*may the Lord who frees you from sin save you and raise you up,* and then a moment later, *Our Father, who art in heaven—*

A chill runs down my spine. "Is it that bad?" I ask quietly, my voice so hushed that it's hardly audible. "To need last rites?"

Max pauses, looking at me. "If I'm being honest, no," he says calmly.

"It's a sin to lie."I hand Max one of the wet cloths as I stack the towels on the edge of the bed, looking at Alexandre's pale face. I reach out to touch his hand, wincing at how cold it is, and Alexandre's eyes flutter open at the touch, glazed and pained.

Max smiles at me. "See? He's awake. It's not a lie. But I have seen in the past how such injuries can take a turn for the worse very quickly. I thought it best to do it anyway, as a precaution." Max's mouth twists in a wry smirk. "After all, considering what you and Liam have told me, I think his mortal soul is already in enough danger."

"*Petit,*" he whispers, and I try to force a smile, my hand still on his.

"Alexandre, I'm sorry—"

"Don't be." He winces as Niall cuts his shirt away to reveal the wound, being none too gentle as he yanks the cloth free. "Ah!" Alexandre groans as Max presses the wet cloth to the wound, wiping away and staunching the blood, reaching for a clean towel to help with the blood as he cleans the area.

"You're going to be okay," I whisper through tears. "I didn't mean for this to happen, I swear—"

"It's not your fault, *petit*. It's his," Alexandre says, narrowing his eyes. I turn to see Liam standing at the foot of the bed, his hands empty now, the gun put away. His face is drawn, as if he's regretting what he's done, only now it's too late.

He was right about one thing, this has all gone too far. More than anything else, I want—*need*—it to end.

"He isn't who you think he is, *petit*," Alexandre murmurs, sucking in another deep, struggling breath. "*Petit—*"

"Shh. Stop talking." I squeeze his hand, reaching out to pass Max another clean towel as he sets the bloodied ones aside. "Now isn't the time. You need to save your strength."

Alexandre smiles weakly. "I have almost no strength left, *petit*. But you must—" He takes a deep, rattling breath, his body convulsing slightly as his hand tightens around mine, his eyes fluttering shut with pain. "Ask him—ask Liam—ask him about—Franco—Bianchi."

He sags backward, his breathing evening out as he falls unconscious, leaving me standing there stunned with his words echoing in my head.

Franco Bianchi.

Those two words, that name, spoken aloud, is enough to make me freeze in place, the horrible memories rushing back in a tidal wave of remembered panic and pain that is nearly enough to knock me off of my feet. I can hear myself gasp, feel myself stumbling backward, but I feel like I'm somewhere else, like it's all happening to someone else, like I'm out of my own body. I feel my toes curling against the carpet, sharp phantom pains shooting through my feet at the memory of what Franco did to me, hot tears dripping down my cheeks.

No, no, no, not again, please stop, make it stop, no, no, no, no—

I don't realize I'm gasping it aloud until I feel Max's hands on the back of my arms, steadying me. "Ana, it's alright," he says, his voice low and calming. "Franco isn't here. He's dead, Ana. He's still dead. He can't hurt you anymore."

The room feels like it's tilting. I look around for something, anything to ground me. I see Liam still standing at the foot of the bed, his face pale and stark against his reddish auburn hair and beard, looking as if he's been stabbed in the heart.

"What is he talking about?" I whisper through tears, looking at Liam. "What is Alexandre talking about?"

I've never seen a man look as defeated as Liam does in that moment as if his world is falling apart around him. "I'll tell you everything," he says quietly, like a man beaten. "But not here. We'll go home and talk."

"What?" I whisper, staring at him. It feels like an ocean has opened up between us, miles separating us instead of the inches between the side of the bed where I'm standing and where he is at the foot. "What do you mean?"

"Ana, please." Liam looks miserable. "Just come home with me, and I'll tell you. I don't want to talk about it here."

"Go with him, Ana," Max says gently. "I'll stay with Alexandre for now, until he's stable again—for your sake," he adds. "Not Alexandre's. Liam can give me the contact for his doctor, and Niall can help with Yvette's body. We'll deal with everything here."

There's a groan from the bed as Alexandre briefly comes back to consciousness, and we all turn nearly as one to look at him. "I heard you giving me—last rites—" he manages hoarsely, looking up at Max. "Are you really a priest?"

Max frowns. "I used to be," he says flatly. "But any layperson—"

"I know that." Alexandre's jaw clenches against the pain. "What did you do, Maximilian? Kaito and I talked about it, you know. He had theories." Alexandre laughs, a thick, pained sound. "The fallen priest. Was it love? It usually is—love or hate."

Max hesitates. "It was revenge," he says quietly.

"Ah, so love." Alexandre pauses, clearly out of breath from saying so much, and I cut in quickly.

"Alexandre, you need to rest. This doesn't matter—"

He ignores me, though, still focused on Max. "Was it a woman?" Alexandre asks with some difficulty, though a small smile is playing at the corners of his lips. "It couldn't be, though. You were a priest. You have never loved a woman."

"It was my brother," Max says, his voice still quiet, and I look at him, startled. He's never said so much about it before. I wonder why he's chosen now, if it's because he feels some kinship with Alexandre, if he understands the lengths that someone can go to, the things he'll do, and sacrifice for someone he loves. "But I have loved a woman," he adds wryly. "Two, in fact. Love can come without physical intimacy, you know."

"I am a Frenchman," Alexandre says with one eyebrow raised. "So no, I do not know." He goes quiet for a moment, his jaw working as pain blooms across his face again. "What happened to them?" he asks. "Talk to me, Maximilian, so I don't pass out again."

Max glances at Liam and me, the tension still hovering between the two of us, and then back at Alexandre. "The first one," he says quietly, "I was wise enough to know that someone else could love her better and when to let her go. And the second—" Max hesitates. "I've broken every vow but one," he says finally. "And I hope the distance will keep me from breaking the last."

"A man who is truly in love will break *every* vow," Alexandre says, his gaze flicking to Liam, who is still standing at the foot of the bed, looking at Alexandre as if he'd like to kill him still, here and now. "Except the one he's made to the woman he truly loves."

Alexandre's head turns towards me, and his hand slides forward, seeking out the tips of my fingers as his eyes find mine with something like pleading in them. *"L'amour s'en va comme cette eau courante,"* he whispers. *"L'amour s'en va, comme la vie est lente, et comme l'Espérance est violente."*

The room goes completely silent as he speaks, Niall at Liam's side as Max stays by mine and Alexandre's, all of us watching him. I can feel tears sliding down my cheeks all over again, silent and warm on my skin as the whispered French takes me back to Alexandre's library in Paris. I can almost smell the firewood, hear the crackling in the fireplace, taste the rich port on my tongue.

"All love goes by as water to the sea," Alexandre murmurs, repeating the poem he'd once read to me in English on that romantic night in Paris. *"All love goes by, how slow life seems to me."* His fingers tense against mine. "Look at me, Anastasia," he whispers. My gaze has dropped to our hands, and I can't bring myself to look at him, the tears dripping off of my cheeks onto our fingers, and yet he doesn't move his away. I know the next line, and even as he says it aloud, I can't bring myself to meet his eyes. I can't.

"How violent the hope of love can be."

"Apollinaire," Max says quietly. "I know his work."

"A priest as cultured as a Frenchman," Alexandre smirks, a look I know so well. "How pleasant. It will be a pleasure to have you at my side tonight, as I wait to see if I will make it until the morning."

"Ana, please." Liam's voice floats towards me, as cracked and pleading as Alexandre's now. "Let's go home, so we can talk. We *need* to talk."

I lick my lips and taste salt. "You read me another poem, too," I whisper to Alexandre, still unable to meet his eyes. *"Tomorrow, at dawn,"* I start to recite, the words catching in my throat as I try to say it through my tears. *"at the hour when the countryside whitens, I will depart. You see, I know you wait for me. I will go through the forest and over the mountains."*

"*Petit,*" Alexandre whispers because he knows the last line as well as I do—better, even. How many nights had he read that poetry in his library, alone, wishing for someone to recite those words to, someone to make them come to life?

I had been that person for a little while. But I know, to the depths of my soul, that I can't any longer, even as my heart cracks apart once again with the knowledge. In the weeks between loving Alexandre and leaving him, I have felt my heart break over and over again. But I know, too, that he can't be the one to heal it.

I cannot stay far from you any longer, the last line goes. But when I finally raise my eyes to Alexandre's, looking at him and seeing the grief and pain written across his face, that's not what I recite.

"I cannot stay with you any longer," I whisper.

His hand flinches back, the realization of what I've said filling his eyes as they glisten, and he looks away. "*Petit,*" he murmurs. "Anastasia—"

But I'm already turning away from him, walking towards Liam. "Let's go," I say quietly to him, and then without waiting, I walk out of the hotel room.

TWENTY-TWO
LIAM

I've never felt so completely, utterly defeated as I do at that moment. Even as Ana and I get into the car together to go back to the penthouse, I can feel her slipping through my fingers, as if I'm already losing her. I'm very afraid of what telling her the truth about Franco will mean for us, what will happen when I do. And yet, I feel angered too, hurt by hearing their whispered words to each other, the evidence that they'd loved each other spoken right in front of me.

There's so much hurt in my history with Ana, so much pain and so many secrets, and so much of it is because of Alexandre. Even this, the secret of who Franco was to me, I might never have had to tell her if not because of him.

I wait to say anything about it until we're in the penthouse. The silent car ride only builds the tension between us until we finally walk into the living room, the city lights outside of the glass doors illuminate the room, and Ana and I face each other.

"What was that in the hotel?" I ask, trying to keep the accusation out of my voice. "That–poetry."

Ana looks as exhausted and utterly defeated as I feel. She reaches up, pushing her blonde hair out of her face and over her shoulders, and she looks out towards the view of the city as she wraps her arms around herself, her voice quiet and tired. "There was a night in Paris," she says softly. "When we started to fall for each other, I think. It was after his punishments, when he started to trust me again, to forgive me–"

"Forgive you?" My voice is hoarse, angry. "Ana, I don't want to hear about his ridiculous ideas of punishment and forgiveness again or how he treated you so terribly–"

"Liam, if you want to know, if you're going to ask questions, then let me tell you." She looks up at me with those sad blue eyes. "If we're going to get all of this out tonight, whatever secrets are left, if you're going to tell me yours, then let me tell mine too in the way I choose to."

My jaw clenches, but I nod. "Alright," I say quietly, and she lets out a long breath.

"He cooked me dinner, and we ate at the table together. It felt special, like a new beginning for us. I thought that I would never leave. I didn't think you were coming for me–I didn't think *anyone* was coming for me, Liam. I wanted to be happy. I wanted to feel safe. It was *all* I wanted, and if there was a chance Alexandre could give me that, if I could find something in him to love–"

She bites her lower lip, looking outside again. "After dinner, we went upstairs to the library. We drank port by the fire, and he read me French poetry. It was–it was romantic. It was the best thing that had happened to me in a long time. It was the night before he took me on a date, before we made–we slept together for the first time, and he told me about his past, about the terrible things that had happened to him, too. We fell in love in those two days, and those were the poems he recited to me tonight. But Liam–"

Ana takes a breath, looking at me. "Didn't you hear what I said? I changed the last line. *I cannot stay with you any longer.* But now–" She shakes her head, swallowing hard. "I don't know if I can stay with you, either."

"Ana–"

"I found a way to be happy again in Paris," she says sharply. "After some of the worst things that can happen to a person happened to me, things that broke my body and my spirit and my mind, I found a way to be happy with Alexandre, a kind of kinship and love between the two of us–an *understanding*, even if it was rooted in pain. I won't be judged for finding that or what I did for it. And then I had it taken from me."

"I *saved* you, Ana–"

"I know." She cuts me off. "I know you did. I know there was no real future for Alexandre and me. I thought that maybe–maybe I'd found that chance for love and happiness again, with you. Better, even–a real love, an equal love, a partnership. But maybe you were right when you said that Alexandre ruined us before we ever had a chance."

I can't stop myself. Her words feel like knives in my heart. I stride forward, closing the space between us in two steps as I grab her upper arms, pulling her against me as I look down into her pale face, her glistening blue eyes.

"I don't believe that," I tell her sharply. "How can you believe it after everything we've shared?"

Ana wrenches herself away from me. "Maybe it was just lust." She won't meet my eyes, and I shake my head.

"It wasn't." I can hear the desperation leaking into my voice. "You *know* it wasn't, Ana! Be honest with yourself and me, at least. You know I love you, I know that you–"

"Is it love if you're keeping secrets from me?" Ana rounds on me, her voice rising. "Can it be love? What else are you keeping from me, Liam? First Saoirse and now this–how did Alexandre know about Franco? What does that have to do with you?"

I can feel the room closing in around me, my throat choking with emotion. I don't want to tell her or watch as the truth splinters apart everything we are to each other. And yet now I have to.

"Alexandre stalked me," I say harshly. "He went to the same people I went to in order to find him, the Yakuza, to get information on me. He dug into my life, my family, my business–and not just mine. Luca's, Viktor's–anyone that has anything to do with me. He's deranged, Ana, obsessed with you, and he–"

"That doesn't answer my question," Ana says flatly. "You mentioned Franco once before, on the plane here. You knew him somehow. What does Franco have to do with you?" She shakes her head, biting her lower lip as she walks close to the doors, looking out over the city. "It doesn't make sense," she says softly. "How something about Franco and you could be this huge secret. He was Italian mafia, Luca's underboss."

She turns back to face me, confusion written plainly across her face. "What was it, Liam? Were you close with Franco? Were you friends?"

I shake my head, and I can feel tears burning in my eyes. I look at Ana, wanting to memorize her at this moment, to remember her in these last seconds before I say the words that could sever her from me forever. Words that I know will change everything between us forever.

Even exhausted and sad, she looks more beautiful to me than any other woman I've ever seen, illuminated by the Boston lights, ethereal in the dimly lit room.

"I love you," I whisper helplessly. "I love you, Ana, like no one else in this world–"

"Liam." Her expression is implacable, and I know the moment has come. I can't escape it any longer.

"Franco and I weren't friends," I say quietly.

"Then what, Liam? Please, just tell me the truth–"

I swallow hard, and I feel a tear fall from one eye, sliding down my cheek as the words spill from my lips, hanging between us in the silence of the living room.

"We were brothers."

TWENTY-THREE
ANA

For a moment, I can't breathe. I can't think. I feel as if the room is spinning, as if everything has come to a screeching halt, my heart cracking open with the pain of this new information that I can't bring myself to actually believe.

"That can't be true," I whisper. "I don't believe it. Franco wasn't even Irish–Sofia told me about his family, his mother–"

Oh god.

I remember it then, Sofia telling me about how Luca and Franco were so close because he'd protected him from bullying as a child– bullying that had come about because of Franco's red hair, because of rumors that his mother had cheated with the Irish King when he was in the Rossi territory on business, and that Franco had been the result.

"No," I whisper, shaking my head as my eyes fill with tears. "No, Liam–"

"I didn't have a relationship with him, Ana. I didn't even know him until we were both adults. My father didn't even acknowledge him as his son for most of his life. But my father wanted to take over the Rossi's territory. He got greedy. He wanted to use his friendship with Don Rossi and then Luca's trust to partner with the Bratva and infiltrate them. He was in talks with Viktor Andreyev, but my brother

Connor pushed back against it. He said it was wrong, that he wanted no part of it, that the Kings he planned to inherit wouldn't lie and cheat and betray to expand their territory. I was at the table by then, old enough to be a part of things even if I had no real rank, and when my brother fought with my father over it and then disappeared, I thought he would turn to me next."

"But he didn't." My voice is flat, my heart aching in my chest. Out of everything I've ever imagined happening, I never considered this. It's more horrible than anything I could have thought of.

"No." Liam swallows hard, his Adam's apple bobbing. "He went to Franco. He promised Franco the inheritance of the Kings if he would betray his friendship with Luca and use it to work with Viktor to take over the Italian territory. My father had bartered with Viktor that they would share it, but he intended to betray the Russians too and take it all for himself. It was a huge, greedy play that might not even have worked. But then you and Sofia–" Liam breaks off, because he knows as well as I do that he doesn't need to say the rest. I know very well what happened after that.

I'll bear the scars of it for the rest of my life.

"It ended with both Franco and my father dead, my brother missing and unable to be found, and me the only McGregor left to rule. That's how I ended up at the head of that table, Ana. The default son. The one my father called a changeling, blamed for my mother's death, forgot about for most of my life. He chose his bastard son over me, and *still*, I ended up ruling. And yet–I've been willing to risk it all for you, Ana, because *I love you*–"

I hear him, I hear the pleading in his voice, and yet I can't. All I can think about is what Franco did to me, that Liam *knew* about that and kept the secret anyway.

"Why didn't you tell me?" I whisper brokenly. "On the plane, why didn't you tell me then? In the hotel when you saw my feet? Why didn't you tell me literally *any* time that Franco came up, instead of keeping it a secret from me–"

"I couldn't!" Liam's eyes are full of tears, his hands clenched at his sides. "I couldn't tell you, Ana. I've lost too much–first my brother to my father's plans, and then my father himself. Franco took *everything* from me. I couldn't let him take you too, to keep tearing me apart from beyond the grave–"

"He took everything from me, too!" The words tear from my lips in a shriek, the sound of my scream making Liam step back, startled as the blood drains from his face. "He took everything from *you*? You rule one of the biggest crime families in America, you have this penthouse, you have–" I gasp, the words catching in my throat. "He took everything from *me*. Everything. Everything that's happened to me has been in one way or another because of him, because of what he did to me. My career, my mind, my strength, my body, *everything*. And now this–I wish I'd died," I gasp brokenly, staring at Liam with my own fists clenched, a fine tremor running through me. I'm crying again, hardly able to breathe, feeling as if I'm crumbling to dust.

"I wish he'd fucking killed me," I whisper brokenly. "Because I've had enough. I've lost everything and almost everyone that matters to me. Now *you*–the man I thought I was falling in love with, *in* love with even, that I thought I could build a life with and start over with, I find out has been lying to me from the start." I shake my head, wrapping my arms around myself as I feel a chill settle over me, crawling down my spine and into my blood. "I would tell you to go find Saoirse," I whisper painfully. "But honestly? Saoirse deserves better, too."

I can see those last words strike him, making him physically flinch back. Liam is crying, too, soundlessly, tears sliding down his face as he looks at me.

"I'm so sorry," Liam whispers, and he tries to take a step closer to me. I put my hands up, warding him off, and he stops in his tracks. "I didn't want you to be reminded of Franco every time you looked at me," he whispers helplessly. "I couldn't bear the thought of it, Ana."

"You're reminded of Alexandre every time you look at me." I throw my hands up, staring at Liam. "We see the worst things that have happened to each of us reflected in each other." My voice breaks as I say the words, my heart splintering. They feel so final, the final admission of how ruined we are for each other. "We're each other's worst kind of mirror."

Liam shakes his head fiercely, and this time he does step towards me, a hand's length between us as he looks down at me, his face taut and full of pain.

"I don't see Alexandre when I look at you," he says, his voice a tortured whisper. "I only see the woman I love. The woman I want to fight for, even now. All I want, Ana, is for you to see me too, for you to love *me*. Ever since I met you, you've made me want to fight for more than I ever, ever knew I could have. I was wrong to keep secrets from you–but every single one I kept, Ana, I kept to protect you. To protect *us*." He's a breath away from me now, close enough for me to feel the heat of his body, the tension coming off of him in waves.

"What Alexandre made me do to you broke me, Ana, in ways I never knew I could be broken. But you?" He reaches out, his fingers brushing over my cheekbone, and I shudder at his touch, my eyes fluttering shut. "You, Ana, are the only one who can shatter me completely–and the only one who can put me back together again."

I open my eyes and look up at him, this handsome man who I've come to love so much, who has torn me apart and put me back together in a dozen different ways. "It's bad luck to break your mirror," I whisper, and Liam smiles the tiniest bit, his full lips quirking up on one side.

"I'm Irish," he says quietly. "I'm supposed to have luck in spades."

"I'm not, though."

Liam looks at me sadly, his fingers still brushing against my face. "I've never felt lucky a day in my life, Ana–not until I walked into that gloomy Russian safehouse and saw your face. It was like the sun came out that day. I knew then–I knew I needed you."

"I was broken when you met me." I shake my head, pulling away a fraction from his touch. "*Franco* broke me. Your *brother*."

"He was never my brother!" Liam shakes his head fiercely, reaching for my hands. "He might have shared a bloodline with me, but that doesn't make him my brother. He was a coward and a traitor, and I'm *glad* he's dead for everything he did."

There's a moment of silence, hovering thickly in the air between us, and to my shock, Liam drops to his knees on the floor in front of me, still clutching my hands. "I'm so sorry, Ana," he pleads. "Forgive me. I'm sorry for the lies, the secrets, for keeping things from you. I know it was wrong, I *knew* it was–but I was afraid. I was weak, Ana, afraid of losing you. I see now that you're so much stronger than I knew, that you could have handled it, that I should have told you everything from the very beginning." He squeezes my hands, his bright green eyes shimmering, wide and begging me to understand. "I'm sorry for what's happened to you, Ana, for the part my family played in it. I'm sorry that Franco broke you, that he took so much away from you. If I could, I'd kill him for you. I'd kill Alexei with my own hands all over again, Alexandre too, if it would wipe it all away."

He's crying now, tears sliding down his face, as utterly broken as I am. "I'd die for you, Ana. I need you to know that–"

Something cracks open inside me, and I sink to my knees in front of him, my hands wrapping around his. We're both crying now, leaning into each other, and I reach out, cupping one side of his face in my hand. His beard feels soft against my palm, and I feel Liam lean into the caress, his green eyes fixed on mine. "Ana–"

"I don't need you to kill for me," I whisper. "I don't need you to die for me. I need you to be *honest* with me, Liam. I need you to *live*–to trust me. And I need–I need you to love me."

Liam's eyes widen at that, but before he can say another word, I grasp his face in both of my hands, my thumbs wiping at the tears on his cheekbones as I lean forward.

And then, tasting the salt on both our lips as I do, I kiss him.

TWENTY-FOUR
ANA

I feel Liam's gasp as I kiss him, the way the touch of my lips reverberates through his entire body. His hands go to my waist, his lips parting as I lean into him, and I feel the vibration of his groan as he surges forwards, his hands tightening on me as he spills me back onto the floor, the kiss turning savage as he stretches over me.

"Ana–Ana–" he whispers my name against my mouth, his hands tearing at my clothes, shoving my dress up as my lips part under the onslaught of his mouth. Every emotion comes flaring to life, pain and hurt, and longing and love all tangled together. His tongue plunges into my mouth, twisting with mine as I grab at his shirt, pulling it out of his trousers.

I hear the rip of chiffon as he drags my skirt out, feel the pop of buttons as I yank his shirt open, my nails against the smooth skin of his chest as he moans my name against my lips. I gasp his, too, fumbling with his belt, both of us a frantic mess of hands and mouths as we struggle past the layers of clothing between us.

There's no stopping now. He tears my panties off, his fingers hooking under the edge and dragging them halfway down my thighs, his hard cock between my legs in an instant as he surges against me, groaning with need. "I need you, Ana," he whispers against my mouth as I feel the head of his cock parting my folds, pushing against my entrance, "I need you—"

I cry out as he thrusts into me. He gasps with pleasure, groaning as I tighten around him, pulling him deeper, and my hands go to his face, his hair, tangling in the strands as I look up at him. "I need you too, Liam," I whisper as he rocks against me, thrusting hard and fast with an almost primal need. "Oh, god, Liam, Liam—"

He surges inside of me as deeply as he can go, and I lock my legs around his hips, my back arching as I feel the pleasure starting to unfurl, crashing over me. "I'm going to come, Liam—"

"Yes," he growls, his mouth slanting over mine as he slams his cock into me again, fucking me with a frantic, urgent pace that has us both on edge. "Come for me, Ana, come on my cock, *fuck*—"

I gasp, my nails digging into his back as I arch against him, and I hear the groan that tears from his lips. "I'm going to come too, Ana, *fuck*, I can't hold it back, I can't—"

"Liam!" I scream his name as I feel his cock throb inside me, his entire body shuddering with the force of his orgasm as it triggers mine, both of us grinding against each other to draw it out. "Liam—"

"Ana." He whispers my name against my mouth like a prayer as he shudders against me. "God, Ana—"

I feel him throbbing inside me, the hot rush of his cum filling me, my own pleasure rippling over my skin in seemingly endless waves. He goes very still atop me, his mouth against my neck, and I think for a moment that he's going to pull out of me. But then a beat passes, and another, and I feel him starting to move again, slower this time.

"Liam?" Startled, I look up at him, and he grins down at me, groaning softly as he reaches for my hands. He threads his fingers through mine, raising my hands above my head and holding them there against the cool hardwood of the floor as he starts to thrust, long slow strokes that let me feel every inch of his rigid cock inside of me.

"I'm still hard for you," he whispers. "This is how much I want you, Ana. You make me come harder than I ever have in my life, but I'm still rock hard. I still need to be inside of you, to make you come again, to fill you up until you're so full of my cum." He rocks his hips as he slides into me again, grinding against me as he sinks as deeply into me as he can. "I want to make you come over and over, give you as much pleasure as you can take, with my fingers and my tongue and most especially my cock." He thrusts again, hard, as if to emphasize his point. "I could spend the rest of my life like this, inside of you."

"Liam–" I breathe his name, tilting my head back for his lips against the side of my throat, feeling another orgasm start to build as he slides out of me and back in again. He feels as if he fits perfectly inside of me, as if his body were made for mine. I look up at him–at his handsome, chiseled face, the reddish beard glinting in the city light coming through the glass doors, the burnished auburn hair falling over his forehead. "Oh, Liam."

"You're mine, lass," he grunts, thrusting into me again, rocking his hips so that I can feel how solidly he is inside of me, filling me. "Mine always. I will not let you go, not ever. And I will not let harm come to you again, not ever. When I say I love you, Ana, I mean with everything that I am–with my body, my heart, to the depths of my soul. I will be yours. I *am* yours, before anything else."

I feel tears come to my eyes, swimming to the surface, but they're a different kind of tears this time. I tilt my chin up, looking into his eyes as he moves inside me. "I love you, Liam," I whisper, and I feel the shudder that goes through him as I say it. His eyes close, his hips jerking against mine as he thrusts into me again. "Open your eyes," I whisper, and he does, his green gaze fixed on mine with a kind of desperate hope that breaks my heart and heals it all at once. "I love you."

"And I love you." He kisses me again, deep and hot and fierce. I lose track of how many times we murmur it to each other as he thrusts inside of me, again and again, slow and inexorable as the pleasure builds for us both.

"Come with me, lass." he finally groans, his body shuddering atop mine. I meet his lips in another fierce kiss as I wrap my legs more tightly around his, pulling him against me and holding him there.

"Come *in* me," I whisper, and the tremor that rocks his body vibrates to my bones. He groans against my mouth, his hands tightening around mine. When I feel him harden even more inside of me, throbbing with the first wave of his orgasm, I cry out too, the sound lost in our kiss as we come together for a second time, my body clenching around his as he fills me. It feels better than anything I'd ever imagined, better than anything we've done before. I can feel him melting into me, our bodies liquid against each other as we cling to one another, shuddering as the pleasure wracks us both.

He stays inside of me even as he starts to soften, both of us panting. "You're going to have to do that every day," I tease him breathlessly. "Maybe twice a day, to make up for how long you made me wait for it."

Liam pushes himself up on both of his hands, leaning over me as he looks down into my eyes, his face filling with hope. "Are you going to stay then, lass? Do you forgive me?"

"I forgive you," I whisper, reaching up to touch his cheek. "But as far as me staying–" I slip out from under him, feeling the soft weight of his cock against my thigh as I move away, pulling my dress down around my hips as we both sit there on the floor, looking at each other. "We're not free yet, Liam. Alexandre is still here. You're still engaged. We don't know whose baby this is–"

"I meant it when I said I didn't care." Liam grabs my hand, looking into my eyes. "I meant it, Ana. All I care about is that you love me. I'll deal with Saoirse–I *have*. I've told her and her father both that I can't– that I *won't* marry her. All that's left is to tell the Kings my choice. And as for Alexandre–"

"I know I can't go back to him," I say softly. "But Liam–I *need* you to understand that he once meant something to me. What I needed at that time, in Paris, he gave me. In his own way, he saved me, too, even if it couldn't last. It was like a dream, some kind of strange dark fairytale, and I need you to find your peace with that, Liam. If I can make peace with Franco being your brother, with the secrets you've kept from me, then you can find a way to be at peace with the fact that Alexandre and I did share a certain type of love."

"A dark fairytale." Liam gives me a sad half-smile. "Does that make me the knight that saved you, then?"

I laugh softly. "Yes," I murmur. "I think you could say that."

"That makes Alexandre the villain," Liam points out.

"Every villain has a story too." I shake my head. "Liam, he's been punished enough. He's lost me and any chance of us having this child together. I've chosen you, Liam–that has to be enough. If Alexandre can let me go, then you *have* to promise me that you'll let Alexandre go, too–that you can put this behind you, behind *us*, and that we can move on. It's the only way this will ever work."

Liam is quiet for a long moment. Finally, he looks up at me, and he nods. "I'll do that, Ana. I'll put it behind me, I swear."

"Can you do that?" I search his face, trying to find the truth there. "You swear to me that you can?"

"Yes, Ana. For you, I would do anything."

And then his lips are on mine again, sealing the promise with a kiss.

—

We go back to the hotel together. When we walk into Alexandre's room, he's awake, propped slightly up on pillows, with Max sitting next to his bed. Alexandre's eyes widen when he sees me, and Max starts to get up to leave, but Alexandre puts a hand out to stop him.

"Please stay," he says quietly, and Max sinks back into the chair, glancing at us as he does so.

"Alexandre–" I start to speak, but he shakes his head.

"*Petit*, please, let me go first. You must at least give me this if you are going to say what I believe you are."

I hesitate, but Liam squeezes my hand, and I nod. "Alright," I say softly. "Go ahead."

"When the two of you left, *petit*, after I regained consciousness, Maximilian stayed here and talked with me, all through the night while the two of you were gone. And he has helped me to–understand some things."

Alexandre pauses, breathing with some effort, and I can see the pain on his face–whether physical or emotional or some mixture of both, I'm not entirely sure. "I love you, *petit*," he says quietly. "I know that you may believe I do not know real love any longer, but I assure you that I do. I wanted–" he pauses, swallowing hard. "It does not matter, though, not any longer. I love you, I love the child that we might have made together, but I also know now that you are right. There's no future for us, especially not with a child." He smiles sadly. "There might once have been that future for me, with the first woman I loved. Perhaps I could have had all of it–the wife, the house, the *bébé*, the life that Margot and I dreamed of."

"I'm sorry, Alexandre–"

"I was angry with you, *petit*, and I am sorry–sorry for taking it out on you. I was angry that you broke your vow not to leave me. I wanted to punish you for lying to me, to see you suffer the way I have suffered seeing you with *monsieur* McGregor, losing you."

I open my mouth to speak, feeling the pain of his words, his accusations cutting into me, but Alexandre puts up a hand.

"Please, *petit*, let me finish while I have the strength." He coughs, wincing in pain. "I no longer believe, *petit*, that you lied to me or that you deserve to suffer for leaving me. The good father–"

"Max is fine," Max cuts in. "I'm no longer deserving of that title."

"Maximilian has helped me understand that sometimes you make a vow out of necessity–knowing you will have to break it, no matter the cost." Alexandre looks at Liam as he says this and then back at me, his voice softening. "And sometimes you make a vow out of love, believing you will keep it–but sometimes you cannot."

I bite my lip, feeling tears come to my eyes. "Alexandre, I–"

"I see now that a broken vow does not always mean it was a lie. You can mean it, this promise you made, and still break it. I see that you could have loved me and wanted to stay and yet still had to leave in the end. You are, after all, not so broken as you once were. How could I keep you?" There are tears in his eyes too, and he motions for me to come closer.

I glance at Liam, who lets go of my hand and nods. That small gesture goes straight to my heart, because it means that he trusts me–trusts me to come back to him. To go to Alexandre and say our goodbyes, honor what Alexandre and I meant to each other, and return to my future once I've settled the past.

"I thought you were like one of my paintings," Alexandre says softly, when I'm sitting on the edge of the bed next to him. "Beautiful and damaged, forever changed by what happened to you. But now I see differently."

"What do you mean?" I whisper, and I feel the first tears dripping from my eyelashes as I grip the edge of the bed. "Alexandre, what are you saying?"

"I see now you are not those paintings, Anastasia. You are the Japanese vase instead, the one that I once paid Kaito Nakamura an obscene amount of money for. The Irishman you love has filled in all your cracks with gold, and you are stronger now because of it. Strong enough, even, to leave me behind."

"You filled in some of those cracks too," I whisper, crying softly now, my voice breaking. I can feel him letting me go, forgiving me as I forgive him, and it heals us both in a way that neither of us could have expected. When he reaches out to take my hands, I let him, feeling his long fingers enclose mine for the last time.

"I have learned something else from Maximilian's stories tonight," Alexandre says softly. "I, too, have loved two women–but it is the opposite for me. The first woman I loved, I still do, and the distance of time and the grave has not changed that. But the second–"

He reaches out, letting go of one of my hands to brush a tear off my cheek. "The second I see that I must let go of, because someone else can love her better."

I bite back a sob, looking into his crystal blue eyes as I reach out to touch his face gently. "I did love you, Alexandre," I whisper. "It wasn't a lie. I–" I take a deep breath, trying to hold back the rest of my tears. "I don't know if I'll choose to find out who the biological father of my baby is. But if I do, and it is yours, I promise you this." I press my hand against his smooth cheek, feeling him lean into the touch, his eyes closing as I lean closer. "I'll only tell them the good, Alexandre. I will only ever tell them about the beautiful, eccentric Frenchman who, in his own way, saved my life as much as Liam did. I promise you, that is one vow to you I will not break."

Alexandre's eyes open, and he reaches up to cover my hand with his. "No," he says softly, smiling at me. "If the baby is mine, when they are old enough, they should know it all–the good and the bad, the ugly and the beautiful, the cracks and the gold. It's all a part of me, Ana, and of you. All a part of our story. And while it lasted–"

He takes a deep breath, his eyes closing again momentarily before locking with mine as he takes my hand and brings it to my lips.

"It, too, was beautiful, *petit*."

His lips brush against my skin, cool and dry, and I can feel them linger a moment longer, as if he wants to memorize this one last caress. And then he lets go of my hand, letting it fall back to the blankets as his gaze holds mine one last time.

"*Au revoir, petit*," he whispers. "Goodbye, Anastasia."

TWENTY-FIVE
ANA

There are still tears sliding down my cheeks when Liam and I step out of the hotel room, and I half expect him to be hurt that I'm so upset. But instead, he turns towards me, brushing his thumb gently over where the tears have fallen, and tilts my chin up so that I'm looking into his eyes.

"I don't know if this is the right time to ask this, Ana," Liam says quietly. "But I think I need to know. Do you know what it is that you want?"

There's no hesitation in me. "Yes," I tell him firmly, looking up into his green eyes. "I know it might feel hard to believe right now, after what just happened, but I do know. That last moment with Alexandre was the closure I needed, and Liam–I want you. Forever."

"There may be more hard times to come," Liam warns me gently. "It won't be an easy path to us being together. But I want you too, Ana–and I'm willing to fight for us, whatever comes our way."

"I am too," I promise him, reaching for his hand.

"Then I want you to marry me."

I blink up at him, startled. "What? When?"

"Now," Liam says firmly. "I know this isn't a traditional proposal, and I don't have a ring, but nothing about the way we've done this has *been* traditional. I want to marry you now, Anastasia Ivanova, before something else happens or something else tries to stand in our way." He reaches out, taking my face gently in his hands, the smooth skin warm against my damp cheeks. "I want you to be my wife, Ana. It's all I've wanted since I found you again."

The door opens behind us, but I barely hear it. It's not how I'd imagined a proposal would be. Liam isn't down on one knee, there's no romantic location, no sparkling ring. I feel a little jealous, thinking of the oval diamond on Saoirse's finger, the grand church where he promised to marry her–but the feeling flees as quickly as it comes.

Liam was forced to sign that contract–in part because of his eagerness to find me–but no one is forcing him to stand here and say any of this now. We might be in a hotel hallway making hurried plans, but he's asking me because he loves me, not because anything else is forcing his hand.

"Yes," I whisper, and the way his face lights up makes every bit of it worthwhile. "Yes, I'll marry you, Liam."

"When is the date?" Max's voice comes from behind us, and we both turn to see him standing there. "Sorry I missed the proposal."

"Is Alexandre stable?" Liam asks, and Max nods.

"He's in rough shape, but he'll survive. The doctor you sent managed to get the bullet out and stitch up the wound nicely–he won't be going back to Paris for a little bit yet, but he will soon enough. Niall took care of Yvette's remains. She won't be coming back to haunt us. And you don't need to worry about Alexandre bothering you any longer," Max adds. "He was serious when he said we had a long talk. We talked for hours, in fact. And it clearly made a difference."

"You should probably call in that favor with Viktor sooner rather than later," Liam says wryly. "You clearly were meant to be a priest."

It's meant to be a compliment, but Max's face goes somber at that, his gaze flicking away. "Well," he says finally. "We'll see what Viktor can do for me."

"Who was the second woman?" I ask suddenly, looking at Max's shuttered expression. "The one you said you were keeping your distance from?" Based on what I saw when we were all in Russia, I have a glimmer of suspicion that it's Sasha. Though I know it's technically none of my business, I'm too curious not to ask.

"It doesn't matter," Max says firmly, as I'd thought he might. "She's unreachable for me, and that's as it should be." He glances at Liam. "I'm going to stay in Boston a bit longer to decide what I want to do next while keeping that distance. Who knows," he says with a faint grin. "Maybe I'll be here for the wedding once you set a date."

"The date is now," Liam says firmly. "Tonight. I want to marry Ana as soon as possible. Can you do it for us?"

Max looks slightly taken aback. "I'm ordained to perform secular marriages as well," he says slowly. "But I'm defrocked–you know that. If I marry the two of you, it will be technically legal, but not done properly in the Church. It won't be recognized–"

"That's fine," Liam says firmly. "I want Ana and I married, that's all. We'll confirm it with Father Donahue later, the next time we're in New York. Maybe we'll have a celebration afterward. But it's us being married, legally, that's the most important part right now–I don't want to wait, and neither does Ana," he adds, looking at me.

I nod. "I want to do it tonight, too," I tell Max, squeezing Liam's hand. "I don't want anyone to be able to separate us."

Max frowns. "Liam, can we speak for a moment?"

Liam glances at me, but follows Max halfway down the hall. I watch as they speak in low, urgent voices, a concerned look on Max's face as he says something to Liam, who shakes his head and replies, though I can't hear anything they're saying. I feel awkward waiting in the middle of the hall as they talk, but the conversation is brief, and Liam comes back to get me.

"What was that about?" I ask as we walk towards the elevator.

"Nothing," Liam says quickly. "Max had some worries about the marriage not being confirmed, that's all. But I told him it's nothing to worry about. We'll get Father Donahue to handle it sooner rather than later." He squeezes my hand as we ride down in the elevator, the driver already waiting for us at the curb. "I want us to be married, Ana. That's all."

I feel the same way. The Kings might be angry at him for the snap decision, but they can't force him to marry Saoirse if we're already married. And with us legally married, he will have a legal right to claim my child as his.

It solves a great many of our problems. Still, I also know it's being done out of love between the two of us, an affirmation of our relationship and choosing each other, which means more to me–and to him– than anything else.

Liam calls Niall on the way back to the penthouse, one hand still firmly holding mine, asking him to come to witness it and to bring two gold bands if he can get ahold of them.

"What should I wear?" I ask Liam as we head up, and he grins at me, pulling me close to him for an exuberant kiss.

"Anything you want," he tells me firmly, and I lean into him, my arms going around his neck as the kiss deepens.

After what happened between us earlier tonight, there's nothing left to stand in our way. All of our secrets are out in the open, and even now that they are–perhaps especially because of that–I know that there's no one else for me. Liam is willing to stand beside me no matter what, and I know that he's the one *I* want beside me, for better or worse, 'til death do us part. I know that he loves me, and I love him.

Love isn't everything, but it's the most important thing to me. And I believe that it is for Liam, too.

He's willing to risk everything to love me.

While he changes clothes and waits on Niall, I slip into "my" room, which doesn't feel so much like mine after nights of sleeping in Liam's bed as a place to store my things. I take a quick shower, washing the tears from my face and the flecks of blood from under my fingernails, blow drying my hair and brushing it until it falls smooth and straight like silk around my face and shoulders.

I put the emerald dress he'd bought me for our date and the matching jewelry, my skin flushing a little at the memory of what he'd done to me the last night that I wore this dress. It's a far cry from a traditional wedding dress, but it looks beautiful on me, and it's something that Liam chose for me himself. There's something fitting about it, too–the Russian girl dressed in Irish green, trading my Ivanova name for McGregor.

I don't bother with shoes, going barefoot up to meet Liam on the rooftop. It's a gorgeous night, the last hour before sunrise, the moon still glinting off of the dark water in the pool, and the city still lit up beyond the edge of the building. The air is warm with a faint breeze, and the world is quiet. Everyone else around us is still asleep in their beds, while Liam and I make our promises to each other in the last still hours before dawn.

When I get up to the rooftop, Liam, Max, and Niall are already there waiting for me. All three men are in suits, though Niall looks slightly less comfortable in his than either Max or Liam does. Liam looks as handsome as I've ever seen him, his burnished auburn hair ruffling lightly in the wind. When he sees me, the look on his face lights him up, his green eyes glowing with more joy than I've ever seen on his face.

I don't have a wedding dress or an engagement ring, a bridal party, or a bouquet–there's no wedding march or aisles of guests–but none of that matters. There's a strange, buoyant sensation filling me as I walk towards Liam, making me feel so light that it's almost as if I could float away, my heart racing in my chest with an emotion so strong that it brings tears to my eyes. I don't realize what it is until I'm standing in front of Liam, and he takes my hands, and I feel as if I could burst with the intensity of it.

It's been so long that I'd forgotten what this feeling was, but in the instant Liam's fingers slide through mine and I look up at him, I know.

I'm *happy*.

"You look beautiful," Liam whispers.

"So do you," I tell him, almost giggling as his hands tighten around mine, almost giddy with the joy of the moment.

Max clears his throat, and both Liam and I turn to look at him.

"Liam McGregor and Anastasia Ivanova," he begins, "have you come here to enter into marriage without coercion, freely and whole-heartedly?"

"Yes," Liam says firmly.

"Yes, I have," I echo, and Max smiles.

"Are you prepared, as you follow the path of marriage, to love and honor each other for as long as you both shall live?"

"I am," I say clearly, and Liam says it almost in unison with me. My heart leaps as I hear it, and Max hesitates slightly before speaking the next part of the marriage declaration, glancing between the two of us.

"Are you prepared to accept children lovingly from God and to bring them up according to the law of Christ and his Church?"

Liam's gaze goes instantly to my still-flat stomach, and I know what he's thinking. We didn't plan for this child, weren't even thinking of it, but he's already accepted this baby as his, whether or not it truly is, before Max ever said those words. He's told me already, more than once, but that doesn't lessen the rush of emotion I feel as he looks at Max without hesitation and answers clearly.

"I am," Liam says firmly, and I echo it.

Max smiles. "Now repeat after me, each of you–"

It feels like I'm in a dream as I stand there, facing Liam with his hands in mine, repeating the vows as Max recites them to us. *"I, Anastasia Ivanova, take you, Liam McGregor–"*

"I, Liam McGregor, take you, Anastasia Ivanova–"

"To be my husband–"

"To be my wife–"

"I promise to be true to you–"

"In good times and bad–"

"In sickness–"

"And in health–"

"I will love you–"

"I will honor you–"

"--all the days of my life."

"Do you have rings?" Max asks, and Liam glances at Niall, who digs quickly in his jacket pocket.

"They're not much," he says apologetically. "But it's what I could get, calling in a favor with a jeweler friend. Just plain gold bands–I hope they fit."

He holds out the box, and Liam and I each take out a ring–a wider, flat gold band for me to slip on Liam's finger and a narrower, rounded one for me. They're both plain, but to me, they look more beautiful than anything I could have imagined–because these rings will bind Liam and me together, a symbol of the promises we're making tonight.

My heart is racing as we repeat the exchange of rings after Max. "Liam," I whisper, reaching for his hand. "Accept this ring as a sign of my love and fidelity, in the name of the Father, and the Son, and the Holy Spirit." I slip the ring onto his finger, and it's the slightest bit tight, but it fits. So does mine, as Liam slides it down my finger, repeating the same words.

"Ana, accept this ring as a sign of my love and fidelity–"

His eyes lock with mine as he says *fidelity*, and I know he's thinking the same thing I am. We've never been unfaithful to each other, but up until now, we haven't each been exclusively the other's, either. Liam had to disentangle himself from his first engagement, and I had to grapple with my feelings for Alexandre. But tonight, as we promise love and fidelity to one another, the cool metal sliding over our skin, it feels as if all that has blown away on the warm summer breeze.

The sun is just starting to rise as Max looks at the two of us, painting the greying sky with brilliant strokes of purple and pink and yellow, the rising sun illuminating both of our faces as Max pronounces us man and wife.

Liam pulls me into his arms a second before Max tells him to kiss his bride, his lips already on mine as Max is saying the words. I arch against him, my arms going around his neck as Liam kisses me deeply, and I hear Niall whistle from the other side of Liam.

"I think it's time we left the two of them alone, eh?" Niall says to Max, grinning, and Max laughs.

"Congratulations, you two," Max tells us. "We'll be going. Niall, breakfast?"

"Sure thing. I know a diner–"

As the other two men leave, going down the steps to the penthouse and out of the building, Liam turns to me. His face is glowing as his fingers thread through my hair, pulling my mouth back to his.

"Should we go downstairs?" I ask him, and he grins.

"We can go down and do it in the bed if you want," Liam says slowly. "But I, personally, think we should have our wedding night right here."

"Morning, technically." I grin up at him, and he kisses me again, hard and firm.

"All the better. I love seeing you naked in the sunlight," Liam says. "And this is our private rooftop. No one will come up here."

His hand goes to the zipper of my dress as the sun slowly rises, and there's not a single part of me that's going to tell him no.

TWENTY-SIX
ANA

I t feels deliciously wanton in the best way to let Liam strip me naked on the rooftop, as the sun comes up above us, with the city all around us as if we're the only two people left in the world. I'd foregone wearing anything underneath it once again, and Liam's groan as the silk slithers over my bare skin to the warm surface beneath our feet is the most erotic thing I've ever heard. I pull off his jacket, tossing it to the ground as he yanks his tie free with one hand, my fingers making quick work of his shirt buttons as his hands slide over my bare skin, up to my breasts, where his fingers toy with my nipples as I undo his belt. I gasp with pleasure as his lips find my neck, his fingertips pulling and pinching at the stiff rosy peaks of my breasts as I arch against him, shoving his suit trousers down so that he's naked too, his hard cock springing free against my belly as he pulls me against him for another deep, ravenous kiss,

"I know exactly what I want to do with you," Liam murmurs against my mouth. "I've been dreaming about it for as long as I've had you here," he adds, and then he scoops me up into his arms, carrying me towards the sunken hot tub on the other side of the long rooftop pool.

He sets me on the edge, stepping down into it as the jets come on, the water foaming and bubbling around his hips as he comes to stand between my legs, spreading my thighs as one hand slides upwards, his other hand cupping the back of my head as he brings my lips to his. "I want to fuck you here," he murmurs against my lips. "But I'm going to make you come for me first. I want you drenched for me, Ana, so wet and wanting that you can't bear it any longer by the time I'm inside of you."

His fingers slide over my clit as he whispers against my mouth. I gasp, my lips parting for the onslaught of his tongue in the same instant that his fingers plunge inside of me, curling inside of my tight, clenching pussy as he kisses me deeply. The pleasure is sharp and instantaneous, bursting over my skin as he thrusts his fingers into me, his thumb finding my clit and rolling over it in the familiar sensation I know so well. "That's my good girl," he murmurs, sucking my lip into his mouth, his teeth grazing over the edge of it. "Come for me, Ana, let me feel you squeeze around my fingers–*fuck*, you're so wet already for me, god yes–"

I love how Liam talks to me during sex, encouraging me, making me feel as if my arousal turns him on, rather than something to be embarrassed about as I feel my pussy dripping over his fingers, tightening as I grind into his hand, my thighs spreading as I lean back, gasping with pleasure as the orgasm builds. Liam's mouth is on my jaw, my throat, dragging downwards as I grip the edge tightly, my back arched as he fucks me hard and fast with his fingers. The instant his lips fasten around my nipple and his tongue circles it, I feel the knot of pleasure deep in my belly come unfurled, the tidal wave of pleasure crashing over me as Liam brings me to my first orgasm of the morning.

I know it won't be the last. He keeps going as I come, his fingers thrusting and rubbing, his tongue flicking over my nipple as he sucks my small breast into his mouth, my moans and gasps filling the open air. Even as it starts to slow, he doesn't stop, his fingers still moving slowly inside of me as he kisses his way down my stomach, his thumb brushing gently over my throbbing clit as he works his way down, sliding deeper into the water until his mouth is between my legs, and he looks up at me, kissing my inner thighs lightly.

"I love the taste of you," he murmurs, and then he holds me open, spreading me with his fingers as his mouth fastens over my clit.

I nearly scream with pleasure, gasping as he eats me ravenously, licking and sucking at the tender flesh as his fingers thrust inside of me. It's clear he wants to make me come again almost immediately. I can feel the orgasm building almost instantly, pushing me to the edge and holding me there as he slides his tongue and fingers over all of my most sensitive spots. "Liam–" I gasp his name, shuddering with pleasure as he laps at my clit. "I want you inside of me, please–"

He pulls back, looking up at me with a wicked grin as he runs his tongue over the length of my pussy. "Come for me again then like a good girl, and you can have my cock."

Oh god. It's like he flipped a fucking switch. I cry out, my back arching deeply as I come hard on his tongue, grinding shamelessly against his face as my thighs tighten around his head, and I hear him groan with pleasure. I've never known any man who loved eating pussy as much as Liam. He devours me like I'm his last meal, his tongue lashing against my oversensitive flesh through wave after wave of my climax, until I slump back onto my elbows, gasping. He slips his fingers free of me, reaching for my waist and pulling me down into the hot, bubbling water with him.

My legs go around his waist instantly, my body buoyant, and Liam angles himself between my thighs, groaning as his cock slips into my drenched, fluttering pussy. I clench around him almost instantly, making him moan against my lips as his hand wraps in my damp hair, his mouth finding mine and kissing me deeply as he leans me against the edge of the small pool and starts to thrust.

I can feel how hard he is inside of me, how eager he is, but nothing about his movements is hurried or rushed. He slides into me, again and again, his hips moving in steady thrusts as the water laps around us, his lips brushing over mine, over my jaw and my throat, and up again, his breath warm on the shell of my ear as he makes love to me, steady and slow.

This time my orgasm builds by degrees, a little higher with each thrust of his rigid cock inside of me, filling me as he moans against my lips, gasping with the pleasure of being inside of me. "I can't wait to do this every day for the rest of our lives," he murmurs, and I laugh softly.

"Every day?" I ask him, raising an eyebrow and then gasping when he thrusts into me again.

"Just wait and see," Liam promises, and then he thrusts again, shuddering with pleasure as I clench around him. "Oh god, Ana, I'm so close–"

"Come for me, then," I whisper, kissing him again as I wind my arms around his neck and my legs around his hips, moaning softly as he thrusts into me harder, his thighs tensing with his oncoming orgasm. "I'll come with you, oh god, Liam–"

I feel him swell and harden, feel his cock starting to throb as he presses his mouth to my shoulder, his whole body tensing as he grinds against me, the beginning of his orgasm triggering mine as I feel the first rush of his cum inside of me, his arms holding me tightly against him, skin to skin, the hot water splashing around us.

We stay like that for a long moment, breathless and panting as Liam holds me up. Then somehow, we manage to get out, stumbling naked to one of the wide lounge chairs and falling, dripping, and steaming onto it.

Liam pulls me into his arms, kissing my neck as I curl against him. "I love you," he murmurs, and I let out a soft sigh.

"I love you too." I turn in his arms, my breasts pressed to his smooth damp chest as I cup his cheek in my palm. "I love you, Liam McGregor."

"And I love you, Anastasia McGregor."

"Mm, I like the sound of that." I smile against his lips as I kiss him again.

We stay like that for a little while, kissing and touching lazily, the sun fully up by now. I run my fingers through his still-wet hair, pulling back slightly to look at Liam's face. "What happens now?" I ask softly. "Sofia–and especially Caterina–were worried about the alliance and what the Kings would do if we stayed together. Caterina practically begged me to leave you and come back to Manhattan. She made it sound like–" I take a deep, shaky breath, some of our reality crashing back in. "Are you in danger, Liam? Are *we* in danger?"

"I don't want you to worry," Liam says gently, pushing my hair away from my face. "I'll keep you safe, Ana, I swear."

"But what about *you*?"

"I'm going to call a Kings meeting tomorrow," he explains. "I'll tell them that it's too late for them to push me to marry Saoirse, that I've informed her and her father that I was breaking the engagement, and that I've married you–and that besides that, you're already pregnant with my heir."

I laugh softly at that, grinning at him as his hand slides possessively over my hip. "What if it's a girl?" I ask teasingly, and Liam laughs.

"In that case," he says, rolling me onto my stomach on the soft lounge chaise and nudging my legs open again, "I'll just have to get you pregnant again as soon as possible, once the baby is here."

I gasp as he pushes his hard cock into me again, my sensitive inner walls spasming around him as he thrusts all the way to the hilt, wrapping his hand in my hair and making a fist as he bends down, kissing the back of my neck as he starts to thrust.

He feels so fucking good. His cock fills me perfectly, just on the good side of almost too big, making me feel every inch as he plunges into me again and again, long and slow and then faster as he holds onto my hip with one hand, tugging my head back so that he can kiss and bite down the column of my throat. I arch my back, pushing my ass up and into him, meeting each thrust as Liam groans aloud. He lets go of my hair, running his hands over my back and waist and hips, and then he reaches for my wrists, pinning them over my head as he pushes me down flat on the lounge, fucking me hard. I cry out, my muscles spasming with pleasure as he pounds his cock into me, sucking at the tender flesh of my throat.

"I fucking love you, Ana," he whispers. "I love making love to you, eating your sweet pussy, and fucking you hard and fucking you slow, fucking your mouth and pussy and ass, every inch of you. You feel so perfect, so fucking good–"

Liam pulls out of me then, and I moan in protest, but he's already lifting me up, pulling me astride him as he lays back on the lounge. "Ride me, Ana," he groans. "I want to watch you come on my cock–*fuck*–" he groans as I wrap my hand around his shaft, guiding him between my thighs as I sink down onto him again. "God, that's so fucking good–"

I've never been on top of him before. "You're so handsome," I whisper, looking down at my husband as I grind atop his cock, squeezing my thighs around his hips as I press my hands to his chest. "God, you feel so good. I'm going to come, Liam. I'm going to–"

"Yes," he growls, the sound reverberating in his chest. "Come for me, that's a good girl, *yes*—"

I throw my head back, arching and grinding down onto him as I start to spasm, rolling my hips so that I can feel him rubbing against every sensitive spot inside of me. He feels incredible, the orgasm crashing over me in waves as I rock atop him, and I feel him grabbing my hips, pulling me down tighter as he thrusts up into me. I open my eyes just as I hear him groan, just in time to see the flash of pure ecstasy on his face as his cock starts to throb, filling me with his cum again as I ride him. The sun glints off the gold band on my finger as I scratch my fingers down his chest, gasping with pleasure as I watch him. I think at that moment that I wish we could stay up here forever, doing only this, with no one else to interfere.

We fall asleep afterward for a little while, sunning like housecats, naked on the lounge. When I finally wake up, it's to the sound of Liam walking across the rooftop, a tray of food in his hands and a robe thrown over one arm, dressed just in a pair of swim trunks. He looks gorgeous, bare-chested, with his burnished hair shining in the sun.

"I brought us some food," he says with a grin. "And some water," he adds, handing me my short-sleeved satin robe. I shrug it on, tucking my legs under me as Liam sets the tray down. There's fruit and crackers and prosciutto and cheese, and I reach for a piece of cheese and the glass of water he hands me.

"What happens?" I ask nervously as we eat, looking at him. "When you tell the Kings? Are they going to just accept it, just like that?"

Liam pauses. "I don't know," he admits. "It won't be pleasant, I know that–I've broken a vow made before God and a fellow King, in order to keep mine to you. As far as I'm concerned, the most important one of all," he adds. "There will be consequences, but I'm prepared to pay them."

"What consequences?"

"You don't need to worry about it, Ana–"

"Please tell me." I set down my glass, looking at him. "No more secrets, remember?"

Liam sighs. "There will be a physical punishment, more than likely. Lashes, for disrespecting the O'Sullivans–"

"That sounds medieval!" I stare at him, completely aghast. "They can't–"

"They can," Liam assures me. "Our customs are ancient, as are our punishments. But Ana–" He grabs my hands, looking deeply into my eyes. "Listen to me. It doesn't matter. I'd take any punishment to be with you, break any vow, except the one I made to you tonight–to you and our child."

He leans forward, kissing me gently. "I'll be okay, Ana. I'll come back to you."

I look up at him through eyes gone watery, clutching his hands as fear wraps cold tendrils around my heart. "Do you promise?"

"I do," Liam says gravely. "I will always come back to you, Ana. That is one vow I'll never break."

TWENTY-SEVEN
LIAM

I expected the meeting of the Kings to be unpleasant when I called it. What I didn't expect was to find Luca and Viktor there, waiting for me as I walked into the building, both of their faces grim.

"What are you doing here?" I ask, none too kindly, as I catch sight of them. "This doesn't concern you–"

"Oh, but it does," Viktor assures me, his voice terse. "If you've done what I've heard that you've done and intend to say what I think you're going to say, it concerns me a great deal." His expression is colder than I've seen it in a very long time, and it sends off alarms in my head. "But we'll find out soon enough," Viktor adds, pushing past me to stride into the room where the Kings meet, Levin at his side.

"What the fuck were you thinking?" Luca hisses, the second Viktor is out of earshot. "Viktor and I both warned you–"

"If you're referring to my marrying Ana–"

"Of course, that's what I'm referring to." Luca glares at me. "Sofia told me about it. We warned you not to do this, Liam, that there would be consequences–"

"We have an alliance," I remind him. "This isn't a democracy–"

"The Kings are a hell of a lot closer to a democracy than the mafia or the Bratva," Luca snaps. "And the alliance was made with the *Kings*, not with you personally. If you can't do what needs to be done to lead them, someone else will."

"What the fuck is that supposed to mean?" I growl, but Luca is already striding away, along with his underboss, Alessio. I'm left where I stand, my anger mounting by the second when I hear a familiar feminine voice behind me.

"Today isn't going to be a good day for you, Liam, from what my father says."

I turn to see Saoirse standing there, her strawberry hair falling loosely over her shoulders, pulled half-up in the front. She looks as if she's dressed for a funeral in wide-legged black pants, black heels, and a sleeveless black chiffon shirt that buttons down the front, emerald studs in her ears. She's as beautiful as always, but she looks sad, her eyes barely meeting mine. I glance down to see that the ring is no longer on her finger, as I'd expected.

"Your father should worry more about himself," I say curtly. "I'm sorry, Saoirse, for what happened between us. I–"

"No." She cuts me off brusquely. "You're the one that's going to be sorry, Liam." Saoirse bites her lower lip, looking up at me. "You should have married me," she says softly, and then she pushes past me too, following the others into the meeting room as they start to arrive.

The mood of the room is intensely somber when I take my place at the head of the table, Niall on my left as always. The other Kings look unsettled by Luca and Viktor's presence there, except for Graham, who looks only angry. He glares at me with a grim expression as he goes to sit at the end of the table instead of his usual spot at my right hand, a clear message to the table. He's quite literally facing off with me, with Saoirse just behind him with a wounded expression on her face.

Once everyone is assembled, I stand up slowly. "What I have to say to you today, some of you may not like." I look around the table, avoiding Luca and Viktor's gazes. "But I assure you, I have considered my place here when making this decision. It was not made lightly."

"What are you on about, lad?" Colin O'Flaherty speaks up, and it's clear from his tone that he has some idea of what's going on. "Out with it."

"Have some respect when you speak to the McGregor," Niall says harshly, stepping forward. "He's your leader, aye?"

There's a rumble around the table, but I ignore it, pushing forward with what I have to say. "I have informed both Saoirse O'Sullivan and her father of my intent to break the betrothal contract between us. It was not my wish to hurt her or insult her family name. Saoirse is a good woman, and any man would be lucky to have her as a wife–it is not my intent to devalue that in setting her aside. But my heart and soul are with someone else, and it would be a lie before God to stand up and swear her my fidelity."

"What are you saying?" It's Flynn O'Malley who speaks up this time, his eyes narrowed in his wrinkling face. "Lad, who is it you intend to wed, then?"

"It's who I *have* wed," I say firmly, and the table erupts, drowning me out. "Anastasia Ivanova is my bride," I say, raising my voice above the din, and every head turns to face me.

"A Russian?" Denis Mahoney fairly spits the word. "You'd put a Russian half-breed heir in that seat after you?"

"Not only that," Graham says, rising slowly to his feet. "He's already put that heir in her. He's come to you today to tell you that you'll accept a Russian woman in his bed and a half-Russian child to lead you some years hence, and what if that child doesn't choose a good Irishwoman to marry? There won't be a drop of Irish blood at the head of this table a generation or two hence, and where will we be then? Not the Irish Kings I've helped to lead, I'll say that!"

"We won't stand for it." Colin O'Flaherty bangs his fist against the table. "This is an insult to a good woman, to Graham O'Sullivan, who served your traitorous father faithfully up until the day of his treachery." He turns to look at Saoirse. "Will you confirm this, lass? That Liam McGregor told you he intended to break a lawful contract made with you for your hand?"

"It's true," she says clearly, her voice strong and emotionless though her face is pale, her gaze sweeping over the table. "My father told me, too, that he'd gotten her pregnant. I'll confirm that. This marriage is news to me, though." Her eyes lock with mine, and I can see in that instant that whatever feeling Saoirse O'Sullivan might have had for me is gone.

Graham holds up a hand to quiet the rumble of conversation that breaks out around the table. "This man has broken a contract, married outside of the families without the approval of the table, insulted my honor, and disgraced my daughter's. By the laws of the Kings, the table should sit in judgment on him. Up to and including death or banishment, this table should decide the punishment for the man who would so disgrace the seat that he holds."

The rumble of agreement shocks me into momentary silence. I'd expected anger, outrage even, but I hadn't expected them all to side with Graham so easily or consider such harsh punishment. In the back of my head, I'd known that it was a possibility. Graham *had* threatened it–but I'm the last of my family's line. I hadn't expected them to consider, even for a moment, exterminating the bloodline that has held this seat for generations.

But then again, perhaps this table is more power-hungry than I'd realized.

"Set the marriage aside," Flynn suggests. "Force him to marry Saoirse."

"What's done in the eyes of the Church cannot be undone," Colin argues. "The marriage is valid, lad? Done properly, by a priest?"

I tense. According to what they're asking, it's not. Max is defrocked–the state of Massachusetts considers Ana and I husband and wife, but I also know the Irish Kings don't give a fuck about that. They care if the marriage is valid in the Church–and it's not.

But I'm not about to tell them that.

"It is, and it was," I say firmly. "Anastasia is my wife, and nothing can undo that."

"Then you've signed your own death warrant, lad," Michael Flanagan says. "We might ally with the Russians, but I'll not have one leading us at our own table. I vote that Liam follows his traitor father to the grave."

"You fuckin'--" Niall steps forward, his eyes narrowed with rage, but I put up a hand.

"These are valid proceedings, Niall," I say quietly. "Let it go."

"I won't let them kill ya." Niall's hand is already twitching towards his gun. "I won't stand for it."

"We're not there yet. Hold your peace." I glance at him, and Niall steps back, but I can feel the tension coming off of him in waves.

"Who would take the seat then?" Denis speaks up. "One of our sons? Who decides who inherits if a McGregor no longer holds it–"

"I could take the seat." Graham stands again. "As the former McGregor's right hand, I suggest that it ought to go to me. My daughter–"

"Can only marry one of our sons. You're not of an age to take that seat now, as greatly as I know you want it." Colin looks at Graham. "We choose the son of one of the other families here to marry Saoirse. Execute the traitor son like his treasonous father, and wipe the McGregor name from the lips of the Kings for all eternity." Colin spits on the floor, looking at me as he does so. "That's my vote on the matter."

"It's a shame the only good McGregor left abandoned this table to his father and brother's treachery," Denis says. "The elder son wouldn't have done such a disgraceful thing." He looks squarely at me then, and for the first time, I feel cold fear snake down my spine.

Three of the most well-respected Kings at the table have now called for my death. It's not beyond the realm of rational thought that others might follow. I know Niall will go to his own death trying to stop them, but I'm stunned that it's gone so far.

Was I a fool not to see it?

"What do you have to say for yourself, lad?" Denis asks, and I clench my teeth, looking around the table at the men I was supposed to lead and who have largely turned on me for the simple crime of not marrying the woman they demanded.

"I ask your forgiveness," I say simply, and I'm sincere in that as I meet each of their eyes in turn. "From Saoirse, from Graham, from Luca and Viktor, from everyone here at this table, I humbly ask that you forgive me." I pause, taking a breath as I consider what to say next.

"It was not my intent to besmirch the honor of Saoirse O'Sullivan or that of her father. But I could not in good conscience stand up and make vows to a woman for whom I had no feeling other than respect and duty. I know a good many of you will say that is what makes a marriage for men like us. That love and passion can be found elsewhere, but I tell you now that I intend to be a faithful husband to my wife and always have, regardless of who I chose to marry. I broke my betrothal vow to Saoirse in order to keep from breaking vows after our marriage and to keep the vow I made to the woman I love–to cherish and protect her.

I let that sink in for a moment, speaking with careful intent. "Though we have more equality at this table than most, the Kings have never been a true democracy, to vote on their leaders. For generations, this seat that I hold has been handed down from McGregor to McGregor. But in this," I say slowly, "I'll defer to the table, according to the laws of the Kings. I can't promise you that I will bow to your edict if it is death, but I will go if you choose to oust me. But I remind you this, each and every one of you–when my brother abandoned you and my father nearly ruined you with his treachery, I stayed!" I raise my voice, loud and stern, commanding in the small room. "I have kept the McGregor vow, devote myself to this table, uphold the interests of the Kings, and who I marry won't affect that. If it is your edict that my heir marry a daughter of this table, I will vow that on his behalf. But I will not easily walk away from what I have fought for. I love my wife, and our child will begin the next generation of McGregors. If my actions have cost my children their legacy, then I'm truly sorry for that, above all else. But here, now, I ask for your forgiveness and that you place your faith in me one more time."

I look around the table once more, at the impassive faces of the men sitting there, at Graham's angry expression. *"Ní éilíonn mé go nglúine tú, ach iarrfaidh mé ort bogha,"* I repeat the words of the Kings that I've said to them before when asking for their loyalty. "I do not demand that you kneel, but I do ask that you bow."

And then, lowering my head, I grip the edges of the table. "I will not kneel for your judgment," I say quietly. "But I will bow to your decision."

I keep my head lowered as the vote is taken. It's disheartening to hear how many of them argue for my death, and it sends cold fear through me. I do believe that if I were killed, Luca would at least see Ana safely back to New York–but I'm not certain that she would survive something else so terrible. *She's been through enough,* I think grimly, my knuckles turning white as I grip the edge of the table. *I won't allow them to kill me. Anything but that.*

A vote for my death would have to be unanimous. My blood feels like ice in my veins as I stand there, waiting to see who at my table will call for not just my removal, but my *death*. I can feel Niall, tense and as ready to spring as a hungry wolf, but I know that it's unlikely either of us would leave this room alive if it comes to that. Niall and I are both skilled with a gun and our fists alike, but we're far outnumbered.

We'd take a few of the shites with us for certain, though.

Graham straightens, his eyes meeting mine with a dark, certain anger as he raises his hand. "Death," he says coldly, and I see Saoirse flinch the slightest bit next to him, but she remains unmoved.

For a brief moment, I think he'll be the only one to call for it. But then Colin O'Flaherty stands, glancing at Graham before raising his hand.

"Death," he says, his voice clear and cold in the small space of the room.

Denis Mahoney is quicker to stand with two men having called for it. "Death," he says gruffly, adding his voice to the tally. "I'm sorry for it, lad," he adds, glancing at me. "But it's clear you've got your father's traitor blood. I'll not have the Russians running this table.

"Anyone else?" Graham looks around. There's a beat in which no one moves or speaks, and then Lawrence Monaghan stands, raising his hand.

"Death," he says, his voice less certain than the others. His glance at Graham gives away his uncertainty, too, and his refusal to meet my eyes.

It's doubly painful to hear because Lawrence was once one of my father's closest friends, like Graham.

"Feckin' traitors, all of ya!" Niall shouts, his Gaelic the thickest I've ever heard of it. "It should be you kneeling for a bullet."

"Quiet!" Graham's voice rings out. "For death or for removal, it must be unanimous rather than a simple majority. Does anyone else call for the death of the Irish King, Liam McGregor?"

I can hear my heartbeat pounding in my ears, my face paler than I'd like it to be. All I can think of is Ana, back at the penthouse alone, waiting for me–and Graham's words in the garden of his estate. *You'd rather give the girl a corpse to cry over than a breathing man to miss.*

I might be a corpse by day's end. I want to believe Luca will keep her safe, but I don't know who I can trust anymore–with the exception of Ana herself and Niall. Even Max, who I trust greatly, is under Viktor's protection. My circle of true allies has become frighteningly small.

The table is still silent, and I can hear the faint regret in Graham's voice when he calls it. "Not enough votes for death," he says clearly. "Now–for the removal of the Irish King, Liam McGregor, to be replaced with a chosen son of one of the men seated here, the seat sealed with marriage to my daughter."

Once again, there's not so much as a flicker of emotion on Saiorse's face, though she's being sold like a trophy or a broodmare by her own father. *Duty*, her father had said, and that's all I see on her lovely face. A commitment to stand by her duty, whatever it costs her.

When the vote is cast again for my removal, it is nearly unanimous–with the exception of Luca and Viktor.

"Are ya fuckin' kidding me?" Colin O'Flaherty stands up, his fist coming down on the table. "The Kings have voted as one, and this Italian bastard and Russian shite will be the difference?"

"These men are in an alliance with us," Graham says coldly, speaking before I can as if I've already been removed. "Luca Romano, say your piece."

Luca looks at me regretfully, he and Viktor both standing in unison. "Our alliance was made with a McGregor at the head of the table," Luca says. For a moment, I feel a pulse of hope that he's going to stand at my side, have my back, as I'd once believed he would. But the expression on his face tells a different story.

"We are not in favor of another family taking the seat," Viktor says firmly. "But it has come to our attention that there may be another option."

I stare at him, the blood beginning to rush in my ears. "What the fuck are you talking about?" I snap angrily, but Luca is already speaking, refusing to meet my eyes.

"Graham O'Sullivan, I believe the floor is yours," Luca says, and he and Viktor both sink back down into their seats as Graham stands.

Slowly, Graham looks around the table, meeting each man's eyes except for mine. Next to him, Saoirse looks calm and composed, and I know in that instant whatever he's about to say, she's aware of already.

"Connor McGregor is alive," Graham says, his voice clear and loud in the small room. Every face turns towards him, a low hum passing through the room as he commands the complete attention of the Kings. "I know where he is," he continues. "And if I can bring him home, the rightful McGregor can take his place–here, at this table."

TWENTY-EIGHT
LIAM

There's a brief moment of stunned silence, and then the table erupts. I feel the room tilt as I stand there, shocked, gripping the edge of the table just to keep myself upright as I stare at Luca, who is still refusing to meet my eyes. Viktor does, though, his glare cool as he watches me.

"You said he was dead," I hiss at Niall as the table argues, and when I look at him, his face is as pale and shocked as I imagine mine is at this moment.

"I had heard good evidence that he was," Niall says quietly. "But if this is true–"

"If this is true–then I can't hold it." I grit my teeth as the table settles down, the men voting once again.

When it comes back, this time, it's unanimous. There's a moment's discussion with Graham, who then stands up. As the one holding the right-hand seat, it's his right to pass judgment, no matter how much it rankles with me that he does.

"Liam McGregor will be punished today, in sight of all gathered here for his broken vow," Graham intones. "There will be no changes in leadership here today, but it is determined that all efforts will be made to find Connor McGregor and bring him home. If he returns, the table will take another vote." He smiles grimly. "I don't think you have to think hard, lad, to guess what that edict will be."

Luca still won't meet my eyes. The sharp, piercing sense of betrayal runs deep–I might have expected it of Viktor, but I would never have thought that Luca wouldn't have my back in the end when it truly mattered.

"You promised to bow to our judgment, lad," Graham reminds me, and I slowly straighten, feeling every muscle in my body tense at what's to come.

But I refuse to flinch. I wouldn't have allowed them to kill me without a fight, but I'd known there would be a punishment. I'd told Ana I was willing to accept it for her sake, and I'd meant it.

Whatever I have to do to show the table that I am capable of leading them, that the seat should remain mine, I will do.

Slowly, I unbutton my shirt, stripping it off and handing it to Niall. He takes it, his expression grim, staying nearby in case I need him to defend me. But I'm not worried about them killing me–not today.

"Saoirse." Graham turns to look at his daughter. "Liam McGregor broke a solemn vow made to you. The first part of his punishment is yours to administer."

She stands gracefully, taking the thin iron rod he holds out to her, the length of a hand and the width of one of her fingers. Graham lights a candlestick, holding it to the end of the rod until the first inch or so of it glows brightly. Then Saoirse meets my eyes, coolly walking to my end of the table and holding the rod outstretched.

"For the hand that proved false when it signed the contract that bound you to me," she recites, her voice smooth and flat, emotionless–as if she weren't holding out an instrument to burn me. "For five seconds, Liam."

"Jesus, Mary, and Joseph," Niall swears behind me. "Liam, for fuck's sake, man–"

It's one thing to have something done to you. It's another to be forced to do it to yourself. But there's no choice here. If I have any hope of holding this seat, I have to face my punishment fearlessly, to accept the will of the Kings up to a point, to show them that I can be the leader my father wasn't.

Saoirse holds my gaze, and I see something in them, daring me not to do it. To humiliate myself and her further, in front of this table, and see what happens.

I reach out and pinch the glowing tip between the thumb and forefinger of my right hand, as is custom, the hand I used to sign the document.

It's all I can do not to scream. The pain is sharp and immediate, searing the skin, and burning away nerve endings that will never be the same. The hand won't be crippled, that's not the intent, but the pain is blinding, the urge to jerk it away mingling with the sudden inability to move at all. I hear Niall curse behind me, Graham counting down the five seconds, and even when he says *five*, I find myself unable to move, my hand frozen in place.

"Liam!" Saoirse's voice cuts through my pain. "Let go."

She can't pull back, she might take skin with her. My mind is screaming at me, the pain shuddering through me, and somehow I manage to pull my fingers apart. Tears swim to my eyes, but I manage to keep them from falling.

Saoirse looks at me, her expression carefully blank. "I hope it was worth it," she says quietly. "You've lost everything today."

I meet her eyes, gritting my teeth, forcing myself to speak through the pain. "What I haven't lost, Saoirse, is the only thing that matters."

"I hope that's true," she says softly, glancing at me once more. "She's all you'll have left."

Then, she turns away, setting the rod aside and returning to her seat as Graham takes her place, a leather strap in his hand.

"Ten lashes," he intones. "Five for the insult to me, and five for the insult to my daughter. Grip the table, lad, and take them like a man."

I don't protest. I wouldn't have, at any rate, but after the pain of the burning rod, the lashes seem like nothing. I grip the table with my left hand, bending forward at the waist, my head bowed as my right hand hangs uselessly at my side.

Graham puts all his strength into it, that's for certain. My entire body jerks with the first lash across my back, but I don't make a sound, nor with the second or the third. By the fifth, my jaw is clenched so tightly against the pain that I'm unsure if I'll ever be able to pry it apart again. However, I still keep silent, refusing to give him the satisfaction of so much as a whimper.

By the time he finishes and steps back, panting, I can feel blood trickling down my back. Niall steps forward, holding out my shirt for me to slip back into. I do so slowly, careful of my injured right hand. I can feel the fabric clinging to the bleeding welts as I straighten painfully, looking around the table.

"I have bowed to your judgment," I say carefully, forcing myself to speak clearly, without a break in my voice. "I ask that you consider that–my faithful service to you and my willingness to humble myself before you, paying for my insult with my blood and body–when you think of replacing me with my faithless brother." I square my shoulders, surveying the table. "This meeting of the Kings is adjourned."

Not a single one of them speaks or looks me in the eye as they file out, leaving only Luca and Viktor there with Levin and Alessio, and Niall at my side.

"I'm sorry, Liam–" Luca starts to say, but I shake my head.

"You betrayed me," I say quietly. "You should have stood with me, but you didn't."

"It's not lost yet. If Connor isn't found or won't return–"

"You should have stood with me," I repeat. "I won't forget this, Luca. Or your failure, Viktor."

"We have our own families to think of," Viktor says sharply. "They, and others, depend on us–"

"And now I'm going home to mine." I glance at Niall. "See to it that they leave here shortly."

Niall nods. "They'll leave now," he says pointedly, and I turn away, heading for the door.

At this moment, all I want in the world is Ana.

I'd promised her I'd come back. And I mean to do precisely that.

Nothing else matters. Only her.

TWENTY-NINE
ANA

I hadn't known, really, what sort of condition Liam would be in when he came back to me after the meeting. He'd said that he'd be punished, but he hadn't been willing to explain to me what that meant. My mind had been racing the entire time he'd been gone. Still, nothing could have prepared me for what I'd see when he walked through the door, his shirt stuck to his back with blood and his face grey and ashen, his forehead broken out in a cold sweat.

His driver had to help get him up to the front door. "Liam!" I exclaim as Ralph helps him inside, only for him to half fall into my arms as I reach for him. "Ralph, call the doctor–"

"No," Liam says, with some difficulty. "No doctor. Just you."

I stare at him. "Liam, you're bleeding–"

"I know," he manages wryly. "There's a first aid kit in the bathroom. Just help me sit down, and you can patch me up. I only want you."

Part of me wonders if I can manage that. But I tell Ralph to go, helping Liam into the bathroom and to the edge of the tub, where he sits slumped as I get the first-aid kit out from under the bathroom sink.

"You'll have to help me with my shirt," he says. "My hand–"

He raises his right hand, and I feel faint. Some of the skin on his forefinger and thumb is burned away, the remaining flesh red, raw and blistered. "Liam," I whisper in horror. "What happened? What did they do to you–"

"It was my punishment," he says quietly. "For signing a document I intended to break. The lashes were for the disgrace done to the O'Sullivan family."

"The lashes–" My eyes widen as I look at the blood-soaked shirt clinging to his back. "Oh god, Liam–"

I manage to get his shirt off, his groan of pain as I peel it away from his flesh, cutting straight to my heart. I feel faintly sick at what I see there–the welted, torn flesh from where he was struck bleeding down his now-marred skin. Tears well in my eyes, but I force them back. Liam needs me to care for *him* now, and I can't do that if I'm sobbing.

It's a long process. As I tend to his wounds, he tells me about the meeting–all of it. He tells me about Luca and Viktor siding against him, as Sofia and Caterina had feared, about Graham's speech to the table, distracting himself from the pain as I clean the burns first with cold water, layering antibiotic ointment and loosely wrapping a bandage around the raw flesh.

"You're going to have to have the doctor look at this," I tell him sternly.

"I know," Liam says contritely. "I just couldn't right now–not today. I need you and only you right now, Ana."

Gently, I start to clean the wounds on his back, hating each time he winces or sucks in a breath of pain. "So, is this the end of it?" I ask quietly. "Is it over?"

"No," Liam says, and my heart sinks like a stone in my chest.

He turns to face me then, pulling away from my touch to hold my hand in his instead. "I'm sorry, Ana," he says quietly. "It's worse than I thought it would be. Some wanted to have me killed. Niall would have stopped them–or tried–if it came to that, but Luca and Viktor and a few others kept that from being a unanimous vote. Luca and Viktor prevented a unanimous vote to replace me with one of the other families' sons–but only because Graham had something else up his sleeve."

"What?" I look at him, frightened. "Liam, what are they going to do?"

"Graham says my brother is alive. They're going to find him and bring him back. And if they do–there's not a man at that table, including Liam and Viktor, who will speak up for me. It was always meant to be Connor's, and they'll likely give it back to him if they can."

I stare at him, trying to let it sink in. *Liam's brother is alive.* It should be happy news, but it's not, and that breaks my heart anew for him, in addition to the rest of it. "What about Niall?"

"He's not a King, only my friend and enforcer. He doesn't get a vote, unfortunately." Liam lets out a long breath. "I could try to stop it. But it would mean war, Ana. With my own brother–and very little in the way of allies to help me."

He reaches for me then, pulling me into the circle of his arms, careful of his injured right hand. He looks up at me, and I can see the guilt and sorrow in his eyes, written on every line of his face. "I'm sorry, Ana," he whispers. "I don't know what's going to happen now, if I'll hold the Kings or lose them, who I will be–what our child's legacy will be. But I swear to you, I will always love you. I will never leave you, so long as I draw breath. It won't matter to me if I lose all of it as long as I have you." He lowers his head then, and I can see the slump of his shoulders. "Except for the fact that I will have nothing left to give you or our child."

"Liam," I whisper his name, tears welling in my eyes as I reach down, cupping his face in my hand and raising it so that he looks at me. His green eyes are glistening too, and I gently stroke his cheek with my thumb. "I don't care who you are, Liam, an Irish King or an ordinary man. You crossed the world to find me. You'll always be extraordinary to me. I'll never leave you–and I will always love you, as will our child. What you are has never mattered–only *who* you are, a good man down to the depths of your soul." I bend down, kissing him gently, brushing my fingers over his lips as I pull back. "That's my husband and the father our son will have, King or no King."

Tears slide down Liam's cheeks, and I kiss them away, whispering that I love him repeatedly, as I sink down to sit next to him, clinging to his good hand. "Aren't you afraid?" he asks, and I lay my head against his shoulder, biting my lower lip.

"Yes," I admit. "I've seen what happens to an ousted man with no allies, to my own father, murdered by the Bratva. I was terrified for you today, Liam, terrified that I'd live my own mother's life, a mob widow, running for her life with her child. I'm still afraid of that, afraid of the future and what it brings for all of us now. But what was our choice?" I sit up, my gaze locking with his. "You love me, and I love you. We'll love our child together. And whatever comes of that, comes."

Liam kisses me again, slow and gentle, and I stand up, turning him so that I can finish cleaning and dressing the wounds on his back. When he's finally bandaged, I help him up and undress him, helping him to the bed so that he can lie on his stomach, with pillows under his head and hips to keep him comfortable.

I lay down next to him, brushing his hair away from his face, holding his good hand until he falls asleep. "I love you," I whisper, and I've never meant anything more in all my life.

Despite everything, I could swear I see him smile even in his sleep.

—

FOUR WEEKS LATER

I stand in our living room, an envelope in my hand, Liam next to me. There's an answer inside it, and I don't know if it's one I want to know.

We both had doctor's appointments today–first Liam to check on the healing of his back and hand, and then me for the baby. The baby itself is fine, healthy, and growing nicely, according to the doctor, but we were handed something else on the way out–the results of the paternity test we'd requested.

Now, I'm holding it in my hand, wondering if we should open it.

Everything is uncertain. The Kings haven't met officially since that last fateful meeting. Liam continues to run the business as usual, always aware that Graham is searching for his lost brother, making contact with those who know where he could be. We look over our shoulders on a daily basis now, waiting for the bad news to come.

This could be good news or bad. Or it could be nothing at all, if we choose for it to be.

"Do you want to know?" I ask Liam softly, looking up into his green eyes. In the first month of our marriage, as tumultuous as it's been, our relationship itself has only grown stronger. Without Alexandre or Saoirse hanging over us, we've felt free. And though his injuries meant we've barely been able to be intimate, I feel as if a different kind of intimacy has been growing, bringing us closer together than we've ever been before.

There's a ring on my left hand now, an emerald-cut diamond on a yellow gold band, with a sapphire baguette on either side. My birthstone and Liam's. Next to it is nestled the plain gold band he gave me on our wedding day, a ring I love more than any other, even the beautiful engagement ring he gave me to make up for not having one when he proposed.

I'll never take either of them off. Liam is mine, and I'm his, now and forever. No matter what happens, nothing can break that–not even the potential contents of the envelope. But still, I wait for his answer, feeling faint as if I can't breathe.

"It doesn't matter to me," Liam says firmly, as I'd thought he might. "You're my wife, the love of my life." He touches my cheek gently with his healing right hand, smiling down at me, his eyes full of love. "As far as I'm concerned, the baby is mine. *Ours.*" He pauses. "Do you want to know?"

I think about it for a long moment, turning the envelope over and over in my hands. And at last, I walk to the fireplace, squatting down in front of it.

It takes a few minutes to get the fire started. Outside it's a hot summer day, but in here, the central air is cold enough that the heat from the fire almost feels pleasant. When the flames are leaping, I look at Liam to give him a chance to stop me.

"No," I say finally, when he doesn't move or say a word in protest about what he must know I'm planning to do. "If the baby is yours," I continue, my hand tightening around the envelope, "then everything would be fine. We could put the past behind us, forever, with no trace of it left."

"Of course." Liam's gaze searches mine. "But?"

"But what if it's not?" I look up at him. "What if it's Alexandre's? You can claim the baby as our child and love it, but we'll always know. We'll never be able to forget it, and I'll never be able to fully let him go. I don't want to know, Liam. I want this baby to be ours, regardless of what the biology says. Like you said, it doesn't matter. So we don't need to know."

"I agree," Liam says softly. He steps behind me, his arms going around my waist, and I take a deep breath as I step forward towards the fire.

"I love you," I whisper. "I love you, and only you."

"And I love you, Ana. Only you, now and forever–and our baby." Liam kisses my cheek gently.

"That's all I need to know–and all our child will ever need to know."

I reach out, throwing the envelope into the fireplace. It catches immediately, my heart leaping in my chest along with the flames as it starts to burn. As the edges curl, I turn in Liam's arms, and he pulls me closer, his hand going to my face as he bends to kiss me.

It's been nearly a month since we've really been able to make love. I'm hungry for him, ravenous, and I arch against him, my lips parting for his tongue as he tugs me backward, sitting on the couch as he pulls me into his lap.

"Careful of your hand," I whisper, but he's already pushing my dress up, fumbling with his zipper as he kisses me, hard and hot and deep, his fingers pushing my panties aside so the tip of his cock can find my entrance.

I cry out when he slips inside of me, his hand on my hip as I sink down onto him, and I clutch his face in my hands, kissing him fiercely as he starts to thrust, filling me completely.

"I love you, Liam McGregor," I whisper, the way I had the morning of our wedding as we lay next to each other on the roof."

Liam smiles against my lips, his hand in my hair as he rocks against me, the two of us as close together as two people can possibly be. "And I love you, Anastasia McGregor," he whispers. In one swift movement, he topples me over onto my back on the couch, thrusting into me hard and fast as I cry out with pleasure.

I lose myself in him, in the sensation of his body inside of mine, his lips on mine, his body against mine, skin to skin. And as we make love, the fire crackles just beyond, the envelope turning to ash inside of it.

Burning every last trace of the past away.

EPILOGUE
LIAM

One Month Later

It's taken a bit longer than expected, but as I get into the car for my driver to take me home, I'm anxious to get home to give Ana the good news.

I'm fully healed from the wounds inflicted at my trial of the Kings, if not without scars. My back will always have a few ridges of scar tissue and thin lines marking where the belt hit, and the flesh on my right thumb and forefinger is left with a divoted scar on the tip of each, the print gone.

The doctor had tactfully mentioned that there's an excellent plastic surgeon they could refer me to, but I declined. I don't mind the scars—they're a reminder of what I endured to try to keep my place at the head of the Kings' table and what I endured for Ana's sake. To be with her. To have our family, our child.

I want to tell my driver to hurry as I text her that I'm on my way back to the penthouse. Since the trial, we've been forced to have careful sex, always conscious of my wounds and not reopening them or hurting me further, but now I can do whatever I like.

I'm fully healed, and I intend to put that to use just as soon as I walk in the door.

But when I get home, stepping inside and locking the door behind me, Ana is nowhere to be seen. The living room is dim, just the light from the balcony coming in through the sheer drapes, and I feel a sudden pulse of fear.

What if something's happened to her?

Alexandre is gone back to Paris, I know that for certain—but what if I'm wrong? What if he changed his mind and came back for her and the child he thinks is his—or what if it's something else? Graham, abducting Ana and taking her away to punish me further, or force me to marry Saoirse once I was a widower—

A dozen terrifying scenarios go through my head in a dizzying rush. "Ana!" I call out, turning down the hall to her former bedroom to see if she'd maybe fallen asleep in there, or gotten engrossed in her current project—turning it into a nursery for the baby. But it's empty other than the mess of clothes and furniture scattered around waiting to be put into some kind of order, and I feel the fear ramping up. *I can't lose her*, I think, my heart pounding in my chest as I rush back through the living room towards the master suite we now share. "Anastasia!"

"I'm in here."

Her voice, soft and sweet, comes through the door of the master suite, and my knees go weak with relief. *She's here. Nothing happened.* I feel as if all the air has been sucked out of me, and I have to fight to draw a breath as I push open the door—only to see her kneeling there on the plush rug next to the bed, waiting for me.

The sight steals my breath for an entirely different reason. I stop in the doorway, staring at her, my cock so instantly rock hard that the sudden rush of blood makes me momentarily dizzy. I blink at the vision in front of me, more aroused than I think I've ever been in my entire fucking life.

Ana isn't just kneeling there waiting for me. She's wearing the pink and white lingerie set, the one that I bought her the day we went shopping, that I never actually expected to see her in. And she looks stunning.

The tiny white lace panties barely cover anything. They're just a scrap of lace between her thighs, a thin ribbon tied on either side of her slender hips. From the shadow I see between her slightly spread thighs, she's already wet for me, just from kneeling here waiting for me to come home to her. A lace garter belt just above the ribbons, clipped to the white lace-topped stockings stretching over her long elegant legs, and a scrap of lace covering her breasts that could barely be called a bra. There's the tiniest bit of lace over her nipples and then the white straps that arch over the tops of her small breasts. Her head is bowed, her hands folded on her knees, but I can see the one other element of the outfit that makes my cock lurch against my fly, straining to harden even more than it already is.

The pink and white leather collar that had come with it, with the gold ring, is buckled around her neck.

"Anastasia."

I say her name, her full name, which makes her look up slowly, her wide blue eyes meeting mine. I can see that they're already glassy with desire, which makes my cock throb all over again. She wants me. I can see it in every inch of her, in the eager, submissive look on her face, the way her lips part instantly as if wordlessly begging for my cock.

This is my wife. My perfect, beautiful wife.

And now I get to fuck her whenever I please.

"You look beautiful, kneeling there like that," I tell her in a low tone as I start to walk towards her. "But you made me worry, Ana. I thought something had happened to you."

"I'm sorry," she whispers, her eyes huge and plaintive as she looks up at me, and the ache in my cock feels nearly unbearable. "I wanted to surprise you."

"And you have. It's a lovely surprise." I stop in front of her and see her eyes flick to the bulge in my pants, the fabric straining to contain my thick length. "But I'm afraid I'll have to punish you for making me worry."

I'm not truly angry with her, and it's hard to contain a smirk as I see the light in her eyes at that, a sparkling eagerness at the idea of how I might exact my punishment.

"Of course," she says demurely, looking up at me from under those long lashes, and I can see her sharp intake of breath as my cock twitches in my pants.

"First though—" I reach down, running my fingers over her silky blonde hair, and she lets out a soft sigh. "I think a beautiful lass such as yourself deserves my cock in her mouth."

"Oh yes, please," Ana breathes, her lips parting even more, and I feel a white-hot jolt of lust shoot through me at the eagerness on her face. She keeps her hands in her lap, letting me get my cock out for her, just the way she knows I like. For the last several weeks, sex has been—with a few exceptions—her hands and mouth on me and mine on hers, the exertion of actual intercourse too much for me while I was healing. I'd missed fucking her, but we'd made the best of it, each learning all the other ways that the other liked to be touched. One of the things she'd learned was that I enjoyed making her wait for the cock she loves to suck so much, getting it out slowly and teasing both her and myself until I chose to push it between her soft, full lips.

But this time I can't wait. I'm aching for her—I have been all day, and I can't undo my belt fast enough, dragging down my zipper and reaching in to fist my rigid, throbbing cock. I can feel the pre-cum pearling at the tip when I pull it out, slick and hot. Ana's mouth opens instantly as she leans forward, her eyes fixed hungrily on the dripping tip of my aching length.

"Greedy lass," I murmur as I guide it between her lips, sucking in a breath at the feel of her hot, wet tongue encircling my cockhead, lapping up the arousal there before her lips tighten around me. She slides downwards, inch by inch, her wide blue eyes looking up at me for approval as she sucks my cock expertly.

"Fuck, that feels so good," I groan, my hand in her hair, curling around the back of her head as she slides down. "No one has ever sucked my cock like you do."

Ana lets out a small hum of pleasure, her eyes still locked on mine as she sucks, sliding up and down slowly as her tongue slides over every ridge and vein. My hand slips around to cup the side of her face, stroking her jaw lightly as I groan with pleasure. Then, my fingers drop lower, hooking in the ring of her collar and pulling her closer so that I can thrust more of my swollen length into her mouth.

I feel my cockhead pressing against the back of her throat, the clench of her muscles as she swallows against it. I bite out another groan, my fingers tightening on the ring of the collar as Ana moans around me. I look down at her, the sight only intensifying my desire, and thrust my hips forward, pushing every inch of my cock into her willing mouth with a sensation so pleasurable rippling down my spine that my knees feel almost weak.

"I want to come in your mouth like this," I growl. "Not tonight–tonight I'm going to come in your pussy, but soon. I want to hold you by this ring, so every inch of me stays buried in your throat while I shoot my hot cum down it, and you swallow–*fuck*–"

Ana moans helplessly, squirming on the rug as she looks up at me with those huge blue eyes, the vibrations surrounding my saliva-slick cock as I pull out reluctantly. Her mouth is too good, the pleasure so intense that I know if I stay there too much longer, I will do just that tonight and come down her throat before I have a chance to fuck her.

I've come in her mouth plenty these past weeks. I want my wife's pussy.

But first, her punishment.

"Stand up, little lass," I say hoarsely as I pull back reluctantly, slipping out of her mouth. My cock throbs as the cool air strikes my swollen, straining flesh, and I grit my teeth against the urge to push it back between her lips instantly, thrusting until I fill her mouth with my cum. "Bend over the bed."

"Yes, Liam," Ana says softly, that glitter of anticipation in her eyes. "Should I spread my legs for you too, so you can see my pussy?"

Jesus, Mary, and Joseph. My cock lurches upwards at that, so hard it's nearly touching my belly, at the sound of those words slipping off my sweet wife's tongue. "Yes," I tell her firmly, my hand wrapping around my cock at the base and squeezing to try and stave off my imminent climax. "Spread those pretty thighs wide for me, little lass."

Ana obeys, bending over the side of the bed and spreading her legs far apart. I can see that I was right–the white lace of her panties pressed against her pussy is positively soaked, drenched with arousal. There is even less fabric in the back than in the front. Her puffy, aroused folds swallow the scrap of lace that turns into nothing but a string between the delectable swells of her ass cheeks.

I touch her, my palm rubbing over one of those round cheeks as Ana gasps, arching upwards into my hand. With my other hand, I reach between her thighs, stroking her swollen folds and the wet lace as Ana cries out.

"So wet for me already," I murmur. "But you always have been. You've always been my good girl, so aroused and hungry for my cock whenever I want to give it to you. Aren't you, little lass?"

"Yes," Ana gasps. "I want it, whenever my husband pleases–oh god, Liam, please–"

She moans as my fingers press against the lace, pushing against her entrance as she grinds back against me. A mew of frustration slips from her when I pull my hand away, and I chuckle.

"Punishment first," I tell her sternly, though I know it's less of a punishment than a means to arouse her even more. "Do you want my hand or my belt, Anastasia?"

She moans at the sound of her full name on my lips. "Hand," she whispers. "I want to feel your hand on me, punishing me for being a bad girl, Liam, please–"

"Who am I to tell my wife no?" I chuckle, rubbing my palm over her ass once more, and then I pull it back, bringing it down hard on one side.

Ana cries out, arching, her hands clutching the duvet as her thighs spread wider. "Liam–"

Another, on the other side. She moans, and I feel another trickle of pre-cum sliding down the shaft of my cock, my desire almost unbearable.

Two more spanks, the flesh of her ass reddening, and I pause. "Do you need more, Ana?"

"Yes, please," she begs. "I know I was bad, Liam. Please, I need more."

Another, and another. Her pussy is drenched, her arousal dripping from the lace of her panties, and I can't wait any longer. I give her two more well-placed spanks, feeling the way she arches back, wanting more, begging for me, and then I can't bear it a second longer.

"That's enough, Ana," I tell her, stroking the curve of her ass with my hand. "I need to fuck you, *now*."

"Oh god, yes. Please." She scrambles up onto the bed, kneeling there as I follow her, my hands on her waist as I tumble her back against the pillows. "Please, Liam, I need you–"

I reach for the ribbons holding her panties on, undoing them at the same time as I pull the bows free and snatch the scrap of lace from between her thighs. She has the most perfect pussy I've ever seen, bare and pink and so swollen with arousal that the lips are parted, allowing me to see her small hard clit peeking out from between the folds.

My cock is pulsing with an almost unbearable need, but I have to taste her.

Without teasing, I slide down, pushing her thighs wide with my palms as I go straight between them. I need to fuck her so badly that I can hardly stand it, but I want this first, to feel her come on my tongue, taste her arousal flooding my mouth.

The second my lips fasten around her clit, my tongue fluttering over it, Ana lets out a cry of pleasure that's nearly a scream, her back arching as she grinds against my mouth. I push two fingers into her, feeling her clench as she reaches her climax nearly instantly, her head thrown back as I feel a gush of her arousal over my tongue, her pussy tightening around my fingers. She comes hard on my tongue, moaning with a high-pitched sound that drives my own desire to the brink, crying out my name as I suck fiercely on her clit.

I have to be inside of her. I'm so close to my own orgasm, my balls tight and aching, and I pull back, kneeling between her thighs. My cockhead brushes against her swollen folds, making her cry out again, and I look down at her beautiful, lust-filled face as I reach for the ring of her collar.

I grab onto it, tugging on the ring to pull her up in the same moment that I drive my cock into her in one hard thrust, my other arm going around her waist as my mouth comes crashing down on hers.

Fuck. She feels so incredible, hot and wet and impossibly tight, her pussy fluttering around me with the aftershocks of her orgasm, and I know I'm not going to last long. I pound into her, thrusting again and again as I devour her mouth, my fingers curled tightly in the ring of her collar, and I think I'm going to go mad with lust and desire for this woman, my Ana, my beautiful wife.

"I love you," I whisper fiercely against her mouth as I fuck her, driving into her hard, filling her with every inch of my cock. The feeling of her hot pussy around me feels like coming home, like anchoring myself in the place where I always belonged. I feel as if I can't get deep enough, close enough, and Ana arches against me as if she feels the same, her small breasts pressed against my chest, the lace rubbing against my shirt as I wrap my arm around her more tightly, pulling her astride my lap as I thrust up into her.

"I love you too," Ana whispers, her hand on my stubbled cheek as she grinds against me, riding my cock as I get closer and closer to the edge. "I'm so close again, Liam. I'm going to come for you. I'm–"

She gasps, her back arching more deeply as her hips roll down onto mine, and I groan aloud. "Yes," I growl, thrusting harder, faster. "Come for me, Ana, come for me while I fill you up with all of my hot–fucking–cum–*fuck*!"

I feel her tighten around me, hear her strangled cry as she throws her head back against my grip on the ring of her collar, and I hold onto it, using it as leverage as I pound my cock into her as hard as I can, feeling her tighten around me as I swell with one last burst of pleasure before my cock explodes into her.

"Ana!" I cry out her name, clutching her to me as the first spurt of my cum shoots into her, her cries of pleasure mingling with mine as we come together. It feels so good, *she* feels so good, and I lose myself in the white-hot bliss of it, of her body wrapped around me, of the two of us experiencing it together.

We fall back into the bed together, her clasped in my arms, and I press my forehead to hers, trying to catch my breath.

"You didn't tell me how your appointment went," Ana says softly after a little while has passed, still curled against me.

"You didn't exactly give me a chance," I tease her, pushing a strand of blonde hair out of her face. "I was a little distracted."

"Good." Ana smiles up at me, her fingers toying with one of the buttons on my shirt. "I tried."

"You succeeded." I lean down to kiss her softly, then push myself up against the pillows, holding her against my chest as I lean back. "It was good news. I have a few scars, but I'm fully healed. The doctor said I could return to–regular exertions."

"Oh, good." Ana laughs. "We can do it again, then?"

"Just as soon as I have a minute to recover," I promise her, but her hands are already on my pants, pushing them down, undoing the buttons of my shirt.

I roll over as she strips me naked, turning her onto her back again as I look down at her in the pink and white lingerie. I run one hand down her stockinged leg and pull it up around my hip, my cock already hardening again as I look down at her. "You're so very beautiful," I whisper.

"Are you still glad you married me?" Ana asks, her voice half-teasing, but I can hear the note of worry in it. "After everything, now that you're healed–was it worth it?"

"Yes," I promise her, and I nudge forward, my cock once again rigid enough to pierce her instantly. "Always, Ana." Another inch, and another, until I'm buried inside of her, and she gasps, tightening around me as she looks up and I hold myself there. "Always and forever. I love you, and you have made me the happiest man in the world. No matter what happens next, that will always be true."

"And you've made me the happiest woman." She pulls me close, tilting her chin up for a kiss. "I love you too, Liam McGregor."

"And I love you, Anastasia McGregor." I kiss her deeply, tangling my tongue with hers as I begin to thrust, the pleasure of it sweeping over me once again, mingled with the emotion that wells up inside of me. "Tonight," I tell her firmly as I slide into her, "I plan to make love to you all night long, until we're both exhausted. I've been waiting for this night far too long."

"Oh god, yes." Ana leans up to kiss me, her back arching. "And tomorrow?" she whispers, and I can hear the hint of fear in her voice, even now.

"Tomorrow, we'll face whatever comes together," I promise her. Then I bend down to kiss her again, all words swallowed up in the fierce kiss and the tangled moans of our pleasure that come after.

But later, as we're lying together, sweaty and satisfied once again, I feel Ana press her lips against my chest. "Are you sure we'll be safe?" she asks. "From Graham and everyone else who wants to replace you? They won't find Connor?"

I want to lie to her at that moment, to tell her that nothing will ever hurt us again, that nothing will change. "I have a plan," I tell her instead. "They might find Connor, but I'm going to do all I can to keep him from coming back."

Ana tilts her chin up to look at me, her blue eyes still full of worry. "But he's your brother," she says softly, biting her lower lip. "Won't it hurt you to not see him again? To know he's alive but not be able to have him come home?"

I touch her face gently, my arm around her tightening so that I can hold her close. "What would hurt me more," I tell her firmly, "is losing you. Whatever they do, Ana, whatever they throw at us, whatever happens–I'm going to fight. I'll fight to the bitter end for my empire, my place at the head of the table, for you and our child. I promise you that."

"I know," she says softly. "But more than anything, I need you safe, Liam. And here with me."

I feel her head against my chest again, and a little later, her rhythmic breathing as she falls asleep. But as satisfied and exhausted as I am, sleep doesn't come to me for a long time. Instead, I lie there looking at the ceiling, with my wife cradled in my arms and one thought repeating over and over in my head.

Try to come and take it from me, brother.

For Ana and my family, for everything I love and everything I have, I'll fight you to the end.

Whatever it takes.

. . .

Keep reading for a preview of *Irish Betrayal*, the next book in the *Irish Kings* series, meet Connor, whose return threatens everything.
Irish Betrayal
Irish Kings #4

Irish Kings #4

Chapter One

Saoirse

This isn't me.

I don't recognize the girl in the hotel room mirror, despite her having my features, my dark strawberry hair, my green eyes, my figure. In these new clothes, purchased just for tonight, I feel like an unfamiliar person in a foreign place. My heart skips a beat in my chest as I run my fingers anxiously through my bone-straight hair, all the usual waves ironed out of it.

On the foot of the bed next to me, there's a file, open with documents and photos spilling out of it, like I'm some kind of agent or one of Viktor Andreyev's new assassins-in-training on a mission instead of the daughter of an Irish King, the closest thing to royalty there could be on American soil. I glance at it, feeling my heart speed up a little as I catch sight of the pictures again—pictures of a man I also hardly recognize.

When I knew him, he was polished, smooth, and elegant, always with a clean-shaven face and his dark reddish-brown hair carefully styled back, always in a suit or a button-up and slacks. If those arms were ever visible, they were smooth and bare, without a speck of visible ink in sight.

This man in the photos is someone else. More muscular than before, stubble where his cheeks used to be smooth, a scar running down one side of his face from the corner of his eye to below his chin—something that might make another man look less handsome, but only serves to make him look even more handsome and more dangerous, a roguish sort of sex appeal.

I push the pictures around the duvet, glancing at each of them as I try to steady my heartbeat, but seeing his face in every one doesn't help matters at all. In some, he's wearing a t-shirt and jeans, tattoos covering every inch of his exposed arms and crawling up his throat. In others, he's wearing a well-worn leather jacket, sometimes a beanie in the colder weather, other times with that thick reddish-brown hair that I remember so well, loose and messy around his face.

Connor McGregor.

The man I was once supposed to marry—and that tonight, I'm supposed to pretend to seduce. A concept completely unfamiliar to me. I've spent my whole life protecting my virginity, a thing that was drilled into me from a young age contained the majority of my value to my family. I'm not expected to give it up tonight—but I'm supposed to seduce this man into thinking he's coming to my hotel room to fuck me.

It's not as if I've never thought about sleeping with Connor McGregor before. Once upon a time, it was understood that he'd be my husband. But I'd always pictured it as a cold, transactional kind of thing. A clinical coupling to join our families and produce an heir. I hadn't thought much about pleasure or passion back then.

But this man—even in still images, he oozes sex appeal. This man doesn't look like the kind to spend fifteen minutes thrusting into a woman in missionary and then rolling over to sleep. This man looks like he'd throw a woman up against a wall. Toss her over his shoulder and carry her into the bedroom, whether she wanted him to or not. *Demand* things from her, filthy things, things that I'm not even sure I have the capacity to describe, with my narrow concept of sex and complete inexperience.

Connor never really excited me, not the way Liam had. But looking down at the photos, I feel a throb between my legs, an unfulfilled ache as my mouth goes dry and my pulse speeds up. Between my thighs, I can feel my arousal, dampening the lacy panties that I'm wearing underneath the abnormally tight jeans.

Jesus, Mary, and Joseph, Saoirse. If you're not careful, he'll be the one seducing you.

I grab the photos, shuffling them into a pile and turning them over quickly. The only way this will work is if I maintain control of the situation. I can't do that if I'm salivating over a man I haven't seen in years, who doesn't even know I'm coming.

The documents in the file, all procured by men my father has sent out looking for information on Connor these past months, tell me a few very important pieces of information. First, Connor is running his own gang out of London now—a mid-level operation dealing in things like party drugs, a bit of money laundering, weapons between them and Ireland. He hasn't cut off all Irish ties, that much is clear, but he's going by an English name, a fake identity.

William Davies.

There's a knock at the door. "Come in," I call out, my heart pounding a steady rhythm in my chest as I close the file, turning towards the door as it opens. It's my father, as I knew it would be— Graham O'Sullivan, right hand to the Irish King, as the O'Sullivans have been for generations. Tall, bearded, handsome, the one that I take after more than my mother, a commanding presence who instilled in me a strength that's served me well all these years, even if it causes us to butt heads at times. Though I've always known it was my place to serve the family through marriage to the right man, my father taught me that didn't mean I had to be weak or subservient.

An Irish rose is no wilting flower.

"You look perfect." My father looks me up and down from head to toe. "He won't be able to resist you."

"I don't feel like myself." I glance in the mirror again. It's not as if I've spent my entire life in evening gowns and jewels—I went to college, after all. I wear normal clothes. But this—the black jeans are skin-tight, outlining every curve I have, made with some sorcery that makes my Pilates-firm ass look bigger than it actually is. The top I'm wearing is dark green, sleeveless, and with a draped wrap neckline low enough that I can't wear a bra. It shows off the swell of my full breasts, and god help me if I move too quickly to one side or the other —someone might catch an eyeful of an entire breast, nipple and all.

Which, I suppose, is the point.

The rest of it feels just as out of place. Huge silver hoop earrings, biker-style Doc Martens with the jeans tucked in, a buttery-soft black leather jacket to cover up against the chilly London rain, which seems to persist here even in summer. The jacket I actually like—I might keep it. But the rest, including the dark eye makeup and false lashes, feels so antithetical to my usual style that it's like wearing a different skin.

The last time I wore green to meet a man I was supposed to marry, I was in silk and diamonds, swathed in candlelight, dressed like royalty to have my betrothal to the Irish King blessed by the priest.

Tonight, I'm dressed to seduce.

"Good," my father says. "We don't *want* you to look like you, Saoirse. The less likely he is to recognize you until you get him up here to the room, the better. He knew you for a long time before, after all, and while you've certainly changed in the years since he left, he might remember you. The less you look like that girl he was supposed to marry, for now, the better."

"He probably doesn't remember me." I press my lips together, frowning with remembered annoyance. For all that I was always meant to marry a McGregor son, neither of them ever noticed me much. Connor was too busy learning his place as the McGregor heir, and Liam—well, Liam was too busy being himself, the reckless, playful, funny younger brother who had no responsibilities and no one watching him.

Except for me.

"He'd be a fool not to," my father says gruffly. "But for our sake and the sake of the plan, let's hope you're right. Now come on, lass, let's get you downstairs." He looks at me, his gaze hardening. "This is an important night, Saoirse, for all of us. Everything depends on you getting Connor back here, to this room, for him and I to talk."

He reaches for my left hand, thumb rubbing over the space where a ring used to be. "Liam left you in disgrace," he reminds me—as if I needed reminding—"with a broken engagement. This is your last chance to do what you were born for, lass. If you don't succeed, who knows what man will take you. If Liam keeps his seat, it's likely that I won't keep mine. The O'Sullivan family will fall, and I'll be forced to marry you off to whoever can offer us some alliance and cushion that blow."

I meet his gaze unwaveringly. "Don't worry," I tell him calmly—more calmly than I feel inside. "I know what this means for us. I'll do my duty."

"Don't let him take liberties with you, either," my father adds. "It's important that he's your first man—*in your wedding bed*. Don't let him take for free what he has to earn. Seduce, but don't give in."

I feel a flush creeping up my cheeks. "I understand," I tell him through gritted teeth, looking away.

If there's one thing I'm looking forward to above all else out of being married, it's that the endless conversation around the state of my virginity will finally come to an end.

We take the elevator downstairs, where four other women are waiting—all strangers to me, women that my father has paid to be here tonight, to flesh out our plan. They're all dressed in tight, revealing clothing too—short bandage dresses with sky-high heels, tight jeans and lowcut tops, big earrings and flat-ironed hair, heavy makeup. They look as foreign to me as I feel to myself, and I feel a wave of discomfort as I step away from my father and go to join them.

"Nice evening out, ain't it, luv?" one of the women says in a thick accent, as we pile into the town car that my father rented for us while we're in London, complete with driver.

"Ah—is it?" I frown, squinting against the still-falling rain as I follow her into the car. "It hasn't stopped raining since we landed."

"New to London, I see," one of the others, a pretty blonde, says. "It never stops raining here. Just whether it's cold rain or warm rain, y'see."

"It feels like cold rain to me." I'm grateful for the leather jacket, at least, even if I'm supposed to leave it in the car before we go into the warehouse where I've been told we'll find Connor and his men. "But yes, it's my first time in London."

Truthfully, though I wouldn't say it to anyone, it's my first time out of the States. I'd always pictured that first trip being on my honeymoon, somewhere warm and sunny with sand between my toes and a fruity drink in my hand. When I'd imagined that honeymoon with Liam, it had been full of passionate sex in a crisp white hotel bed with salt air coming through the windows, while he taught me everything I never knew about how to make love.

Things have turned out—a bit differently.

"And thanks to you, we're riding in style!" The first girl crows, leaning back against the smooth leather seat. "Not how I usually go to my outcalls, that's for sure." She eyes me, picking up on my nerves as surely as only someone who is a veteran of this sort of thing could. "New to this, are you, luv?"

"Mm. A bit." I'm careful with my words. Once I get Connor's attention and get him away from the warehouse, I won't see these women again. They're just my in, a way to make my arrival there look less conspicuous, and sell the whole story that I'm just taking him back to my hotel room for a quick fuck. I don't want to give anything away.

"And that man in the hotel, he was what? Your pimp?"

I clench my teeth at that, a flare of anger flushing my cheeks at the thought of anyone insulting my father like that. But I rein it in. I'm not Saoirse the Irish princess tonight. Tomorrow, when things are more settled, I can sink comfortably back into the identity that I know so well and be myself again. But for tonight, I have to be someone else. A woman of the world. A seductress. Someone who hears a sentence like that and laughs it off.

"Something like that." I look out the window at the rainy streets passing by, wanting the conversation to end.

"Not very friendly," I hear muttered from one of the women, but I ignore it. The closer we get to our destination, the more my heart races to the point that I feel almost sick with nerves, and I wish I could run back to Boston. That I could rewind time and make everything go differently.

That I could make Liam never have become obsessed with that Russian ballerina and break our engagement—along with all my dreams of marrying the McGregor brother I preferred and that sunny, sandy honeymoon.

You can do this, I whisper to myself in my head. *You're an O'Sullivan. You're strong. You're brave.*

You can do better than marrying a disappointing man. You can be the heroine of this fucked-up fairytale.

The one who brings the prince back home.

The car turns down several roads that take us into a less well-heeled part of London, darker and more industrial, with less well-kept roads and buildings in disrepair. It doesn't look anything like the kind of place where I'd find the Connor I remember—the cool, collected, passionless man who used to sit at his father's left hand—but from what I read in the file that my father put together on him, Connor has done quite well for himself here. It reminds me of just how much rides on tonight. Connor has been happy enough to let everyone think he was dead—disappearing into a false identity, leaving his family and everything else behind, and starting a new life here. Now my father wants to forcibly resurrect him, and I can't imagine he'll be happy about that.

As the car door opens and I step out, my boot splashes down into something wet—some kind of puddle that makes me suddenly glad I'm not wearing the heels I would have chosen. The smell of the nearby alley wafts towards me, making me wrinkle my nose, and I grit my teeth, refusing to let any of it rattle me.

The warehouse door is slightly ajar, and buttery light streams out, the sounds of loud drunk men spilling out into the warm night air. I pause at the edge of the door with the other four women surrounding me, my heart hammering in my chest, and I take a deep breath—something I quickly regret, thanks to the heavy smell in the air that I can taste on the back of my tongue.

And then, with my jaw clenched against the fear coiling around my spine, I step into the glow of the warehouse.

I see him instantly, at the same time that I hear the cock of weapons. "Stop right there, ladies," two heavily Cockney-accented voices say. Still, I don't bother looking at them, despite the fact that they almost certainly have guns pointed at our heads. Instead, ignoring both them and the pounding of my heart, I look straight ahead at the poker table set up in the middle of the warehouse and the man seated at the head of it.

It's him. For all that he looks so much different, scarred and stubbled and tattooed, in a charcoal t-shirt and dark jeans with that leather jacket slung over the back of his chair, I recognize him instantly. I recognize the burnished auburn hair and those piercing bright blue eyes, and all I can do is hope that he doesn't recognize me.

"Nah, let them in, boys," William—*Connor*—says, leaning back in his chair with a smirk on his handsome, stubbled face. "The game was getting a bit dull, but I'm sure these ladies can liven the night right up, am I right?"

There's a roar of laughter from around the table, Connor's men giving their raucous assent, and the other women push forward, heading straight for their marks. But I hang back a little, my gaze fixed on Connor, my heart beating so hard in my chest that I feel as if I can hardly breathe.

He'd been handsome in the photos, dangerously so, but here—in the flesh and up close—there's something else to him, too. Everything about this room, from the armed guards to the table scattered with cards, chips, and money, the fugue of cigar smoke hanging in the air, and the clank of ice in highball glasses, screams *power*, and it's all his.

He built this from scratch. It wasn't handed to him. Connor McGregor was the heir to an empire, but William Davies is a self-made man. Looking at the man at the head of the table, his eyes fixed on me as he takes a sip from his glass, I wonder how much of Connor is left in him.

The Connor I remember was smooth, polished, arrogant, without a piece of clothing or hair out of place. He would never have sat at a table with men like these—brutish and dressed in denim and canvas and leather, boots and bears and messy hair, scars on their faces, hands, and arms, weapons visible rather than carefully concealed. The Connor I knew didn't gamble or smoke, and he drank socially. This man has a pile of chips in front of him, a cigar in his hand, and a bottle of expensive cognac at his elbow. He oozes power, money, masculinity—and something else, too.

Sex.

The other women are already in the laps of the men around the table, high-pitched giggling filling the air. Still, it fades to an echo as I walk towards the table and Connor, feeling as if time has slowed down, each second punctuated by the beat of my pulse, and I can feel my mouth going dry, just as it did in the hotel when I looked at his photos. His gaze hasn't left mine, and he watches me almost hungrily, like I'm prey. A meal.

He smiles lazily as I approach, and I see a droplet of cognac still clinging to his full lower lip.

What would it taste like, if I kissed his mouth and licked it away?

The thought startles me and makes me suck in a breath. The offensive smells of the alleyway are gone, replaced with the heavy scents of vanilla and tobacco, cigar smoke and expensive alcohol, gunpowder and something else—a smell that stirs something warm and heavy deep in my belly as I circle the table towards Connor, his gaze following me as if I'd caught his attention from the very moment I walked through the door.

Something masculine, musk and cologne, and I know it's him.

I feel that ache between my legs again, that gathering dampness of arousal, and swallow hard. I can feel the eyes of every man in the room on me, even the ones with women in their laps, but all I can see is Connor. And from the way he's gazing at me, it seems as if all he can look at is me, too.

Good. You're doing well. Keep going.

The words whisper in my head, urging me forward until I stop a hand's length from him, my heartbeat so fast that I can hear the blood pounding in my ears.

"Well, hello there, love," he says slowly, that same smirk curling his lips as he looks up at me. "And what could a fine-looking girl like yourself be looking for in a place like this?" His eyes rake over me as he speaks, lingering on my breasts, my narrow waist, lower down before sliding back up the length of me in a blatant show of lust that makes my pulse quicken all over again.

If I hadn't seen the file, the pictures, the evidence, I almost wouldn't believe it's him. He looks so different, speaks so differently—everything about him is rough, hard, dangerous, all of the polish wiped away and replaced by something else—but it doesn't make him less attractive. If anything, it makes him *more* so, spiking my arousal in a way that the old Connor never had, and I don't know what to make of it. I can feel the heat of him as he looks up at me from his seat, the scent of cigar smoke and warm leather wafting off of him, and something so deeply masculine that it makes my knees feel weak. After all these years, I'm so very close to him again, but the feelings washing over me now are nothing like the ones I remember.

It makes me feel uncertain, off-balance, and then before I realize what's happening, his arm snakes around my waist, and I *am* quite literally off-balance as he pulls me down into his lap.

His arm is tight around my waist, pulling me against him, and I can't breathe. Connor reaches out, touching my jaw with rough-tipped fingers. "Pretty girl like you, so much prettier than the others," he muses. "You must be here looking for something. Or *someone*?" He grins at me, and I feel a shiver ripple through me from the top of my head to the tips of my toes, my skin heating everywhere, but especially in all the places he's touching me. His arm around my waist, his fingers splayed against my hip, his strong, muscular thighs underneath mine. His fingers still resting gently against the line of my jaw.

Say it. Before you lose your chance, say it. You might not feel like yourself, but you're still Saoirse O'Sullivan, and you're here for a reason—not to go weak at the knees at the first touch of a man who turns you on. Do what you came for.

I reach up slowly, and for the first time in my life, I touch Connor McGregor. I slide my fingertips over his cheek, feeling the stubble scraping against my soft skin, in a mirror of how he's touching me. I take a deep breath, and I meet those bright blue eyes, doing my best to ignore the jolt they send through me, as if they could electrify me with a look.

"I've heard about you, William Davies," I say teasingly, and I see his eyes widen at his name on my lips. "So when my friends said they were coming here, I just had to come along." I lean forward, my voice hushed, as if my next words are a secret just between the two of us.

"I came here looking for you."

Order Irish Betrayal here.

Were you Team Alexandre? Alexandre get's his on Happily Ever After in November. Order it here.

THE COLLECTORS GIFT PREVIEW
THE COLLECTOR

O nce upon a time, there was a man who had loved two women.

The first was forbidden to him, but he loved her anyway. They met in secret, under the cool and watchful glow of the moon, innocent to everything except for their love. He was her first, and she was his. They knew that her evil stepfather and his wicked stepmother would never allow them to be together, but they dreamed anyway. They dreamed, loved, and made promises, and in his innocence, the man who was a boy then believed that all of their dreams could come true.

But the evil stepfather and wicked stepmother discovered them, and in a jealous rage, the stepfather took all of their dreams and cut them to shreds. He killed the boy's first love in front of him and left him to ponder the ruins of the future they'd imagined.

The boy grieved, cried, and changed. He ran away from the evil stepfather and wicked stepmother, and he grew into a man.

A man they called the Collector.

He didn't think himself an evil man, although many did. He saw himself as broken, his heart and soul buried in the countryside where his first love lay, and he swore he would never let another broken thing suffer if he could help it. So he collected all the beautiful, damaged things he could—art, books, arti-

facts, once-priceless things ruined by the folly and carelessness of men, and he gave them a home.

Girls, too. Broken girls, injured girls, girls with defects who made them ugly in the eyes of the world. But not to the Collector. He gave them a home, and he thought he could keep them there, safe from those who would bury them.

But he lost them all, one after another. Until he found her.

His second love. His little doll.

He rescued her, he said, from an evil man who wanted to do her harm, just like the evil stepfather from so long ago. She was broken, damaged, in her mind, body, and soul, and he saved her. His pet, his little dancer, his Anastasia.

For a while, they were happy. And in his newfound bliss, the Collector believed that he might have love again, after all. His little doll had saved him, and not the other way around.

But then, as in all fairytales, there was a handsome prince. He came to rescue the damsel, believing, as everyone else did, that the Collector was an evil man who only wished her harm. He defeated the evil villain, the Collector, and whisked the damsel away to his own country to ask for her hand in marriage. And as in all fairytales, the damsel fell in love with the prince who saved her. She accepted his proposal and sent the Collector away, and she and her prince lived happily ever after.

The end.

Or is it?

The Collector went back to his lair, broken once again, his love lost to him once again. He locked himself away with his other broken things, and he swore he would never love again—that he would shut out the world and live alone until he died, at last, alone.

After all, he told himself, who could ever love a man without a soul? Who could ever love a monster?

Who could ever love a beast?

THIRTY
NOELLE
LONDON, ENGLAND

My brother is sitting in front of me in our shabby living room, blood trickling from his split lip. His eye is already blackening, and I can see the lump rising on his cheekbone. Beneath his shirt, there are likely more bruises. His ribs, his kidneys. Internal injuries that might heal or might not.

We can't go on like this.

Our father is dead. Six months now, he died of liver cancer that swept over him so suddenly that it took him from us in a matter of weeks, and now we're left to pick up the pieces.

Pieces that, specifically, involve gambling debts and back-alley loan sharks who don't care that our father is dead. He borrowed money from them, and they want their money, however it comes. If our father is six feet under and unable to hand it over, then as far as they're concerned, we've inherited it—my brother and I.

No matter that I waitress at the local pub for just enough to scrape by on our rent and cheap groceries or that my brother is barely sixteen, too young to hold down a job. They want their pound of flesh, and since my brother is ostensibly now the man of the house, they've come to him for it first.

From the look of him—quite literally.

"Georgie, we can't keep doing this." I sit on the arm of the chair he's sunken down in, trying to reach for his face so I can get a better look at his injuries, but he bats my hand away.

"Stop calling me that."

"It's your name." I reach for his chin, but he slaps my hand harder this time, enough to sting. I yank it back instinctively, cradling it against me, though he didn't really hurt me. It's more of the shock—my brother has never been rough with me, even as children. He's always been the quieter one, the shy one, the one who skipped sports to focus on academics in school.

"My name is George." He looks away from me. "I'm not a little boy anymore, Noelle."

"George was our father. You've always been Georgie to me. You think that stops just because he's dead, and you think you're almost a man now?" I grab his chin more forcefully this time, turning his face into the light. The bruises and bloodied lip are worse than I thought. His face is already swelling.

"Are there more injuries? Did they beat you up badly?" I lean forward, reaching for his shirt to tug it up so that I can see, but my brother gets up so abruptly I almost topple over into his emptied seat, glaring angrily at me in the lamplight as he backs up.

"I don't want to talk about it! It's not fair—these were father's debts, not ours. How dare they come after us, as if we were some, some—"

He turns away, and the ache in my chest only intensifies. If our ages were swapped, Georgie might have been George to me, a big brother who watched over me and protected me. But I was four when he was born, a late baby after our parents had given up getting pregnant again, and I'd watched over him all my life, his big sister. Even as he outpaced me in nearly everything—smarter, funnier, even more attractive as he got older—I still loved him devotedly. I hadn't wanted to go to university—instead, I'd opted to stay home and work. Our mother had died when I was fourteen and Georgie was ten. By the time I finished my exams and could have gone, our father had sunk so deep into his alcoholism that I'd felt obligated to stay and care for him and Georgie, who was fourteen by then.

Now he's sixteen and I'm twenty, and he needs me more than ever. I hadn't seen how deep our father's grief had gone, that he'd turned to gambling as well as drinking to cope, but what I missed back then, I'm determined not to miss now. I'm determined to protect Georgie and keep him safe.

I don't want to hate our father. But it's hard not to feel angry, looking at my sweet brother's face. He's never been a fighter. And I can't let this happen to him again.

"What happened?" I ask quietly. "Where did they find you?"

"Outside school, like bullies." Georgie still won't look at me, shifting out of the light. "They said I needed to come up with a way to pay. They didn't care how. Or they'd find you next." When he glances at me, I can see his eyes are shimmering, and he looks much younger than his sixteen years.

He looks like my baby brother. And the wave of vicious emotion that sweeps over me is so strong that I know what I have to do.

The thought of facing down these men terrifies me. But I'm his big sister. It's my job to protect him.

To protect what's left of this family.

"Let me help you clean it up," I say gently, standing up and crossing the room to where he's standing in the shadows. "You don't need to do it on your own. And then I'll—I'll handle this."

"How?" Some of Georgie's earlier bravado is slipping, and I hear a small quaver in his voice, the fear that we've lived with on a daily basis since our father died. *Will we have enough food this week? Will the lights stay on? Will there be cooking gas? Will the rent be late?*

"I'll find a way," I promise him, my hand on his back as I guide him towards the small bathroom, the only one in our three-bedroom flat. One of those bedrooms I can't bear to go into any longer. It still smells like our father to me, but not the father I remember from our childhood, who smelled like cigar smoke and exhaust and petrol. It smells like him at the end, a sick, wasting smell.

The smell of death.

It makes me sick just thinking about it.

"You can't, Noelle," he protests as he sits down on the edge of the toilet, giving in and letting me pull the half-empty first aid kit out from under the sink. "We don't have anything left. We barely had enough for food for the week—if you can call what we got from the grocery *food*."

Chipped beef, bread for toast, half a dozen eggs, some noodles, and sauce. It certainly wasn't much, and my stomach aches just thinking about it. I give Georgie as much of the food as I can manage without starving myself completely. There are nights now when I dream about a full English fry-up, a roast dinner, a takeaway curry. The kebabs from the street vendor we used to eat at when we were children.

Before our mother died. Before our father gave up living.

"I'll fix it," I promise him again, and I mean it.

But as I get out the things to patch him up, the gnawing dread in the pit of my stomach reminds me that I don't know how I will, either.

I might not have been a genius in school—more out of a lack of ability to focus on the boring subjects we were taught rather than any real lack of intellect—but it doesn't take much for me to figure out where I might find my father's debtors. I force myself to go into his sickroom, holding my breath until I finally let it out all in a rush, a little lightheaded.

It's actually quite clean. The bed is just a mattress now, stripped of the sheets and pillows it was made up with while he was alive. They've been binned now, the empty bed looking all the more bare and stark for the fact that it's surrounded by the detritus of my father's life, all of it still untouched because I haven't been able to bear to go through it.

The liquor bottles are long gone, the pills thrown out, and all traces of the sickness that ravaged him disappeared. But his books and papers and all the rest are still scattered about, and I dig through them until I find the notes from his debtors, telling him long before he died that he needed to pay up.

He didn't, of course. And now those chickens have come home to roost.

I take the IOUs, all of them, and retreat back to the other side of the flat. Georgie is in his own room now, sleeping. I check in on him before leaving the IOUs in my bedroom and going to the bathroom to take a quick shower, conscious as ever of the length of time I'm in there using the hot water.

Tonight, though, I make sure to wash my hair and use what's left of my good soap, the kind I got from a farmer's market that's made with goat's milk and smells like lavender. I wash my hair with it too after my usual cheap shampoo, just to give it some extra fragrance, and examine myself critically in the mirror as I towel off, going over in my head what I came up with to say when I saw the evidence in my father's room, the amount that he'd amassed. More than I'd thought at first, for sure.

I'm Noelle Giles. My father was George Giles. I know he's left a great many debts, and I'm here to pay them. How, you ask? Well, I don't have money. What do I have?

I'm twenty years old, and I'm a virgin. You can have someone check if you like. But that's the only currency I have, and I'm here to use it to pay off those debts, so that my family can be left alone.

I have no idea if it will work. Just the thought makes me shudder—I don't want to imagine what's ahead of me—a night, or nights, spent working off my father's debts by letting the sharks have their way with me. I don't know how, exactly, I can make sure they stick to their word and write off those debts once I've "paid." But I'll figure that all out when I get there. All I can think is that when tomorrow comes, they'll go after Georgie again and again, until those debts are paid. And we have no money.

Even if Georgie got whatever after-school jobs are available to a fourteen-year-old boy, it wouldn't be enough to pay off those debts. Definitely not in the time frame the sharks are bound to want them paid off by—probably not ever, if I take into account the kind of interest they probably charge.

I have one thing of value, and I'm prepared to surrender it in whatever ways I have to if I can fix this. If I can keep my little brother from coming home bruised and bloody—or worse, beaten to death in the street.

Just the thought is enough to make me furious.

It ought to work. I'm pretty enough—a bit on the thin side; my breasts are a little smaller than they used to be from the lost weight, but my stomach is flat and my hips still have a slight curve. The thinness of my face makes my blue-grey eyes look that much wider, huge like a doll's and with thick feathery lashes inherited from my father and my black hair just down to my shoulder blades. I'd cut it all off a couple of years ago when I graduated, into a razor-sharp bob that I thought was stylish at the time, but now I'm glad it's grown out. The length and slight wave that it has makes me look softer, younger, and more innocent—all things that I'm sure will help plead my case when I go to trade on my body to pay the debt.

I fish my nicest dress out of the closet, a blue collared party dress made out of a rich taffeta that matches my eyes. It has a sweetheart neckline that makes my breasts look fuller than they are right now, a fitted waist, and a slightly flared skirt that comes down to just above my knees. It's a relic from a birthday years past, and I'd thought about selling it on consignment many times for a little extra money, but I'd held onto it. It's not designer, just a high street dress, so it wouldn't have been worth much—not as much as it was worth in nostalgia to me. I'd worn it to the last birthday before my mother died, and she'd helped me pick it out. Now more than ever, I'm glad I hung onto it, even if I know deep down she'd be ashamed of the reason I'm wearing it.

She wouldn't be ashamed of *me*, though, I don't think. She'd be ashamed of my father, if anything, for putting me in this position. For leaving Georgie and me this desperate.

I leave my hair down, slipping on the nude patent heels I bought to go with the dress, and tap a little blush onto my pale cheeks. A swipe of drugstore mascara and a little rosy lipstick, and I'm ready to go.

My stomach is in knots as I check in on Georgie, who is still sleeping. I leave a note on the table, *Gone to speak with debtors, be back soon,* and close the door carefully behind me, stepping out into the cold chill of the London evening.

Somewhere in the city, it's bright with holiday décor, lights strung up and streetlamps wrapped with garlands and bright buttery light glowing in decorated shop windows, but not in our part of the city.

The neighborhood where we live is run-down and shabby. I step around dubious puddles and am careful not to look at the men who pass by as I pull my worn black wool coat tighter around me, my old leather gloves not doing much to keep my hands warm.

We haven't even had a snowfall yet. Even though it would make it harder for Georgie to get to school and me to work, I still would have been glad for it, if only because it would make the streets seem a little prettier, bring a little holiday spirit into our rundown part of town. As it is, my heart aches every time I think of Christmas. It hasn't been much of a holiday since our mother died. Still, I tried to do something every year for Georgie—a few decorations, a small tree, a gift underneath it for him and our father.

There won't be anything this year, though. No tree, no presents, because there's no money. At this point, the greatest gift I can think of would be for our father's debtors to leave us alone, so we can try to figure out how to start fresh.

I don't even know what my life is going to look like now. But I'd like a chance to figure it out.

I look down at the address on the slip of paper. *Market Street.* I turn down street after street, only to find myself in a nicer neighborhood than I'd imagined. It's no ritzy part of London, but at least the houses and flats don't look like they're falling in on themselves, and the sidewalks are less cracked. The address leads me to a street with a handful of exotic restaurants—*L'Orange, Bistro Italia, The Genie's Lamp,* and a few bars, all the way to a dark building that, when I glance into the windows, looks like a speakeasy. When I step inside, the smell of cigars and alcohol hits me in a warm wave, and I look around, taking in the Art Deco décor and the long mahogany bar. It's all meant to look luxurious and high-end, but a closer glance reveals that the velvet seats are a little threadbare, the tables scuffed in places, the bartop not quite as shiny as it could be.

The bartender looks at me. It's a Tuesday night, so it's a bit dead—there's a handful of patrons but nothing too busy. He's shining glasses, and I notice that he looks like he's in his late twenties and handsome. He doesn't look like the kind of ruffian that would have beaten my brother up earlier. It makes me wonder if I'm in the right place. "You lost, little lady?" he asks, not unkindly. "You look lost."

I swallow hard, taking a step up to the bar. Behind him, a row of glass bottles wink and shimmer in the light, with names I've never seen before. I've never tasted a drop of hard liquor in my life, just the wine I'd be allowed a glass of at holidays—once again, before my mother died. Now, after my father's descent into alcoholism, I wonder if I ever will.

They all look like the enemy to me, culprits pointing directly to the reason I'm here, the reason I'm about to offer myself up like a lamb to the slaughter just so my brother and I can have a chance at a fresh start.

"I don't think I'm lost." I clear my throat, taking a step closer. "I'm Noelle Giles. My father was George Giles—I'm here about his debt."

The bartender's eyes narrow. "You *are* lost then. I don't know about any debt. But all the same, I don't think this is the place for a pretty little thing like you. You should get going."

It's tempting. I could turn tail and run. I could go home and tell Georgie I tried. Maybe get our things together and leave town for good. Surely they won't chase us out of London. I wouldn't have to offer up my body to pay off a debt that isn't even mine, give my virginity to god knows how many men before they're done with me. We could leave, start over somewhere else. Make new memories, a new life.

With what money? Georgie was right earlier when he said we'd spent our last bit leftover from rent on food. I don't even have the money for a train ticket out of London for us, let alone lodging or food wherever we end up. And outside of London, it will be harder for me to find a job. It'll be difficult to get Georgie enrolled again without a permanent address. People would come asking questions.

In time, I might save up enough to solve the money problem—in a week, or two, if I picked up extra shifts. But these men aren't going to wait that long.

In a week or two, they might kill Georgie. They might come and see me anyway, and then what little power I have won't be in my hands anymore.

This is the only way.

I take a deep breath and hold up one of the IOUs. "I'm not lost," I say with as much bravery as I can muster. "This is the address, right? Whoever here my father owed money to, they beat up my little brother today. I'm here to set things right. So just go and get—"

"Miss, you need to leave." The bartender's voice is harder now, more urgent. "You shouldn't be here. You shouldn't—"

"Now, now, no need to be hasty." There's a deep, Cockney-accented voice behind me, and I freeze in place, afraid to turn around. "George Giles' girl, hmm? Turn around, so I can take a look at you."

My heart is pounding in my chest. The bartender gives me a look, as if to say *I told you to leave*, and I force myself to stay calm as I turn to face the man behind me, feeling myself pale a little as I look up at him.

He's tall, over six feet, dressed in grey trousers that have seen better days, a moth-eaten sweater, and a plaid vest with a newsboy cap. His eyes rake over me in a way that I'm familiar with from the pub, but there's something different about it this time. This is a man who knows he could have me in his pocket and will, before the night is over.

It's just a matter of whether or not I can negotiate the terms I want.

"That's me," I say with as much bravado as I can muster. "I wasn't aware of the debts my father incurred while he was alive, sir. But I'm here to discuss how they might be paid. If you're the man I need to talk to—"

"I'm not," he says, a smirk curling one side of his mouth. "But I can take you to him. I daresay he'll be interested to hear what you have in mind." His eyes drift over me again, and I have to fight the urge to clutch my coat tighter around me.

A moment passes, and then he shrugs, motioning for me to follow him. "Come on, luv," he says, his accent thickening as he turns away, heading towards a doorway at the far end of the bar. "I'll take you to the man himself."

I don't want to go with this man, through that door, into whatever unknown lays beyond. But I think of my brother, bruised and bloody and sleeping in our flat that we're clinging to by our fingertips and everything we stand to lose if I don't.

Stiff upper lip, I think to myself. The man is holding the door open for me in a parody of chivalry, and all I have to do is walk through it, down the stairs, and into the darkness below. I do that, and we have a chance. I don't—and we might lose much, much more than we already have.

I glance at the man and see not a single speck of emotion on his face. There's no help for me here, not that I won't have to buy. But I knew that already. The bartender might have been the last one who had my best interests in mind.

The choice is made—as if I ever really had one to start with. The stairs stretch out in front of me, the black mouth at the end opening up into an unknown room, with unknown men, and an unknown night ahead of me.

I take a deep breath and walk through the door into the darkness beyond.

Order The Collector's gift here.

Printed in Great Britain
by Amazon